FIRECHILD

"Do you – do you know anything?"

"Nothing. Except that Vic called me last night. What he said troubles me. It sounded too much like a final farewell. Could he be sick?"

"Obsessed. With this Alphamega project. That's sickness enough."

"Something dangerous?"

"I wish I knew. It's terribly important to him. He's high when it's going well, in the dumps when it isn't. Yesterday morning he –" She paused uncertainly. "He frightened me. He'd set the alarm to rush off early the way he always does, but then he came back into the bedroom and took me in his arms. That terrified me, because he never liked to show that sort of emotion. I asked him if anything was wrong.

"'Not after today.' The words puzzled me, because of the half-cheerful way he grinned and squeezed me again. Grinned with tears in his eyes. 'Something has gone dreadfully wrong, but I'm about to set it right.'"

Jack Williamson

FIRECHILD

A Methuen Paperback

A Methuen Paperback

FIRECHILD

British Library Cataloguing in Publication Data

Williamson, Jack
Firechild.
I. Title
813′.52[F]   PS3545.I557

ISBN 0–413–16330–X

First published in Great Britain 1988
by Methuen London Ltd
11 New Fetter Lane, London EC4P 4EE

This book is fiction. The characters and the events are invented. Any resemblance to living individuals or actual events is entirely coincidental.

Printed and bound in Great Britain
by Cox & Wyman Ltd, Reading

In Memory
of
Blanche

Prologue

Alphamega's history might begin with a small child in rural Ohio, the free-minded boy who left the footprints of his country-doctor-father to become a creator of something like divinity. It might begin with the sordid years of child abuse and festering hate that deformed a less fortunate child into the iron man who fought to stop that creation. It might begin on a bleak day in midwinter Moscow, with a lovely woman receiving orders from her KGB superiors to assassinate the American monster-makers.

Skipping back in time, it might begin four billion years ago on a long-gone savage planet near the young galactic core, with the hatching of a mutant predator, an unlucky hunter that died because it couldn't kill and lived again through the ages in the accretion disk of a spinning black hole as the Father-Mother of the people of fire. A better starting point might be at the EnGene Laboratories in the unlucky little city of Enfield, with the Petri dish where the first spark of Meg's brief and tragic life on Earth was lit.

However begun, her story belongs to our own uncertain time.

1

The Soldier of God

Clegg liked people to listen.

He never made it easy. He was a gaunt, big-boned man with fire in his eyes and an air of righteous might. His thick black hair had receded to show an imperial forehead, splashed with a big, wine-red birthmark. Commonly hidden under by a brown beret pulled low, the mark looked like the print of a bloodied hand.

A sense of holy mission drove him.

On a windy spring morning, he arrived at the Enfield municipal airport in a sleek Learjet. Marching from the plane to the terminal building in a slept-in brown business suit, he took a taxi straight to the EnGene plant. That was a long brick building once used by a maker of radio and TV receivers, back before those industries went overseas. A tall woven-steel fence surrounded it now, topped with barbed wire. The gate carried a neat green-lettered sign that read ENGENE LABORATORIES, INC.

The guard stopped him there. He produced an embossed business card that identified him as Adrian Clegg, Director, Bioscience Alert. He asked to see the management. The guard knew what to say.

"Sorry, sir. With no appointment, you can't see anybody."

Not visibly ruffled, Clegg went on to his hotel. The taxi waited while he checked in, changed into a neat black suit, and spoke on the phone. He returned to the plant. He had left the beret in the room, but the birthmark was covered by his heavy gray makeup.

An apologetic security officer was ready by then to give him a badge and escort him to the staff lounge. Research people had gathered to wait for him there. They wore clean white smocks embroidered in green with the EnGene logo.

Six men and a woman, most of them with names known to him as enemies of God, however revered they were by their ungodly peers. They fell silent when he entered, rising to meet him with an air of uncertain concern. Seven devils, as he saw them, gathered in this unholy coven devoted to the Satanic arts of genetic engineering:

Dr. Victor Belcraft, the slight, myopic little man who was said to think and even dream in the four-letter language of the double helix.

Dr. Nick Blake, the restless biochemist whose fingers were always busy, forever stringing bright plastic beads into experimental models for new shapes of DNA, toylike patterns for experimental life.

Dr. Glendel Endrich, heavy-eyed and lazy-bodied, sitting motionless as Buddha, playing his own ceaseless mental games of nucleotides and codons with the silent concentration of a blindfolded master moving chessmen.

Dr. Aristide Sorel, the gangling mathematician who dwelt among the multitudinous dimensions of his own private hyperspace and blinked with seeming surprise when anybody told him that his abstruse equations had revealed some new law of life.

The doll-dainty woman was Dr. Carole Bliss, a specialist in electron microscopy before the laboratory accident that had left her wide blue eyes half blind, her mind undimmed. Listening to her colleagues tossing off untested new ideas, she held her place among them with an uncanny instinct for false trails and true ones.

The other men were Arnoldo Carboni and Dr. Bernard Lorain. Arny ran the computers. A moody, owl-eyed youth, he had no degrees at all and seldom much to say. Absorbed in writing his own computer games when the press of work allowed, he seemed to find his machines better friends than people.

Lorain was the arch-fiend, as Clegg saw him, the leader who had recruited and organized the team. Bliss called him their catalyst. Soft-spoken, almost shy, he had a rare ability to crystallize all their gifts into unexpected new potentials.

One by one, they came to shake Clegg's muscular hand and then settled back to the clutter of coffee cups and soft drink cans around the long table, watching him in puzzled expectation.

He wanted no coffee, no Coke, no Danish or doughnut. With no time to sit, he stalked to the end of the table, planted a thick black brief case like a rampart before him, and stood scanning the group as if searching out their sins.

"Dr. Clegg?" Lorain broke an uneasy silence. "May we ask your field of expertise?"

"I am a soldier of God." Clegg cleared his throat, a short, harsh, bark. "I have been a student of divinity and a West Point cadet, but I hold no degrees. I retired from the Army as a colonel to set up Bioscience Alert."

He paused, waiting for them to wonder.

"We are an informal watchdog group. Volunteers concerned with the ethics and morality of what we believe you are doing here. Even more gravely concerned with a terrible public danger."

"Danger?"

"If you are blind to danger—" A tone of icy accusation. "We have information that you are prying into the most sacred secrets of creation."

Lorain came half to his feet, but sat back silently, trembling with emotion he failed to conceal.

"We're doing genetics research." It was Sorel who spoke, concealing whatever he felt behind a sleepy-seeming mask. "Do you object to that?"

"It frightens us. Because of what you are trying to create."

"We are not creating anything," Sorel protested. "Not yet, certainly. Rather, we're revealing truth. Do you call that a danger?"

"We do." Clegg bristled. "Because we foresee the outcome of your wickedness."

Carole Bliss gasped and shrank from a sudden raw savagery in his voice.

"Who knows the outcome of anything?" Sorel shrugged. "Faraday once inquired what a baby is for. We're doing pure science, which requires no end except itself."

"Pure?" A snort of contempt. "Prying into God's forbidden powers! Can you call that innocence?"

"Sorry, sir." Sorel waved a lazy-seeming hand. "The actual facts of life were never the monopoly of any god. Through all the ages of evolution, they have been written into the DNA of every living cell, lying open to anybody with the wit to read them. That's what we've learned to do."

"Evolution!" Clegg mouthed the word like something foul. "Our information suggests that EnGene was established to invent new kinds of life."

"Perhaps." A bland Buddha smile. "No law forbids it."

"Why not, Dr. Clegg?" Victor Belcraft was a brown little imp, grinning now through thick-lensed glasses as if amused. "Natural evolution has been creating new forms of life every day for several billion years. Ever since the first mutation of the first protoform."

Clegg stiffened, his big hands gripping the briefcase tighter.

"Suppose we should master the craft of creation?"

Belcraft met his cold stare with a wider grin. "Look at mankind. Don't you think our defects ought to be removed? Our behavior improved?"

"If that is what you are up to—" Clegg shook his dark-maned head and paused to scowl into their faces. "Have you forgotten that you—even you!—were created in the holy image of God? Can you do better than God?"

"Not yet, Dr. Clegg."

"But someday—" Sorel smiled his Buddha smile. "Someday we will."

"Not if we can stop you."

"Please!" Lorain rose, protesting with a soft-voiced eloquence. "Let's keep the peace. We aren't attacking God. We don't know where our research may lead us —we could hardly call it research if we did. But what we hope to learn can benefit all mankind. Applied by future generations of genetic engineers, it could create new food plants, new medicines, new industries. Its best creations may be new weapons against hunger and pain and death."

"We're sick of your sophistries." Clegg glowered into Sorel's bland serenity. "You may laugh at me now, but you won't laugh long. I speak for God." He stopped to glare at Belcraft, whose hand had lifted as if he had been a doubtful schoolboy. "Do you challenge God?"

"The God you claim to speak for, I do." Belcraft nodded. "He was invented by primitive men who had to explain their world and its life. We have gained powers of creation they never even claimed for Him. Perhaps we can do better—" He paused to smile, eyes shining through the heavy lenses. "If He was the maker of men, perhaps we can be makers of gods."

The birthmark darkened.

"You—you—" Clegg caught his breath, and that first startled stutter turned to booming fury. "If I speak for God Almighty, you squeak for Hell. The new Lucifer? Daring to battle your own creator, and destined to fall behind your Satanic master into the eternal fire!"

"You honor us too much." Belcraft's impish grin grew wider. "If you credit us with rebellion in Heaven—"

"Hellish rebellion!" Clegg shook a quivering fist. "Arrogant insolence that will damn your pitiful souls forever! But I warn you now that I won't let your judgment wait for God. I intend to stamp your insane deviltry out, and I don't stand alone. Bioscience Alert commands human power, enough to burn your whole nest of demons in the holy fire you seem to crave. Get me?"

"Just give us time." Belcraft turned graver. "I think we'll get you."

Sorel had chuckled, and Clegg responded with a scowl.

"Remember King Knut?" With an air of lazy innocence, Sorel murmured his query. "The story that he tried to sweep back the tide with a broom? Not quite biblical, but still a lesson you might look at. Whatever devil has got into your soul, I doubt that you can command the ocean. The secrets we look for are contained in every living cell. Genetic research will surely go on, and not just here. What we learn—all of us, everywhere—will be a tide of knowledge old Knut never imagined. God or not, new science will sweep your kind away."

"Blasphemer!" Clegg's birthmark showed through his makeup as his face reddened with anger. "We don't debate Satan's vile disciples. And we aren't naive."

He stopped to frown at each of them in turn, as if to memorize their faces.

"We know genetics enough to foresee the Armageddon your folly is inviting. If you persist in this mad infamy, we can mobilize force enough to stop you. We can pass laws against you. We can rally the media to warn the nation. If you force us into action, we have measures to take that even you will have to understand."

"Mr. Clegg—" Trembling, Lorain was back on his feet. "Is that a threat?"

"Ignore our warning, exhaust our forgiving grace,

and you'll find out." Clegg swept up his briefcase and swung to the security officer waiting at the door. "I'm ready to go."

He returned to his hotel. During the day a number of men in business suits came to his room, most of them grimly grave as he was. When he went out for dinner, a private car stopped at the curb to pick him up. After midnight a different car brought him back. He flew out of Enfield early next morning, his destination Denver.

At the EnGene Labs, genetic research continued.

2

"The American Weapon"

The long midwinter night had fallen over Moscow. Kutuzovsky Prospekt lay armored in black ice and nearly bare of traffic. The Hotel Ukrania brooded above it, wedding-cake towers dissolving into low-scudding clouds, Stalin's red star only a rosy nimbus around its high pinnacle.

Sleet rattled on the windows on the fourteenth floor, but the suite inside was stuffily hot. The man in the canopied bed was sensitive to chills. He was overweight and ill. Wrapped in a blanket and propped against a mound of pillows, he lay listening to the woman, pale old eyes watching her fondly.

She sat very straight in a hard chair by the side of his bed, reading aloud from a volume of Shakespeare. Beneath a sheer white nylon robe, her fine skin shone from the heat. She was slender enough, with long platinum hair and a shape that had excited many men.

" 'Methought I heard a voice cry, 'Sleep no more!' " She had been an actress. She read with lively animation, and her accent had always charmed him. " 'Macbeth does murder—' "

"Pardon, mademoiselle." The nurse spoke behind her. "Monsieur Shuvalov has arrived."

The man in bed wheezed for his breath, blinking indignantly. "Who's Shuvalov?"

"An official. From the Kremlin." The woman laid her book on the coffee table, bent to kiss his lax old lips, and reached for a heavier robe. "Sorry, darling. He's a man I must see. World-Mart business. I won't be long."

The nurse had seated the caller in a gilt-columned reception room beside a table where a samovar was steaming. He was a stocky and heavy-bellied man, his blue-jowled face sleekly shaven and odorous with cologne.

"My dear Miss Ostrov!" He came to meet her, scanning her with small shrewd eyes that took no part in his smile. "Fetching! More fetching than ever." He liked to practice the English he had brought home from embassies and trade missions abroad, but he still had a thick accent. "Apologies, if I'm intruding."

Her own long eyes a little narrowed, she offered tea.

"Urgent business for you." He shook his head. "The news you brought requires a quick response. You will return to America at once. The Center has new orders for your special cell."

"At once?" Her voice sharpened. "We can't. Mr. Roman has trade negotiations all this week, and he wants to see Dr. Rykov. His emphysema—"

He waved a heavy hand to stop her.

"The trade discussions will be postponed. Dr. Rykov can call tonight. The Roman party is booked for New York on Aeroflot, leaving at noon tomorrow."

"Listen, Boris!" She was on her feet, her face grown white. "I'm not your slave—"

"Anya, you forget that we made you." He paused deliberately to pour his tea. "You were a failed actress. Your family was in disgrace. We took pity on you, saved you from Siberia, or worse, to make you what you are." Gold teeth glinting, he gestured toward the bedroom. "Mistress of a great American industrialist, permitted to wallow in decadent luxury." He paused to sugar and sip the tea. "Do not forget—you still belong to us."

"I don't forget." Trembling, she sat down. "But Mr. Roman will be unhappy."

"He must be persuaded."

"We can't go till he feels better. His emphysema makes travel very difficult—"

"Anya, dear, that's enough." He shook his head as if she had been a stubborn child. "Perhaps you failed to understand the disturbing implications of what you report."

"Computer printouts. Most of them from something called the engine laboratories." She shrugged. "I can recruit and organize, but I am neither a chemist nor a computer programmer."

"You have been competent." He squinted at her keenly. "But you must understand that this affair is going to require a most extraordinary effort. Frankly, comrade, we discussed replacing you with a more senior officer. I advised against that because you know your agents and they are already in place. However, you must learn more, know more than you seem to be aware of about the crisis—a very grave crisis—implicit in what you report."

She waited while his passionless eyes weighed her again.

"EnGene!" He spoke the name like a curse. "It has nothing to do with engines. It is a laboratory the Americans have set up for secret military research. This new information from your apparatus indicates that they are very near success."

"Success with what?"

"The *Glavni Vrag*!" He burst into explosive Russian. "The *Amerikanski*! They are about to grasp a deadlier secret than anything atomic. One of our own genetic engineers has called it the final weapon."

She sat staring, her eyes grown violet.

"You will be more fully briefed by our own master biologists before you leave." He returned to sober-toned English. "But here, in outline, is your task. Your special cell must act at once to secure complete technical information on the research at EnGene Labs. When that has been accomplished, the laboratory must be sabotaged. The top researchers must be identified. So far as possible, they must be eliminated."

"Comrade!" She shivered. "That's too much!"

"As I said, it will require extraordinary efforts, but you must understand that Mother Russia is facing a new and deadly danger. The Americans must be checkmated. Now, comrade! At any cost! Before they possess this weapon. That is your assignment. The nation depends on you. And I must warn you, comrade." His tone turned bleak. "You must act with the utmost secrecy, without delay!"

"There—there'll have to be delay." She had half risen, but now she sank back into her chair. "We are not prepared—not for this. I do have informers in EnGene, but nobody—no experts in genetics. No fit staff to sabotage the plant and dispose of the researchers. Even in America, foolish as their leaders are, some things are impossible."

"Make them possible! You'll find means." He lifted his teacup as if to drink to her success. His gaze grew thoughtful. "I regret Mr. Roman's illness, because he has been so generous to you. Certainly, the association with him has given you an excellent cover, and I believe the trade ministry has found him a valuable partner. Even now—" The gold teeth lent a glint of malice to his grin. "Sick as you say he is, I think he will serve us one more time."

Jules Roman died in his bed that night. The cause, as reported by Dr. Vladimir Rykov, was a pulmonary embolism. His trusted private secretary, Anya Ostrov, carried his ashes back to his widow in Palm Beach, that island haven where so many senescent capitalists retired to die in luxury.

Exit permission denied, the nurse stayed behind.

3

The Limits of Life

Summer had come early and hot. On that breathless Monday night in Fort Madison, Dr. Saxon Belcraft stayed at the hospital with a recovering cardiac patient longer than he was really needed. He stayed for a second Bud with his sirloin at Stan's Steak Place, and finally killed an hour at the office, frowning over his bank statement and the file of past-due bills. Since Midge left, he hated going home.

Tara Two—that was her fond name for the old house on the river bluffs. Timbers decaying and foundations settling, it had cost too much, certainly more than a beginning physician should have mortgaged himself to pay, but the white-columned entrance was still impressive, and it overlooked a magnificent sweep of the Mississippi. Midge had loved it. Without her now, it had become an empty hell.

The phone was ringing when he let himself in, too loud against the silence. He rushed to answer, spurred by the crazy hope that she might be coming back.

"Hiya, Wulf." His brother's voice, so unexpected that he didn't recognize it until he recalled how Vic used to call him Beowulf. "Happy birthday!"

The greeting surprised him again, because the years

had let them drift so far apart. Even when he married Midge, there had been only that short note on the EnGene letterhead. *Sorry, Sax, but I can't be there. We've just broken into something new here at the labs. Something too big to be neglected.*

"Thanks, Vic." He paused, remembering. "It's been a long time. What's new at EnGene?"

"Nothing I can say much about." Vic seemed gently hesitant, no longer the brash kid brother. "How's the young riverboat doctor? And the beautiful bride?"

For a moment he couldn't speak. The empty house got to him again. Midge had walked out just last week. Still crying for herself, blaming herself for wanting too much. There would never be anybody else. It was just that the hospital and the office and the night calls took too much of him. The grand old house was too lonely for her now, no longer enough.

"So-so." He didn't try explaining anything to Vic. "I'm on the hospital staff. Financial sunlight maybe in sight." And he asked, "Is anything wrong?"

"There has been, Wulf." A rueful voice, older and graver than he recalled. "But I'm on top of it now."

He waited, wondering about EnGene.

"Listen, Wulf." A sober-toned appeal. "I don't think I've ever thanked you. Till now, I guess I never really wanted to, because I don't think you ever forgave me for being brighter than you were. When you used to look after me, I always thought it was just because you had to, because I was your baby brother."

"Maybe." He had to agree. "Maybe so."

"Not that I ever blamed you. I guess I didn't care, not that much. I must have been pretty obnoxious, and I've been thinking lately that I do owe you something for wiping my nose and beating up the bullies that beat me up. Remember, Wulf? You taught me how to tie my shoes, and you signed for library books everybody said I was too young for. You even played chess, so long as I let you win now and then. I guess I loved you, Wulf, even if I never wanted to admit it.

"I had to tell you that."

"You didn't need to." He felt a throb in his throat. "Though now and then you were hard to take."

"Anyhow, Wulf, I've just mailed you a letter. Marked personal. Make sure you open it yourself. When you're alone. It will tell you why I called. And, well—" An odd little pause. "Thanks again for a lot of things. And so long, Sax."

The phone clicked.

He slept fitfully that night, thinking and dreaming of the scrawny, myopic, loud-mouthed kid Vic had been. Seven years younger. A lot brighter in fact than he was, but too much given to letting it show. Getting into playground battles with kids who resented his brains and his arrogance. Kids big enough to maul him.

Was Vic in need of help again?

Before the night was gone, he knew he had to find out. Up at five in the creaky house, he made instant coffee in the microwave, gulped it with a slab of cold pizza, and dialed information for an Enfield number for Victor Belcraft.

The phone rang a dozen times before a young woman answered, sounding sleepy and annoyed. She hadn't seen Vic since yesterday morning. She didn't know where he was, and she didn't like being blasted out of bed in the middle of the night.

Her voice warmed when he gave his name.

"Wulf? The doctor-brother? He spoke about you just the other day. Seemed fond of you. Sorry if I sounded nasty."

She was Jeri—the way she said it told him how she spelled it. A commercial artist, she'd met Vic when she was doing PR for EnGene "back when EnGene wanted PR." They had lived together the last two years. Planning to marry if his job ever left him time for a honeymoon.

He asked her, "Is Vic okay?"

"I don't—don't really know." Her voice had slowed. "He never talks much about the lab, but I know something has disturbed him terribly. Some project he calls Alphamega. Keeps him there night and day. Something he won't talk about. When I kept asking, he tried to get me out of town. Wanted to ship me off to a graphics exhibit in Memphis, and then to see my folks in Indiana. Of course I wouldn't go. All I can do is sit here and fret.

"Do you—do you know anything?"

"Nothing. Except that Vic called me last night. What he said troubles me. It sounded too much like a final farewell. Could he be sick?"

"Obsessed. With this Alphamega project. That's sickness enough."

"Something dangerous?"

"I wish I knew. It's terribly important to him. He's high when it's going well, in the dumps when it isn't. Yesterday morning he—" She paused uncertainly. "He frightened me. He'd set the alarm to rush off early the way he always does, but then he came back into the bedroom and took me in his arms. That terrified me, because he never liked to show that sort of emotion. I asked him if anything was wrong.

" 'Not after today.' The words puzzled me, because of the half-cheerful way he grinned and squeezed me again. Grinned with tears in his eyes. 'Something has gone dreadfully wrong, but I'm about to set it right.'

"He wouldn't say what he meant. Just kissed me and rushed off." Trouble dulled her voice. "Last night he never came home. Never even called. I tried the lab a dozen times. The switchboard girl always said his line was busy. I wondered if he just had no time to talk. Anyhow, I was worried so much I nearly never got to sleep last night."

"Neither did I," he told her. "If you reach him, tell him I'm on my way to Enfield.

"If I can—" She hesitated. "I'd better warn you that lab security has got awfully tight. I've never been inside. Once he promised to show me around, but security wouldn't let me in."

"I'm driving. I'll be there tonight."

"If we could get him out of EnGene—" A longer pause. "I'm sick about it, but he's a stubborn man."

"I remember that."

Driving hard all that long midsummer day through fields of tall green corn and golden wheat and fat cattle grazing, he had time to think of the boy Vic had been. The arrogant oddball. Victor—he wanted people to use his full name because he said it meant winner, but nobody did.

The scrawny little kid, always wanting too much, somehow often winning it. Grimly taking on bullies too big for him, projects too hard for him, begging for books too old for him. Reading them too late by a flashlight under a blanket in spite of his myopia. Always trying to build things his allowance wouldn't buy: a steam engine and a microscope and finally his own computer. Sometimes they worked.

Vic had always surprised him. He kept recalling their last night together, the night of moody silences and solemn recollections after their father's funeral. They sat up late in the Cincinnati hotel room. He was sipping bourbon and water, which Vic refused.

"I've got a fine brain. I want to keep it running."

He set his own drink aside.

"A damn shame." He knew Vic was thinking of their father. "After all he'd done—done for others—" His voice had broken. He gulped and went on. "But I guess he knew what was coming. I remember how he used to quote what he called the first and second laws of medicine. We're machines. Machines wear out."

He nodded, recalling the reek of the pipe and the rasp of the rusty old voice and medical smells that always filled the front room where the old man met his patients.

"Life—it isn't fair!" Vic's voice quivered. "He died too hard!"

A bitter silence. He reached for his drink.

"Too hard!" Vic paused and slowly brightened.

"Someday we'll do better." He sat abruptly straighter, as if his grief had lifted. "I never liked those two laws. I always felt that we're more than just machines—I know Dad was. I never wanted to wear out. And Sax, you know, perhaps—"

Vic's voice changed.

"I hate to say this, Sax. Because of Dad. But I'm getting out of medicine. I never had your bent for it. Or his, though I never told him. I guess I'm—well, maybe just too restless. I never had Dad's total dedication. Now that he's gone, I'm giving it up."

"For what?"

"Genetics."

"Why genetics?"

"It's where we'll build the future." Vic's eyes shone behind the heavy lenses. "Here's what I mean. An idea I've been incubating ever since I first began to see what's possible. Dad would have called it a crazy dream. But listen!"

He listened, a little awed by Vic as he had always been.

"The genetic engineers are redesigning life. Give them a few more years, and they'll be able to create nearly anything."

"Supermen?"

"Could be." Vic shrugged. "But let's look first at something simpler. For example, microorganisms."

"Genetic weapons?"

"I hope not!" Vic looked hurt. "A lot of bugs are bad, but others are benign. You've got benign symbiotes in your own gut, Sax. Suppose we could create a better symbiote."

"Like what?"

"Call it a virus of life." Vic's voice had lifted. "A virus that could spread through your body, infect every cell —but to heal instead of kill. To repair damage and reverse the decay of age. People could be perfect. Eternal as gods. Think of that, Sax!"

His own dark mood was slow to lift.

"Wake up, Wulf!" Vic was the blithe child again, eagerly intense, dreaming impossible dreams. "Open your eyes! Even such a virus wouldn't be limited. We don't know the limits of life. We've never tested the limits of evolution. Suppose we could?"

"How do you mean?"

"Experiment!" An eager gesture. "We all evolve. You remember the old saying that ontogony recapitulates phylogeny—that the growth of every individual replays the whole process of evolution? Suppose we design a new being able to keep on adapting till it reaches some final limit—if there is a final limit."

He couldn't help shaking his head.

"You're just like Dad." A sad little shrug, but Vic went on. "It could be—it will be done. I mean to be on the team that does it."

"If you think you can—" He raised his glass. "Dad would have told you to try."

Pushing the car all that blazing day, he kept wondering. He had seen Vic only briefly since that night. Twice at symposia, where Vic had been reading papers a little too technical for him to follow. Once at their mother's hospital bedside, and again at her funeral. He had never spoken again of that utopian dream.

Suddenly, he wondered if Vic had really been pursuing it. EnGene, to guess from the name, must be devoted to genetic research. Could Vic's Alphamega project have been an effort to realize that wild vision? An effort now gone perilously wrong? Why else Vic's air of mystery about trouble at the lab and that alarming hint of final farewell in his voice?

Night had fallen before the road signs named Enfield. A few miles out of town, the red-winking lights of a police car stopped him. He pulled up beside it and rolled the window down.

"Road closed, sir."

Stiff from sitting and chilled from the air conditioner, he peered groggily into the hot dark to ask how he could get into Enfield.

"No way, sir. All traffic diverted."

"What's wrong?"

"Disaster area—"

A radio was squawking in the police car. Muffled shouts, maybe curses, somewhere off the mike. They faded into crackling static. The cop had turned from him to stare toward the town.

"Disaster? What sort of disaster?"

A cricket chirped in the brush beside the road. Heat lightning flickered far away. The cop ignored him.

"My brother lives there!" He raised his voice. "I've got to reach him."

The cop stood fixed.

He heard an overdriven engine, far off at first but whining nearer. Headlights stabbed through a thin gray groundfog. A quarter-mile away, they dimmed and went out. A long second later, he heard the squeal of skidding tires, the thud and shriek and jangle of the crash. The cop stood blankly staring at a yellow fireball lifting out of the fog. He shouted at the cop.

"Listen! I'm an M.D. Let me get down there—"

The cop wasn't listening. In that sudden stillness, the cricket shrilled again.

"Officer, please!"

"Huh?" A blink of blank surprise, as if the cop had forgotten him. "Nothing you can do."

"People could be dying—"

"Mister, they are dying." Shambling into the headlight glow, the cop grimaced at him. "God knows from what, but there's something hellish loose down there. Killing—killing the city! All we can do is try to keep people out."

"If the problem is medical—"

"God knows what it is! If you'd heard what's coming out—" The cop's head jerked at the crackling radio. His face looked lax and sick. "We're diverting everybody."

"Sir, I've got to look for my brother—"

"Turn your damn car!" A drawn pistol glinted. "Back the way you came."

Damn the cop! He wanted to gun the car past him and on toward Enfield, but you didn't defy the law—not if you were a new doctor trying for a start in old Fort Madison, where the legends of Mark Twain's river still mattered more than modern medicine.

He turned the car on grating gravel and drove away. In his rearview mirror, the burning wreck was a tall golden tree, the bright yellow trunk branching into reddish smoke. The cop stood motionless, a black stick figure at its foot. Beyond, only the dark. Suddenly shivering, he turned off the air conditioner.

4

Scorpio

Anya delivered the ashes to Jules Roman's family, with no thanks from anybody. With no display of grief she could see, the funeral was a private graveside ceremony in an exclusive cemetery in West Palm Beach. A long black limousine brought the widow and her daughter across the lagoon from the family mansion, along with the widow's nurse and her wheelchair. She sat happily through the service, smiling at her own fleeting illusions, or rousing herself now and then to ask the nurse who all those people were.

They were only a handful. Julia, the daughter whom she no longer knew. A few long-time friends, most of them as old as she and very little fitter. Old Roman's lawyer, almost as old as he had been. Two attorneys Julia had hired. The head of the New York office and a World-Mart attorney. Anya kept discreetly apart from them.

Julia was a hawk-faced blonde, recently and bitterly divorced. She stood possessively behind her mother's chair and kept staring watchfully at Anya Ostrov through dark-lensed sunglasses. When the brief service was over, she demanded a look at the will.

Back at the beachfront mansion, the old man's lawyer

found it in a wall safe. He gathered them around a table in what Roman had called the cathedral room, a long dim hall that shone with the color and gold of old Russian icons and a huge photomural of an ancient iconostasis that framed the doorway to his study. The lawyer's voice changed as he read, and he stopped once to stare hard at Anya. Listening, the company men scowled and blinked in consternation.

Roman-World-Mart was to be liquidated. Half the proceeds would be used to establish a foundation for Soviet-American studies. To be the administrator of the estate, the guardian of his beloved wife, and the first director of the foundation, he had chosen "my faithful private secretary and a loyal member of our corporate family," Anya Ostrov. There was a final provision that the bequests to "my wayward, headstrong" daughter, Julia Rose, be reduced to one dollar in the event that she contested the will.

"You c-c-conniving huh-huh-whore!" White-faced and stammering with wrath, Julia shook a red-nailed forefinger at Anya. "You and your cr-cr-crooked commie pals! I'll see you never get a penny." She appealed to the attorney. "Barry, tell the filthy b-b-bitch!"

The lawyer scanned the will again and went into a huddle with the muttering company men and Julia's attorneys. She waited impatiently, glaring at Anya through her dark lenses and gasping for breath as if her legacy had been her father's emphysema.

"Julia, I don't know what to think." The attorney left the huddle to shake his head at her. "This is certainly not the document I drew up a year ago." He gave Anya a scathing glance and turned again to the quivering daughter. "As I had informed you, Julia, the instrument I saw named you as executor, your mother's guardian, and the ultimate heir. It contained no provision for this Anya Ostrov or any Soviet-American foundation."

"Mr. Roman changed his mind." Anya had risen, her fair skin flushed and her accent stronger. "He made this new will last month, just before he left on his last trip to the USSR." She paused to smile at Julia, a happy malice in her eyes. "It was drawn up by the lawyers for our new foundation. They have signed and notarized copies, kept where they are safe. The will expresses Mr. Roman's wishes, and it is legally correct. The courts will support it."

Early next morning she was on her way to Enfield, leaving legal matters to the lawyers. From the airport, she called Scorpio, the agent she had first known as Ranko Barac. He was now working as a night guard at EnGene Labs, where he used the name of Herman Doerr. Her call woke him. Muttering angrily, he agreed to let her pick him up at a bus stop a few blocks from his apartment.

Though Scorpio's competence had been well proven, she hated him heartily. Probably of some mixed Turko-Balkan ancestry, he was muscular and bald, with cold, lead-colored eyes set wide apart beneath heavy black brows. She had met him first in Miami.

Using yet another name, he had come across from Cuba with the Mariel boat lift in command of a death squad. His targeted enemies of the Cuban revolution had been efficiently removed, but, reporting his success to her, he had displayed a proficient willingness to kill that appalled her. Though enemies of the people sometimes had to be neutralized, that was a duty she always tried to avoid.

She knew he hated her. He disliked working under a woman and resented her for rejecting him. Once, drunk on straight vodka at the Miami safe house, he called her a cheap Ukrainian whore when she laughed off his clumsy passes, and then tried to rape her when she said she wasn't cheap enough for him. Now, climbing into the car beside her, he greeted her with a snarl.

"What crap is this?" He was good at many things, his English convincingly native. "You can get me killed."

"Or both of us." Careful with the unfamiliar car on unfamiliar streets, she pulled away from the curb and drove slowly on toward the few tall buildings in the city center. Just as careful in dealing with him, she kept her voice emotionless. "A necessary risk. I protested. I was overruled. I've brought you a revised assignment."

"And the CIA tramping on our heels?" He twisted in the seat to glower at her. "What is wrong with the O'Hare drop?"

"Time. The Center wants action now." She glanced into the rearview mirror. "I know the danger. I take good care. I have been driving for an hour. We are not followed."

"I told you not to come here. If Moscow is unhappy with me, let them find somebody else—"

"They are pleased." Detesting everything about him, even his unbathed, animal odor, she rolled down the car window. "Your reports have been extremely important. They asked me to commend you. But they want action. Now."

"What action?" His dark features hardened. "Do they think I'm this cartoon Superman? You have read my reports on EnGene. Too many spies swarming in, trying to bribe everybody, to steal everything they can. Spies from the people's republics and imperialist nations. From American companies and foreign companies. As well as the CIA."

"Are you afraid of spies?"

"Afraid?" An insolent snort. "Of these bungling idiots? All of them looking for more than I think the EnGene scientists have yet discovered. Leaving clumsy traces of their stupidities. Locks broken. Papers out of order, important records missing. They've got the whole staff uptight about security. Made my own work almost impossible. No more shop gossip worth picking up. Nothing in the wastebaskets."

"You have good contacts."

"I've already milked them for all they know."

"Which has been useful." She hated to say it. "To encourage their good service, the Center wants them well rewarded for those recent printouts."

"Reward Arny Carboni?" A scornful shrug. "That

crazy kid? No friend to anybody. No loyalty to anything except his damn computers. Bleeding us dry for jumbled stuff that makes no sense to—"

"It makes sense to Moscow. Experts there read enough of it to frighten them. They want action. That's what I've come to tell you."

"Okay!" He sneered. "You tell me."

"You are to execute a two-stage plan." She tried to contain her loathing for all he was: a hairy, stinking, evil-natured animal. "It will have the highest priority, supported with all our resources. There can be no delay—"

He muttered a word she didn't catch.

"Those printout—" Another driver honked and drove fast around her. "They reveal that the Americans are very near success with a genetic weapon. More dangerous, our own experts believe, than anything nuclear."

"So?" He shrugged. "Experts have been wrong."

"The errors of experts are not your problem." She let her voice ring cold. "You are to follow the research here, reporting every detail as soon as you discover it. If any weapon is developed, you are to obtain technical data on its nature and its means of production. You are then to sabotage the weapon and the laboratory. If possible, you are to neutralize every person who has been entrusted with any genetic secret."

"Hah?" He mouthed a contemptuous-sounding word in some tongue she didn't know. "Can you send me a batallion of the KGB?"

"The growing American alertness has forced the Center to rely on agents in place." She enjoyed her authority and the angry way he reddened at her words. "I am to keep in closer touch with you. We now have a confidential source of abundant American funds from the Roman estate. Further instructions will be coming, as Moscow analyzes our reports."

"Moscow!" He glared at her. "Moscow expects miracles."

"The Center expects results." They were in the outskirts of the town. In her tension, she had pushed the car too near the speed limit. She slowed, turning into an empty residential street. "I understand that we are working on genetic weapons of our own. Our own mission is to buy time for our own genetic engineers."

"You speak as if we were generals," he muttered, "given armored divisions—"

"Our mission would justify generals." She raised her voice to cut him off. "Divisions, if we could deploy divisions around Enfield. We cannot. Comrade, the task is no smaller because it has fallen to us. We have been promised full support. If we need weapons, we can obtain them. Weapons better than tanks—"

His sardonic grunt checked her.

"Listen, comrade!" She hated to call him that. "I am speaking of military biologicals. None of our own are yet fit for deployment, but the Center has hinted of some powerful new instrument that might be made available for use in emergency. Only as a last resort, however. And only if we are confident that the Americans can be deceived into believing the deaths were due to an accidental mishap with their own experiments."

"Kill ourselves?" He scowled at her sullenly. "With some synthetic plague? I know knives and poisons and bullets. I am not a laboratory rat."

"You are a soldier." She let her voice sharpen. "We are fighting a war. Fighting for the future of all the people's democracies. Perhaps even for human survival—"

"You quote *Pravda*?"

"Here in Enfield, we fight at the front." She ignored his sarcasm. "Not because we volunteered. Just because we happen to be the agents in place. Believe me, our failure here at EnGene could cost Mother Russia more than the loss of an army. The Center made that very clear.

"The American weapon—it must be obliterated!"

Herman Doerr was late for work that night. He had spent four unwilling hours in the rented car with Anya Ostrov, most of the time parked at malls and supermarkets, outlining a series of contingency plans, discussing resources he might require, planning ways of getting quick reports to her. She left Enfield the next morning, flying back to Florida to begin her own legal battles with Julia Roman and the Roman-World-Mart attorneys for control of the dead capitalist's estate.

Enfield had not yet died.

5

Task Force Watchdog

Driving back in the humid gloom, away from the cop and whatever had struck Enfield, Dr. Saxon Belcraft felt as utterly dazed and blank as the cop had looked. On impulse, recalling the squawk of the police radio, he twisted the dial of his own. A burst of rock music. A deodorant commercial. A country singer wailing. He snapped it off.

Red neon flashed ahead. ENBARD MO EL. The building looked shabby and deserted when he slowed for it, no cars in sight. He drove on to look for a phone, for any news from Enfield, perhaps a room for the rest of the night.

A yellow light slowed him again, blinking in the middle of the road. His headlamps picked up two farm tractors and a battered station wagon parked in position to block the pavement. He stopped and rolled the window down.

A thick rank scent swept over him, the jungle reek of weeds and undergrowth the tractor wheels had crushed. Nothing moved anywhere. The hot night seemed oddly quiet till he heard the throb of a helicopter far overhead. A sudden searchlight blazed into his face.

"Listen! You at the barrier!" A bullhorn behind the searchlight, hoarsely braying. "Stop where you are. Turn back now."

He climbed out of the car and stood squinting into the glare, trying to shield his eyes.

"Get this! You by the car. You are in an emergency safety zone, created under military authority, now policed by Task Force Watchdog. The flasher marks the perimeter. Exit forbidden. Get back and stay back."

"Why?" He blinked into the blinding light. "What's hap—"

"Warning! The perimeter is closed. Turn your car. Get away and stay away!"

He tried to shout again, but his voice had dried up. For a moment all he could hear was the chopper's steady beat.

"Get this!" the bullhorn boomed. "You on the road. You are a suspect carrier. You are confined to the quarantine zone. If you don't move, we'll obey orders. Fire to kill!"

He backed away. The searchlight followed. Still blinded, he felt the car jolt off the pavement. He stopped till the beam went on to light a narrow bridge and pick up black shadow-clots of brush and trees in a shallow valley below. He saw no movement anywhere. The bullhorn gone silent, all he could hear was the chopper's throb, the heart of the dark. When he could see, he drove back toward Enfield.

Suspect carrier?

The words echoed in his mind like a tolling gong. The city's knell, perhaps his own. The darkness settled suddenly on him, suffocating. All he could see was the yellow flasher, growing fainter in the rearview mirror. Breathing hard, he shuddered.

Could he get out?

With luck enough, perhaps he might. Whatever the forces on the perimeter, they must have been called up on very short notice. Perhaps he could find some back road not yet watched. If he drove without lights, perhaps the chopper couldn't follow. Or would the crew have infrared detectors?

At worst, he might abandon the car and strike out on foot. The moon had been full last weekend—the night Midge left, he had walked under it for endless hours, fighting the truth and the pain. Now it would be rising soon after midnight, perhaps in time to help—

That panic impulse died. The shape of danger was still invisible, remote enough to be denied. Speaking to Jeri only this morning, he had heard no desperate alarm.

He left the headlamps on. Deliberately, he took a deep breath and slowed the car, searching for all he could recall about EnGene. Pharmaceutical reps calling at the office had told him more about it than he had ever heard from Vic.

A pioneer among the hopeful new outfits set up to exploit genetic engineering, it was rumored to be creating miracle endorphins and interferons, magical antibiotics, and fabulous new vaccines, but no EnGene salesman had ever called on him to offer any such wonders.

Had Vic been involved? Perhaps with some synthetic microbe meant to heal but somehow turned malign? He shook his head, trying not to consider that. The imagined perils of genetic research had always alarmed a few crackpots, but crackpots were everywhere, shouting alarm about every chimera they could invent. Such paranoias had no place in medical science, and he refused to entertain them now. Evident panic had hit the town, but it had to be—surely it had to be—merely hysteria.

He tried to relax at the wheel, taking cautious stock of his own sensations. His seat felt numb, his shoulders stiff from driving too long. His head ached a little. That slab of cold pizza heavy in his stomach, he had eaten nothing till late afternoon, then only a quick double cheeseburger. Now, longing for a cold beer and a good rare sirloin, he certainly felt no symptom of any synthetic virus working in him.

Again he tried the radio. A slick commercial for an album of country music stars. A drawling local newsman, reading official estimates of a bumper wheat harvest. A hoarse evangelist screaming threats of hellfire in the hereafter. Nothing of any hell in Enfield, here and now.

Ahead, the ENBARD MO EL still flashed its gap-toothed invitation. Though the flickering neon said NO VACANCY, the place looked empty. Nowhere better in view, he stopped and walked inside. The jangling bell brought a thin little woman out of a dark hallway. Limping a little, she wore the penetrating turpentine stink of some patent liniment.

"Yes, sir?" She squinted warily though steel-rimmed glasses. "Want a room?"

"Maybe. If I can use a telephone."

"Pay phone yonder." She nodded vaguely.

He found the phone on the wall beyond the Coke machine and dialed the number Jeri had answered. A busy signal beeped. The woman stood waiting till he came back, both bony hands flat on the cracked glass counter, dourly patient.

"Single is thirty-seven eighty-nine if you want to stay. Cash now."

"VISA card?"

"Not tonight."

"Why not tonight?"

"Pay now if you want the room." She pushed an index card across the broken glass.

"What's going on tonight?" He tried to decipher her pain-pinched, pale-eyed face. "Has something happened in Enfield?"

"They's some crazy tale." She rolled a tape-wrapped ballpoint after the card. "On the room TV if you want to hear about it. Channel Five."

"The roads are closed," he told her. "Both directions."

"So you got stuck?" Her bird-quick nod reflected no regret. "Hope you ain't hungry. We don't serve meals. Not even breakfast since Mr. Bard died—my late husband." She shrugged toward the vending machine. "Fritos and candy bars if you want a snack."

"Later, maybe."

He signed the card, and her yellow talons took his cash.

"I'll put you in number nine. Straight back. Has to be tidied up."

She gave him the key on a heavy wooden ball. He parked outside number nine, and she limped after him into the room. The bed looked unused, but soiled towels littered the bathroom floor and empty beer cans had been tossed at the wastebasket.

"Full up before sundown, but that fool tale scared everybody out."

She collected the clutter and took it away. He used the bathroom and tried Channel Five. A national network news show was just ending on heart-rending shots of big-bellied infants dying of famine in the Sahel. A cosmetics commercial followed, then one from Enfield Federal, "where we take interest in you and you get interest from us."

Mrs. Bard rapped and shuffled in again with a water-stained glass and two skimpy towels. He asked what she had heard on Channel Five.

"Hokum!" She hung up the towels and flushed the toilet. "From nobody regular. Some crazy guy there in the news studio. Drunk as a skunk. Making up wild lies that panicked all our guests till they jumped in their cars and took off. Most never settled for their rooms. I'd like to sue him." Her gaunt jaw set stubbornly. "It's got to be another hoax, like way back the year I married Mr. Bard. That radio thing about the monsters from Mars."

"Just a hoax? I saw a car go off the road and burn."

"Crazy!" Back at the door, she squinted at him through dirty lenses. "Simon-pure craziness. I know they ain't nothing to it, because my own son's down there. A security guard at EnGene. Anything bad, my Frankie'd a-called me before—"

Her knobby hand darted at her throat, and he saw her gulp.

"Before the phones went out."

"My brother works there." He stepped closer to her, into that sharp turpene reek. "Do you know what they do—what they did at EnGene?"

"Nothing bad. That's certain sure." Her head jerked for emphasis. "Frankie calls it bio research. Inventing new *farmer sooticals.* Frankie says they'll wipe out cancer and asthma and my neuralgia. I just hope it's soon!"

She pushed a stringy gray wisp off her face.

"All hush-hush, Frankie says, because the formulas—"

She stopped to stare at the TV. A toothpaste commercial had broken off to show an empty news desk. The logo on the wall behind it read ENFIELD TONIGHT.

"That crazy drunk, coming back. Claiming he's the last man alive in Enfield—"

6

Pancho Torres

The ladies and ladylike men of the Enfield Garden Club had toiled long to enhance "the tiptop lifestyle of the city magnificent," planting ornamental pines in traffic islands and supporting the antilitter ordinance and phoning the mayor to gripe about weeds in vacant lots, but their civic benevolence had never reached the county jail. Filth festered there. The air conditioning had been broken all summer, while commissions and contractors squabbled over who should pay for repairs. In the baking heat, it was an evil-odored oven.

Pancho Torres had been there since winter, when it was an evil-odored icebox. Lying naked and sweating through that last night in the solitary cell, he slept little and uneasily, escaping at last into a happy dream of San Rosario, back when he was small and dreams were real. It was morning in the dream. He lay listening to the slap-slap-slap of his mother patting out tortillas and the mouth-wetting smell as they toasted.

"Hombres! Desayuno!"

Men! His mother's voice, calling him to breakfast with his father. No longer would he have to wait with Estrella and Roberto and little José until his father and Hector had eaten. For this was his *cumpleaños*! Today he was seven, and his mother had called him a man!

She had bought him his first huaraches, made from a worn-out tire, and today he was going to the *ejido* with his father. Estrella and Roberto would have to take over his old tasks, carrying water to fill the *olla* and learning to work with their mother, climbing the hills for firewood and grinding *masa* for the tortillas.

Barefoot no longer, he would be proud today, walking with his father in the strange-feeling huaraches. On their way out of the barrio and through the plaza and down to the growing crop of *frijoles* and *maíz,* people coming home from early mass would see them and know that now he was a man.

"Hey you, killer spic! Hit the deck!"

That mocking shout shattered the dream. He woke to the heat and the stinks of old sweat and old piss and old vomit and the dark flat face of Deputy Harris grinning through the bars.

"Up and at 'em, greaser boy! Good news for you." Harris stopped to chuckle. "You're leaving us today. Your lawyer won't be down to see you off, but he left a message. Says he's found no grounds for appeal. Ain't that just too bad?"

"A disappointment." He nodded, trying hard not to show how much he hated Harris and the court-appointed lawyer and every Mexican-hating gringo. "No surprise."

The game of life had been rigged against him from the start. He had tried to play it by the hard rules the gringos taught him, against odds he had never really understood. A tantalizing game, because it let him win enough to think he was born lucky, until the *mala suerte* snatched everything away.

A cruel gringo game, where his unlucky people always lost.

"Listen up, greaser boy." Harris raised his taunting voice. "You can pack your things and kiss your girl good-bye. You'll be riding upstate this afternoon. They'll be hooking up your chair."

"Okay, Mister." He looked hard at Harris, taking care not to let his Spanish accent show. "I'll be ready."

An endless morning after Harris was gone. He had no girl to kiss good-bye, no sign of sympathy from anybody. The Anglo prisoners all despised him, perhaps the blacks and Latinos too. With nothing to pack, nothing at all to do, he walked the narrow cell and sat slumped on the narrow bunk, hating all gringos.

Most of all, even more than Deputy Harris, he hated the gringo *marijuaneros* who had put him there. Gringos who didn't want Mexicans to pilot airplanes or make money or have beautiful women. Ugly *cabrones* who called him and his people bungling fools, who laughed at them and cheated them and bullied them. Those jealous rivals had helped set up the sting, to get him and Hector and all their compadres out of the way.

His one visitor that last morning was another hateful gringo, a fat Protestant preacher who came with a guard to stand outside his cell and beg him to kneel and pray for one final precious chance to escape the roaring fires of hell.

"Believe with me!" The preacher's pale eyes lifted toward his Lord. "Cast yourself into the loving arms of Jesus. I beg you, brother! Open your damned soul to admit His holy light. Believe and receive—"

"That's enough." He cut the preacher off. "I've believed too many lies." He turned to the guard. "Take him away."

His lunch came on a paper plate, a heavy gray slab of what the jail cook called meat loaf. A dead cockroach lay on top of it, legs up. Thanks, he thought, to Deputy Harris.

It was Harris again who came with two guards to shackle his wrists and escort him down the corridor, past those stares of silent scorn and out to his cage in the police car. Two deputies drove him away.

"Your final ride, killer boy! To something hotter than your *cucaracha* pie!"

Harris stood waving. Glad to have no more of him,

Torres moved his arms to ease the pressure of the handcuffs and sank into bitterness. *Tierra de Dios,* his brother Hector used to call it. God's country. So it had seemed through all his hard childhood years in San Rosario. He remembered his father struggling to sound out the letters from fabulous Los Angeles.

The city of the angels. Letters from his mother's brother, Eduardo, who had become *el tío rico.* Later, those from Hector, who had gone north to share Eduardo's good fortune and discovered enough to begin coming back to land his own airplane on the narrow airstrip the *marijuaneros* had made in the rocky *campo* above San Rosario.

At last, when he had grown old enough, Hector had taken him north in the roaring airplane, all the way to *la tierra de dios.* There, sharing Hector's *buena suerte,* he had learned to shoot guns and pilot *aviones* and date stunning gringo girls.

God's country, *en verdad* till those envious gringos set up *la picadura.* Their poison sting. Eduardo had posted a million-dollar bond and gone back to buy the hacienda where he had been a peon. Left with nothing for the mocking gringo lawyers, he and Hector had gone to prison, sentenced to twenty years. Hector died climbing the wall. Outside and on the run, but very little luckier, he had jumped off a freight train on a bleak winter night and found himself in Enfield.

Penniless and shivering, he tossed a rock through a pawnshop window. The owner had left no cash, but he found a gun and tried a 7 Eleven for cash. The counter girl screamed. He waved the unfamiliar gun. It exploded. And now, many years and many miles and many disappointments since that first one, the day he discovered that digging weeds out of the *ejido* strip was really no fun at all, he was on his way to die.

A dull concussion roused him. He felt it jolt the car. Distorted voices on the radio began squawking code numbers that meant nothing to him. He leaned to peer out. They were still in Enfield, crawling down a crowded street. Another dull explosion. The men in the front seat turned to scowl at each other. He heard sirens shrieking, and they had to stop.

The signal lights went green and red and green again, but all traffic had been halted. He saw ambulances and fire trucks racing up the street ahead. The driver listened to the blasting radio and turned again to squint at his partner. They nodded together. The driver bent to the wheel. The car roared, lunged ahead, careened across the median into the other lane.

Their own siren howling, they barreled back across the town. He shouted questions through the steel mesh, but the men in front ignored him till the car slowed and stopped beside the road. The driver stayed at the wheel. The other scrambled out and ran to unlock the door that held him in.

"Okay, Pancho. Let's see your cuffs." He held out his hands. "With all hell bustin' out behind us, corrections won't have time to ask what we've done with you."

"*Qúe hay?* Spanish came in spite of himself. "What's going on?"

"God knows!"

7

The Cato Club

The day Enfield died, Adrian Clegg called the executive council of the Cato Club into emergency session. They met at the Holy Oaks Hotel. That historic monument, just off Pennsylvania Avenue, was now owned by the club. Built to be the Washington residence of a railway tycoon, the noble old mansion had been refurbished for another tenant every generation since: to house an Asiatic embassy, an exclusive residential hotel, a philanthropic foundation, a museum of primitive art.

Now, for all the world knew, it was once more a hotel, through its public rooms were always closed for renovation and most would-be patrons never found reservations available. The sole occupants now were the sworn and tested members, a few of their well-screened guests, and the discreet black staff. As the Cato Club, they remained zealously invisible. No club activity was ever announced; no untrusted outsiders were ever admitted. Staffers wore the historic gold-braided Holy Oaks livery, but also badges and guns.

The meeting on that fateful afternoon was in the old library, itself monumental, the high wainscoting and tall bookcases and great table all dark mahogany. An isolated island, the room seemed untouchable by any hazard from Enfield, remote even from the capital around it. Traffic noise was muted to a faraway whisper, and the air carried the faint fragrance of good cigars and the mellow aroma of old leather from the massive chairs and the gold-stamped books moldering on the shelves.

Though the club itself strove hard for namelessness, few of those seated there had ever shunned their own publicity. Clegg himself, like the lobbyist and the ex-Secretary of State, had always courted it. The pollster made a science of it. The oil baron, the shipping magnate, the banker, the media tycoon, the newspaper editor, two or three journalists and a few others too secretive to be classified: they all were or longed to be brokers of power. Their talk ceased when Clegg came in.

"Got anything?" the editor greeted him eagerly. "Anything new?"

"Enough to make us move." He stalked to the end of the long table. "Gus is on his way from the White House now. He'd have the latest, but we won't find comfort in it. They're buzzing like a nest of stirred-up hornets with nobody in sight to sting."

He paused to clear his throat, and his voice rose enough to fill a larger hall. "Gentlemen, when we've heard whatever update Gus may bring, I'll have news for you. Before we get to that, however, this is a moment when we should all renew our solemn pledges. Beginning with our oath of secrecy."

Hands on their hearts, they echoed the ritual he intoned. Again he made them wait, while he turned to frown at the liveried black waiting at the door.

"So?" The editor ventured the question. "What's happening in Enfield?"

"Up to now, nobody knows." He kept his cavernous eyes on the doorway. "I pray to God it's what we Catonians stand ready for. I pray again that such procrastinators as Gus haven't been able to delay us too long." He paused for effect, and his voice fell solemnly. "Gentlemen, I'm afraid we're the nation's only chance, though all I've seen up to now is those first unconfirmed AP bulletins. Which the government is hushing up."

"The facts will get out," the editor muttered.

"Not from us." Clegg's cragged features stiffened forbiddingly. "I should remind you that our pledges are enforced." He nodded at the guard. "Here's Gus."

Gus was Dr. Gustave Kneeland. Washed out of the Air Force Academy after a crash that left one eye almost blind, he had entered academe to earn an engineering degree from Cal Tech and the Ph.D. from M.I.T. Nearing fifty now, he had kept himself straight and fit as the young cadet. He attired himself with an effect of stylish elegance—strangely broken now and then in moments of emotional stress, when his bad eye went suddenly askew.

After a brilliant beginning—rumored to have come at least in part from his shrewd choice of research associates—he had been director of a science foundation and then an arms expert for the Pentagon. Now National Security Adviser, he stood high among the secret founders and directors of the club.

Uneasily silent, Clegg beckoned him to the end of the table.

"Fellow Catonians—" Tight-lipped, he paused to shake his head. "I'm afraid you're expecting more than I can say at this point. I have to tell you that we have every indication of a grave national disaster, but its actual dimensions are not yet known. No outcome is yet predictable."

"Why not?"

"Panic." A helpless shrug. "Civil defense, the police, the media—all in the dark. Nobody can confirm anything. Hundreds dead in Enfield before communications got cut off—the worst reports say thousands. Nothing at all for hours now. Disorder spreading out across the state. Total breakdown."

"What hit it?" Clegg was still on his feet, the words

a hostile-seeming challenge. "Some devil's brew out of EnGene?"

Kneeland shrugged, his dark, hawkish face carefully blank. "Nothing confirmed."

"What else could it be?"

"We don't know. We may never know."

"We can guess." Clegg's knobby forefinger stabbed at him accusingly. "We know Lorain and what he's been up to. Gathering Victor Belcraft and his gang of devils there to pry into God's power of creation. Stealing His holiest arts to create genetic monsters—military monsters, since you decided to allow Pentagon funding. Can you deny—"

"We admit nothing." Kneeland's lean mask stiffened. "There will be no official comment. Not from anybody. That's an order straight from the top. No comment whatever. Not until we have something confirmed on the nature of the disaster—if it is an actual disaster."

"It is. Gus, you've got to know it is." Clegg was patronizing, almost sneering. "Proof enough of that got out before anybody tried to muzzle the media. A disaster I expected—and warned you to expect. Lorain and Belcraft should have been scotched a year ago. Instead, you let the Pentagon funnel secret millions—"

"Colonel Clegg, you don't make military policy." Kneeland's voice took on an edge of its own. "The President does, in consultation with people who have earned his trust. EnGene has been receiving confidential funding because his expert military and strategic advisers approved confidential funding."

Lifting a hand to hold off Clegg's rejoinder, he lectured the others like the professor he had been.

"I must clarify the basis for that decision. Progress in science isn't something you can turn off or on. When the time has come for a new step forward, it won't wait for any man or any nation. Lorain and Belcraft aren't the only genetic engineers who have reached what you might call the brink of creation. Others—in Russia, in half a dozen countries—are only one jump behind us.

If a biological superweapon is going to be possible, we want America to own it. Even if lives must be lost—"

Clegg rapped a question, "How many lives?"

Kneeland's wild eye darted at the ceiling, but his voice flowed evenly on.

"The nukes are bad enough, but genetic war could become a worse nightmare. Genes don't have to be mined and run through billion-dollar refineries. Each of us carries our own. Bioscience labs are cheap enough to build. If anybody does perfect a weapon, genetic proliferation will come soon and come fast. The weapons could be spores, deployed by the wind—"

"God's first power, desecrated into an instrument of death!" Clegg had come without the brown beret, and the blood-colored handprint had begun to show through his ashy makeup. "And you admit—"

"We've nothing to admit." A rap of anger. "Whatever we've done was done in good faith, planned to bolster the national defense. If genetic weapons are to exist, we need them in time to develop defenses against them. Perhaps it's true that we've lost a city. Its sacrifice may well save the nation."

"If you and your Pentagon friends are willing to sacrifice innocent cities—" Clegg's hard jaw jutted out. "What else must we expect?"

"That's impossible to say." Kneeland shrugged again. "At this early point, our field reports don't make much sense. When I left the President, he was tied up with the Secretary of Defense and the Joint Chiefs of Staff and the Strategic Air Command in a conference call. Cheyenne Mountain has been alerted, but up to now NORAD hasn't picked up any hint of missiles.

"Pending something definite about what the hell is happening, we're alerting everybody. Civil defense, the military, the CIA and the FBI, state governments in the threatened areas—but very quietly, not to ignite a greater panic. We are confident that the danger can be contained and eliminated—if in fact any widespread danger does exist."

"If Enfield is dead," Clegg muttered sourly, "I think a worldwide danger does exist. A danger even to our own survival."

"You don't know that." Kneeland's odd eye stabbed suddenly aside, and his voice rose sharply. "We don't in fact know anything. We won't until broken communication links can be restored." Both eyes back in focus, he squinted at his watch. "At this early point, that's all I can say. If you'll excuse me, I'll have to get back—"

"Not quite yet—" Clegg cut him off. "I've got something else you'd better hear."

8

Arny Carboni

Anya Ostrov had been called back to Moscow. A plainclothes lieutenant met her at Sheremetyvo airport with a black Chaika limousine and carried her fast into the central city. He parked outside the old Lubyanka prison, now converted into office space for the KGB headquarters, the Center.

The shabby old building had been scrubbed and repartitioned and repainted, but agony and terror and despair still clung like the scent of death to its dingy corridors. Inside, the lieutenant identified her for the sentries. They grinned in appreciation of her figure, but she found no pleasure in their admiration.

Though the bright summer day was hot for Moscow, she shivered a little, following the frayed red carpet down into the guarded offices of the Surveillance Directorate. Boris Shuvalov rose to meet her in a gloomy little room that once had been a torture cell.

"My dear Anya!" His voice seemed too warm, his smile mechanical. "We've been waiting." He sent the lieutenant outside and locked the soundproof door. His quick animal eyes tried to read her features. "Have you brought the Belcraft file?"

"Not yet, Boris."

"Nyet?" His voice lifted. "Why not?"

"The situation—" She spread her arms as if a gesture could explain. "It has become unexpectedly difficult."

"Your earlier reports led us to believe—" His sallow face turned savage. "We have told Colonel Bogdanov that you would have the file with you. Today! He'll be unhappy."

"You promised too much." The room was hot. Brightness shone on his bloodless face, and his cologne failed to hide the odor of his sweat. Keeping her distance, she sank into the chair before his desk. "Who is Bogdanov?"

"A senior officer of the First Chief Directorate. Now acting secretary of Group *Nord.*"

"Group *Nord*?" In spite of her, the words came huskily. "Must *Nord* be involved?"

"Naturally." An impatient shrug. "*Nord* was formed for just such contingencies. It includes the chiefs of all our foreign operations divisions. Call it a general staff in command of all our outposts along the invisible front. The colonel has just been named acting head. He is deeply concerned about the American genetic experiments. Most eager to receive your reports." He shook his head, thin lips set. "The colonel does not forgive failure."

"We haven't—haven't failed!" Angry with herself, she knew she had spoken too hotly. "I hope the colonel can understand we had no way to foresee this—this most unfortunate situation."

"Comrade, let me warn you." His tone grew as cold as his emotionless ferret eyes. "This is no game with nice fat prizes for whatever clever ploys you may have invented. It is war for the survival of Mother Russia, perhaps for the survival of all—"

"I know." She caught a weary breath and wiped at the moisture on her own fair face. In spite of her makeup, its lines of sleepless strain betrayed more years than she liked to show. "I hope the gravity of the situation will persuade the Center to arrange the price my informer is demanding."

"Why any price? Can't you use old Roman's millions?"

"They aren't enough." With effort, she drew herself straighter. "If you'll let me explain—"

"The colonel accepts no alibis."

"Comrade, here is the situation." Her voice turned crisper, as if the words had been rehearsed. "Our most useful informer in the EnGene laboratory has been a man called Arny—Arnoldo Carboni. He is employed as a computer programmer. His exceptional abilities have forced most of the research staff to trust him with the details of their discoveries. Working long hours, often at night, he has been able to make the duplicate printouts that I have secured for the Center."

"But the Belcraft file?" A brittle accusation. "Which you promised—"

"Comrade, if I may speak—" She let her own voice rise. "Dr. Victor Belcraft has become a special problem. Our own experts now call him the ablest man on the EnGene staff. They keep demanding his research notes. Those are difficult. He came to mistrust Carboni. He is also at odds with other members of the staff, perhaps because of some idealistic objection to the production of a biological weapon. Recently, he has worked almost alone. He understands computers. For the past few months he has been writing and running his own programs—"

"You've reported most of that." He waved impatiently to stop her. "But you led us to understand you would bring copies of his private—"

"I was wrong." She shrugged. "If I've failed anywhere, it was a failure to understand Carboni. I thought all he wanted was money. He presented himself to us as a pathological gambler obsessed with an idea that he could beat the casinos at the Las Vegas resort with systems of play designed on his own computer. We've paid him many thousand American dollars, which he seems to have thrown away—all just to trick us."

Her fair skin flushing, she caught an indignant breath.

"We taught him skills to open the office safe where Belcraft kept his laboratory notes and paid him eighty thousand dollars to photograph them. He has done that. He has delivered convincing copies of cover pages and a few revealing passages, but he won't give up the entire file. Not for money. Not even for a million, unless we also meet his main demand."

"Which is—?"

"Alyoshka."

"That traitor?" Shuvalov's wet face reddened. "Impudent idiot! Does he think he commands the Kremlin?"

"He expects to," she said. "He offers what he calls a reasonable trade. Freedom for Leon Alyoshka and his wife and daughter to migrate to Israel or America, or anywhere they like, with suitable guarantees that they will never be molested. In return—and the same guarantees for his own safety—he will surrender the Belcraft file."

"Impossible! The Colonel couldn't—" Shuvalov surged to his feet. "It's blackmail! The USSR will never submit. Never! Not to some American hoodlum."

"Carboni is no idiot." Feeling calmer, she wanted to smile at his agitation. "He knows well enough that his offer is hard for us to accept, but he has refused to give us any other option. He demands Alyoshka's freedom in exchange for the files—and he knows how much we want them. He has been keen enough to work out the exchange like a seasoned professional."

"Don't you employ your own professionals?"

"Who have failed." She shrugged. "I have discussed the problem with the agent Scorpio, who has been my contact with Carboni. Professional enough, though I despise him. He reports that Carboni no longer has the photos in his own possession. Carboni says they have been placed where they will reach the American CIA if anything happens—"

His hostile headshake checked her.

"Comrade—" She caught her breath and lifted her head to face him. "I'm convinced that Alyoshka must be released if we want the photos."

"I don't know—" He stood scowling at her for half a minute, then retreated abruptly into an inner office. She let herself sag wearily back into the chair till he returned. "I have referred the matter to Colonel Bogdanov. He wants to question you himself." He moved toward the door. "At once!"

9

Marty Marks

Standing with that withered little woman in the stale heat of number nine, Belcraft turned with her to watch the TV. A gangling, mud-spattered youth was sliding into the chair under the newscast logo. His face was grimed and swollen, and new blood beaded a jagged scratch down one unshaven cheek. His breath rasped fast, as if from a run. He sat a moment, peering behind him, and then turned to blink into the camera through black-rimmed glasses. One lens was cracked and smeared.

"Folks, I got—got back!" His voice came out with a nervous squeak, and he gulped to smooth it. "Back to the KBIO newsroom on the downtown tower. Here again to continue my own exclusive report on disaster in Enfield. Dunno how long—"

He paused to get his breath and mop his face with a dirty rag that smeared the oozing blood.

"Needed that break. On the mike since six, all by my lonesome. Stopped for a bathroom break. And something else I needed. Another good swig of Old Smuggler out of the news director's private bottle." He tried to grin. "Don't think he'll mind—"

"Hogwash!" Mrs. Bard sniffed. "A stinking drunk."

The door slammed behind her.

"—back on the penthouse terrace," Marty Marks was rushing on, as if in terror of interruption. "Looking down on Central and Grand from eighteen stories up. A whole new scene since last time. Streets worse than a madhouse then. Wrecked cars and trucks and buses piled up at every intersection. Most on fire. People swarming out of houses and running everywhere, wild to get away. Except a few crazy kids smashing into a liquor store, staggering out with bottles they never had time to tap.

"No motion now. Bodies piled on top of bodies they'd tried to crawl over, crazy to get away. Bodies everywhere, on the sidewalks and the pavements and the roofs I could see—and not a soul alive anywhere. A stillness in the streets that's worse than all the car horns and the engines roaring and the sirens and the screaming. All I heard was a chopper overhead. Somebody looking, I guess, for what they'll never—"

Abruptly silent, Marty Marks came half to his feet and turned to listen, his lank frame tense. Poised for a moment as if for flight, he sank slowly back into the chair.

"Nothing, folks." He pushed the glasses higher on his nose. "A nasty minute when I thought I had company. Anybody coming up here would likely bring something I'm in no hurry to get. Can you blame me?"

Swabbing his face, he flinched when he touched the scratch on his cheek.

"A funny feeling, folks. Ever since I was just a whimpering kid I wanted to be a TV anchorman. Somebody like Dan Rather or Tom Brokaw. A crazy dream, because I never had the looks or the voice or the wits for it. But tonight's my night. As long as I last—"

Shivering a little, he twisted to listen again.

"For anybody just tuning in, I'll try to sum it up—what I know, which ain't all that much. Like I been saying, it all began early today, out at the EnGene Labs. Maybe forty blocks southwest of downtown. What is it?" Eyes wide and strange, he stared into the camera. "Who knows?

"Nobody never told us nothin'. First thing anybody outside knew, they were calling from the labs to report an accident. Some hazardous substance escaping. Never said what it was, but they wanted the cops to seal their premises off.

"Demanded a news blackout. Under orders, they claimed, from Washington. The cops did divert traffic away from the plant. One of our mobile units went out to get the story, but the cops wouldn't let 'em in. They did catch an EnGene scientist while he was held up, yelling at 'em to let him inside, but he claimed not to know a thing.

"The cops kept him out till he called Washington. In a few minutes they had orders from the local FBI to let him in. His last mistake, I reckon. Never came back out. The G-men went to work on our news director. Claiming they had a red alert—if you know what that is.

"They made him agree to sit on the story, but the mobile crew kept taping what they could, digging for answers. Trying to run down the truth about EnGene and what it was to Washington. Prying for comment on crazy tales they picked up. Rumors EnGene had been doing illegal biological research that must have got out of control. Never got a word from anybody that admitted knowing anything."

Marty Marks stopped to listen again.

"Okay, folks." Gingerly avoiding the scratch, he mopped sweat off his grimy forehead and pushed the broken glasses back up his nose. "That's all I know about how the thing began. Just past noon, the labs blew up. Could have been a gas explosion—our news people had smelled escaping gas."

Explosion? Belcraft shivered in the hot room, wondering if that blast had killed his brother.

"—other buildings caught." He heard Marty Marks again. "Cops let the first fire trucks inside the lines, but they hadn't done much before something knocked them out. Something—you tell me what! Equipment still there, but standing still. Nobody fighting the fires. A lot of buildings still blazing now, all across the southwest side of town.

"Middle of the afternoon, bigger wheels got here from Washington. Our mobile unit caught 'em at the airport, landing in a military transport. Claimed to come from an outfit we'd never heard of before. Bioscience Alert.

"A funny thing about Bioscience Alert. They claimed to be unofficial. Just a handful of scientists concerned about what they called the promises and the dangers of genetic engineering. But they all had special badges and emergency authority straight from the top. Giving orders to the FBI and the CIA and the state police and everybody else. Threatened to have our own people shot if we reported anything about them."

Marty Marks grinned bleakly into the camera.

"They ain't here to stop me now, and I'll say what I know. They took things over. Ordered the cops to pull back their lines and evacuate everybody in six blocks of the lab. Our camera crew climbed on a roof to take what happened when they went in. Half a dozen men looking like spacemen in masks and plastic suits. Went in toward the fire and never came out. What did come out—"

Marty Marks stopped to listen, sweating, yet still shivering.

"What it is, I don't know. Don't reckon they did. Nothing you could see or hear, but it kills people. Quick! Wherever it catches 'em. On the streets and in their houses when they try to hide and in their cars when they try to get out. Never any warning they've got time to tell about.

"It spread from the dead. With the wind, I reckon, because the cops kept calling our weatherman for wind forecasts. As long as he stuck around. Winds light all day, which I guess is lucky. It hit the cops and firemen first, close around the lab. Those that tried to run never got far. Not if they'd already caught it—whatever it is.

"The cops still alive—along with whoever was left of the G-men and those Washington bigshots—they tried to stop the spread of it. Moved the roadblocks back when it got past their lines. Dynamited the river bridges and the viaduct over the railroad yards.

"The last I heard of McGrath—he is or was our news director—he was reporting a run-in with one of those Bioscience wheels. About the news blackout. If the country is in danger—sure as hell it is—McGrath thought the public ought to be told. The wheel said no. McGrath said to hell with him. Called the studio to stand by for a direct broadcast from the mobile van.

"We stood by, but he never came on. The rest of the day crew checked out to cover the story—or more likely to get out of town. I stayed here to put McGrath on the air. Night crew never showed up. Not that I blame anybody. Good friends of mine. Just hope to God they took off in time. Could be the wheels had somebody shoot McGrath. Could be the wind from the lab caught them all.

"Suicide to try the streets now, so I'm still here. On the air!" A haggard grin. "At six o'clock, when nobody turned up and I felt damn sure nobody would, I decided to tell what I can, as long as I can talk—to hell with Washington and Bioscience Alert!

"One thing more—not that I know what it means." Biting his lower lip, Marty Marks twisted to listen again. Blood-pinked sweat oozed down his dark-stubbled chin. He squinted again into the camera. "All quiet down below, last time I looked. But things are—shining.

"Everything, I reckon, that ever was alive. Bodies. Clothes they had on. Grass and trees down the street in Eisenhower Park. Shining with a pale gray light. Burning, I first thought, but there ain't no smoke. Not except from those blazes, off toward where the lab was.

"Don't ask me what makes the shine. I don't know. Don't know if anybody ever will. But I'm signing off for now. Time for a break, and another good snort of Phil's

Old Smuggler. Maybe a snack, if I can find anything—a couple of the staffers used to bring lunches, and I don't think they ever had time to eat."

Behind the desk, Marty Marks stood up and stretched himself.

"So that's all for now. Can't guess how much time I've got left. Or what time you've got—anybody out there still cool enough to listen. But I'll take another gander from the penthouse terrace and get back to tell you what I see. If I can get back. Just one more word, while I can talk."

Suddenly swaying, he sat down again.

"If you see anybody comin' out of Enfield, don't let 'em—"

The nasal voice faded. The blood-streaked features relaxed into an empty leer. The mouth yawned open. The dirty lenses slid off the vacant eyes and struck the desk with a tiny clatter. Marty Marks slumped slowly out of view. Nothing else moved. The studio was silent.

10

Alyoshka

Anya followed Shuvalov out of the Lubyanka. They found the plainclothes lieutenant waiting with the Chaika. Fast again, he drove them out of Moscow, southwest across the ring road and on into the empty-seeming greenbelt.

Well inside the forest they passed a billboard that read HALT! NO TRESPASSING! WATER CONSERVATION DISTRICT. Out under the dull sky again, he parked beside a guardhouse identified with a gold-lettered sign. SCIENTIFIC RESEARCH CENTER. Khaki-clad sentries checked Shuvalov's pass, frowned over the visas in Anya's passport, and telephoned the colonel before they were passed through the turnstile.

Inside the tall chain link fence, the seven-story office building of the First Chief Directorate made a striking contrast to the grimy old prison, its window-walls of aluminum and glass shimmering out of well-kept lawns and flower beds.

Bogdanov was a dark massive man with thinning gray hair and a face like the nose of a battle tank. He sat facing them across a wide, uncluttered desk. As if to accent his air of implacable iron, the room was fragrant with a mass of fresh cut roses in an antique brass vase on the end of the desk. His career had begun on a livestock collective, and he still had the manner of a butcher. He kept them standing while his slaty eyes narrowed to inspect Anya as if she had been a fallow heifer. She had reddened in spite of herself before he nodded curtly for them to sit.

"This ultimatum?" His guttural Russian exploded at her. "Are you insane?"

"Colonel Bogdanov, we—we have tested every alternative." She held herself stiffly upright, trying not to tremble. "If anybody is insane, it is our informer in the weapons laboratory. A computer programmer named Carboni. He has demanded freedom for this dissident and his family, with adequate measures to assure their safety. He refuses to consider anything else. I think—" She had to catch her breath. "I think you should know why."

"So!" A grunted command.

"We have gathered a dossier." Eyes still on him, she tried not to see him. "Information that seems to explain his behavior." She spoke rapidly and flatly, almost as if reading the words. "This Arnoldo Carboni was born in the American city of Boston. His mother's family had once been wealthy, but while she was still an infant her father failed in business and killed himself. When her mother died, she used the insurance money to attend Columbia University in the city of New York. She met Leon Alyoshka there—"

"In New York?" The colonel squinted at her. "When?"

"Many years—"

"Comrade Bogdanov," Shuvalov broke in, "the traitor was once a trusted man, though he had never joined the party. His Jewish ancestry had been concealed. He had earned honors in science at Moscow University. He was allowed to spend two years in America as a graduate student in nuclear physics."

"True." She nodded. "And Carboni is his bastard son."

"A son?" The colonel blinked at Shuvalov. "Is that possible?"

"Not likely." Shuvalov shook his head, scowling at her. "I aided the investigations of Alyoshka. I never heard of any American son."

"Neither did Alyoshka." She straightened to face their disbelief. "Comrades, if I may explain. Alyoshka was married. Here. His wife was not permitted to go abroad with him, no doubt to guarantee his return. It is not surprising that he fell in love with an American girl. A fellow student at Columbia. Although he seems to have told her about his wife, she allowed him to involve her in a passionate affair.

"When his two years ran out, that had to end. The girl had become pregnant, but she never told him. She kept the child—named for him; he used to sign himself Arny Ames when they checked into motels. Later, she was briefly married to a laborer named Carboni. He adopted Arny, but she was still obsessed with Alyoshka and the marriage soon dissolved.

"She raised Arny—raised him to love the father he had never seen. She tried to follow Alyoshka's career through the news reports of his achievements in science and his later deviations. His photograph hung at the foot of her bed above a little shelf of momentos. A sort of shrine to him. Russian novels he'd given her, a doll in Cossack costume, a photo of St. Basil's on a postcard that must have been the last message she ever got from him.

"After her death, the son kept those items in his own room. He is described as a lonely oddball who knows computers better than people, but he seems to worship his father—or, rather, that saintlike image he got from his mother. It became the only human value in his life. He has brooded over the sensational speculations in the capitalistic press about Alyoshka's current troubles. He has always longed to know him, longed for a chance to show his love. Now this freak of circumstance has given him a weapon. He's determined to—"

Beneath his blank stare, she had to stop for breath and courage.

"Colonel, I think the dissident will have to be set free."

"Nyet!"

Bogdanov shook his head, considering her. Absently, pale eyes still upon her, he took a rose from the vase to sniff its sweetness. Angry at herself, she knew she was flushing again.

"You must be told." He nodded at last. "Alyoshka is dead."

"Oh—" Her voice was gone.

"He died in a psychiatric hospital." The colonel seemed almost smug. "As you know, before the onset of his paranoid deviations he had been considered a brilliant scientist. Our foremost psychiatists did everything possible to correct his tragic antisocial delusions, but their best efforts failed. They reported a bad reaction to the drug aminazin. The illness destroyed his mind."

"I—I see." She tried not to shiver. "Could we—could we possibly inquire if Carboni would bargain for the wife and daughter?"

As if surprised to find the rose in his hand, the colonel tossed it abruptly aside. His face turned bleaker. "They suffered from similar delusions. They attempted street demonstrations in support of the traitor. Loyal Soviet citizens were so much incensed by their activities that they were forced into hiding. Their whereabouts are not now known."

Silently, she nodded.

"Your problem, Comrade Ostrov." A tone of cold command. "You will return to America at once and proceed to solve it. I advise you not to tell anybody what you have learned about the fate of the deviants. You are free, however, to choose your own plan of action. In the past you have done excellent work, but never anything so important. You must not fail! If means to secure the Belcraft file do not now exist, you will create them."

"If—" She gulped. "We'll do our utmost."

"Get them!" The colonel rose. "You may ago."

He bent to bury his nose in the roses.

Anya Ostrov left Sheremetyvo by Aeroflot that same afternoon. In flight, she saw attendants gathered in the galley, whispering in a seeming alarm which they denied when she asked what was wrong. The weather ahead was excellent. The pilots had not reported any difficulty with the aircraft. It landed at Kennedy without incident. In the terminal building, she found excited people clustered around a man holding up a newspaper to show bold headlines:

GENE PLAGUE
KILLS CITY!

11

Plan Black Cat

Clegg waited at the end of that massive mahogany table in the Holy Oaks library, watching Kneeland turn and move uncertainly back toward to group.

"Please, Gus! For the good of the club—the good of the country—please sit down and listen." Though he seldom smiled, his dark granite face had softened a little, and he kept his tone carefully placatory. "We're going to need the best you can give us."

He paused again, while Kneeland hesitated and finally, almost sheepishly, sank into the big leather chair.

"Thank you, Gus." He cleared his throat and scanned the silent circle. "I've more to say to all of you. If things are as bad as they seem, we Catonians will have a new role to play. We can—we must seize the lead. The iron hand concealed of course, but we must act at once to defeat this newborn evil that our best efforts have failed to abort."

His shadowed eyes came slowly back to Kneeland's red-flushed face.

"We're going to need you, Gus." Again he tried to smile, but his voice had an imperative edge. "I hope you never forget that we depend on you as a founding member, your total loyalty duly sworn to the club. You are obligated to share in our decisions, and to let us share in the nation's. We will continue to require your aid and advice. The whole nation will require ours.

"I have news all of you must hear."

"Keep it brief," Kneeland muttered. "The White House staff will be expecting me."

"The White House can wait." Clegg stood silent for a moment as if to organize his thoughts. His voice, when he went on, had begun to ring with with oratoric overtones. "Gentlemen, in this grave emergency, I want you to recall the noble Roman whose name we honor. I want you to remember why we call ourselves Catonians."

He paused to scowl forbiddingly at Kneeland's sullen headshake.

"Founding the club, we pledged our lives—and our sacred honor, gentlemen, if you recall our oath—to defend a precious legacy. We—the founders of the club—stand among the privileged best of a nation God has favored greatly.

"As Americans now, standing in the shadow of Armageddon but looking back across a magnificent past, we are the fortunate inheritors of four great millennia. Heirs to all that priceless legacy we call civilization. The faith of the Jews and the word of Christ. The glory of Greece and the splendor of Rome and the best of all the ages since."

Kneeland moved restlessly, looking at the door.

"Gentlemen," that solemn chant rolled on, "this dark moment has to make us all aware that our noble national heritage has fallen into desperate danger—a danger most of us have long foreseen. Our precious America has long been in danger from the foul decay of faith, from the corruption of democracy, from liberalism and Marxism and a hundred other idiotic delusions. Through decades of moral rot, everything we cherish has been sinking into gathering peril from all the hordes of apish fools rising up to riot and strike and fight for rights they never earned.

"Unless we act at once, with resolute vigor and every resource we can command, this last chapter—this gene-spawned terror spreading out of Enfield—can be the end of us and everything we love."

He stopped to shake his lean-boned head at Kneeland.

"We are banded together as the world's last best hope, sworn to defend the sacred temple of mankind, to rescue and preserve the precious faith and wisdom that have made us what we are, to give our fortunes and our lives if need be to insure the safe survival of that holy heritage that can erase the ancient curse of Cain.

"That is our holy mission. To defend that precious legacy that can transform the savage animal—the untamed creature that comes from the womb—into the statesman, the scholar, the minister of God. We founded the Catonians because we know that miracle can be wrought, acting in faith that we are chosen to perform it. This demon raging out of Enfield has come sooner than we had foreseen, its guise more dreadful. Even now, however—if you will trust my leadership—we still have a chance.

"Because we are not naive. We have read the lessons of history and gathered the reins of power. Even now, here in the shadow of terror, with luck enough we can hope to avoid the fatal blunders that have always trapped those misguided leaders of the past who have tried and always failed to gather up and patch the fragments of toppling democracies. Democracies rotting and falling, as they all rot and fall, because they are finally infected with the virus of mobology."

Kneeland turned in his chair, frowning a silent question at the editor. The editor shook his head.

"Look at the list!" Clegg boomed on. "Look at Alexander and Caesar and Napoleon and a thousand others, even down to Hitler. All caught in the same dilemma, trapped between the mobs and their own grand designs. To hold the mobs behind them, they had to wage foreign wars. Victorious or not, they wasted their nations and the nations around them, and they died by violence.

"Our own hazards are the same. Those mobs would murder us gladly if they had any hint of what we are and what we plan. That's why our oath of secrecy must be enforced so sternly. We have chosen a safer strategy than the best of our famous predecessors—and we must hold to it, gentlemen, even under this threat of genetic doom. Our control can be firm as any emperor's, but we must use it with skill and caution.

"We Catonians must remain invisible. Our rule must be through indirection, through all our means of influence, through our command of money and the media, through electronics and psychology, through a shrewd control of proxy politicos who must never know they're proxies—not even those few unfortunates we may have to sacrifice.

"Okay, Gus?" He swung to challenge Kneeland. "Are you with us?"

"Of course I am!" Kneeland's voice rose testily. "But you've got to remember where I am. Most of you are free to act. I serve two masters—"

"You swore an oath!"

"I'll keep it. The Catonian Plan will always come first. But I should tell you that my other master has grown new teeth. In this emergency, the President wants total discipline. It isn't martial law—not for us and not quite yet. But he was close to panic when he got us together in the Oval Room early this afternoon.

"Can you blame him?" Kneeland moved as if to rise. "Suspecting everybody. The Russians. The Puerto Ricans. The revived Weathermen. Determined to hush up the crisis till we know what's going on. If there's any news leak from official sources, he threatens to have his Secret Service people run the new omnigraph on everybody and shoot suspects without further trial." His

Adam's apple rose and fell. "I'm in danger, revealing even that."

"We're all in danger." Clegg shrugged. "Thank you, Gus, for your update on that chaos in the executive branch. Fortunately, we Catonians are in a better situation. The difference is that they're trapped and helpless in their ignorance and indecision, while we know what to do. We're going to do it."

He swung to face the group with an air almost of triumph.

"Gentlemen, I have spoken to the President since that session in the Oval Room, and I was able to cool his panic. Slightly, anyhow. I doubt that many of you know that he has always been a secret Catonian. He has agreed to let us activate Plan Black Cat."

The men around the table stirred, exchanging puzzled glances.

"A top secret plan," he told them. "Developed by our Inner Council. An executive program designed to call up our resources for emergency action. As you are all aware, we do have resources. We have members in the military and the major corporations. People with money. People in the laboratories. We have Bioscience Alert. We have—"

Kneeland was squinting at his watch.

"Hold it, Gus. Just a moment more." Clegg paused again, staring away at something beyond the old mahogany walls and the tall shelves of never-read Victorians. His deepset eyes came back to Kneeland, his tone harshly accusing. "You need to hear this, Gus, because you've let those fools at Enfield open the gates of hell. In spite of all your stonewalling, it's clear enough that you've conspired with those fools in the Pentagon to let this demon out of hell.

"In plainer English, that devil's crew at EnGene has stolen God's secret power of creation and abused it to create a monstrous weapon. I warned them, a year and more ago. In their Satanic arrogance, they ignored me. Now most of them are doubtless dead.

"And we Catonians are going into action."

He waited until all their eyes were on him.

"I have been recalled from retirement with the rank of brigadier general to mobilize and command Task Force Watchdog." His voice rang with the sheer joy of new authority. "The President has assured me of total support from every arm of government. It should interest you, Gus, to know the true purpose of that conference call you are itching to be party to. The President is going to alert the Chiefs of Staff and order them to expedite our mobilization."

He swung as if to challenge Kneeland. Kneeland blinked and shook his head until that outlaw eye had focused on Clegg.

"The President—" He gulped. "You say the President will approve?"

"He has approved. As soon as we adjourn, I'm flying to the Enfield area to take personal command."

"One—one more question." Kneeland was pale and trembling. "Under Plan Black Cat, what is to be the status of our own weapons research?"

Clegg's gaunt form drew straighter. "I never wanted a genetic weapon. I warned and fought those hell-sent fiends who sought to forge it. If they were the first victims, that is heaven's justice. But if an actual biological weapon does exist—if God is pressing the blade of Armageddon into my hand—I intend to seize it."

He turned back to face the group, a righteous pulpit power returning to his voice. "Gentlemen, we stand in the awful shadow of Armageddon, with God's final judgment close upon us. Whether or not some new hell weapon has been perfected, evil men from many nations will be scrambling to rule the monstrous fiend now loose in Enfield. Task Force Watchdog will challenge and defeat them, wherever their leering heads may lift. We fight for God, this sword of His wrath ready for our righteous hands, and we will not fail."

He nodded at Kneeland, his tone gone flat.

"Okay, Gus. Now you may go."

12

The Burning Dust

Belcraft sat stunned and torn in number nine, staring at the silent TV. Fixed on the empty news desk and the KBIO logo behind it, the camera showed no motion. A faint scent of hot asphalt came through the open door. He heard choppers throbbing far away. Several of them now.

Vic? Had Vic stayed in Enfield to die with Marty Marks and all those others? Stayed in a trap he knew was closing? That looked probable. But why? Guilt for his own share in some unthinkable scientific blunder?

Not likely. On the phone last night, he had shown no hint of terror or remorse. Rather, his voice had rung with a sort of grim elation.

Jeri? That young-sounding woman who had answered Vic's home phone. The live-in companion whom he had never taken time to marry. Was she, too, among the dead? If Vic had known what was coming, and cared for her as he surely did, why hadn't he gotten her out?

Haunting questions. He found no answers.

Here and now, what for him? Should he run for his life? That panic impulse swept him again. With more choppers arriving, the quarantine around Enfield must have been drawn tighter. Yet gaps would be left. If he waited for the moon and drove without headlamps, he might get through—and carry death for thousands more?

Shuddering, he took fresh stock of his own sensations. Still stiff and dull from that long day on the road, he wanted food and drink. Later a good workout and a good night's sleep. Certainly he felt nothing deadly consuming him. But perhaps there were no warning signs. Marty Marks had reported none.

The killer? What could kill a city, so silently, so totally, so fast?

Grappling again with that riddle, he recalled a winter night back in Ohio when their parents had bribed him to baby-sit. Vic, the spoiled and willful four-year-old, wouldn't go to bed. Trying to frighten him into it, he had read him Poe's "Masque of the Red Death." Before he came to the end, his own voice had been hoarse and trembling with dread of the mysterious red-cloaked killer, but Vic had merely fallen asleep, so soundly that he had to carry him to bed.

Now he felt dazed and helpless again in that same spell of implacable terror, even though Enfield's unknown nemesis was not red, as Marty Marks described its aftermath, but shining white.

A synthetic microorganism? Created by some insane project to forge genetic weapons? Or Vic's own virus of life gone dreadfully wrong? Had Vic known or suspected what he had done, stayed to make some forlorn effort to undo it?

With no answers apparent, he decided to risk a closer look.

Even in that hot room, the notion chilled him. Yet he couldn't put it down. Suddenly, he had to see the killer for himself. As closely as he dared. The way should be clearing by now. Even if every exit road had been sealed, those toward Enfield would surely be open. If that highway cop was still alive, he would have been called farther back.

If he caught the wind right, if he stayed in the car—

The room went dark.

That asphalt stink suddenly seemed stronger, the stale air suffocating. He stumbled out of the room into the hot night. The choppers filled the sky with their drumbeat, but all he found around him was the empty dark. The ENBARD MO EL sign was dead. No lights anywhere. The power system must have been abandoned.

He groped his way to the car and stopped beside it, uncertain of everything and trembling with a shapeless dread of the killer working in the dark. He wanted light. In this total blackout, he could hardly move without the headlamps. Yet any moving light would surely draw the choppers. Louder now, flying lower, they seemed hostile as the killer itself.

He stood by the car till his eyes adjusted. He found stars. Arcturus overhead, red Antares low in the south. Virgo, Bootes, Libra: the constellations he had learned that long-past summer when Vic pestered him into helping grind the mirror for a flimsy little telescope.

Eastward, he found a pale gray glow. The moon? Too early, he thought. The streak of light looked too long, stretching all across the horizon in the direction of Enfield like a mistimed dawn. The white shine Marty Marks had seen?

The shine of death?

A line of ragged trees and a weed-clotted fence row loomed dark against it, showing a road that ran past the parking lot and dipped out of sight toward its pale blaze. A back way into Enfield?

Breathing faster, he climbed into the car. Starting the engine, he felt an odd elation, all his senses sharpened by the stress between fear and daring. Joy of action lifted him like a heady wine, till dread came back to quench it.

The lights on dim—he thought it shouldn't really matter if the choppers picked them up—he eased off the empty parking lot and through a straggling hedge to the road. After a mile or so, it dropped into the trees and brush along a narrow stream.

Another loop, perhaps, of the same creek where he had been stopped at the quarantine perimeter. The land beyond lay featureless and black, sloping up again toward that bright horizon line.

Close enough. He stopped on a low bluff above the stream. The road ran on, over a narrow bridge and into the shadows beneath that shine. He turned the car. Ready for a quick retreat, he stepped out and lifted a wet finger to test the wind. The hot night seemed breathless. He stood by the car, watching that silent fire, waiting for the killer.

Hardly aware of the passing time, he found himself stiff from standing, sat back in the car till his legs cramped, climbed out to walk around it, stood again, staring at that slow tide of brightness. He saw the half moon rising. He was dimly astonished to discover it again, suddenly midway to the zenith.

Now and then one of the choppers came near, flying low along the edge of the brightness, seeming to ignore him. He wondered if the crews knew any more than he did about what they were observing.

The white glow crept toward him. Never fast enough for him to see the motion, it was always closer, crawling over grass and weeds and brush, somehow crumbling them into luminous dust. Touching trees, it turned them silver, cloaked them in fleeting glory, dissolved them at last into showers of pale sparks. There was no sound he could hear, no heat he could feel, no smoke he saw rising, no odor—

Alarmed at the notion of odor, he got back into the car and rolled the windows up, but still he sat there, groping back through all he had ever learned about bioluminescence, recalling nothing that made any sense. No familiar biological process could do this. No familiar virus or bacterium, however magically mutated. Nor anything else that he could imagine.

The killer had to be something—something midway between life and fire. Slower than fire, faster than life, it seemed to consume everything organic. Perhaps only its makers had ever known what it was. They were probably dead. He doubted that anybody else would ever know. Yet, trapped by its lethal mystery, awed by a sense of implacable power in its devastating march, he kept on watching and half forgot to fear it.

It spread by contact, he decided. Metal was apparently left untouched. The spidery steel of a farm windmill stood alone where a home and a barn had shone and crumbled. Fence wire hung from thin steel posts. An old hay rake lay like a black steel skeleton against the shine of what had been a meadow.

What it consumed was organic: life or matter that had been alive. Was it something—something not quite alive yet parallel to life, using the tissues of life as fertile soil where its germs or seed or spores could root themself and multiply into more of those luminescent germs or seed or spores? Could it—

What if the wind came up?

He reached to start the car but checked himself to roll the window down and put his hand out to test the air again. It had grown cooler. When he wet his finger, he felt a very slight movement, still from the west. Reassured at least for the moment, he closed the window and sat back to watch that creeping glow at least a little longer.

EnGene?

The need to know stronger than his alarm, he returned to that cruel riddle. Had EnGene labs really been a weapons shop? Vic a worker at its fearful forge? He shook his head, thinking of Canis. The spotted mongrel Vic had found hurt on the street and lugged home in his arms—that was back in Ohio while their father was still a country doctor; it must have been the summer Vic was seven.

He had refused to let their mother have the injured dog put to sleep. Tearfully defiant, he had built a shed for it in the backyard, nursed it to recovery, loved it while it lived, cried half the night when it was run down again. Vic couldn't have made the killer dust. Not knowingly. Not willingly.

Would anybody? It was hard to believe that any sane scientist would allow any risk of causing such disaster. Yet—thinking of Hiroshima and Nagasaki and all the stockpiled nukes that sane patriots had built, he had to battle a sudden flood of dread.

If the dust overtook him—

In a sudden waking nightmare, he fled from it. Those shining sparks pursued him. He ran faster, gasping, desperate. Spinning in a fire-bright tornado, the dust overtook him. He was trapped and suffocating. He was instantly blind, sobbing for breath that wouldn't come. Overwhelmed with agony, he felt the burning film searing all his body, imagined hands and feet and all his skin crumbling into a glittering cloud that swirled away from his glowing bones.

Was this the end of all mankind?

The chill of terror clung and probed and paralyzed him, overwhelming reason. Nuclear genocide had never seemed really likely. Even if civilization fell, the human species had always seemed tough enough to somehow survive absolute extinction from the worst the nukes could do. This silent dust seemed deadlier. Already, it must have killed all who knew its secrets. It looked unstoppable.

Shaking, he bent to start the car. A glimpse of motion checked him. Something beyond that little bridge, coming down the road just ahead of that shining tide. A boy on a bicycle, pedaling desperately.

Carrying the killer?

He started the engine and waited again, delayed by a sudden hunger for human company. If the boy had taken flight in time, escaping infection, it would be a coward's trick to leave him here alone.

Yet—

Shivering from a sudden sweat, he watched the bike

go off the road. It spun into the ditch, went down into a mass of weeds that hid it. Watching, breathing harder, he couldn't help a sense of sick relief. Now he wouldn't have to risk a rescue.

He watched the weeds. For a time, he saw no change. He was almost convinced that the boy had brought no infection, but then the weeds again began to shine and shatter. They crumbled away, finally revealing the unharmed bike and at least the small bright skeleton flaking slowly into dust.

A chopper startled him, passing low overhead. He found the moon, suddenly almost at the zenith. An actual dawn shone pink in the east, the uneaten steel of that windmill tower stark against it. The chopper slowed above him and then drummed on, so low it raised a pale gray plume.

A plume of deadliness. Dull against the dawn, it hardly seemed to move, but he thought day might bring rising winds. It was time to go. He drove back up the road toward the motel and slowed on the curve to look across the creek. The shine of the dust had faded beneath the brighter light of day, and he was struck with a sudden hope that somehow it had been slowed or even halted.

He turned to frown at the little patch of bare gray ash around the bicycle. It was still an isolated island. It had grown no larger. He sat there, watching a line of tall sunflowers along a fence row, watching the clump of trees around a more distant farmhouse—the boy's home, perhaps. The rising sun was suddenly higher, hot in his face—

And nothing more had been touched!

Nerved with hope, he waited. Waited through a dragging eternity, not an hour by the clock on the dash. The sunflowers tipped a little, following the sun. The trees stood unharmed, dark against an ash-white desert. He counted five of the choppers still patrolling, most of them miles away.

Reporting—what? That Task Force Watchdog had

stopped the killer? That the quarantine could soon be lifted? Not very likely. Whatever they reported, the quarantine would surely be kept in force until more was known about the nature and the origin of that mysterious lethal vector.

In truth, would anything more ever be known?

Nearly too groggy to care, he drove back to the motel and parked at the door of number nine. Stiff and achy from sitting too long, he walked around to the office. The bell jingled when he went inside, but nobody came.

He turned to the vending machines. With the power off all night, the drinks would be warm. Not that he cared for Coke anyhow, unless with rum and a twist of lemon. His stomach churned when he thought of Snickers for breakfast, but he found cheese wafers and salted peanuts.

Back in number nine, he pulled off his shoes and scrubbed his hands as if for surgery before he touched his face. Sitting on the creaky bed, he washed the wafers down with tepid water out of the lavatory tap. The little bag of peanuts half open, he let it slide out of his fingers—

His own scream woke him.

He had been dreaming about that boy on the bicycle, racing the dust, swerving into the ditch. In the nightmare, however, the victim had risen out of the weeds, run desperately on toward him across the little bridge.

It had been Vic!

Vic, the age he was in the photo their mother took back on that Ohio farm, the Christmas he got his first bicycle. The picture showed him standing beside it, grinning proudly through his freckles, a front tooth missing, straw-colored hair uncombed. She'd had it enlarged, kept it hanging in her room the rest of her life. Her baby boy.

The grin had become a grimace of terror in the nightmare, and the dust was alive again, flowing fast after him, a glittering sea that overtook him, washed him with liquid fire, dissolved his clothing and his flesh into dancing sparks. He became a skeleton, still running up the road from the bridge, that gap-toothed grin grown hideous. If he came too near—

Belcraft's own scream ended the dream.

In the first dazed moment of waking, he thought he was back in his familiar bedroom in Fort Madison. He sat up, calling Midge's name because he needed her arms around him to drag him back to sanity. In another moment, the roar of a low chopper recalled Vic's phone call, plunged him back into the Enbard Mo el and real-life madness.

The room had become an airless oven. Yellow sunlight blazed through the faded curtain on a west window. Hot sweat drenched him. Blinking sticky eyes, he stumbled toward the bathroom and stopped to listen at the chopper, suddenly deafening. It was over the parking lot when he looked out, so near he could read US ARMY lettered on its dark-mottled camouflage.

A rescue mission!

Thinking that, he ran for it. It had almost touched the baking asphalt fifty yards ahead, but it hadn't come to rescue anybody. It didn't land. A man in uniform leaned out, waving a gun to warn him back. A cardboard carton tumbled to the pavement. The chopper rose quickly, hammering him with searing air.

Anger flared in him, because he was no carrier—he was nearly sure of that. The dust had never touched him. He felt no hint of any invisible killer working in him. Nothing worse than an ache of hunger and the thirst bitter in his mouth. Yet, if the crewmen knew no more than he did about what the killer was, perhaps he shouldn't blame them.

The hot tar was burning through his socks. He limped back to the room for his shoes and carried the carton into the motel office. Again, the bell brought no response. He walked around the counter to try the inside door. It was locked. He rapped and heard the quavery moaning of old Mrs. Bard:

"Jesus save us! Jesus save us! Jesus save—"

He opened the carton. A sheet of flimsy yellow paper lay at the top. Bold red letters headed a blurry block of duplicated typescript.

NOTICE!
TO PERSONS INSIDE QUARANTINE ZONE:

General Clegg is happy to announce that the emergency in Enfield appears to have been controlled. The spread of the not-yet-identified contagion is believed to have been arrested. Regrettably, however, continued uncertainties require all suspect areas to be kept under strict surveillance while investigations continue. Violators of quarantine orders are to be shot without further warning, but all possible aid will be rendered to those affected until the situation has been resolved.

(signed) Major Malcolm Forrest
Acting Air Commander
TASK FORCE WATCHDOG

He opened the carton. A brown bag of soggy hamburgers that set his mouth to watering. Loaves of bread. Cans of corned beef and tomato soup. Oreos and chocolate bars. A six-pack of cold Bud, which had smashed the bread when the package hit the pavement. Candles, matches, aspirin. A Kansas City newspaper with a head that caught his eye:

GENETIC CRISIS ENDING?

He skimmed the story. Washington sources were repeating earlier assurances that the reports of many thousands dead in "the Enfield incident" has been vastly exaggerated. General Adrian Clegg had deplored the incident, calling it "a moment of tragic public hysteria," unjustified by any actual national hazard. Biological scientists were pressing urgent inquiries. Governor Bronson had deplored fresh outbreaks of irrational alarm. The quarantine would be lifted as soon as possible. The public, in the meantime, would be kept fully informed.

Grinning bleakly over the story, Belcraft divided the contents of the carton, stacking Mrs. Bard's share on the counter. Sure she wouldn't mind, he kept all the beer for himself. He carried his own lot back to number nine. Sitting on the doorstep, feasting on cold hamburgers and beer, he found spirit to savor the hot vitality all around him.

A musky breath of fecund growth rose out of the jungle of weeds and brush behind the motel. Cicadas were shrilling. A mockingbird in a lone cherry tree scolded an intruding jay. A bright-winged butterfly drifted past him. A dove cooed somewhere, its gentle voice almost lost in the sky-filling drum of the choppers.

Eight of them now. One in the northwest was probably dropping more food cartons. The rest cruised low over the dust where Enfield had stood. Black vultures, searching for carrion—

Not so. Not quite. He shook his head. The crewmen were brave men, no doubt, able scientists among them, risking everything to probe for that unidentified biological vector. Doomed to fail, because all who had ever known the answers had dissolved into that creeping dust.

Should he test it?

Its advance had stopped. Perhaps the danger had actually passed. He was here on the ground. He knew the basics of genetic science and epidemiology, maybe well enough. His two Peace Corps years had been spent in Zaire, working with Reinberg in tropical medicine.

Why not?

The men in the choppers had given no orders to keep him out of the dust. Energized with food and drink and at least a thin new hope, he got into the car and drove back toward the creek and the bridge and new gray desert where Enfield had been.

13

Three-Footed Coyote

Standing in the shower of gravel as the deputies raced away, Pancho Torres frowned blankly after them and turned to look around him. He was alone. The empty road fell toward straggling trees and a thin shine of water at the bottom of a shallow valley. It rose again beyond, toward a lone grain elevator and the little clump of downtown towers, miles behind him now. Greasy smoke smudged the blue summer sky above them. An open field sloped up from the road toward a windmill and an isolated house. Whining away, the car went out of sight beyond it.

Buena suerte! Luck had smiled again—or maybe not. He couldn't guess what was happening back in the town to jolt the street and raise that smoke and frighten lawmen into flight. He shook his head and started walking up the hill the way they had fled. Behind him, another car came fast from the town. He dropped into the weeds and watched it pass. Another police car, red lights flashing. In pursuit of the fugitives? Or joining their flight?

When it, too, was gone beyond the ridge, he left the road and climbed toward the trees. Another car came howling from the town, then a line of them behind it.

He walked on, hoping they would have no time for him, till he heard tires screaming and turned to see a blue sedan veering off the highway as if to follow him.

Again he fell flat. It raced past him, up a side road he hadn't seen. Watching from the weeds, he saw it lurch to a stop in front of the house. The driver ran inside. Minutes passed. Behind him on the highway, he heard tires shriek again, heard the slam and jangle of a collision, then a hollow boom. Yellow flame exploded in the valley below, where a car had gone off the bridge. He heard far screaming. Nobody stopped to help.

When he looked again, people were running out of the house on the hill. A woman and two small girls. The woman carried clothing in her arms. The larger girl dragged a piece of luggage too heavy for her. The smaller carried something, perhaps a doll. They tumbled into the car. It came skidding back down the hill and spun into the traffic too close to another car, which braked and lurched and rolled into the ditch.

The woman drove on. A man crawled out of the overturned car. A young woman followed. They tried to roll it upright. Failing, they climbed back to the roadside and stood waving desperately. Nobody stopped.

Back at the house, a garage door was rising. A red pickup shot out. It stopped. A small boy in jeans ran after it. A dog came from somewhere and jumped after the boy into the pickup. It roared past him to the highway, slowed as if to stop for the waving couple, lunged ahead before they could reach it. They ran on in the ditch, the woman limping.

Why the panic? He shaded his eyes, peering back toward the town. Thicker smoke had veiled the grain elevator and those far tower buildings. It had begun to spread a low brown cloud against the sky, but he found nothing more alarming, nothing that should have frightened people from this isolated dwelling.

He turned again to frown at the stream of refugees. Should he follow? Not yet. Whatever the terror, it could hardly be anything deadlier than the chair waiting upstate. He walked farther from the road and stopped again to watch the house and the town and the speeding cars. Nothing moved around the building. Smoke floated slowly higher over the town. Smaller clouds boiled up along the highway, where he thought more wrecks were burning. The passing traffic thinned and finally ceased.

He walked on toward the dwelling. It was cream-colored brick, the grass around it neatly mown. Red roses bloomed beneath the windows. No sound came from inside. He tried the doors and windows; they were locked. He went on to peer into a wooden shed sagging into ruin beside the windmill tower. The dirt floor was stacked with rusting farm equipment, but the absent owner had been no farmer. Weeds grew high in the abandoned field beyond a sagging barbed-wire fence.

The windmill was out of use, replaced by an electric pump. Vanes were gone from the motionless wheel, staves broken from the side of the empty wooden water tank on a platform beside the tower. He climbed the old wooden tower to look back again toward Enfield.

Smoke had blotted it out. The highway was empty until a lone motorcycle burst out of the smoke. It came past him, driven fast. Two people on it, a woman with a small child clinging behind her. A police car stopped them on the ridge, red lights flashing. The woman waved her arms, as if protesting. They turned at last, raced past him again back toward the town. He lost them in the smoke and heard another engine throbbing.

Searching for it, he found a brown and green military chopper flying from the north as if circling the town. It hovered over the cop car and then came on to sink again toward the house. He dropped flat on the platform, hoping not to be seen.

"Warning!" He caught a hoarse electronic bray. "Enfield area is under emergency quarantine. Perimeter is closed. Entry and exit forbidden, on pain of death. Warning!"

The chopper drifted on, the bullhorn fading.

In the winters, his father had trapped coyotes in the hills above San Rosario. He used to pity the caught animals, limping on broken legs to drag the trap to the end of the chain and crouching there, snarling, waiting to be clubbed to death. Even if they gnawed their feet off to get away, they could never run well enough to overtake game again. They were going to die.

He felt trapped like those coyotes, dodging something deadlier than his father's club. That guarded perimeter had become his own strong chain. Even if he somehow broke it, even if he managed to escape the law and the chair, even if he somehow got back to San Rosario, he would still be a hunted animal, crippled for want of friends or money, still a three-footed coyote.

Watching the empty road and the distant chopper, he decided to stay where he was. At least till he learned why people had run. He climbed down the tower. With a rusting hammer he found in the shed, he pried a screen off a back window, broke the glass, and climbed into a bedroom. It had belonged to one of those little girls; clothing she'd had no time to pack lay tossed on the floor, the doll's bed was empty beside her own.

He explored the house. The boy's room: the walls were covered with posters of planets and the moon; model spacecraft hung from the ceiling. A larger room with pink curtains and a huge water bed; he sat on it to feel the waves, grinning when he thought of his hard cot in the jail.

An office desk stood in an alcove off the hall, the door of a wall safe ajar. Searching hopefully, he found no money. A badge in the wastebasket carried a photo with a number and a name. *Guadanolo, Rudolph, CPA. Comptroller, EnGene, Inc.*

In the den, a *M*A*S*H** rerun was on the TV. It stopped while he stood there. Blank for a moment, the screen came lit again with an empty desk under a rainbow arch lettered ENFIELD TODAY. A thin little man in a dirty sweatshirt limped to the desk.

"I'm Marty Marks—" He was out of breath and trembling, half his face streaked with grime and blood as if from a fall. "Trapped here alone in the tower newsroom. Reporting what I can. Which is pure hell! Hell I never imagined! Fires burning out of control. Panic in the streets. People dropping dead—I can't guess why. All I can do is tell what I see. As long as I can talk."

Marty Marks told what he had seen. Fire and panic and sudden death. Nothing he said explained anything. He had been alone all afternoon, since the rest of the staff ran or died. He had fallen on the stair, climbing to the tower room—people were dead in the elevator. Rasping out the story, he kept pausing to peer anxiously behind him. Abruptly, he stood up.

"Excuse me, folks. Got to use the bathroom. And get another gander. Be right back—if I live that long."

He left the picture, but Pancho Torres sat a long time in Rudolph Guadanolo's easy chair, watching the empty news desk, trying to understand what he had heard, to decide what to do. Was he still too close to Enfield? Or was he safer here, where others might fear to come?

He held his breath to listen. No sound except the TV humming faintly. But the killer, *la muerte,* would it be soundless? He pushed on again through too much silence to find the front door of the dwelling. He opened it cautiously, peered outside. He saw nothing moving—but would the killer be visible? Dread spurred him back to climb the windmill again. The cop car had vanished from the ridge. The road lay empty. Thicker smoke veiled the town and that tower studio.

"Por qué?" He shrugged. Why watch, when he had no notion what to watch for? *"De nada."*

He went back to the house. Inside, the fragrance of food drew him to the kitchen. Two loaves of fresh-baked bread had been left to cool on the counter. A baked ham, glazed with pineapple slices, was still warm in the oven. Golden oranges in the refrigerator, and cold beer! He sliced the ham and bread to fill a plate, opened a beer, carried them back to sit in Rudolph Guadanolo's enormous chair and watch the humming TV.

A feast unknown to the Enfield county jail, yet he ate it almost without tasting. For Marty Marks soon came back to rasp another jittery report. Watching from windows and the terrace, he had seen fires burning nearer, panic grown madder, unseen death knocking more people down.

"No cause I could see." A baffled shrug. "No damn sign of anything to kill 'em."

Pancho Torres left Marty Marks babbling in his panic and went back to climb the windmill again. The sun was already setting. It lent a lurid tinge of red to the smoke over Enfield, but the nearer landscape seemed strangely peaceful. The highway wrecks had burned out. The little valley lay green and still, a few spotted cattle grazing toward the road.

Nothing else was moving. The air felt cooler. He had eaten again, and he didn't have to run. Not yet, anyhow. Marty Marks seemed strangely far away. If thousands had fled from the dying town and thousands more had fallen in the streets, he found that he didn't really care.

"No importa," he muttered. *"No hay hace nada."*

Nothing mattered anymore.

Nothing could, after all they had done to him. After the bullets that left Hector torn and screaming on the prison wall. After Deputy Harris and the Enfield county jail. After too much of too many gringos.

They hated and despised him, hated and despised all his people—humble, hungry people who had to break their cruel laws to sneak into their ugly country and slave for little pay at the hard and dirty and dangerous jobs they were too good to touch. A rotten race, rotted with too much money and too much ease and too much pride in their own stuffy righteousness. A ruthless race, defying the world with their frightful nukes and corrupting his own misused people with the billions they paid for illegal drugs they needed to endure their rottenness.

He couldn't really care, not even what happened to him. For he was the trapped coyote. Even if he gnawed off his foot and somehow got back to San Rosario—

"Nada. Todo por nada."

Nothing to hope for anywhere. Nothing whatever. His father dead of want and toil, his mother of some illness the *curandera* couldn't cure. He had sent money to José and Estrella when he had money, but they hadn't even written since he went to prison. Eduardo, the fat *haciendero* now, Eduardo would probably alert *la policía* if he ever did get back.

He had no reason to run. Not just yet. Whatever demon had escaped from hell to kill Enfield, it was no worse than Enfield had earned for itself, no worse for him than the jail and the chair upstate, surely no worse for anybody than the nukes sitting in their pits, ready to kill the world when a computer went wrong or some loco punched a button. He went back inside to open another beer and watch that empty desk on the TV screen.

14

To Sting the Glavni Vrag

Anya Ostrov's reports brought Boris Shuvalov from Moscow to take command of the KGB response. Traveling as Tass correspondent Yuri Yerokhin, he was accredited to the Soviet Mission at the United Nations and assigned to cover debate on a proposed U.N. resolution for international control of all genetic research.

A driver waited at Kennedy to take him straight to the Manhattan headquarters of Roman-World-Mart, Inc. Arrangements had been made for Anya to meet him there. He found the office suite deserted while attorneys for the company and for Julia Roman battled over the liquidation of World-Mart and funding for the new Soviet-American foundation. A security man escorted him down empty corridors to the top-floor boardroom and asked uneasily if he had heard anything new about "the Enfield holocaust." He hadn't.

Anya was late. He swept the room for hidden bugs, using an electronic detector built into the small tape recorder he carried in a black attaché case. Finding none, he sat down to scan the *New York Times* for anything about the disaster. He found long columns of alarmed editorial speculation and hollow-sounding appeals for public calm, but no more facts than Tass had reported.

He looked at his watch and walked the floor and stood at a window, looking far down on Fifth Avenue and across at the sunlit towers beyond it, wondering how soon the genetic monster might come to empty the buildings and stop the racing traffic forever. Unless it could be tamed—

He shook his head and walked the floor again.

An ugly assignment. He hadn't asked for it, or really been persuaded by Bogdanov's assurances that the Center would remember his service to the party and the people. The risks were too enormous.

The CIA and the FBI and military intelligence were swarming everywhere like dug-up ants. The American immigration officers had grilled him too skeptically about his background in biology and his experience in journalism, as if they already suspected his true mission. His U.N. cover was flimsy, and he was sweating before the guard brought Anya in.

Her long-limbed allure had always tempted him, but now she looked travel-worn, her greenish eyes hollow, her face pinched and pale. She offered her hand and tried to smile, but he stood scowling until the guard was gone.

"You're late!" he snapped at her then. "Have you got the files?"

"I've tried everything." She sank into a chair. "I'm afraid we'll never get them."

"Fail, and you'll regret it."

"The world will regret it."

"Forget the dramatics," he advised her sourly. "You aren't playing Chekhov."

She was fumbling into her bag. "At least I have one more report from Scorpio."

"On your person?" Anger edged his voice. "The Americans already suspect me, and your own status here is barely legitimate. They are well enough aware that Roman was a friend of the USSR. These offices are probably under surveillance. At any time, either of us could be seized and searched."

"We take risks."

"We also expect results. Can't you deal with this Carboni?"

"We've lost him." His harshness had turned her half defiant. "He was to meet us last night in a bar near the Chicago safe house. Scorpio waited there with me till three this morning. That's why I'm late—that and the panicky mobs at O'Hare.

"I thought we had a deal. Scorpio had promised him photos and letters from the three dissidents assuring him that we had arranged their safe release. In return, he was to give us the key to an airport locker where we would find the films. I had the letters with me.

"Professional forgeries, complete with doctored snapshots of the old rogue Alyoshka and his women. The letters confirm his joy at discovering that he has a son and the happiness of the whole family in being liberated. But"—her breath went out—"Carboni never came."

"He didn't die in the Enfield disaster?"

She shook her head. "An odd thing. You know he was our only good source at EnGene. Scorpio thinks he must have learned that it was about to happen. Previously, they had arranged to meet that night at his Enfield apartment to finalize plans for the exchange. Carboni called on very short notice to change the meeting place to a Kansas City motel—he said he suspected that the CIA had bugged his place.

"Scorpio says that Kansas City meeting saved both their lives."

"Let's get to the point." His voice sharpened impatiently. "What happened to the Belcraft files?"

"Who knows?" A baffled shrug. "Scorpio hates me. Recently he has been difficult. Demanding more money. He seems afraid of his work since the disaster, and I hate to trust him. As for Carboni—I've never even seen him. Scorpio says the FBI and the CIA have been collecting dossiers on all the EnGene employees. He and Carboni are both on the list, subject to interrogation if they can be captured. Carboni may have simply gone into hiding." Her voice sank. "I just don't know."

"Find out!" Shuvalov turned shrill. "I don't risk my neck for nothing."

"Operations are getting sticky." Her brow furrowed. "The Americans are desperate. They apparently know even less than we do about what hit their city. They suspect nobody and everybody. As you say, they may strike at us." A weary shrug. "Anyhow, here's something for you." She dug into her bag. "Scorpio did deliver another report."

"If you've lost Carboni and the films, what's left to report?"

"Scraps of fact that Carboni kept offering to justify his arrogant demands. Scorpio carried a hidden tape recorder and later dictated his own report of each encounter. I have transcribed the tapes—Scorpio refuses to put anything on paper."

"But you are bolder?" He turned sardonic. "You risk us both?"

"Read it." She produced a thick envelope. "Evidence enough that EnGene was in fact working to create a biological super-weapon. The effort was based largely on Belcraft's work, but never with his cooperation. He was bitterly opposed to all military research, and he had remained at the laboratory only because he was allowed to use the facilities for a project of his own—a strange project.

"Carboni says he was attempting to create a new kind of life."

"A madman?"

"A genius, Carboni calls him. Looking for genetic discoveries that might transform mankind. Carboni calls him an idealistic dreamer, driven by visions that he could somehow recreate the human species into beings nobler and wiser than we are. Too noble even to think of genetic warfare."

Shuvalov snorted. "I think he was a madman."

"Mad, perhaps, but also something greater!" Her voice quickened. "Perhaps he hadn't done much to impress most of his fellow Americans, but Carboni knows genetics enough to feel terrified. He told Scorpio that Belcraft was creating what he called para-life. A stranger stuff than just a clone or a mutation or genetic recombinant. Something wholly new. As different, Carboni told him, as some alien form that might have evolved on another planet."

"Not very likely."

"It is described, Carboni swears, in the lab notebooks he photographed. Described in very convincing detail, with outlines for lab processes that he hopes will synthesize it."

"So?" Shuvalov shrugged. "What is it to us? Colonel Bogdanov will hardly care to play creator. Or allow experiments that might bring this plague to Russia."

"Knowing the lesson of Enfield, our own genetic engineers might perhaps do better."

"Perhaps. But you have not obtained the files." His small eyes sharpened. "Did Carboni speak of anything of greater interest to the Center?"

"Carboni says there are notes made on a word processor for a letter Belcraft was planning to write his brother. Carboni got into the computer to make his own printout of the notes. Sketching Belcraft's whole career at EnGene. His disagreements with the weapon-builders and his ideas for some new creation. If the letter was actually written, it would be a fascinating document. Even the notes should be revealing."

"This brother? Where is he?"

"He's a physician in Fort Madison. A town on the Mississippi. We sent an agent there, who found him away. His office nurse says he called her on the morning of the disaster to say he was driving to Enfield. He has not returned. She has heard nothing more."

"Was he involved in the genetic research?"

"Apparently not. On the night before the disaster, he received a telephone call from his brother at EnGene —a call Carboni was able to record. We have a transcript here." She nodded at the envelope. "The brother —Victor Belcraft—speaks of a letter, which he says has been safely mailed. Perhaps he was anticipating the disaster. Something in his call seems to have alarmed the doctor-brother."

"He reached Enfield in time to die there?"

"No. I don't think so." A troubled headshake. "Scorpio is not my only agent. We have informers in the American task force. One of them has reported a survivor picked up inside the quarantine perimeter—a Dr. Saxon Belcraft. He must be the brother from Fort Madison."

"If that's true—" His eyes narrowed. "The Americans are doubtless interrogating him. We must learn what he says."

"There's something stranger." Her voice dropped. "The informer reports that this brother ventured into the devastated area, where all life had been erased. The task force is still afraid of contagion, but he came out alive. He brought a creature with him. A queer little animal that had survived whatever destroyed the city." She caught her breath, leaning a little toward him. "It is said to be a sort of thing never seen before. Perhaps the para-life discussed in the Belcraft documents."

"The file you failed to obtain."

"We made every possible effort." She tried not to flinch from his rasp of accusation. "Scorpio says Carboni is afraid of us and afraid of the CIA. He has refused to reveal where he is hiding. Since he failed to meet us in Chicago, we have no way to reach him. With military law in effect around Enfield, and the whole nation under emergency alert—" She shrugged unhappily.

"The American investigators have accomplished nothing. I'm afraid we'll do no better."

"Comrade!" he scolded her. "We are never negative."

"I'll make every possible effort." Gamely, she tried to brighten. "Even if we have lost Carboni, we have others as competent. I believe we are still ahead of the Great Enemy."

She used the familiar Russian phrase, *Glavni Vrag.*

"They appear to know even less than we do about the deadly agent. The evidence indicates that all its makers died in the disaster. Though Carboni once threatened to have his films given to the CIA if harm came to him, that has not yet happened."

"If that is the case—"

Shuvalov paused, hard little eyes fixed unreadably upon her. She had begun to flush before he reached across the table for the envelope. His sallow smile relieved her.

"Comrade, I commend you." His tone was suddenly too warm. "The fact that the Americans don't know what is killing them will be welcome news at the Center. You have done well in a hazardous emergency, and I shall forward a commendation along with my analysis of this material."

"Thank you, comrade!"

He was rising. "I'll have new orders for you later today. Based on revised instructions from the Center. I believe our plan of campaign is already clear. The panic in the American military seems to indicate that the secret of their super-weapon was lost in the disaster.

"We are to make certain that it is not recovered. If Carboni's photos still exist, we must obtain them. If Belcraft's letter to his brother was mailed in time to escape destruction, we must secure it. If the brother and the creature from the ruins can offer clues to the nature of the weapon—"

He paused, quick little eyes probing into her.

"I understand." She came slowly to her feet. "The

brother and his queer little creature must be eliminated, though." She had to shake her head. "The Americans will have them under heavy guard, somewhere inside the quarantine perimeter. They may be hard to reach."

"They can be—have to be erased." The pale smile turned him uglier. "Our best chance to sting the *Glavni Vrag!*"

15

Born of Fire?

Before Belcraft reached the bridge, a chopper dropped and hovered ahead of him. A little blizzard of bright flakes swirled down around him. He stopped the car and climbed out to read smeary black print on an orange-colored leaflet.

DANGER! KEEP OUT!
AREA CONTAMINATED!

All persons are hereby warned that the ruins of Enfield and the surrounding area are under a strict quarantine required by public safety and enforced by military law. Trespassers are in danger of infection by an unidentified biological vector.

WARNING!
LOOTERS WILL BE SHOT ON SIGHT!
By order of General Adrian Clegg
Commander, Task Force Watchdog

Waiting in the car, Belcraft looked across the bridge into that forbidden ground. It was now an ashen gray, as if from a fall of dirty snow. He saw nothing in it moving, but closer to him sparrows were flitting around the untouched trees along the creek. The bicycle lay unharmed where that luckless boy had fallen. His dust had eaten no farther into the weeds. Higher up the slope, those straggling sunflowers stood where they had been, bent now toward the western sun.

Had the contagion really stopped?

Heart beating faster, he watched the chopper rise and then drove on across the bridge and up the slope. A hundred yards into the dust, he stopped again to look around him. The road was still nearly bare; all the growth beside it had been dissolved into that fine gray powder. A tall chimney stood starkly alone where a home must have been, a red-brick monument to death.

He felt surprised to find so much unchanged. The dust was almost the color of ashes. Everything wooden had been consumed: buildings and signposts and telephone poles. It seemed strange to him that there had been so little actual fire to blacken brick or stone, crumple or darken the still-bright metal.

The chopper was circling back, hammering the stagnant heat, flying so low that it lifted a thick gray cloud. A breath of that reached him, edged with a queer dry sharpness a little like vinegar, more like new paint.

He scrambled out of the car. Fighting the impulse to shake his fist, he stood waving the chopper away. It kept drifting closer, the hot blast stirring up dust to wash him. His eyes began to burn. His nostrils stung. He sneezed. Gasping, close to panic, he waved both arms.

It sank closer. His eyes had blurred, but he caught the glint of lenses. Men in uniform, leaning to watch him with binoculars. Eager to observe and report what the dust did to him.

So far, nothing worse than a fit of hay fever. He didn't like the stink, but it was no worse than anatomy labs he remembered. With a grin of bleak relief, he climbed back into the car and shut the windows. At least, he thought, they weren't likely to shoot him for a looter. Not so long as he was their live guinea pig.

He blew his nose and waited. The chopper rose a little, pulling back until the dust cloud no longer reached him, but still it hung there. He counted eight others farther off in the shimmering heat, all cruising low. Metal vultures, wheeling over this alien desert where only metal could survive.

The closed car grew suffocating. He started the engine and turned on the air conditioner. The chopper dropped again, circling him. He opened the door for a moment and waved to let the crewmen know he wasn't dead. Not yet, anyhow. They kept on watching.

Overheating, the engine slowed and bucked and died. He sweated again, watching the chopper and scanning the ashen landscape. A little cluster of taller downtown buildings stood undamaged on the dancing horizon. One of them, no doubt, was the Enfield Trust tower, where Marty Marks had watched the last convulsions of the dying city. A Chevron station, nearer, glistened red and white and blue, bright as an unwrapped Christmas toy. When at last the chopper rose and roared away, he got a can of water there and cooled off his engine.

He drove ahead. Beyond that shining Chevron station, a pile of burnt-out vehicles clogged the entrance to a divided highway. He jolted over curbs to get around them, then turned south toward where he thought the EnGene labs must have stood.

The road led him through what had been a residential district. The homes were gone, their flattened sites left littered with brick and metal: naked chimneys, uncovered plumbing, dusty appliances still in place on concrete floors or tumbled crazily where wooden floors had gone to dust. A business section looked oddly half intact, signs still bright and masonry walls still standing, though most roofs had caved in.

The skeleton of a burned fire engine lay more than half across the EnGene exit ramp. He scraped around it, reckless of damaged paint. Half a mile beyond, bare steel beams rose out of toppled ruin. He picked a wary way toward them across fields of dust, avoiding dead fire trucks and police cars and the empty van from KBIO, until he had to stop before a wall of blast-tossed debris.

What now?

He sat sweating in the car for half a minute, then climbed gingerly out into ankle-deep dust. The new-paint reek rose strong around him, the stink of starkest tragedy. This dismal ruin marked his brother's grave. The tomb, he thought, of all the EnGene staff—if Task Force Watchdog had found survivors, it would hardly be raking the dust so avidly for clues no longer likely to exist.

Certainly, he had seen no hint of any answer. Yet this was the spot where the disaster had begun. If any evidence of the killer's origin did remain, here was his chance to be first upon it.

He caught a breath that almost choked him and plodded toward a gap in the shattered wall. A louder drumming checked him, and a rush of burning wind. A chopper floated closer, blinding him with dust. He bent to a spasm of sneezing. With a handkerchief to his nose, he pushed on—and saw a flash of pink.

Something moving!

Something small, slowly crawling, searching its way out of a mountain of shattered mortar and broken concrete blocks. The handkerchief slipped out of his fingers. Dazed by the thing's total strangeness, he stood watching while it squirmed across a scrap of fire-scarred metal. Pausing at the edge as if to look ahead, it dived out of sight into the rubble.

Life!

How could anything be still alive, here in the killer's very cradle? Gasping, trembling, he recovered the handkerchief and blew his nose and stumbled closer. There! He found it crawling over a broken brick. It paused, almost as if it had perceived him. The head end rose toward him. In a moment, it came on.

They met. He knelt in the ashes to peer down at it.

The blunt pink head appeared as if to look up at him, though it had no eyes that he could see.

"In God's name, what are you?"

In all he knew of zoology, there had been nothing like it. The skin was slick and bright, unbroken anywhere. It had no legs or wings or antennae, no appendages at all, no apparent sense organs, yet he knew it was aware of him.

He reached for it, and it leaned to rub against his fingers like a friendly cat. When he spread his hand, it curled into his palm. Its skin was warm and dry, and he felt it throbbing like a purring kitten. He stood up and held it close to study it again. It looked featureless as a pink sausage.

"What are you?" he muttered again. "How'd you stay alive?"

Its blunt head moved as if to study him, but it made no other response. Squinting at it, he recalled that long-gone night with Vic in Cincinnati after their father's funeral, recalled Vic's crazy-seeming dream of writing a new genetic code to create a new family tree engineered to grow something better than humanity, perhaps closer to divinity. Was this small thing the first fruit of that new tree, shaped of something different from any familiar natural protoplasm, its laws and limits unknown?

He shivered at the notion—but only for an instant. For he liked it, in spite of its shape and its strangeness. He trusted it without needing to know why.

"Whatever—" He shrugged, grinning down at it. "You're okay, but still I'd like to know—"

He started walking with it back into the tangled ruin, trying to follow the wavering track it had left in the ashes. It moved on his palm, shrinking back toward him as if it didn't want to return, but he went on until he lost its trail at that gap in the wall.

It had come out of the blackened wreckage beyond, a jungle of broken masonry and tangled steel too thick for him to penetrate. Fallen beams, shattered concrete and brick, burned wire, torn and flattened air ducts, twisted pipes and burned metal fixtures, all were covered with actual ashes darker than the dust, the bitter stink of recent fire sharper here than the new-paint reek.

Born of fire?

The notion stuck in his mind, not quite rational yet oddly appealing. Its actual womb must have been some test tube or petri dish now shattered and fused and forever lost, but its survival seemed to hint at some remarkable immunity to flame and chaos. He peered through the gap, wondering if it had endured the explosion in some basement space too deep for blast and heat to reach, but any search for such a site would have to wait for bulldozers.

It squirmed and shivered in his hand. He found the chopper roaring close behind him, kicking up a suffocating cloud that rolled in around him. Two men with binoculars leaned out to study him. He gasped and wiped his stinging eyes. Trying desperately with his free hand to wave them off, he shielded the pink thing against his chest and stumbled back to the car.

Keeping too close, flying too low, the chopper followed him back out of the ruin, back to the highway. He found a National Guard jeep parked on the bridge. A man in Army camouflage got out as he neared it, one hand lifted to stop him, a pistol ready in the other.

He stopped and rolled down the glass. On the seat beside him, the pink thing nestled against his hip as if to hide. He felt it shuddering.

"Halt!" A brittle-toned command. "Identify yourself."

"Belcraft," he said. "Dr. Saxon Belcraft. I practice general medicine in Fort Madison, Iowa." He climbed out of the car. "Who are you?"

"Fair enough." A tight-lipped grin. "Lieutenant Joseph Dusek, US Army. On temporary duty with Task Force Watchdog. My orders now are to find out what you're doing here."

"I came here to Enfield to see my brother. He is—or was—employed here at EnGene labs. A state cop kept me out of town, but I was caught inside your quarantine line."

"You're lucky to be alive. I doubt the cop is." Impatient accusation sharpened Dusek's voice. "You're a trespasser here. Don't you know that?"

"I picked up a leaflet."

"You were seen picking up something else." Dusek stepped closer. He hadn't shaved. He smelled of sweat. His eyes were black-rimmed and bloodshot, as if he hadn't slept. "Just now. In yonder." His gun gestured. "What was it?"

"If you want a look—"

He reached for the pink thing. It recoiled, but he slid his hand under it and lifted it out of the car. It shuddered away from Dusek, trying to crawl up his sleeve. Dusek gaped at it, backing away with an equal aversion.

"What the hell?"

"I found it crawling out of what used to be the EnGene labs. That's all I know."

"It was alive in there?"

"Evidently."

"Could it—" Dusek shrank farther. "Could it carry the plague?"

"The plague—the lethal effect, whatever it was—seems to have stopped." He lifted the pink thing higher. "It seems harmless. Affectionate, in fact."

"You're crazy!" Dusek blinked at him glassily. "Where are you going with it?"

"For now, back to that motel." He drew the pink thing back away from Dusek, and it snuggled gratefully into his palm. "Afterward—" He shrugged.

"Stay there!" Dusek waved the gun. "Keep your monster with you. Away from anybody else, in case it is the killer. Watchdog will want to see it." Retreating toward the jeep, he paused to add: "If you try to claim you didn't know, just remember the contaminated area is under military law. I could kill you for trespassing. I won't do that, but you are under house arrest. Stay in your room till Watchdog comes."

He paused, scowling and backing farther from the pink thing.

"Got that?"

"I've got it."

Dusek backed the jeep off the bridge, beckoned him across, and followed him back to the motel. He parked outside number nine. Dusek stopped on the road, shouting into a mobile phone. Inside the stifling room, he heard the jeep roar and burn rubber, getting away.

The pink thing wrapped itself around his forefinger when he tried to lay it on the unmade bed. He pushed it off gently. Starting to the bathroom, he heard a faint squeak and looked back to find it squirming off the bed.

"Dry?"

It shrilled again, and he saw a tiny mouth open now in the middle of its head. He picked it up and brought it with him. Whistling eagerly, it leaned toward the lavatory. When he opened the dripping faucet, it dived off his hand into the basin.

"You were dry!"

It played five minutes in the water, swimming and leaping and diving again before it climbed to the basin rim and raised its tiny mouth to whistle at him, he thought happily. He carried it back to the bed and left it there while he looked for a beer. Three cans were left from the six-pack. He opened one. When the warm beer spewed, the pink thing whistled, leaping eagerly toward the spray.

"If you want a drink—"

Its eyeless head turned alertly to follow while he filled and offered the water-stained glass. It stretched for the frothy beer, sucking thirstily.

"Hungry?"

He dug again through the box the chopper had dropped and found a can of tomato soup. No opener had been included, but he split the top of the can with his pocket knife and poured cold soup into the glass. Tentatively, he offered a drop of it on the tip of his finger. The pink thing leaned daintily to taste and squealed for more. It had sucked up almost half the can before it drew lazily away to pipe a tiny note of what he took for contentment.

He opened a can of corned beef to make himself a sandwich that he ate with another tepid beer. Escaping the hot room, he went out into the building's slightly cooler shade and sat on the step with the little creature on his knees. It snuggled toward his body and lay still, coiled like a small pink snake.

Its mouth had vanished. Its purring throb slowed and ceased, as if it had gone to sleep. Its scent rose around him in the humid heat, faint but clean and pleasant. Vaguely like fresh-cut hay, he thought, but really like nothing he knew.

He thought it had to be a product of genetic science, probably Vic's own creation, yet it remained a tantalizing riddle. If it really belonged to another kind of life, engineered from a new protoplasm never known on Earth—what could it unfold, for biology, for medicine, perhaps for future history?

He shivered again, a little in awe at all its unknown potentials, but more afraid for its own future. For Dusek would be reporting it. Men from Watchdog would soon be here to take it for examination. It wouldn't want to be examined, and suddenly he felt certain he didn't want to give it up.

He watched the road the jeep had taken. Nothing came back along it. All he could hear was the unending beat of the searching choppers, half a dozen of them low in the east, forever crossing and recrossing the ash and dust of Enfield.

Toward sunset, another arrived from toward the perimeter. It circled the motel and settled over the parking lot, so low its hot engine fumes took his breath. A crewman leaned out with binoculars focused on him and the pink thing. Aroused, the little creature raised its head and shuddered against him until the chopper lifted.

"Better watch 'em." He stroked its quivering coils. "They could hurt you."

He heard the TV thump. The air conditioner came on, and the room was cooling when he came inside. The KBIO newsroom had vanished from the tube. He twisted the dial, searching for news. A blast of rock music. A feminine hygiene commercial. Finally a special documentary, the title just fading. BIOGENETIC BLACKOUT.

A network anchorman came on with a roundup of what he called official information sources, though he had gotten very little actual information. Washington was denying a rumor that Enfield had been devastated by the accidental malfunction of a secret military biological. Though the Secretary of Defense remained unavailable, State had issued a white paper formally denouncing all biological warfare.

"With no accusations stated or implied, and regardless of anything known or suspected about the intentions and capacities of other nations, the American government has solemnly and repeatedly assured the world that it never had and never would undertake any preparations whatever for genetic aggression."

The White House had condemned all such weapons. The President described them as "demoniac inventions, devised to turn the most secret and sacred forces of life against themselves." Although interrupted communications were yet to be fully restored, civil defense officials still insisted that the "Enfield incident" had been, in fact, merely a needless panic due to baseless rumors and unfounded media speculation.

The documentary continued with shots of sleepy people in airline terminals waiting for canceled flights to be resumed; shots of National Guardsmen called up without notice to serve on the quarantine perimeter; shots of indignant congressmen demanding information.

In reply to questions about yellow rain in Asian wars and a rumored anthrax epidemic in the USSR due to experimental mischance, unnamed spokesmen had denied knowing of genetically engineered weapons under development anywhere. The American government had no connection whatever with EnGene.

The corporation was privately held. Attorneys defended the innocence of the unidentified owners, claiming that EnGene had been totally devoted to the creation of new lifesaving pharmaceuticals. Nothing under development there had any possible military use.

That was all.

The night sky was alive with throbbing choppers when he looked outside. Searching now, he supposed, with infrared detectors. Discovering nothing. They never would.

Waiting for Watchdog to come for the pink thing, he opened the last warm beer. It made that tiny mouth again to share it with him. Relaxed with that, it coiled in his lap and seemed to sleep. He laid it on the bed and lay back beside it, uneasy for it but uncertain how to help.

Its small whistle woke him.

Gray daylight filtered through the dingy curtains, and another chopper was roaring low outside. The pink thing shrilled again. Blinking groggily, he found it at the door, its eyeless head turned hopefully back to him.

"If you think you can get away—"

He stumbled to open the door.

16

La Pendeja

Pancho Torres spent most of that hot night on the windmill tower, lying flat on the high platform under the broken wheel, watching Enfield burn. There was no moon till midnight, but towers of flame and red-lit smoke revealed the fire. Steadily it spread, a bright streak running far along the horizon, the nearer trees and buildings standing black against it.

Strange fire, because it ceased to smoke. No smoke was left to dim the late moon's yellow curve when it rose beyond the town, yet still the fire burned on. Like a white sea rising, it reached and drowned those closer shapes. Slowly crawling, it seemed to burn everything. Trees and houses, fields of corn and grass. The highway cut a black slash across the glowing white. Before dawn, it had crept almost to the bridge where that wrecked car had burned.

He saw motion. Animals running. The cattle he had seen, grazing so peacefully then. Bellowing, at first far away, they came racing out of that slow bright tide, down toward the stream he had crossed. At first they were black silhouettes against the brightness, but in a moment it had washed them. The bellowing died away. One by one, they staggered and went down into the grass. Shining, their bodies flattened and dissolved. New fire spread from where they had fallen.

Shivering, even in the warm and windless dawn, he knew he had to run, even if he didn't care. But not quite yet. The strangeness of it held him. The eastern dawn had already grown brighter than the fire, but still he saw no smoke. He felt no heat. No common fire had ever burned so strangely.

Even if it had come to burn the whole world for too many centuries of sin, he wanted to avoid it as long as he could. Stiff from lying too still too long on the splintery boards, he stood up to go. Looking again, however, while he flexed his achy joints, he thought its deadly march had stopped. Had sunlight somehow quenched it?

He lay back on the platform to keep on watching.

It had come almost to the stream. Its edge was a sharp-drawn line. Closer to him, grass and weeds still grew green. A red pony grazed, unalarmed. Beyond the line, gray ashes spread as far as he could see. Only a few scattered objects had somehow escaped, a row of steel towers that carried power wires, the grain elevator, the downtown buildings where that man on TV had taken refuge.

He lay a long time there. Unharmed flies came to buzz around him. The ashes shimmered under the driving sun, smokeless and dead. No wind stirred them. He watched the red pony. Grazing to their edge, it trotted on into a wide gray tongue of ashes, lay down to roll in them, stood and shook off its own small gray cloud and ambled on down to the creek. Waiting for it to shine and die, he saw no sign of harm. The pony drank and grazed back along that line of death.

His feeling of danger fading, he fell half asleep. A drumming engine roused him. Another military chopper, cruising low, men with binoculars scanning the ashes. A hazard he could understand. Motionless till it had passed, he wanted a place to hide.

The old wooden water tank standing by the tower—

it was big enough to hold him, high enough on its own platform to let him watch in all directions. He peered inside, where broken staves had opened a window, and decided it would do.

Back in the abandoned house, he found blankets in a closet, gathered up the rest of the bread and ham and beer. Searching the empty garage, he found a flashlight and a camper's ax. He erased the marks of his presence as best he could, washing and replacing the few dishes he had used. He locked the door again, climbed to the tank with his loot, and used the ax to break out a larger door.

The old tank was a wooden oven, even hotter than the jail cell he had escaped. Yet he stayed there, climbing now and then on a stack of broken staves to look out through the manhole, sleeping when he couldn't stay awake. The whole sky soon throbbed with choppers, flying low outside the dust, a little higher where it lay. Twice one of them came to hover near the house, the crewmen shouting through a bullhorn. They didn't touch the perilous land.

Darkness fell. Waiting till no engines were near, he went back to the house. The power was off, the refrigerator stopped, the TV dead. Wondering how Marty Marks had fared, he ate and drank by flashlight, washed dishes till the water quit running, and returned to the tank.

That night he watched and napped and watched again. The black sky roared with engines. The land lay black below them, no fire burning anywhere. Now and then he slept, dreaming that he was coming home to San Rosario, where he thought there would be no electric chair and his mother would call him *un hombre* and this strange fire could never burn. He woke to weary bitterness. His mother was dead, and he would never be seven again.

The next day was even hotter. Sweating in the tank, he was afraid to leave it. Choppers filled the blazing sky, flying slower and lower than ever. He saw the glint of searching lenses. Late in the airless afternoon, he watched a military jeep that came cautiously toward the town. It stopped on the hill while men climbed out to set up a tripod, perhaps to take photos. They stopped again before they reached the ashes, went fast when they left.

He climbed out of his stifling prison to watch them out of sight. Tired of hiding, he was halfway sorry that he hadn't been discovered. Fear of the law and the chair, fear of that strange fire, fear of all he didn't understand—he had feared too much, endured too long. In the end, unless that cold and deadly fire overtook him first, they surely would find him.

When they did, he would tell the best tale he could invent. If jailors enough were dead, and legal records burned, perhaps they would believe him. Perhaps—but he couldn't really care. His luck was lost. Live gringos were no better than their poison ashes, and nothing would ever matter again.

No le hace nada.

He clambered back down the ladder. In spite of all the gringo choppers, he had to stretch his legs. He started walking down toward the stream. His cramped muscles rejoiced to action, and something changed his bitter mood. Whatever evil things were coming, the air had grown a little cooler. Low in the darkening west, a delicate feather of cloud turned to glowing gold. He caught the sweetness of a honeysuckle climbing the white picket fence.

He came down to the stream and stopped on a grassy bank. The water ran clear, pebbles shining through it. He scrambled down the bank, stooped to wash his grimy hands. It felt cool and good. He dropped on his belly to wash the sticky sweat off his face. Something pink and quick flashed toward him through the ripples. It jumped out to kiss his chin.

Una culebra!

A water snake, striking at his face. His mother had taught him to dread *las culebras de cascabel,* the rattlesnakes that made their winter dens in the rocky slopes above San Rosario. He sprang back from the water and stood trembling with that old fear until he heard a thin little cry from the edge of the water. An odd, anxious sound, almost like the peep of a hungry baby chick.

Snakes didn't speak. He bent to look and saw the pink thing coming out of the water. No snake and no *pollita,* it crawled on four tiny limbs, like *una salamandra.* It stopped at his feet, looking up at him with bright black eyes.

He had whistled in astonishment. Now he saw its minute mouth pucker daintily. Its tiny whistle echoed his own. No longer afraid, he suddenly wanted to help it. He put his hand down to the sand beside it. With a grateful little whine, it squirmed into his palm.

"Qué es?"

It lifted a pink doll-face and squeaked eagerly again, as if trying to tell him what it was. Certainly no *salamandra.* Its skin was too rosy, the tiny features so much like a human baby's that he flinched from a fleeting recollection of the gringo women he had known, those carefully elegant *putas* who took his money and scolded him for mussing their hair and laughed if he ever spoke of his old dreams of marriage and *niños.*

"*Quién sabe?*" he murmured to it. "*La pobre pendeja!* Poor little pink thing! Who knows what you are? *Tiene hambre?*" The gentle Spanish seemed to fit it better than the rough gringo words. "If you're hungry, let's look for supper."

17

"Nothing on Earth"

Belcraft stood that morning at the door of number nine, watching the pink thing drop off the steps and creep along the side of the building. It paused at the corner. The featureless head rose and twisted as if to look back at the roaring chopper and then at him. In another moment it was gone, toward the rank jungle of weeds and underbrush between the motel and the creek.

He stepped outside and waved to the crew, hoping to hold their eyes until the little fugitive was safely out of sight. Nobody answered his gesture, but the machine slid lower and he saw a man in dull-spotted camouflage aiming a big camera at him, perhaps to take back proof that he still survived his excursion into the dust.

He waited in the hot engine reek until the chopper lifted. Back in the room, he stripped off the clothing he had worn all night, showered in tepid water, dressed again. Eating an orange out of that gift carton, he tried the TV.

Channel Five was still dead. A worried anchorman on another network was rehashing stale reports of the Enfield incident. Official Washington, he told his viewers, was repeating assurances that all evident hazards to the public health had been safely contained. The network news staff would be standing by to cover anything—

A rap on the door. He opened it to find Lieutenant Dusek backing uneasily away. The muddy National Guard jeep was parked on the lot behind him.

"Dr. Belcraft?" Dusek's haggard eyes swept him. "You still okay?"

"So far as I can tell."

"Dr. Kalenka." He nodded at another man waiting in the jeep. "A civilian scientist with the task force. He wants the creature you brought out of the ruins."

"He'll have to find it."

"What?" An angry yelp. "What happened to it?"

"It came to me." He shrugged. "It went away."

"You let that monster go? Do you realize—" Dusek checked that heated question. He stood silent for a moment, looking sick, his stubbled face twitching. "Doctor, can't you imagine how it felt to die in Enfield?"

"I've tried."

"Then why in God's name—" His voice quivered, and he stopped to control it. "Doctor, I grew up there. My father had split. Mom brought me up—teaching fifth grade and playing the organ for the Methodist Church. She was going to retire next year. Saving for a world cruise she never got to make."

His lips quivered. "Doctor, that town was my life. I played Little League and rode a paper route and went to high school and dated a girl I was hoping to marry, if—if—" Fists suddenly clenched, he was sobbing. "Dead! They're all dead. Carol and Mom and all the kids I grew up with." His voice turned savage with accusation. "And you—you let that monster go!"

"My brother died in Enfield," Belcraft said, his own voice uneven. "But please don't blame that little creature. It wouldn't hurt anybody."

"You were told—" Dusek caught himself and stalked away to speak to the man in the jeep. "Come out here."

He turned to beckon. "Dr. Kalenka wants to talk to you. Out here in the open."

He went out to the jeep. Kalenka was a compact man in mud-spattered khaki. He wore a flat brown cap and a short black mustache. Anxious brown eyes scowled out of a firm brown face.

"Near enough!" He raised a nervous hand. "Your name's Belcraft?"

He nodded.

"Related to Victor Belcraft?"

"My brother."

"What do you know about his work at EnGene?"

"Nothing, really. We haven't been together since medical school. We never really had a falling out. Just lost touch because we lived and worked so far apart. I think he was totally absorbed in his research. Which he never told me anything about."

"Huh?" A skeptical grunt. "So what are you doing here?"

"The night before—before whatever happened—Vic called me back in Iowa."

"So?" Kalenka looked at Dusek and squinted back at him. "What did he say?"

"Just enough to puzzle me. Nothing at all about his work. He spoke about our boyhood in Ohio. He seemed emotional, more I think than he had ever been. His tone left me troubled, though he seemed more elated than depressed. Next day I drove down here. Afraid of something wrong. I guess something was."

"Plenty wrong." A grim little nod. "You've been into the contamined area? In defiance of military orders?"

"I drove out into the ashes."

"I understand you brought an animal back?"

"A little creature I found crawling from what's left of the EnGene lab."

"What have you done with it?"

"Nothing. It stayed with me last night. This morning it wanted to go. I opened the door and it crawled away."

"Your blunder." Kalenka nodded at Dusek, who moved alertly nearer. "Where did it go?"

He nodded at the weeds where it had vanished.

"We'll run it down."

"It's afraid of you. It may be hard to find."

"Huh?" Kalenka scowled. "What's it like?"

"Worm-shaped. Pink. Looks a little like a raw hot dog. No limbs or visible external sense organs, though a mouth did open in its head. It seemed friendly. Intelligent."

"Intelligent? Something perhaps totally new to science—and you simply let it go?" A scorching accusation. "Why?"

"I don't—don't know." He shook his head, blinking at Kalenka. "My brother used to dream of testing the limits of life. He talked of engineering a new sort of life or para-life, different from and better than anything nature had ever evolved."

"Better?" Kalenka snorted. "Good enough to kill a city? Maybe all mankind?"

"No!" Almost a shout. "You haven't seen it. You haven't felt—" He had to grope for words. "It's somehow childlike. Trusting. It can't have been the killer. I've been wondering if it actually is the new sort of life Vic hoped to engineer. It's certainly different, certainly surprising. I don't really understand it, or the way it affected me. I like it. I want to help it. I don't expect you to understand, but I can't feel sorry I let it go."

A hostile glare. "It had you hypnotized?"

"No—" He caught himself uneasily. "Perhaps I was." He frowned into the weeds. "I don't know what to think. The little being seems really unique. Kin, so far as I can see, to nothing else on Earth. Perhaps nothing else that ever existed. I can't imagine what it could grow to be, but I'd give nearly anything to know—and I hope it does survive!"

"If it's anything like that—" Kalenka stared at him and turned to peer into the weeds where the creature had vanished and swung back to scowl again. "You had it here, and you—you let it go!" A burst of baffled anger. "A physician, trained in science, aware of what has happened here and suspecting what the monster is—" He tried to calm himself. "Doctor, can't you grasp the enormity of what you have done?"

"Saved the little thing from vivisection, I imagine."

"You had no right—no moral right!" Kalenka paused as if to swallow his indignation. "Do you value your pet monster above the survival of mankind?"

"It's no threat. If you had felt what it is—"

"Just look out there!" Still pale with anger, Kalenka gestured at the dust. "Somebody has murdered a city. God knows how many thousand innocent human beings. Killed by a means not yet known. It may be deliberate. I suppose it may have been a laboratory accident, which wouldn't excuse it. If it happened once, it can happen again. I'm going to identify the killer and the cause. As of now, your strange pet—"

His voice was trembling, and he turned again toward that gray waste as if to hide his face.

"Your pet!" Swinging back to glare at Belcraft, he spoke the word like an oath. "Your brother's creation or not, the thing came out of the laboratory where this disaster began. The only clue we've found—a vital clue, if it was somehow immune to the killing vector. And you—trying to conceal it!"

"I can't help the way I feel."

"If you can't—" Eyes narrowed, he shrank back as if he had seen the infection in Belcraft. "Your criminal attitude makes the situation worse than I'd imagined."

"If you blame that little being, you—you're wrong!"

"I'm afraid you are." Kalenka glanced toward the wheeling choppers and turned intently back. "This brother—did you ever suspect that he was in weapons research?"

"No. I can't believe—" Belcraft frowned. "Have you found evidence of any actual weapon?"

"General Clegg is convinced there is—or was a weapon. He has lived in dread of genetic war. That's why he was the prime mover of Bioscience Alert, which was formed to prevent this sort of tragedy. At first we were a civilian group, but he has drafted most of us now, into Task Force Watchdog. Maybe too late."

Kalenka sat silent for a moment, bleakly scowling at nothing, before he shrugged and forced a stiff little smile.

"Doctor, you and I had better understand each other. I hope you have at least begun to get the situation. Our nation is in danger. All humanity is, unless this peril can be understood and controlled. Before it's too late." He tried to warm his tone. "We can't afford to fight. We must work together. Learn to trust each other. Perhaps—perhaps it will help if I tell you something about myself. I—I'm a Jew."

Emotion hushed his voice.

"My parents died in the Holocaust. Along with part of me. I grew up haunted by what I recalled and what people told me. It left a terror in me, a dread I can't shake off—because the world won't let me shake it off. I've always been afraid of a new and greater war. There could be a greater holocaust, wiping out more than just us Jews."

Brown hands clenched on the wheel of the jeep, he stared hard into Belcraft's face.

"Doctor, that's why I'm here. I used to see genetic research as a sort of safe harbor. A new science of life that promised to make us immune to the old sciences of death. I was horrified when researchers began to talk about a possible genetic super-weapon. The notion has always torn me up. I joined Bioscience Alert to help stave that desecration off." His face looked sick. "I'm afraid we've failed."

"Failed?" Belcraft nodded toward the dust. "I hear the danger has been contained."

Kalenka's lean lip quivered and tightened again beneath the close-clipped mustache. "It's panic, first of all, that has to be contained."

"I've walked in the dust. Breathed it. I'm not hurt."

"Not yet, perhaps." A troubled shrug. "But we don't know the incubation time. The initial spread of the lethal vector seems at least to have slowed. If it hadn't—"

He shivered,with a gesture toward the dust.

"You don't know why it stopped?"

"Not a hint, though God knows we've tried." He nodded at the far-off choppers. "The lab records were probably burnt—if not consumed by the vector itself. Nothing tells us anything." An anxious half-smile. "That's why we need your cooperation. And why we've got to have that monster. The only possible key we've turned up."

"I'll be surprised if you find it. Because it's afraid—with good enough reason. I don't know anything about its gifts or its limits or what to expect from it; I do know that it's smart." In spite of himself, he let his feelings show. "It's remarkably perceptive, with no sense organs I could understand. For a being so small, lost and hunted in a world that must be strange to it—"

"Never mind!" Kalenka checked him. "Forget your crazy sympathy. Just show us where it went."

Still keeping a cautious separation from him, they made him lead them the way the pink thing had gone, around the corner of the building toward that gnarled old cherry tree and on beyond into the unmown grass and knee-high weeds around an old farm tractor. He stopped there, with a gesture toward the young saplings and underbrush that choked the slope toward the stream.

"I think it's smart enough and small enough to hide."

"Doctor—" Kalenka stepped sternly toward him, as if fear had been forgotten. "We'll expect your cooperation."

"If that will get me back to Fort Madison—"

"Forget Fort Madison." Kalenka's voice rang harder. "Doctor, you're a prisoner here. Detained under martial law, with very serious accusations pending against you. You won't be going anywhere at all. Not unless you decide to cultivate a more helpful attitude. Not until the charges against you are dismissed and we find you free of infection."

He tried to protest. "Sir, really! I don't know anything about my brother's research."

"Keep him secure." Kalenka rapped the order at Dusek and swung back to him. "Military intelligence will be here. Save your alibis for them."

18

Tim Clegg

Anya waited in the empty tower offices that had been world headquarters of Roman-World-Mart, trying to eat a clammy sandwich a guard had brought up from a deli, trying to nap on a folding cot. Shuvalov came back at last with new orders from the Center. She listened to them stoically. The assignment looked impossible, but saying so wouldn't help.

Rid of him at last, she caught a late flight out of LaGuardia. A little after midnight, she checked into a hotel in downtown Kansas City.

With funds enough from accounts old Roman had set up for her in European banks, safely out of Julia's reach, she could travel in the style she used to enjoy, but her pleasure in it was spoiled by the florid, balding businessman who had sat across the aisle behind her on the flight and followed her to the taxi stand and walked into the lobby while she was waiting for the elevator.

Jittery, she slept badly that night and woke too early from dreams of the happier time, when life had seemed kinder and the whole world brighter. Moscow. Skating in winter. The Bolshoi. The university. The dacha some rich Czarist noble had built back before the revolution, the tall-columned mansion out in the woods on the shore of the Moskva. Her parents, till their luck ran out.

The good time had been when her father still had friends high in the Politburo and she had never even heard of the Lubyanka and the Center and the *gulags.* Still fresh and eager then, aware of her looks and a growing power to command the eyes of men, she had relished everything with the same joy she thought her father must be feeling in the important people he entertained and the huge black limousine always waiting to carry him off to work with important people in the Kremlin.

In the dreams, she had even been on the stage again, young male admirers all around her, happily rehearsing for the role she had won in the Chekhov revival. Awake now in this drably cheerless hotel, here in the very middle of the *Glavni Vrag,* she had to cringe again for her father's stunning fall, that bleak winter day when all his one-time friends turned suddenly against him, accusing him of monstrous things he had never done. Everything had gone so wrong that still she could hardly bear to think about it, so terribly wrong that even the jungle world of the KGB had been a welcome haven.

Once, back in the first exciting months she had known Jules Roman, she had thought those ugly times were gone forever. Old Jules had really loved her, truly loved both America and Russia. Their own love, he used to say, was a symbolic beginning for the great new era of world understanding he wanted to foster.

Hiring her to be his private secretary, he had got her a work permit. Later, in a time of détente, he had helped her obtain a permanent residence visa. Traveling with him, living with him in the Florida mansion and the New York town house, she had almost believed in his visions of a future time of international amity when the nukes could be broken down to fuel power plants.

But Jules was gone. The world he promised, like her father's, had tumbled down around her. She had applied for naturalization—he had wanted it for her, and the Center had commanded it—but she was not yet a citizen. At the whim of the CIA, she could be arrested at any instant for deportation or worse.

She couldn't help feeling that she stood alone against the whole *Glavni Vrag,* all its defenses now alert to trap her. Shuvalov expected courage and cleverness she lacked, miracles she couldn't perform.

Too long under too much strain, she had thought of trying to defect, but that could have no happy ending. The Americans would certainly suspect her of trickery. Even if she somehow perusaded them to believe she'd had some change of heart, they would doubtless want to make her a double agent, working for two masters and in danger from both. She knew how the Center dealt with traitors.

Besides all that, she couldn't quite forget Jules's great hope for the foundation. Just perhaps, if this crisis passed with no greater disaster, if it could be funded in spite of Julia Roman, if she herself stayed free to set it up, perhaps it might really help begin an age of world-wide peace and understanding.

Thus far, however, it was only a device of the KGB, useful cover for her own travels around America on the pretext that she was interviewing people for the foundation staff. A cover too flimsy to save her if things went wrong.

All that dismal morning, she longed for the lost joys that had come back in the dream. She ordered breakfast sent up to her room because she knew American agents would be watching for her in the lobby. The phone rang. A history professor from the University of Kansas. He wanted to talk about a position on the foundation staff, or perhaps a grant to support his research into czarist economics.

Hoping he had brought some message, she let him come up to her room. Black-bearded and fat, hairy as Scorpio, he was so eager to show off his command of Russian, and he asked such searching questions about her plans for the foundation, that she knew he was with the CIA. She got rid of him with a promise to consider his application when funds came through.

He had brought no message. The fact depressed her because she had no way to reach Scorpio. Alarmed when Carboni failed to appear in Chicago, he had refused to set up another meeting. He asked for her travel schedule instead, promising to get in touch when he felt safe about it.

The room had grown too warm, and the professor had left a faint, stuffy scent of stale cigar smoke. She was turning up the air conditioner when the phone rang again.

"Anya Ostrov?" A man's quick voice. "May I come up?"

"Who are you?"

"Nobody you know, but you should see me."

The contact from Scorpio? "Okay, come on up."

He knocked, and she let him in. A lanky young man with pale blue eyes and straw-colored hair. She shut the door behind him. Waiting to see what he wanted, she studied his neat gray business suit, his anxious smile, his own searching glance at her.

"Miss Ostrov?"

She nodded, wondering.

"My name is Clegg." The name startled her, and she saw a flash of amusement in his eyes. "Tim Clegg. My father is General Clegg, in command of the task force at Enfield."

An instant of sheer terror. She tried not to show it. Heart thumping, she scanned him again. He looked harmless enough, even almost shy, but her voice was still gone. She gestured at a chair.

"Wondering how I know you?"

She nodded again.

"Thanks to a man I knew as Herman Doerr."

"Doerr?" Relaxed enough to breathe again, she stepped quickly toward him. "Have you some word from him?"

"From Scorpio?" The code name hit her like a fist. "I don't think you'll hear from Scorpio again."

"Why not?" She tried not to tremble. "Has he—is he in trouble?"

"Too slick for that. But he told me who you are." She was still standing. He nodded at another chair. "Relax, Miss Ostrov. The situation needs explaining."

Reluctantly, she sank into the chair. His face looked open and honest. She couldn't help wanting to like him, but she had lived through too many years of deceit and betrayal to trust anybody.

"Don't shut me out." He smiled again, frankly approving her. "Not before you know why I'm here."

She shook her head, and he saw her apprehension.

"Please, Miss Ostrov. I don't want to harm you. We're players in the same game. I hope we can team up."

"Game—" She had to gulp. "What sort of game?"

"Intelligence."

"Intell—"

Panic took her voice. She saw him move his hand as if to wave her fear away, but his air of easy reassurance meant nothing at all. An American prison might be better than the Lubyanka or treatment in the sort of hospital where Alyoshka had died, but it would be the end of her life. She sat staring at him, feeling cold and giddy. She must have turned the air conditioner too high. She tried to listen, but his voice seemed far off.

"—reason for alarm." He was shaking his head, with a smile meant to calm her. "Just hear me out."

Numb with dread, she whispered, "Okay."

"Okay." He echoed the word and paused as if deciding how to begin. "I'm a soldier's son, grew up an Army brat. Never loved the services myself, but I took three years out of college to serve my own hitch in the infantry—because I'd promised my father when I was still a kid. Last year he hired me away from Hewlett-Packard to join a special intelligence group.

"It was a private unit until he drafted us into the task force. I was on duty in Enfield the last several months before the disaster, with a cover job in security at EnGene. One of my fellow guards was Herman Doerr." Pausing again to watch her response, he added, "Your agent, Scorpio."

In spite of herself, she flinched. Watching his quizzical shrug, she felt like a mouse under the paws of a playful kitten. Should she make a break for it? He had showed no weapon. Though she was unarmed, the training school had taught physical combat. With luck enough, she might disable him and get out of the room. But—

She sank back into the chair. Men in military intelligence didn't work alone. He would surely have somebody in the lobby, maybe even waiting now in the corridor outside. Feeling chilled and almost ill, she listened again.

"—both of us trying to get close to the man who ran the EnGene computers. An odd little guy named Arny Carboni. He never got really close to anybody, though I think I got closer than anybody else. It turned out we were both part-time hackers. Both into hobby cryptography—building computer programs to write and break secret codes. We traded algorithms."

"Carboni?" She hated to trust her voice. "Do you know where—"

She saw his face turning older.

"Arny's dead. Dead in Enfield."

"But I thought—"

She checked herself to hear him.

"Arny saved my life." She saw pain on his face. "Mine and Doerr's. Died for it. I'll tell you how. What we both wanted was what he could tell us about the EnGene project. Arny was a sharp cookie. We knew he had to be picking up secrets from all the work he was doing for the research staff. Your man Scorpio came to me when he saw I was ahead of him—I'd borrowed a name, of course, and he had no notion I was anything except another guard.

"I played along. Doerr had his own cover story.

Claimed he was scouting for an American pharmaceutical outfit that wanted to know what sort of genetic miracles EnGene was cooking up. He had money." He peered at her. "Which must have come from you?"

Silently, she nodded.

"I took what Doerr wanted to pay me. Never much at first, till he thought he had me in so deep I'd never get out. Thousands, later, bribing me to pump Arny harder. So much toward the end that I knew he had to be working for Russia. I told Arny what was up. He saw a chance to get his father out of some Russian prison. We played Scorpio's game, till things got tight.

"Your man Scorpio." A quick little grin. "Not all yours. When we confronted him, he sold you out. Told us what he knew or guessed about you and poor old Jules Roman. What your great friendship foundation really is. Told us where his money came from. That's how I was able to drop in on you here."

"If you've come to arrest me—" Her anger flashed. "Don't play games!"

"Wait! Please!" He raised his hand. "Let me finish."

"Whatever." Stolidly, she shrugged. "Whatever."

"The phone woke me that morning—that last morning. Early, just past four. Arny calling. Told me he'd been tapping phones and heard enough to frighten him. Said we had to get out of town. Get out fast. He didn't have a car. Wanted me to pick him up. Quick. Gave me ten minutes to pack.

"I packed in five. Maybe too fast. In my own confusion, I forgot the car keys and locked myself out of the house. Had to break a window to get back in. I lived across town from Arny, and something over half an hour must have passed before I got there.

"A couple of blocks from his place—he lived in a little house close to the campus—I met a red pickup tearing down the street. When I got there, I found the front door open. Arny's body lay just inside, sprawled in his blood. Knifed through the heart, from the look of it, though I didn't stay to look for a weapon.

"The knifer was Scorpio. He drove a red pickup. Part of his American cover, he told me once. Arny must have called to warn him, but I can't guess why he used the knife."

His level eyes challenged her.

"Can you?"

"I never trusted him." She shook her head, wincing wryly. "Any more than I had to, which I guess was too far. I saw him two nights ago. Sat for hours with him in a Chicago bar, waiting for a contact he said he'd set up with Carboni. Of course Carboni couldn't show—not if he's dead. I let Scorpio talk me out of another ten thousand American dollars, for one more attempt to buy—to buy something he said Carboni had to sell."

"Which we can talk about," he said. "After we've come to terms."

"Terms?" She searched his oddly boyish face. "Do you want to tell me why you're here?"

"Not to hurt you." Quizzical again, he studied her. "Working in a world of double agents, sometimes we have to talk of deals."

She waited. He glanced around the room and cocked his head as if to listen at the door.

"I know that you're with the KGB. Now I'm sure you'll want to reach Scorpio's other contacts in En-Gene. I was one of them. You and I are both playing the tradecraft game. For my own part, I'm unhappy with what I'm afraid some of my countrymen are going to do. I think you and I together might have a stronger hand than either of us playing alone."

"Why?" She met his eyes. "If you are Clegg's son, why should I believe anything you say?"

"Because"—his voice turned savage—"because I hate—hate my father!"

19

El Mal Tiempo

Pancho Torres paused in the warm twilight to look around him. The fires had died. The drumming choppers were all far away. For the moment, he saw no danger.

"*Nada, chiquita,*" he murmured to the tiny creature lying in his open hand. "Nothing to hurt you now."

He carried it up to the farmhouse, holding it carefully and high, where he could keep his eyes on it. He felt it throbbing as if it had a fast-beating heart, and he caught its scent, a faint, clean sweetness like the fragrance of a red wildflower that used to bloom when the spring rains fell in the pasturelands around San Rosario.

He unlocked the door with the key he had found inside. With all the blinds and curtains drawn, he laid the little creature on the kitchen table while he risked using one shaded light to look for food. A long shopping list hung beside the silent telephone, but the buying had never been done. He found a half-dozen eggs and a paper carton nearly full of milk. A nearly empty box of cornflakes had been left in a cabinet over the range, and that was all.

The creature crept to the edge of the table and waited there, peeping hopefully while it watched him scrambling four of the eggs. It hurried hungrily to meet him when he brought them to the table in the hot skillet.

"Caliente!" he warned it. "Better let 'em cool."

It waited, with a soft whimpering sound, as if it understood. The milk was still good. When he offered a little of it in a glass, the creature raised itself to grasp the rim of the glass with both tiny hands. It leaned to taste, turned its head to smile at him, and drank thirstily.

When the eggs had cooled, he offered them in a teaspoon. It took a tiny handful, tasted daintily, gave him another grateful chirp, then began ravenously scooping them up with both hands. Nearly half of them were gone before it pushed the spoon aside and rolled on its side to smile at him, purring happily. He saw then that it was really female.

"Niñita! Querida chiquita!"

His own chest was throbbing suddenly with a happy ache he had never felt before. He didn't even try to understand, but she was something better than the baby he had dimly wished to father on drunken nights with those dollar-hungry gringo *putas.* So small and so helpless, in a world that must be as baffling to her as she was to him. His heart hurt for her.

He left her on the table while he washed the skillet. Before he was done, he heard her whimpering fearfully, heard the air drumming again to another cruising chopper.

"Qué es, chiquita?"

She jumped off the table to a chair and then the floor, and scurried to his feet. He picked her up and found her quivering with terror. When he laid her down beside the sink to finish removing the signs of their presence, she whined again so piteously that he put her in his shirt pocket. There, warm against his heart, she piped softly into silence.

When the chopper had gone on, he carried her back to the windmill tower and went to sleep with her near his face in the old water tank. In the middle of the night, her frightened keening woke him. Thunder was rumbling, and the rising wind smelled of rain. Fine hail was pelting down before they got back inside the house.

"Okay, *chiquita*!" he told her. "*Es nada.* They won't be flying in the storm."

He held her in his hands, crooning the sad Spanish love songs he had learned so long ago, until the thunder and her quivering stopped. They slept the rest of the night on the carpet because he wanted to leave no sign in the bed. When morning came, he cooked the rest of the eggs and poured out the handful of cornflakes. She seemed so ravenous again that he thought she could have eaten everything, but she stopped when half was gone to leave the rest for him.

"*Ah, chiquita,*" he told her, "we've got to find something to feed you."

She wouldn't let him leave her anywhere. Carrying her in his pocket, he climbed the windmill again to look for empty-seeming buildings that might hold food. Waiting till the choppers were far away, he tried a big house a mile or so toward the perimeter.

Too late. Some vandal had splintered the front door with an ax. The house was littered with clothing flung from closets and books tossed from shelves. Some mischief to the plumbing had flooded the floors. There had been food enough, but the raiders had dumped refrigerator and deep freeze into the chaos. A nauseating reek of spoiled meat drove him back to fresh air.

He hid in the empty garage until another chopper had cruised overhead. When it was gone, he followed it back toward the desolation until he found a smaller home that looked untouched since the owners fled. Farm folk, he thought, probably retired. The fields had been turned back to pasture. A wide streak of dust had come very near, but he was cheered to see a big vegetable garden, still alive and lush again since the rain.

"*Buena suerte, chiquita!*" he told her. "We're okay here."

Happily, he patted the warm little bulge she made in his pocket and felt her squirm comfortably against him. She had brought his lost luck back, and here was the promise of all they could eat.

Perhaps in panic, their absent hosts had left the back door open. They hadn't been rich. Brown spots were worn in the bright yellow linoleum on the kitchen floor, but it was neat and clean. The air was rich with the sweetness of a bag of apples ripening on the counter, but nothing had decayed. Pantry shelves were loaded with cans of food and full glass jars. The refrigerator and a huge deep freeze were still running, still thriftily filled.

"*Comemos aquí!*" he murmured again. "*Chiquita,* here we eat!"

He thawed steak and fried potatoes and picked ripe tomatoes to make a feast. His small companion filled herself once more and then begged to get back into his shirt pocket, where she lay crooning contentedly.

There was no lookout like the old windmill, no hide-out that seemed as secure as the old water tank, but the plentiful food made him decide to stay. She would soon be famished again, and her needs had suddenly come to matter more than anything—he hardly paused to wonder why.

Better, however, not to sleep in the house. Vandals might raid again. With the dust no longer deadly, the choppers might land their crews. Refugees might return.

He found an empty tool shed behind the garden. The roof seemed sound, and a wall of brush along the old fence row beyond it might cover their escape if they had to run. He brought blankets, a few cans of food, and water in a plastic bottle.

Their stay there seemed almost a dream. His mind no longer dwelt upon the gringos and all their cruel wrongs to him and his people, because her mystery absorbed him. What was she? How had she come to be swimming out of that desolate field of death? What sort of being would she become?

Her past and her future remained beyond his imagination, but she possessed him as no woman ever had. If now and then he caught himself wondering how she had captured him so totally, he shrugged off the puzzle. He felt happy with her. Happier, even, than he had been on that *cumpleaños* back in San Rosario when he became a man. Beyond all the wonders and puzzles of her being, beyond his sudden deep devotion, beyond her trembling terrors that also frightened him, nothing else could matter.

She ate and slept and grew. Ate eagerly and often. Slept in his pockets as long as she was small enough, slept purring against him. Grew amazingly. The *salamadra* tail shrank away to nothing. Her tiny limbs enlarged, growing into perfect feet and hands. She grew hair, straight and silken fine and astonishing as everything about her.

Astonishing, because of the way its color changed. All her colors did. No longer always pink, her skin turned an instant golden tan when the sun struck it, turned baby pink again in the shade. Her eyes, bright black beads at first, flashed green with vexation when some task made him leave her. They were gray when she groped to understand something he was saying, indigo blue when she was fed and happy against him.

She learned to walk, but not by experimental clinging and tottering and stumbling. One day when he had laid her on the kitchen table while he brought their meal, she glided upright and almost danced across the table and into his hand, piping a triumphant song.

On another day, they had eaten well. She was still hardly bigger than a kitten, and he held her on one arm, snuggled against him. She was purring, trilling softly, her eyes trustfully violet and fixed on his face. Her silky hair had turned pale gold. He stroked it gently.

"*Chiquita querida,*" he was murmuring. "*Chiquita mía—*"

"*Chiquita querida.*" At first he wasn't sure what he had heard, but her tiny treble repeated the words. A carefully accurate echo, they reflected all his fond emotion. "*Chiquita querida! Chiquita mía!*"

Faster than his baby brothers and sisters, she learned to talk. She learned his name. "Panchito," as he called himself at first, because somehow she made him feel a child again. Proudly, she piped her own name. Meg. Alphamega. A strange name. When he first tried to ask what it meant and where she came from, she shrank against him, silent and quivering.

On another day she tried to tell him more. The choppers droning too far away to be alarming, they were in the garden. She was riding on his shoulder, clinging to his hair. He had found squash and green corn and new potatoes for another feast, and they were starting back toward the house when she saw a butterfly. Its brilliant wings enchanted her, and they followed it to the back of the garden, where she could see the nearest streak of dust. The butterfly forgotten, she trembled against him again.

"*Ceniza.*" He pointed into the gray desolation. "*Polvo.* Ashes. Dust." He took her in his hand to ask another question. "Did you come from there?"

"*Sí.*" Half her few words were Spanish. "Meg came. *Polvo malo.* Kill all. Kill Vic." Her eyes went indigo, glistening with tears. "*Pobre, pobre, querido Vic!*"

"Vic?" A puzzling name, because it was nothing he had taught her. "*Quién es?* Who is Vic?"

She lacked words enough to tell him.

"*El polvo toma el pobre Vic!*" The dust had taken Vic, and she shivered in his hand. "*El fuego, fuego malo* hurt Meg. Too hot, too hot!"

A chopper was drifting back, and they retreated toward the house. She never wanted to look into the wasteland again, or to speak of Vic or the evil *polvo.* Most of the time, her terrors apparently forgotten, she seemed as happy as he was, delighted with the food he found her, interested eagerly in everything, learning and growing amazingly. Late one night, however, when they had gone to sleep together on their blankets in the tool shed, she woke him with a shrill little shriek.

"Sax, Sax! Sax, *peligro!*" She was screaming at his ear. "Tell Sax! *La casa! Peligro!* Tell Sax! *Peligro en la casa.*"

"A nightmare, *chiquita?*" He took her in his hand and held her trembling against him in the dark. "We're okay, here in our own little house."

"Sax!" She kept sobbing the name. *"El pobre Sax!"*

"Who is Sax?"

"Hermano." A frightened mosquito voice. *"El hermano de mi querido Vic. El hermano de mala suerte."*

Vic, her dear Vic, was dead in the dust. Sax, at least in her nightmare dream, was the unlucky brother, still alive but now in some danger she lacked words to explain. Patting her, trying to still her trembling dread, he told himself it must have been only a dream, but new alarms kept his nerves on edge. One day he saw smoke climbing from a place where he had seen a farmhouse standing a few miles nearer the perimeter. Two choppers came to wheel around the tall black column, and one of them dropped out of sight.

Vandals, again? And the crewmen landing to hunt them down?

Possible. He must take more care to keep the house the way it had been, doors closed and blinds drawn, to leave no footprints in the garden, to avoid moving around in daylight that might betray them. But nothing, he thought, could hide them forever. Some evil day would come. If the dust stayed dead, men on foot would venture in to study it. The refugees would be eager to return. Lawmen would come to comb the landscape, looking for those vandals and such *desafortunados* as he was.

"El mal tiempo." He shrugged. *"Por la mañana."*

Some evil time must come, but let it be tomorrow.

Until then, he would stay with Meg and try to make her happy. Until the bad time came, he would help her grow and learn and do his best to keep her safe.

El mal tiempo.

It came one morning at dawn, when she was still asleep. The choppers had awakened him. He hated to disturb her, but the beans and peas and squash should be picked before the sun rose and the watchers in the sky came near enough to spot him. Leaving her, he turned back in the doorway to look fondly down at her.

A delicate doll-form as she lay on the bare dirt floor in their stolen blankets. She was bare and perfect in the dimness, not yet grown so large as he recalled his baby sisters, certainly not so chubby. She smiled in her sleep, and her breath was a tiny sighing, faster than his own. How long, he wondered, could he save her from harm?

"Hasta la mal." Until the badness came. He whispered that, cold with foreboding, and tried to be silent, closing the creaky door.

The badness came. He was in the garden, bent over the row of beans, when he heard the tramp of boots and the click of a gun and a gloating voice he remembered.

"Doggone! If it ain't the greaser killer!" The voice of Deputy Harris, who had sent the *cucaracha* pie to his cell in the Enfield county jail. "Livin' high on the hog and laughing at the law? Stealin' yourself a nice mess of green frijoles to fill your ugly gut."

A gun clicked.

"Fall flat, spic!"

He tried to run for the brush that might hide him. Three steps. The gun crashed behind him. His leg went numb and crumpled under him. He fell facedown in the mud.

20

"The Hard Fist of God"

Belcraft watched Kalenka turn the jeep and drive away.

"Okay, Doctor." Still keeping an uneasy distance, Dusek escorted him back into the room and made him lay his car keys and billfold and pocket knife on the dresser. "I'll hold you here till we get other orders."

Careful not to touch them, he used the phone book to sweep those articles into a wastebasket and waited at the door until two intelligence officers arrived in an Army car. Impatient men in gray business suits, afraid to come in his room, they had Dusek send him outside and kept him standing well away while they demanded more information than he could give about EnGene and Vic and the pink thing.

Why had he let the creature go?

How could a fat pink worm command instant sympathy? What had it done to win so much aid from a trained physician, a responsible American citizen, a man who certainly should have known how vital it would be to the investigation? He found no answers that pleased them, none that made much sense even to him.

Why had he come to Enfield? What, exactly, had Vic told him on the phone?

Dutifully, he repeated most of the words he could recall, repeated them over and over into tape recorders. Most of them. A secret urgency kept burning higher in him, a driving need to get home to Fort Madison and dig through his piled-up mail to find the letter Vic had mailed.

He knew he ought to reveal its existence. The dust had been a threat to everything alive. Perhaps it still was. All the thousands of troops and scientists and federal agents gathered around the perimeter were fighting to crack the riddle. The letter might hold answers. He told himself all that, and still he didn't speak.

A Colonel Heydt arrived in another jeep. He was commandeering the motel for his forward control post. As wary as the rest, he sat in the jeep, watching Belcraft through binoculars and shouting more demands, snarling obscenities when Belcraft kept insisting that Vic had never said or written anything about his work or his life here.

Two Army trucks pulled into the parking lot before noon, filled with sunburnt National Guardsmen. Colonel Heydt appeared again, barking angry orders and listening from the jeep while he described the pink thing for them. He watched them scatter into the weeds toward the creek.

They discovered nothing.

He spent most of the next two months in number nine, Dusek in command of his guards. Heydt's staff headquarters were in the front rooms. Meals came from a field kitchen on the parking lot. Most of the choppers had departed. The National Guard company kept searching, mowing weeds and clearing brush, finding only chiggers.

One morning Mrs. Bard was escorted to his room, looking ill and weepily grim, claiming her pay for the extra night he had spent there before the Army commandeered the motel. He borrowed his billfold to find thirty dollars, and let her keep the change.

She wanted to know if he had seen her son when he went across the creek. Her poor dear Frankie. She felt sure he was still alive, trapped and suffering in the ruins of the lab. Next day the guards told him that a search detail had found her wandering in the ashes. Later he learned that she had been sent away to her sister in Colorado.

The colonel was a pudgy little man, with sagging red dewlaps and a raspy nasal voice. A retired Army doctor, unhappy about his recall from a comfortable private practice, he seemed to blame Belcraft for the whole Enfield disaster. Pressing the inquisition, he refused to let him get a lawyer, or call anyone outside, or even see the general.

Kept in isolation, Belcraft spent sleepless nights enduring torments of his own. Guilt grew in him over Vic's letter. In spite of ceaseless appeals to his sense of humanity in danger and threats of a federal prison, in spite of sometimes feeling half convinced that Colonel Heydt had good cause to blame him, he never spoke about it—and never quite knew why. He never found a rational reason to care what became of the pink thing. Yet, to his own surprise, he felt a haunting loneliness for it. Somehow, he missed it even more than he missed Midge.

Kalenka came to trust him more than the colonel ever did. When he set up a laboratory in what had been the motel dining room, he let Belcraft work with him, washing glassware at first, weighing specimens and keeping records, finally running tests on his own.

They found the dust to be sterile, consisting mostly of simple oxides apparently formed from the calcium and other nonvolatile elements in the life it had devoured. Nothing remained to reveal what had made it so deadly then, so harmless now. Mixed with the oxides, Belcraft found complex molecules that baffled him.

"Heat sinks?" he suggested. "The oxidations must have released a lot of heat, but there was never any warmth I could feel. Perhaps this stuff was formed by endothermic reactions that protected the lethal agent from the heat of its own metabolism." And he had to add, "We're dealing with something new in biology—something we haven't learned how to see."

Kalenka merely shrugged.

His interrogators had never seemed to listen when he wanted to take his case to the general. Dusek seemed as surprised as he was one day when a message came that Clegg wanted him at post headquarters.

The perimeter had been extended since the night he got to Enfield. Headquarters was a commandeered mansion on a hill, a safe ten miles back from the ashes but still inside the redrawn lines. Dusek parked the jeep on the drive and took him inside. A black sergeant kept them waiting for an endless hour before he let them into what had been the dining room.

"So you're Saxon Belcraft?"

General Clegg faced him across a big table. A window wall beyond it showed banks of well-kept flowers around a huge swimming pool. Against that strong backlight, the general's features were hard to see.

"I'm Belcraft." He nodded. "I've been asking to see you. I think I've been detained here too long, with very little cause."

"Perhaps." The general kept him standing. "Kalenka has asked me to consider your release, but you'll have to answer my questions first."

He waited under the general's coldly probing stare. Eyes adjusting to the light, he made out a figure of autocratic power, tall and gaunt, sitting very straight, medals glinting on the uniform. On the high forehead, a pale birthmark showed faintly through makeup meant to cover it.

"Better answer carefully." The questions came at last, solemn-toned and slow. "Are you a loyal American?"

"I think so." Bitterly, he added, "I've had to swear that a thousand times since your men arrested me."

"Your loyalty is important to us." The general nodded calmly. "Can you put service over self?"

"I'm a physician."

"Can you accept discipline?"

"From whom?"

"Authority." The general's voice rose slightly. "Legitimate authority, sanctioned under God."

"I try to respect the law, if that's what you mean."

He waited, puzzled and resentful, until the general shrugged.

"Doctor, I had hoped for something more affirmative." A doubtful frown. "In your special case, however, perhaps that will have to do." Yet the general paused again, as if to give him time to wonder. The rawboned face creased with what was meant to be a smile. "Dr. Belcraft, I am going to offer you an opportunity we have always reserved for a very few selected men. I am inviting you to join an extremely exclusive organization —a group that exists and acts in the strictest secrecy."

Belcraft was shaking his head.

"You can trust me." A frosty smile. "You must trust me, because I can tell you very little more before you accept the obligations of membership. Under our very strict rules, I am forbidden to reveal the name of our group, or its meeting place, or the identity of any other member."

"Sir," Belcraft began. "I don't—"

"I can't allow you to decline." The commanding voice never paused. "If you insist on some stronger assurance, I can at least inform you that the organization is devoted to our own high vision of a regenerated America. As a member, you will be required to subordinate your own private concerns to that noble vision. You will submit yourself to a necessary discipline—"

"Sir!" Belcraft nerved himself to protest. "Coming from you, that surprises me. It puzzles me. But it doesn't sound like anything I want to join."

"Better think about it." The general's tone grew colder. "Membership can give you rewards that most men never even hope for. I can't define them now, not until you have been inducted. However, there is something else I can tell you." His long pause seemed deliberately ominous. "If you refuse to join, we'll make you regret it."

Trembling, Belcraft wished he had been allowed to sit. He heard the rasp of wrath in the general's voice, and saw that crimson birthmark turning darker.

"However," he heard himself saying, "I do refuse."

"Fool!" The general came upright. For half a minute he stood trembling, big fists clenched. At last, jaws set, he sank slowly back into his chair. "You've had your chance. Don't forget it!"

"I'm not likely to forget."

"Your best chance." The general scowled and shook his head, his emotion almost controlled. "That's all I can say about our secret group, but I can brief you on two very public organizations that share some of the same high objectives. Those two are Bioscience Alert and Task Force Watchdog. I like to call them the armies of God. Called to battle in a holy Armageddon to stamp out the madness that destroyed the city of Enfield."

His voice had assumed an oratoric roll.

"Belcraft, we serve a sacred cause! A desperate campaign that I had to lead alone for too many years. A year and more ago, I came here to warn your brother and his fellow madmen what their Satanic work could lead to. They laughed at me and returned to their black blasphemy. You have seen the frightful consequences."

The general paused with a savage little grin.

"I hope you don't approve of them!"

"Sir! Please—"

"Your brother!" The general mouthed the word like something foul. "Your brother and those others should have been destroyed like the fiends of hell they are. And they could have been—but for the tragic circumstance that we must also wage another holy war.

"That is our unending campaign to save the freedom and the soul of mankind from the atheistic blight of Marxist communism. The Soviets have their own devil's nests of genetic engineers—most of them, so I understand, unwilling slaves toiling under torture in the prison labs—toiling to perfect genetic horror bombs with which the Kremlin plots to overwhelm the world. Your brother's crew begged for research funds, promising that they could give us a genetic defensive capacity.

"The debate was secret—as it must remain!" The general stabbed a warning finger at him. "But the weapon-makers won. Your brother and his fellow demons were allowed to brew their broth of hell, the genetic terror that wiped out Enfield! I'm delighted that they have met their own divine atonement. A forgiving God has apparently erased the plague they engineered, all but that single demoniac creation.

"Your own pet monster!" His tone turned harsh with accusation. "A literal demon, I believe, conceived in hell and left on Earth to spread the plague again. I am told that it bewitched you, Doctor. True?"

"I never felt bewitched." Almost overwhelmed by the general's air of rightous might, Belcraft shook his head. "The creature did appeal to my emotions. It seemed helpless. Pathetic. I know—I'm certain it is absolutely harmless."

"Hah!" An indignant snort. "It's a child of Satan, left here among us like the serpent in Eden. It has tempted you and escaped to mock us. But it has to be hunted down. It has to be exterminated, like the devil's spawn it is." A raw violence shook his voice. "Crushed like a venomous spider! Burned with holy fire. Its foul dust cursed forever!"

"You'll have to find it first."

"You—you *are* betwitched!" The handprint burned redder, and the general's savage thunder made him almost sorry for that impish interjection. "But I warn you, Belcraft! Your brother and his friends have created death and desolation. They themselves have perished for it, and their evil creations shall not prevail. Almighty God has struck them down and quenched their hellish fire. And His work is not yet done.

"Look at me, you infidel!" The general clenched a hairy hand. "Look at the hard fist of God! Raised to smite these infernal engineers and win our Armageddon. I warn you, Belcraft!"

The general dropped his voice and leaned across the table.

"I warn you not to speak of what I've told you here. Not to anybody, not for any reason—you don't know who our agents are, but they will follow you. They will see to it that you keep silent. And, in time to come—" The general shook his head in mock regret. "You'll repent the witchcraft that has led you to deny the righteous cause of God!"

"Sir, you're dead wrong—"

No longer listening, the general bent to touch a button on the table. The black sergeant came to take him back to the jeep. He was astonished next morning when Dusek returned his billfold and his keys, with the news that he was free.

"To go?"

"Wherever." Dusek shrugged. "Orders from the general. I'm to see you out of the perimeter. No stops inside."

As much puzzled as relieved, he started the car and pulled away from the Enbard Mo el. Dusek followed him in the jeep, out beyond the general's commandeered hilltop mansion to a new chain link fence, barbed wire strung along the top and guards on duty at the gate. The guards frowned at him and questioned Dusek and phoned headquarters and finally let him out.

With an uneasy glance behind, he started back toward Fort Madison.

21

A Dream of Alphamega

Going home!

Dusek and General Clegg and number nine left behind him, Belcraft rejoiced in the speed and power of the car. It drove well, and he rolled a window glass down to relish the rich scents of summer. The day was splendid, bright and windless, not yet too hot, a few small puffs of cumulus budding white against the milky blue.

Getting back at last to pick up his neglected practice. Back to look for Vic's letter and whatever it might reveal. His own man again—or was he, really?

The car swayed from a rough spot in the pavement. Eighty miles an hour. He squinted into the rearview mirror. The guarded gate was already far behind, diminishing fast, and he saw no pursuit.

Slowing to a careful fifty-five, he tried to imagine what might lie ahead. That wasn't easy. The ashes of Enfield were too hard to forget. The pink thing stuck in his mind, a riddle never solved. What had she been meant to be?

Awe brushed him again. If she was really Vic's creation, the seed of a wholly new tree of life, engineered to bear more perfect fruit than the human—what might she mean to the human future? Should he want her to live? Or was she in fact the insidious serpent in Eden, somehow bewitching him into betraying his kind?

He shrank from the thought, shivering a little, but still he longed to know how she had fared since he had watched her crawl away into the weeds. Whatever she might become, he couldn't help hoping that her unknown gifts had been great enough to keep her alive.

Longing to know, hoping for news, he tried the radio. Washington authorities had confirmed more ugly details of what they had at last begun to call the Enfield catastrophe. Just this morning, General Clegg had allowed the first camera crew inside the quarantine perimeter, far enough to see the strange gray killer-dust that science was still unable to explain.

"Thirty thousand killed," the surgeon general had reported. "All that remains is the ashy residue into which the unidentified lethal factor crumbled all organic matter it had touched. Collected specimens now appear totally inert, with no pathogen discoverable. Until the unknown fatal vector can be understood and controlled, we must take every possible precaution against reactivation."

Martial law remained in effect around the disaster area, General Adrian Clegg in command. At his insistence, both the FBI and the CIA had been shaken up, new directors appointed. Four different congressional investigations were in progress, none with findings ready to report.

Once again, the President had repeated his expressions of bewilderment and grief, offering heartfelt sympathy to surviving relatives and friends, trying to restore the courage of the shaken nation. "Though such losses are painful, we have kept the rest of America safe. We'll continue to keep it safe."

Nothing new. Uneasily, he kept looking into the rearview mirror. At first the road was empty, but presently a light-blue car crept up as if to pass and then lagged back again. He slowed to fifty, and still it didn't pass. He pushed the car to seventy and beyond, and still it stayed in the mirror. Finally, he pulled into a Chevron station that shone with the same bold red and white and blue he recalled, shining in the dust.

The blue car went on by. He glimpsed a frowsy-looking woman at the wheel. A heavy bald man sat slumped down beside her, apparently asleep. They didn't slow or glance at him, yet he kept on wondering.

His abrupt release was still a puzzle. Refusing to join Clegg's super-secret group had certainly earned him no favors. If the lethal vector was still unknown, the pink thing still at large—why had they let him go?

He shrugged and pulled the car toward a no-lead pump. If they had no convincing reason to turn him loose, they had none to hold him—not since they had found him uninfected. Nor any cause to follow, so far as he could imagine. Anyhow, whatever the reason, he was on the way.

The attendant eyed him warily.

"Mister, where you from?"

"Back toward Enfield."

"Sorry, sir." The attendant backed way. "Fresh out of no-lead."

"May I use your phone?" He nodded at the curbside booth. "I need to call home."

"Out of order." The attendant waved him toward the road. "Sorry, sir. Uh—a funeral coming up. Got to close the station."

He drove on. At the next town he circled a block to be coming from a different direction when he pulled into another Chevron station, and got gas with no questions. He found another phone and dialed his office number. No answer.

Which was no real surprise. Driving out of town that morning before he thought Miss Hearn would be awake, he had stopped by the office to leave her a note.

Unexpected trip to Enfield to see my brother there. Cancel everything through Wednesday. Will call tomorrow.

That was long months ago. With never a chance to call, he was doubtless on the "missing" list by now, his office probably closed. With no word from him, nor any pay, Miss Hearn had likely found another job.

Trouble behind him. More ahead, even at home. He couldn't help brooding, petty as he told himself his private worries were. He had doubtless been replaced on the hospital staff. Too many bills were far past due. Many of his patients must have gone to other doctors. When people learned he had been shut up inside the perimeter, a suspected carrier, they might become as skittish as that gas pumper. Not that he could blame them.

Night was near before he saw the Mississippi. It lay wide and bright beneath the peaceful-seeming dusk, a long string of grain barges creeping around the bend to meet a white-painted tourist stern-wheeler that might have steamed out of Mark Twain's age. That glimpse of the river gave him more comfort than the President's promise, transforming old Fort Madison into an islet of enduring stability, securely remote from invasion by any monstrous biological creation.

Pulling off the highway onto an empty street, Enfield far behind, he felt a moment of elation. That good moment faded when he saw the tall white columns of the house Midge had loved. Empty now and silent, probably smelling of its own long decay. A pang of loneliness stabbed him. Suddenly dreading the place, shrinking from all its silent reminders of happier times gone forever, he turned abruptly to drive to his office and look for Vic's letter.

The office was hot, the air conditioner off. It had a faint, stale scent of disinfectants and dusty emptiness, but Miss Hearn had left his desk neatly in order. The in basket held a stack of mail she had left for him to read, a sheaf of unpaid bills, announcements of professional meetings. He found a postcard from Midge, now with her mother in California. Signed "With love."

If he had somehow given her more time—but all that was gone. He shrugged and searched again. Nothing at all from Vic.

He phoned Miss Hearn.

"Doctor—" A muffled crash, as if she had dropped the receiver. "I thought—we were afraid you'd been caught in Enfield."

"A close call," he told her. "I was trapped inside the perimeter. Held in isolation till they were certain I hadn't been infected. I'm back at the office now. Looking at the mail. I was hoping for a letter from my brother."

"From Enfield?"

"He died there. I think he had written me."

"Doctor—" Something made her hesitate. "A letter did come from Enfield. The same week you left. A thick brown envelope, marked personal. No return address, but I made out the postmark."

"Where is it?"

"Taken in the robbery—"

"What?"

"I never had a chance to tell you. The office was ransacked the next Saturday night. Professionals, the police think, from the way the lock was picked. Somebody looking for narcotics. Frightened off before they found anything. All the drug samples were dumped on the floor, though little or nothing was actually missing. Except that letter. I looked everywhere. The letter was taken—I can't imagine why."

"I—I see."

"Doctor, I tried hard to locate you." Her voice was distressed. "There was no way. Phone lines were out. When I finally got through to the task force people, they said they had no record of you. If your brother—" Her voice caught. "If your brother was there in Enfield, I'm terribly sorry. I know the letter would have meant a lot. I've kept checking with the police, but they say they don't have a lead."

"Thanks," he muttered. "I know you've done all you could. Glad to find everything else okay."

But nothing was okay. He felt almost afraid to wonder who could have known about the letter, or what might come of its loss, but a thin, cold blade of dread had stabbed him deep.

"Really, Doctor—" Miss Hearn came back. "I've done my best. Not knowing—not knowing if you would ever get back. I've been taking care of everything I could. Coming down every day to go through the mail and bank the checks—what few came in."

"Thank you, Miss Hearn!" He tried to pull himself together. "Can you be here in the morning at eight? I'll have your check, and we can get the office open again."

"I'll be there, Doctor. But I'm afraid—" An uneasy pause. "We've lost a lot of patients. Your landlord wants his past-due rent, and the whole town's on edge about the disaster. The bank will want you to come in—"

"Be here," he told her. "We'll do what we can."

Still dreading the silent house, he stopped for dinner at Stan's Steak Place and lingered over the paper and another beer before he went on back to Tara Two. That name seemed sadly ironic now, and its airless emptiness depressed him again. He opened windows and put a Beethoven sonata on the stereo and spent a long time in the shower.

The bedroom still held a painful trace of Midge's scent, but somehow he was thinking of the pink thing as he get into bed. Would the missing letter have told more about what she was? About what she might become?

He went to sleep wondering. Where was she now? Perhaps already dead? What secrets had Vic hidden in her unfolding genes? What was her link to the Enfield disaster? If any link existed? With the letter gone, would he ever know?

He dreamed about her.

"*Señor* Sax?" In the dream she could speak. Her voice was high and tiny, but very clear. Somehow, the anxious words were Spanish. "*El hermano de mi querido* Dr. Vic Belcraft?"

She seemed to sense at once that he was not at home in Spanish, because she changed to English, or tried to, her faint treble grown hesitant.

"The brother of Vic? *El hombre bueno.* The good man who aided me and fed me and kept me from the *cazadores.* The bad men hunting me."

He told her in the dream that he was Vic's brother.

"*Soy Meg. Alphamega.*" Her voice seemed very far away. "My name. From *el señor* Vic. *El fabricante de vida.* The maker of life."

He asked where she was.

"*En peligro!*" He barely caught the words. "In very great danger. Running from *los cazadores,* I fell into a pit. A strange dark *hoyo.* It is cold and wet and very deep. I can't—can't—" He lost her fading voice, then caught a few more words, "*Me duele . . . me duele—*"

She was in pain, and the dream was gone.

22

Meg Alone

Sleeping on the thin brown blanket Panchito had spread on the hard earth floor, Meg dreamed that he had risen from beside her. Shoes in his hand, careful not to wake her, he moved to the doorway of the narrow wooden shed and stopped there to look down at her. She felt his love washing her like warm rain.

Even in the dream, it troubled her for him to be away. But he was only going out to gather young frijoles and sweet green *maíz* and tender *calabazas amarillas.* She was always hungry, and in the dream she told herself that he would soon be back, loaded with food, ready to wake her and make their *desayuno.*

"Niñita chiquita," he would whisper, touching her tenderly, *"es la hora por comer—"*

Terror broke her dream. Suddenly awake, she knew he wasn't coming back. Yet he had seen no danger. He was still out in the garden, stooping over the row of frijoles, softly whistling a lullaby she loved. But even in the dream she had felt *el peligroso* creeping out of the brush and across the rows behind him like a thick red fog.

Shivering on the blanket, she heard the harsh gringo voice mocking *el pobre Panchito.* She couldn't feel the gringo himself, because there was no love to open him to her, but his voice was like a faint red mist spreading over the garden.

She felt Panchito's shock, and caught his wave of fear for her. She saw him try to run and heard the terrible crash of the gun and felt the numbness in his knee and the cruel stabs of pain when his leg bent where it shouldn't bend and the way his mind dimmed and slowed when he went facedown in the mud.

The red badness was suddenly thick all around her, so thick she could hardly breathe. She knew she had to run and hide somewhere, before the gringos found her. Somewhere, perhaps, in the vacant house. Scrambling off the blanket, she turned to search for danger there.

She didn't have to use her eyes because the house was near and she had fixed it in her mind. Standing where she was in the shed, she could look out through the old wooden walls of the shed. When she found the red fog thick around the house, she knew the gringos were there. Listening, she stopped breathing and stopped her heart until she could hear their ugly voices and the thump of their boots and the crash when they broke down a door.

Searching everywhere, she found a curved piece of rusty iron lying in tall weeds behind the shed. One broken wheel jutted above it, and a dark hole had rusted through the side. *Una carretilla,* Panchito had named it when she asked him. *Hierro viejo. Buena por nada.* An old wheelbarrow, in the language of the gringos. Junk. Good for nothing.

Except, perhaps, to hide her.

Shivering from the red haze that seemed like ice in the air, she slipped out of the shed. Crouching, stepping on rocks and weeds to keep from leaving footprints, she darted to the old *carretilla* and slid under it.

Nobody saw her. Lying there, trembling, she felt the throb of pain in Pancho's leg. When she reached his mind, all she found was a dimming flicker of sadness. All the sadness was for her. He was filled with a sick despair because he couldn't move to help her, but he didn't even feel the hurting and the terrible deadness in his leg.

She heard the gringos shouting, tramping through the garden and the weeds, and the redness of danger grew so cold she had to shiver. Almost afraid to breathe again, she lay very still, feeling the pain Panchito couldn't feel. After a long time, a chopper came down so near the ground shook under her from the roaring of it. Its wind shook the old iron over her and blew dust in her face. The engine died. The voices and the tramping boots came closer.

"That yellow-livered killer spic!" The mist grew thicker, and she heard the near voice of the jeering gringo who had shot Panchito. "Hiding here for weeks, maybe months. Right under old Clegg's nose! Glad I got the sneaky bastard. Not that Clegg will ever give a damn. All he wants is the baby monster."

Another voice said something, and the red-shadowed gringo spoke again.

"Funny little critter like nobody ever seen. Some idiot civilian caught it crawling out of the dust and let it go again. It's got the big brass all uptight, because they think it could have brought the plague. Whatever it is, Clegg's hellbent to hunt it down."

"What for?"

"How the hell do I know? He come out hisself to brief the detail. Got pretty hot about it. Called the critter a demon let out of hell to bring that plague to Earth. A scourge of God, he called it, sent to punish us for letting science freaks meddle into the secrets of creation."

Again that other voice.

"I wouldn't know. I ain't all that religious. A baby demon, maybe, if it really is a demon. Ain't no bigger than a baby." The weeds crackled, closer. "Anyhow, they've got us on the trail—not that I'm exactly hankerin' to catch it, if it does spread the plague."

"Better not let on you got cold feet."

"This ain't the duty I signed up for, but I never got cold feet yet. They know the killer spic had the critter with him here, because they photographed it out of a chopper. Riding on him like a monkey while he worked his garden. Clegg wants it, and we'd better get it."

He must have kicked the iron wheelbarrow. It rang in her ears and tipped suddenly aside. She rolled to keep under it. The red fog clotted and froze like ice around her, until she couldn't breathe.

"—tangle with it," the gringo was saying out of his red cloud. "Devil or whatever. But we're hauling that gizzard-lipped bastard back to the hospital. When he gets fit to talk, they'll persuade him to tell where it went."

Somebody shouted. Their boots tramped away, but the red haze stayed thick around her. They were moving Panchito. She felt his mind half alive again, trying not to show his pain, but they were too cruel with his leg. He moaned, and again his mind flickered out.

The gringos kept yelling. The chopper coughed and came to deafening life. The rusty metal over her rocked in its wind. It climbed back into the sky, taking Panchito away. Listening, she heard no boots or voices.

She was all alone.

The redness had thinned, and its feel of cold was fading out, but still it clung around her, clouding everything. Though the gringos were gone, she was still afraid to move. High overhead, she heard other choppers drumming, watching from the sky. Their cameras would catch her if she showed herself. All day she lay there. The iron above her grew hot under the sun. She longed for cooler air. She didn't know what a demon was, but she didn't want the gringos coming back to hunt her.

Sometimes a breath of cooling wind came through the hole in the iron. She crawled nearer to it and broke more weeds to help it reach her. Waiting for sunset and the coolness and her chance to get away, she lay trying to remember what she was and how she had come to be.

Some things she had always known. The dear Vic Belcraft had been her maker, and she would love his name forever. He had shaped her for a mission that had been too big for him, a duty more important than her life or his. For Vic's sake, she must discover that true goal and do everything to reach it.

There were other things she could never know, because Vic had sadly lacked the skills and the time to make her all she should have been or to teach her all she should have learned. She felt afraid she might never be strong enough or smart enough or brave enough to carry out her mission, even if she were able to find what it was.

The dear Vic could never tell her now, because he was gone, crumbled into dust, along with the EnGene and all his friends there, and those others who had to die because of the terrible harm they were about to do.

Baking under the burning iron, she held her head close to the ragged little window in it and tried to remember her beginning. At first her world had been dark, with nothing she could reach or see. She was floating nowhere in a warm vast ocean, the only being in there.

Yet she had not been alone, because the dear Vic was above her, loving her tenderly, toiling to keep her alive. When at last there was light, she could see the vastness of the ocean and vaster shadows drifting over it. She could feel the huge high shape of the dear Vic himself, like a cloud with brightness in it. Sometimes she heard his voice, a slow far thunder rumbling out of the cloud. The words meant nothing then, but she always felt his shining love.

Through ages of darkness and ages of brightness, he sheltered her and fed her and let her grow. The ocean around her shrank and shrank until she could find its wall. She was larger, until at last she could climb out over the wall to the wide warm plain of his outspread hand.

He could see her then without his microscopes. Speaking words she did not yet understand, he began trying to teach her what she would need to know. That was never easy. She could never understand enough. He always said he didn't know enough, and the good time with him was gone too soon.

"I must die."

He told her that on the dreadful night when she first felt the nearing danger, a faint red stain in the air and a chill that made her shiver, even when he held her in his hand. They were alone together. The lab was very quiet, with the staff all gone, and she wished for words to let her ask him what the danger was.

"Baby, baby! Try not to let it hurt." Feeling her shock of grief, he pressed her to his cheek. "If you can stay alive—you must stay alive! I don't matter."

He stayed in the lab all that night. He spoke on the phone. He sat a long time writing with a pen and went from that to the computer and turned from it to work with the big machines that wrote new codes for DNA and other codes to create stranger things. When at last he had time, he came back to speak to her, trying to explain what the danger was, trying to tell her how to stay alive.

"Baby, I hate it!" He held her in his hand, whispering in the dim-lit lab. "Time gone too soon. Nothing ready. You still need me. Terribly. Still too young. No time to tell you anything. Never know how much your understand. But—but—"

He held her against his cheek, and she felt the wetness on it. She wanted to tell him how sorry she was, but she had no words and no way to say them.

"Stay alive!" he breathed. "Find yourself."

All she could do was hang on to his finger. It was trembling when he pushed her off to lay her back in the nest.

23

Billy Higgs

Belfast sat up shivering. The dream was gone. The hurt and terror he felt in Meg had awakened him, her pain more real than any dream could be. He felt a sudden cold certainty that she was in fact the creation of Vic's genetic science, an equal certainty that he had never designed her to harm humanity or bring death to Enfield.

Somehow, she had reached him with a desperate call for help. That was real. He wished he had some power to respond. Yet it left him trembling with something close to dread. Even in danger, was she still somehow greater than human?

Still groggy with sleep, he shook his head. The claims for ESP had never convinced him. The real pink thing had whistled expressive sounds, but she had never spoken. Whatever the case, the experience had left him shaken with a strange conviction that her danger was actual and deadly. Yet he had no idea where she was, no possible way to find and try to help her.

Alphamega? He said it aloud. Her actual name? Had Vic really been her maker? Or had the dream grown out of his own troubled speculation?

He went to the bathroom and then to the kitchen for

a good shot of Cutty Sark out of a bottle Midge had won at a bridge party and left as a last little gift for him. He prowled the empty house for half an hour and finally went to bed again. At last he slept.

And dreamed again of Alphamega.

"Fuego! Fuego!" Her faint, far-off voice was sharp with desperate urgency. *"Peligro, Señor* Sax! *Salga de la casa!* Get out of your house! Before it burns! *Salga, pronto!"*

He felt her fear before he began to understand the words. Trembling with it, he tumbled out of bed. A sleepy sanity tried to call him back. He's been under too much stress too long. Overtired from the long drive home, his mind was playing games. The smoke alarms weren't shrieking. All the shocks of Enfield left far behind, he was safe at last in his own house.

But her terror overwhelmed that voice of sanity. Certain that the house was somehow about to burn, he was already running for the back door. In pajamas, he dashed out across the porch and into the backyard, where Midge, with no green thumb, had tried with small success to start new roses.

Lit by a high half moon and the first gray glow of dawn, the yard was clotted with weeds from months of neglect, but he caught the scent of a few blooms somehow surviving. A cricket, chirping too cheerily, recalled that night the highway cop had kept him out of Enfield.

The cool air revived his sanity. He caught no scent of smoke. There was no fire. Perhaps the old house itself had gotten on his nerves. Too many tormented memories of Midge had risen beside all the haunting riddles of the pink thing. This had to be nothing more than his own private case of what the media people had begun to call genetic shock.

He shrugged and started back inside. Whatever had awakened him, he still felt too jittery to go back to bed. He wanted another shot of Cutty Sark, but this was no time for a drink. Not with another long day ahead, paying what bills he could cover, pleading with the banker, trying to pick up his practice.

For now, what he needed was coffee to steady his nerves, but he couldn't help dreading the empty kitchen and all its reminders of Midge. He would get his clothes on and drive out to the truck stop for coffee and some human company and maybe ham and—

A heavy crash shook the ground beneath his bare feet.

He had time to see yellow fire exploding out of doors and windows before a hot fist smashed him back into Midge's roses. Dimly, he felt blistering heat. He heard roaring flames and sirens shrieking. Men were shouting, somewhere far away. Cold water splashed him. A stretcher slid beneath him. The ambulance was soon swaying under him. He closed his eyes again, feeling a dazed satisfaction that the dream of Alphamega had to be something more than just a dream. Somehow, though nobody was going to believe anything he tried to say about it, she had saved his life.

"Dr. Belcraft!" A bright new voice, prodding at him in the emergency room. "Dr. Belcraft! Can you speak?"

A new doctor, here perhaps to replace him on the hospital staff. He roused himself to answer clinical queries and ask groggy questions of his own.

"You're a lucky man, sir!" More booming good cheer than he was in the mood for. "The blast knocked you out, but we've found nothing that looks permanent. A few blisters and contusions, but no bones broken. No actual burns. We're admitting you for observation, but I don't think you inhaled any smoke. We'll have you out in a day or so."

"What happened?"

"A gas explosion, the firemen think. Gas trapped in your basement. If you hadn't got out of the house—"

That afternoon he still felt weak and shaky, but the nurses raised the head of his bed and let visitors in to see him. Miss Hearn, first, looking pale and strained with more emotion than he had expected. Trying not to sob, she told him not to worry about his office rent or his note past due at the bank or even her back pay.

"Just get well! Thank God that you're alive. Just put your trust in Him, and everything will be okay."

Reminded of General Clegg and the hard fist of God, he felt more thankful to Alphamega.

Police detectives came in to stand by the bed, asking questions. What had taken him out of town, with no notice at all? Why had he stayed so long? Why hadn't he called home? Had he exposed himself to the Enfield plague? What about his medical practice? Hadn't his unexplained absence put it in danger?

He tried to answer reasonably, but they seemed hard to satisfy.

About the explosion, had he smelled gas or noticed anything unusual when he entered the house? Had he used any gas appliance after he came in? Had he touched a switch that might have made a spark? Or struck a match, perhaps to light a cigarette?

"I didn't smell gas," he told him. "I hadn't turned anything on. I don't smoke. I didn't strike a match. I'd beem in bed for hours. Something woke me—I don't know what. I just had run out of the house before the blast knocked me out. I can't explain anything."

"There are circumstances that have to be cleared up." Both men moved closer, more intent. "What was it that got you out of the house? Before daybreak?"

"I can't explain." Which was very true. "I did have a crazy dream. Call it a nightmare. It left me trembling with panic. I ran outside before I was really awake."

"You heard nothing? No prowler?"

He shook his head.

"Thank you, Doctor." They frowned at each other and looked sharply back at him. "We'll want to talk to you again."

Another visitor came that evening. Billy Higgs, the lawyer-friend who had advised him on the office lease and tried to persuade Midge to let him have another chance and agreed to handle the divorce when she stood fast. He came in grinning.

"Hiya, Doc. I tried to smuggle in a beer, but the nurses took it away. They say you'll likely get out in the morning."

"I hope."

"Listen, Doc." Leaning over the bed, Billy forgot the grin and dropped his voice. "I came out to warn you. Better watch what you say to the cops or the insurance people or anybody else. Doc, I'm afraid you're going to need legal help."

"Huh?" He felt as if another blast had struck him. "Why?"

"Awkward-looking circumstances." Billy looked at the door. "Whatever happened, Doc, I'm afraid you're going to be in trouble."

"I've been in trouble," he muttered. "Trouble enough."

"I don't want to know about that. Not any more than you want to tell me. Or more than I may need in your defense. But listen, Doc. The firemen and the cops have turned up bad news for you."

"I wondered why they had so many questions."

Billy waited, listening to heels tapping down the corridor. The room seemed suddenly too hot, and he hated its faint antiseptic odors. When the heels were gone, Billy continued.

"Doc, here's your problem." A searching squint into his face. "The fire marshal found an open gas tap in your basement, and what was left of what he says was an ignition device. The cops believe the explosion was deliberately triggered."

"You mean—you mean somebody tried to kill me?"

"That could be our case." Billy shook his head. "But up to now, their only suspect is you."

"Me?" A breathtaken gasp. "Billy, I didn't—"

"I know you didn't, Doc. But we may have to prove it. It looks odd to the cops that you just happened to be out of the house when it just happened to blow up, at that time of night. You're going to need a pretty solid reason."

"I had a reason." He lay back against the pillows, feeling sick. "But it's one no cop would believe. Or even you—"

"Sorry, Doc." Billy stepped back with an apologetic grin. "A hell of a thing to be telling you here, but I thought I ought to warn you. Get some sleep. If you can. But think about it. I'll drop by in the morning."

Billy left. He thought about it half the night, till the nurse made him submit to a shot.

Asleep at last, he dreamed again of Alphamega.

24

The Badness

She hadn't cried when she knew the dear Vic must leave her, because that was before she had learned to grow eyes that could cry. She felt the hot tears now when that old sadness came again. Lying under the hot iron shell of the old *carretilla,* she went on remembering. Afraid to move, because the danger-feel still as thick around her now as it had been that night in the lab, she had nothing else to do.

She had been all alone in the EnGene lab when daylight came. The crimson mist still stained everything around her, and she shivered when she heard a security man coming through the corridors, hard heels clicking on the floor. He brought her no security. Even through the walls, she felt the redness like a cloud around him. She lay trembling till his heels clicked away.

The dear Vic came back at last, but even his tired-eyed smile failed to clear the danger haze. He slipped quietly through the door and stopped to lock it before he came in to take her in his hand.

"Baby, it's now." His voice was hushed and tight. "Now or never. We've got to say good-bye."

She wanted to beg him not to die, but she had no words.

"A bad time for both of us." He held her to his beard-stubbled face. "I've had hard choices. Now they're made. The staff will soon be coming in. I've got things ready for them. All that's left is to do my best for you."

She wrapped herself around his finger.

"Sorry, baby." He held her away to look at her, and she saw the shine of his eyes. "An ugly time for you. People will be dying. Maybe fighting one another as long as they can move. Wooden things will be crumbling into dust. I guess there'll be explosions. Likely fire. Bombs, I imagine, dropped out of the sky. The building probably wrecked. You'll have to scramble to keep yourself alive, but I think you have a sense for trouble. You've got—"

His voice was gone, and he held her back to his face. "I think—I hope you've got a chance."

He carried her outside, across a yard where big machines made strange dark shapes. Kneeling beside a row of low-blooming, rich-scented plants that grew inside a tall steel fence, he looked quickly behind him and leaned to put her down among them. She hung tighter to his finger.

"A bad time, baby." He raised her back to his lips, and she felt them tremble to his whisper. "But it just has to be. Hide yourself well. Stay alive—stay alive for me!"

She wanted to promise, but still she had no voice. He pushed her gently off his finger and left her there. The redness seemed fainter, and she wanted to believe no badness could come. Vic was surely strong enough to stop it.

The sun had risen. The air was warm and very still, sweet from the blooms. She saw small, quick things moving in the air above her, making sweet, bright sounds. She knew they must be the birds she had never seen. When more machines came into the yard, she crept farther among them into the plants and lay there hoping for goodness.

No bombs fell out of the sky, but very suddenly the badness came. Red danger hazed everything around her. Men ran out of the lab, yelling ugly words. Some of them fell to the ground. A few scrambled into machines that roared and crashed into walls. One machine struck the fence near where she was. It stopped moving, the man in it dead. She crawled under it for a safer hiding place.

The air quivered to a great hooting signal she had never heard. Police cars came screeching outside the fence. Men yelled with great metal voices. The bodies on the ground began to shine with a pale gray light. Garments crumbled and then the gray flesh and slowly the bones, falling into shining dust. The strange shine spread, dissolving even the plants where she was trying to hide.

It tingled when it touched her skin, but she knew it couldn't really hurt her because Vic had made her different from anything else alive. Knowing that, knowing she was not like anything, not even like the dear Vic, she felt terribly small, terribly alone. Nothing else anywhere was shaped like her, nothing was kin to her.

In her sad remembrance, the ground shook again. Hot yellow fire lifted the roof of the lab and pushed out walls and stung her skin. Torn metal and broken concrete came crashing down around her. The dead machine above her rocked when something struck it, and she crawled deeper under it, hiding from the heat.

More explosions began shaking everything. Fire snapped and crackled and roared in the ruin of the lab. Heavier machines rumbled around her. Men kept screaming. Guns thundered. Great jets of water hissed above her, but they didn't stop the fire. The wrecked machine over her began to burn above her. She crawled away from it, along the bottom of the fence. The machine boomed behind her, exploding into a great ball of hungry fire.

The heat grew very bad, until she learned to burrow under the dust. Squirming deep enough to escape it, she had to wait a long time. Night was near before the surface dust was cool enough to let her emerge.

The fire was gone. Broken walls were black from it. Dark ash and gray dust lay over wreckage all around her, and the sun was setting upon a dreadful stillness. She heard loud machines hammering the air far away, but no sound was near. No voice spoke. No birds sang. The lab was dead.

And Vic.

Vic was dead. Without him, crawling through the hot dust in that dead stillness, she felt weak and empty and helpless. If he were gone, nobody in all the world would ever love her. Nobody anywhere could ever know what she knew, or feel what she felt, or think what she thought. Nothing would ever be like her, even near enough to care whether she lived or died. There was nobody to listen, even if she had been able to speak.

All that night she lay alone in the dust, longing for Vic. When the sun rose again, she crept back into the lab, searching for anything left of him, hoping to find why he had to die and why he wanted her to stay alive. All she found was dismal ruin. Ashes. Dust. A sad tangle of burned iron and broken masonry. Nothing to make her want to live—till she heard a car-machine and felt the man who drove it.

Vic!

Alive! That was what she thought for one happy instant, till she knew it couldn't be. The dear Vic was sadly and forever dead. Yet the man in the car shone like Vic, bright with kindness, luminous with the same gift for love. She heard the car stop. Eagerly, she crawled to meet the sound.

The car door clunked. She heard his feet, and the scraps of torn metal clattering under them. She hurried toward him, and stopped when she saw how different he was. He was taller than Vic. His skin was darker and his hair was thicker. He wore no glasses. Yet still he felt like Vic, and suddenly she knew he must be Sax.

Saxon. The brother Vic had told her about, one long night when they had been alone together in the lab and he was trying to tell her what he was, because he wanted to help her understand what he hoped she would be. That was back before she even knew what a brother was. He must have sensed her trouble understanding, because he stopped to explain about the life that came from nature and the life like hers that had to be engineered.

That was hard for her to grasp, but she had understood enough to be saddened again, knowing she would never have a brother like Vic's human brother, Sax, to teach her and help her and defend her. Vic had helped her bear the sadness while he was with her in the lab, but now—

The dark shock of grief dazed her again, till she saw Sax coming on through the ruin. Closer, he felt more and more like Vic, and that good feeling lit a spark of hope in her. She moved on toward him. He had seen her. He stopped to speak. His voice felt as warm and kind as Vic's. He lifted her in his hand the way Vic had done. She felt the glow of love beginning in him, reflecting her own.

He carried her out of the burning dust and took her into his car. He sheltered her from the Dusek who stopped them at the bridge and shrank away from her with no spark of love at all. Sax gave her water and food and an echo to her love that made her want to keep on living. He kept her safe through another night, till day came again, dreadful with the redness of danger. When she knew she must leave him, he opened the door to let her escape.

Hiding, wandering alone with nowhere to go, she went into the water because she was thirsty. Floating in it, letting it carry her farther from the dust and the danger, she found Panchito. Love had been dead in him when she came upon him lying flat to drink from the little river.

Yet she felt no redness in the air around him, and she was not afraid. Lonely and hungry, she leaped to kiss his chin. When he saw her creeping out of the water, he had no fear of her. He took her in his hand, and a bright spark was born.

Panchito learned to love her, nearly as tenderly as Vic. He sheltered her and found food and taught her all he could, but now he, too, was gone. Once more, lying here under the sun-hot shell of the old *carretilla* with the redness dimming everything around her, she had been left all alone.

Yet she must not die. For the dear Vic's sake, she must stay alive. She must learn what he had shaped her to do. She must get it done. If Panchito had come to love her, there might be love from others. Others, too, might teach and help her. If she could only escape the hunters in the sky and stay alive to seek more good people, they might be open to her love.

Night was a long time coming, but at last the old iron cooled and the beat of the choppers seemed farther away. She came out in the dusk to fill her lungs with fresher air, but still the warning redness hazed everything. Southward, where the city had been, it seemed thicker. Low in the north, the darkening sky looked almost clear. That was the way she must go.

First she went back to empty house. The gringos had broken doors, but they hadn't harmed the kitchen. Missing Panchito, she found the food he had ready for trouble, parched *maíz* and frijoles *fritos* wrapped in cold tortillas. She ate all she could and stuffed what was left into a plastic bag.

Missing Panchito to guard her and cheer her, to teach her what he could and carry her when she needed to be carried, she left the house in the red-dyed dark, walking north. Her sense for danger helped. It made a dull crimson glow all across the south, and it ringed the high-sailing choppers with small red halos, yet it couldn't reveal smaller things waiting to hurt her. Though it let her see the hostility and hatred in living minds, it didn't show the sticks that tried to trip her or the rocks that bruised and cut her naked feet.

Many times she stumbled and fell. Most of the night

was gone, and she was scratched and battered and very tired before she came to the fence. It was a tall barbed-wire barrier, just beyond a new road cut through the empty pastures inside it. The wires glowed red because they were electric and meant to kill.

She crossed the road and found a hollow where she could crawl under the wires. Though she tried not to touch anything, the wires shone suddenly redder. She squirmed on through and ran on across the dark field beyond. Once it must have been a farm, but it was abandoned now, slashed with deep gullies where the soil was gone, scattered with rocks and clumps of brush and broken machines that tried to strip her.

A chopper was suddenly roaring low behind her, coming fast along the fence. Red mist wrapped it, and the redness thickened around her. A strange light that was no light, it didn't help her see which way to go. She fell into a gully. Dazed and aching, she struggled for her breath and fumbled for the precious bag of food. It was gone, lost in the clotting redness.

The chopper thundering near, she dragged herself out of the gully and stumbled on. It followed, as if the gringos aboard it could see her in the dark. Blinded by the redness, she tripped and fell again, and crawled on stinging hands and knees into a dark mass of brush. Groping, she felt a hollow in the rocky ground.

Perhaps—perhaps it could hide her.

She slithered into it, and suddenly fell. It had no bottom. She slid down past narrow rocky walls into chilling dampness and the suffocating dark.

25

Better than Human

Dreaming again, yet somehow aware that it was more than just a dream, Belcraft became one with Alphamega. In flight from the gringos, he shared her grief for Vic and cringed when she felt Panchito's pain. The red-haloed chopper roaring close behind, he crawled with her under the fence and tumbled with her into the arroyo. They hid together in the clump of brush, scrambled together into the little cave.

Together, they dropped into the pit. It was narrow and bottomless, cold and wet and black and dreadful, and the rough walls shrank around them as they fell. It snagged and scratched and bruised them, squeezing closer till it stopped them cruelly, held so tight they could barely breathe.

He woke in the hospital bed, chilled with the sweat of her terror, gasping for his own breath. He must have made some outcry, because a nurse hurried in to feel his pulse and ask what was wrong.

"Just dreaming," he told her. "Jittery, I guess, from that explosion."

But the thing had been too real for a dream. Meg had been her paradoxic self, her trouble desperate. Vic dead, Panchito wounded and probably under sedation in some Army hospital, he was the only friend she could reach. However she had reached him—he tried not to wonder about that.

She had to be helped.

As soon as he could get there. A whole day and more must have passed since she fell into what she called *el hoyo.* An abandoned well, perhaps, which should have been plugged or covered. Wedged there, hurt, barely able to breathe. How long could she live?

He had no notion. Vic had equipped her with resources no merely human being had ever possessed. Her survival in the dust was proof enough of that. Yet, clearly, she had come to the end of what she knew how to do for herself. When the nurse was gone, he looked at his watch. Four-eighteen. He dialed Billy Higgs. The phone rang a long time before he heard Billy's groggy-sounding voice.

"Sax? What the hell?"

"Billy, I hate like everything to wreck your sleep at this time of night." He tried to sound sane. "But something has come up. Terribly urgent. Can you get down here? PDQ!"

"Can't it wait till morning?"

"Please, Billy. I need help—bad! Nothing I can try to explain on the phone. Just get into your duds and come on down."

"Sax, old man, I had a late night—"

"Listen, Billy! If I ever needed you, it's now!"

"Okay," Billy muttered. "But you'd better make sense."

He washed his face and got into the clothing Miss Hearn had brought. He was sitting by the bed when the nurse let Billy follow her in. Unshaven and puffy-eyed, he looked as if his night had been far too late.

"What's up, Doc?" He managed a feeble grin for the nurse. "An OB emergency?"

Belcraft waited for the nurse to go.

"A pretty grim emergency," he said then. "Back near where Enfield was. I've got to get there as fast as I can. Billy, I want to borrow your car—"

He saw Billy's startled dismay.

"They say the fire totaled mine. I need the car and whatever cash you happen to have on you. You know I got out of the house in just my pajamas. Wallet gone. Credit cards. Everything."

"Driver's license?"

He had to nod.

"Really, old man—" Billy stopped to frown as if he had been a difficult witness on the stand. "I can't guess what's got into you, but you sure as hell ain't fit to drive again. Not without a license. Or unless you can do some pretty tall explaining."

"Sit down, Billy. Please!" He gestured at the other chair. "It's nothing you'll want to believe, but here's why I've got to get there. You see—You see—"

He had to search for some sane way to say it.

"I found a—found a little being there in the dust of Enfield that had survived after everything else was dead. Something—well, synthetic, though the word seems too cold for her. She's a creation of genetic engineering. There's evidence that the engineer was my brother."

Billy's eyes had narrowed critically.

"My kid brother, Victor."

"I never heard of him."

"Guess I never talked about him. We weren't close, not in recent years. But I did have a brother. We both studied medicine. Brought up to it. But Vic never practiced. Went into molecular biology. Following a crazy dream that he could create better kinds of life than nature did."

"Or God?"

"He never put it quite that way, but General Clegg does." Jarred off the track, he had to recover himself. "Vic was never satisfied with what we are. Dreamed of something that might repair all our defects, make us better than we are. One notion was a benign virus. An artificial organism that would repair defects, heal every illness. Maybe even reverse the decay of age. He was at EnGene for years. Too busy, I guess, to keep in touch with me."

Billy was frowning, gingerly shaking his hung-over head as if the shaking hurt it.

"Anyhow, there's this new being—" In the face of that stubborn doubt, he had to collect himself again. "No way to tell you what she is until you've known her, but she's different in a lot of ways from any natural being I know about. In some ways at least, certainly superior. Whatever hit Enfield didn't touch her. She called me for help just now, across a good many hundred miles—don't ask me how."

Looking blank, Billy grunted.

"Call her Meg. Vic named her Alphamega. Not human at all, but maybe—maybe better. You have to feel what she is. Good—the first thing you feel is a sort of warm, total goodness. Intelligent. Lovable—really lovable. And in dreadful trouble now."

"Huh?" Billy squinted blearily. "What sort of trouble."

"You see, the military connects her with whatever wiped out Enfield." He looked into Billy's unbelieving face and slowed his voice, trying hard to make some kind of sense. "General Clegg wants to get his hands on her because he thinks she could be the key to a biological super-weapon. She does have powers—gifts I don't understand. But they aren't enough to save her now."

"What's all this got to do with you?"

"I'm a suspect, because I brought her out of the ruins and then let her go. Not that I'm sorry I did it, because they'll kill her in the lab if they ever catch her. Cut her up and analyze the tissues, trying to find out what she is.

"She has been hiding somewhere inside the military perimeter. Night before last she got out. Crawled under the fence. Running from a chopper, she dived into a hole that turned out to be an abandoned water well."

"Sax, you haven't been drinking?"

"Not here."

"If you expect anybody—" Billy shook his head, scowling like a judge on the bench. "If all this happened after you left, how do you keep up with—whatever you say she is?"

He had to shake his head.

"I wish I could explain. I guess I could say telepathy, but I never took much stock in Joseph Rhine and all the claims for ESP. Now I just don't know. It is some sort of mental contact. Seems to happen only when I'm asleep. But, Billy—" He wanted to grab Billy Higgs, shake out the disbelief. "It's real. She used it last night to save my life."

"If all this happened while you were asleep—"

"Listen, Billy! I wouldn't be here if that hadn't happened. Meg knew—I can't imagine how, but she knew the house was going to burn. She warned me—in what did seem like a dream—to get out fast. I woke up, and knew it was more than a dream. I got out, barely in time. One more reason I've got to help her now."

"Why you?" Billy stabbed a knobby finger at him. "If you say she has fallen in a well, why can't you get somebody on the spot to pull her out? Be reasonable, Sax. Get on the phone. Call the local sheriff. The state police. The fire department. Whoever—"

"Billy!" He tried to smooth his desperation. "I can't do that. Not with Clegg hunting her. He has already called in the FBI and the local cops and everybody else. She'd rather die in the well than let him butcher her. You are the only person I feel like trusting."

"Don't trust me too far." Billy stiffened. "I'm your attorney. No co-conspirator. I'm sorry, Sax, but if I thought all this was something more than the shock of whatever happened to you in Enfield and the effects of that blast and the drugs they've had you under—" He squinted like an unconvinced judge. "If you don't realize what you're asking, any aid to you in this time of emergency could be construed as conspiracy to commit high treason."

"All I want is help to get back there. The loan of your car. Cash for gas and whatever else I'll need. Rope, I guess. Maybe digging tools. Is that—" His voice tried to tremble. "Is that too much?"

"Take a minute, Doc." Billy frowned judicially. "Let's think this through. I know your professional situation—Miss Hearn came to me while you were out of pocket. Your—let's call it your odd behavior is going to make people wonder if you weren't exposed to whatever hit Enfield. Unless you shape up and stick to business, your medical practice is dead."

"I'll get back when I can. But Meg's dying in that pit right now. I've got to move—"

"Doc! Look at the facts!" Billy stabbed that skinny forefinger at his nose. "Your practice is already gone to hell. Cash flow down to nothing. Bank balance gone and bills still rolling in. The insurance people and the law asking too many questions about that fire. Your only chance is to stay right here. Forget this Alphamega and your wonder-working brother and whatever you say is going on back there in Enfield. Open up the office and explain what you can to the cops—but I wouldn't tell anybody what you've just been telling me."

"Billy, I can't—"

"One thing more." Billy raised his hand. "Personal, not professional. I called Midge last night to tell her you were home; she knew you were missing, and she's been anxious. I heard her sobbing when she tried to thank me for the call. She was happy you're back, upset when I had to tell her you were hospitalized. Distressed with what I felt forced to say about the story you've been telling to cover your absence.

"She wants to talk to you, Sax. She says there's never been anybody else she really cared about. She misses you and the house and Fort Madison. I think she'd agree to try again. If you'll just settle down to business like that wise old M.D. you say your father was—"

"Call her for me. Tell her I'm terribly sorry. But the fact is, Billy—" He shook his head. "It's something I guess I can't really explain. You won't understand. I know Midge wouldn't. Nobody would without knowing Meg. But the fact is I'm more concerned for her than I'll ever be for Midge. I guess you think I'm crazy, but I've got to pull her out of that well."

"Really, Sax!" Billy looked hurt. "I can't let you throw away all you've got and all you can ever hope to have, just for this wild dream. It does seem crazy, if you'll let me say so."

"Crazy or not, I can't let her die."

"I won't play shrink." Billy shrugged. "I think you ought to talk to Mathis or Meissen. I guess you're in no mood for that, but there are facts you've got to face. You're a patient here, still under treatment for shock or whatever. You can't leave till you're discharged.

"And something else." Billy stopped to squint at him, bleary features suddenly tight. "If you really think there's somebody out to kill you, you're in big trouble, Sax. Bigger than you seem to realize."

"I do realize." He nodded unhappily. "But I'm desperate to get Meg out of the pit." Voice shaking, he caught at Billy's arm. "You're my lawyer. You can cover for me. Let me have your car and whatever cash—"

"Suppose I do?" Billy's frown bit deeper. "Look at what can happen. I don't know who blew up your house. If you really didn't do it, some very clever person is out to get you. No matter who did it, you're under suspicion of arson. They haven't got evidence to nail you, but skipping out now would look like an open confession.

"Driving with no license, you could be picked up for any cause or none. If you're caught lending aid to this Alphamega—assuming your little synthetic friend is real—your friend Clegg will hang you up by your thumbs and use your hide for dart practice."

Owlishly, he scowled.

"Want to risk all that?"

"I do."

"If you really do—" Billy got to his feet. "It's your own funeral. Personally, I don't think this genetic wonder exists anywhere outside your sick imagination. That will be my own defense, if I'm accused of anything. But we've been good friends, and I don't judge my friends."

"Thank—" His voice caught. "I hope you're never sorry!"

"Thank my parents, Sax, if you thank anybody. They swear you've saved both their lives. They can't wait to see you back at the office." Billy was digging into his pockets. "The front doors are locked at this time of night. I left the car in back, parked to the right of the emergency entrance. The tan-colored Buick I bought last year—a sweet little car, and I hope to get it back."

"I can't promise anything."

"I see why." Billy gave him the keys, and dug again. "Here's one stroke of luck for you. I played poker last night. Pulled in nearly three hundred. Just leave me a five for taxi fare back to the house. Here you are." Billy thrust the roll of bills at him. "Wish I could to believe your dream creature is all you say she is."

Tears in his eyes, he stuffed the money into his pockets and reached to grip Billy's hand.

"Better check the gas. And luck to you, Sax!" Billy opened the door. "I'll walk down the hall and try to occupy the nurses. Tell 'em how keen you are to get back to your practice and ask 'em when they think this new doc will let you go. You walk out back; you know the way."

26

Homo Ultimus

He knew the way, and nobody stopped him. Outside, the early summer dawn was already breaking. He found nobody waiting to trap him in the parking lot. Driving out, and on through empty streets to the highway, he watched the rearview mirror. Nobody followed. Nobody he could see. Maybe he was lucky.

The Buick was a sweet little car, but the gas gauge stood on empty. He pulled off the road at the first truck stop to fill the tank and drink two cups of coffee. Driving on, afraid of cops and afraid for Meg, he set the cruise control at a safe-seeming fifty-nine and kept an eye on the little mirror. Cars seemed to follow, but never for long. A few were farm vehicles that soon left the road. Most passed and disappeared ahead. Perhaps his luck would hold.

The day was fine, but it dragged on forever. He wasn't so fit as he had felt. Reaction, he thought, from the blast and whatever medications that eager young doc had ordered for him. His hip ached from a bruise he hadn't felt before, and he got groggy at the wheel. At midmorning, he stopped at a hardware store in a little town beyond the Missouri to buy a flashlight and a hundred feet of nylon rope and a shovel.

He caught nobody watching him, yet his unease

clung. If somebody had blown up the house, intending him to die, they must know the effort had failed. If Watchdog had set him free, hoping he would lead them to where Meg was hiding, they could easily be tracing him by some sophisticated means.

Yet, whatever the risks might be for him, it was Meg that mattered. The gas tank full again, a container of coffee and a hamburger to go lying forgotten on the seat beside him, he drove on. On. On. He caught the car swerving toward the other lane. Shaking, he stopped at the next service station to top off the tank and use the rest room and drink the cold coffee.

It was late afternoon when he came to sign that read ENFIELD 20. The perimeter gate, not yet in view, would be another four or five miles ahead. He pulled off the highway on a narrow side road and bumped west through rocky pastures that must have been forest till the trees were cut, and prosperous farmland till the topsoil was gone. The few homes he passed looked deserted, fallen into slow decay and abandoned now since the panic.

Nobody followed. Nobody he saw.

At the bottom of a shallow valley, he crossed a flimsy-looking bridge and pulled off the road into the cover of a clump of trees beside the creek. He left the car there. Walking on, carrying the flashlight and shovel, the rope coiled over his shoulder, he heard a chopper's heavy throb and soon found it low ahead, cruising along the perimeter.

Maybe alerted to watch for him? Not that it mattered. Whatever the danger, he couldn't turn back. He dropped flat until its beat had faded, and then hiked on. Except for that hamburger, gone soggily clammy before he remembered it, he hadn't eaten anything. Suddenly, now, he felt weak with hunger and fatigue. Though the spot where Meg crossed the fence must be somewhere ahead, he found no landmarks he recalled from the dream. The fence must be farther than he had thought.

Another chopper came out of the east. Or perhaps

the same one, circling the perimeter. He dropped again into a thicket until it was far away. The release of tension nearly overwhelmed him. His whole body aching, he needed all his will to drag himself back to his feet and stumble on. The sun was low before he came in view of the fence, barb-spiked wire strung on tall steel posts, glass insulators gleaming. He stopped on the crest of a barren hill to look for anything he could recall from the dream, but the land still looked strange. Perhaps—perhaps she had crossed farther ahead.

He tramped on west, staying away from the marching fence, following the bottom of a brush-tangled valley. The day was still hot. He needed a cold beer. A beer and a rare steak and a hot shower and a good night's rest. A sticky bitterness filled his mouth. His skin felt parched as if from fever. The bare hills looked strange around him.

The chopper came back. He fell to the ground, listening to the fading thud of its blades. The rest felt too good. He lay there too long, and the sun was down before he could spur himself back to his feet. In the twilight, he failed to see a rain-cut gully until he was sliding into it.

But he recognized its shape!

The same arroyo into which he had fallen with Meg in the dream. He clambered out and stopped to look around him. No chopper near enough to hear or see. No sound or motion anywhere. Perhaps—perhaps his luck still held.

The stony slope ahead was the same one he recalled. And there—there was the mass of brush where she had tried to hide. It had grown up around a broken concrete slab and a few twisted sheets of rusting steel. Relics of a stock tank, he thought, that once held water from the well.

He found the well. A narrow pit, half hidden under the brush. Dropping on his face to peer into it, he shrank back from a cold reek of stagnant mustiness. The flashlight picked up its wall, not quite straight but falling forever, shrinking down toward a small dark point. Nothing at the bottom that he could see.

"Meg! Meg! Can you hear me?"

A strange hollow echo came back from his hoarse yell. When that faded, there was nothing else. Uncoiling the rope, he fed it into the pit. Coil after coil, it went down, down, down. Now and then he stopped to shine the light after it. It dwindled into darkness. Listening for a cry, for breathing, for any hint of life, he heard nothing at all.

A hundred feet of thin nylon, and still no sign. When it was all paid out, he began to pull it up again. It came too easily, lifting nothing. Yet he knew this had to be the spot. He knew Meg was down there. Dead?

The rope tightened!

Trembling, he pulled on it. Gently at first, slowly harder. Too hard, at last. Something held the rope, a force too much for her weight, too much for her strength. Unless, perhaps, she was really more than human. Frightened, trembling, he pulled with all his own strength.

The rope went slack. Staggering backward, he almost fell. If she had somehow caught the rope or tied it to herself, he had lost her.

But no!

He felt weight on the line. Carefully, fearfully, chilled with his own sweat in the thicking dust, he hauled and hauled and hauled, still wondering at the strength he sensed, wondering how she could be alive, wondering if Vic had really launched a new human evolution. Could she be the first specimen of a wholly new species? *Homo ultimus?*

Something came out of the well.

Something he failed to recognize till he blinked in the dimness and knew it had to be Meg. Nothing like the fat pink worm he had known. She had the look of a human child, aged three or four, but far too small for that age, her head too large. She had grown long hair, very fine, cotton-white except where mud had clotted it. Her eyes were closed. She wore a thin cotton dress, torn and soiled, too big for her. Her feet were bare, bruised and lacerated.

Her arms were stretched above her head, her hands knotted into tiny fists on the rope, her teeth clenched on it. Her skin looked deathly white, scratched deep by the walls of the well, yet with no blood showing. She felt very light when he lifted her, her body stiff and cold as if already in the rigor of death. He heard no breath, felt no pulse.

Yet she had been alive to clutch the rope—

The chopper was sudden thunder overhead. Its wind was a hot engine-reek. A blinding light glared down on him, and a bullhorn was bellowing: "Don't move, Belcraft! Stand where you are!"

27

Tradecraft

Old Martha Roman's funeral drew even fewer mourners than her husband's. A handful of loyal servants and aging family friends. The tearless daughter and her lawyers. Attorneys for the dismantled corporation and the new foundation. An officious mortician who was probably reporting to the CIA.

For Anya and Shuvalov, the occasion offered cover for a twice-delayed contact. They stood in the cemetery with the foundation attorneys, well apart from the glaring daughter. When the service was over, Anya drove Shuvalov back to the airport.

Sitting under the Florida sun, the car was stifling. The air conditioner took a long time to cool it, and Shuvalov's strong cologne failed to mask the reek of his sweat. He looked jittery and haggard, dark stubble showing on his heavy jowls. Fingers twitching nervously, he lit a rank-odored Russian cigarette and sat staring at her in a wary silence.

"We're safe," she assured him. "Unless the CIA is keener than I think. They could have got to the Avis car I had reserved in Miami, but I dropped it off at Ft. Lauderdale and picked this one up at the Hertz counter there, with no reservation. It can't have been bugged."

"Safe?" A harsh grunt. "Comrade, I have news for you." He waited, but she wouldn't ask what it was. "The Center is recalling us."

Startled, she glanced at him and shrank from the level malevolence in his dark-circled eyes.

"I am flying to Moscow tomorrow," he told her. "You will receive orders to follow as soon as that can be arranged. I doubt that you'll ever be sent back."

"Your own withdrawal is probably advisable." She tried not to show her own old antagonism. "Since it seems you are under such heavy surveillance."

"Advisable?" A savage-toned explosion. "It's the end of my career!"

"Not necessarily—"

"You're a bungling failure, comrade." He cut her off, speaking with a bitter force. "You lack the tradecraft we expected in you. The hard fact is, you have led us into a whole string of failures. You induced us to trust that snake Scorpio. You let him murder our best informer at EnGene, and then escape with documents you had promised us. You have failed to eliminate Belcraft's brother, or Belcraft's genetic monster. In sum, you have become a stupid tool of the *Americanski.*"

Glancing again, she caught a glint of satisfaction in his quick, feral eyes.

"On my advice," he finished, "the Center is recalling you for a final accounting. If the story of your blundering has made a stupid fool of me, if I'm going to the wall for it, I do not intend to go alone."

She took time to pass a delivery truck and regain control before she could trust herself to speak. "Boris, part of what you say may seem true. Our craft depends on luck as well as on skill. Luck is often bad, a fact I think the Center ought to understand."

"Don't depend on it. We do expect occasional miscalculations. But, comrade, your own bad luck, if you want to call it that, has been remarkably consistent."

"I'll let you speak for your own career." She managed to smile into his cold hostility. "I have news, however, for the Center. News that I have not failed."

"Da?" An ironic snort. "Make your boasts to Bogdanov."

"When I do, he'll send me here again to finish up my work."

"Not likely. A klutz who never learned the trade. Why should you be trusted again?"

"Because I have made progress. I recently established a new contact. A man who was employed at EnGene before the disaster. He knew Scorpio and Carboni—he was in fact perhaps the best friend Carboni had. It was a warning from Carboni that enabled him to escape the disaster. He is close to General Clegg, in a position which gives him freedom of movement inside the military perimeter and excellent access to confidential information."

"Who is this unexpected ally?"

"Comrade, that is extremely sensitive information." She paused to enjoy his baffled mixture of doubt and wrath. "I see no reason to reveal it now. Or to you at any time, not if you are to be replaced as my superior."

"Not yet replaced." She felt his cold eyes probing as if to disrobe her. "I can still warn my friends at the Center of your skill with all these cunning fabrications that have allowed you to wallow in the luxuries of a Romanoff czarina."

She drove on, not looking at him.

"I'll be seeing Bogdanov before you return." His tone turned grittily sardonic. "Have you other such incredible facts to report?"

"I believe Scorpio should receive attention." To steady her voice, she drew a deep breath. "It's true he should never have been trusted. I never liked him, but he was sent to me as a faithful and efficient agent. He is now at large, I don't know where.

"He killed Carboni. It is possible that he escaped with Carboni's photocopies of Belcraft's research notes. I believe he also has another document the Center will be eager to recover. That's the letter Belcraft wrote his brother in Fort Madison just before the disaster. We have traced Scorpio there. I think he got into the brother's office to take the letter—and then booby-trapped the brother's house.

"A stupid beast! He lacks brains to understand whatever the letter and the photocopies may reveal, but our efforts to obtain them must have let him know their value. If he should sell them to somebody who knows genetic engineering, the result might be a new Enfield disaster, spreading—I'm afraid to think how far. I imagine the Center will want Scorpio hunted down."

"Da?" He mocked her. "Comrade, do you expect Bogdanov to swallow such fantastic fiction—and choose you to be the exterminator?"

"Boris, I'd rather leave killing to you." She contrived to smile. "As for myself, I expect more appealing missions."

Watching for road signs, she made him wait.

"You see," she resumed at last, "my informer on Clegg's staff has been passing on new information that I think will be of great interest to the Center."

"I know you, Ostrov!"

She saw that she was getting to him now.

"Still the scheming whore you always were." His dark, fat face had turned even darker, and his high voice shook. "You've no command of tradecraft. You have built a career on cunning invention, the way your gangster father did. You lied to make yourself the mistress of that senile capitalist and get your red-painted talons into his fortune."

She shrugged at his anger.

"In any case, comrade—" He turned the word to mockery. "Your cunning schemes have overtaken you. Here at last, with all your false promises of secret files and private letters and genetic wonder weapons, you have led me and the whole Center into a trap. In Moscow, I shall warn the Center not to swallow this strange tale of some mysterious new informer whom only you can contact. A tale I'll make sure they don't believe."

"Comrade, I'm sure you'll try." She returned his derision. "You're aware, however, that the Center has its own records of my training and the use I have made of it. When your friend Bogdanov hears what this man has told me—"

"He'll send you off for psychiatric care."

"You haven't heard what I've learned. Here's the gist of it."

She let him wait while she bent to turn up the air conditioner fan, trying to get his odor out of the car.

"You may report it to Bogdanov in any way you like." She grinned into his glowering. "The Americans have recaptured this genetic creation. My contact describes it as female. A most astonishing creature!"

She turned again to relish his reaction.

"Described as a fat pink worm when first seen, it has grown and changed in a way that is hard to believe—"

"I'll see to it that Bogdanov does not believe."

Carefully, she ignored his raspy mutter.

"This brother captured the creature but later released it for some reason he seems unable to explain. Later, it was sheltered and cared for by a criminal hiding in the abandoned area around the dead city. The Americans spotted them from the air. The convict was wounded and recaptured. The creature was picked up outside the military perimeter, along with the brother."

"Comrade, your dramatic imagination fascinates me. I recall that you were an actress on the Moscow stage before your gangster father was exposed."

"Thank you, comrade." She gave him her brightest smile. "There is even more to the story. Facts that won't get stupid sneers from Bogdanov. You see, the Americans released the brother, hoping he would lead them to the creature. He was allowed to return to his home in Iowa, where he no doubt expected to find that letter."

"Which we should have recovered."

"True." She made a wry face. "I did have his office searched. The letter had already been removed. Scorpio, evidently, had been there first, to take the letter and set his booby-trap—a device that demolished Saxon Belcraft's home.

"Yet—I don't know why—he persists. He appears to care more for the creature than for his own career. It seems that they are able to communicate by some means not yet discovered. In flight from the Americans, the creature fell into a disused water well. She might have died there, but she was somehow able to call Belcraft back from the hospital to pull her out."

"*Da?* An actress inventing fairy tales—"

"You may believe what you like. The facts will speak for me. Center can soon confirm that American intelligence was able to keep up with Belcraft's travels. They reached the scene at the moment of the rescue. He and the creature have been recaptured.

"She is now being held in a special cell in a guarded laboratory inside the military perimeter. In the time since she was first described, she has grown and changed remarkably, taking on the appearance of a human child a few years old. She seems highly intelligent. She has learned Spanish from her criminal protector—reported to be a Mexican alien.

"The Americans are trying to discover precisely what she is and what she knows. Her mental powers seem to make her dangerous. In spite of that hazard, however, they regard her as a valuable prize. They don't intend to let her escape again.

"They are hoping, of course, to learn the technology used for her creation. The same technology, they believe, that set off the Enfield contagion. The American general, Clegg, hopes to turn it into a super-weapon.

"A critical situation. Yet we still have time for action.

The creature knows very little English. She has no technical vocabulary in any language. So far, she has refused to speak at all, except to inquire about Belcraft and her convict friend—his name is Torres.

"She begs to see them. Up to this point, however, she has been isolated in that laboratory cell, under observation through one-way glass. I understand that she looks as harmless as any little child, but until they know what she can do, they hold her friends as hostages.

"I'm afraid for her, Boris." Anya's resentments were half forgotten. "This Clegg is an evil-tempered sadist who abuses his family and bulldozes his men. The mind of a Hitler! Perhaps the same sort of mad genius. He has built a powerful clandestine organization to support his crazy quest for total control of America, perhaps of the world.

"I'm afraid for her, but more afraid of what Clegg's investigators may learn. If he gets that weapon—"

Shivering a little, she shut off the air conditioner fan.

"That will be the substance of my report to the Center." She turned to glance cheerily at Shuvalov. "I think Bogdanov and his own superiors will send me back here, with instructions to continue contacts with this new source and take whatever action seems necessary to stop Clegg from getting any total weapon. If they refuse to believe me, I doubt that the failure will help the future of their careers—or your own."

She had got her malice back.

"Comrade, what do you think?"

28

The Shadow Men

She had been too long in the cold wet dark of the *hoyo,* too long with no food and no air. The pit's jagged walls bit so hard she couldn't breathe, and her life light had dimmed. The good Sax had been too far away when she found him, so far she was afraid he could never come to help. Even when she felt the rope in her face, she had no strength to reach for it—not till she felt the strong white light of his love at the top of the *hoyo.*

That brought back a spark of her life. The hard rock jaws cut skin off her arms, but she moved enough to lock her hands and her teeth on the rope and cling tight when she felt Sax pull, but cruel rock held her fast. The rope hurt her teeth and the rope began to slip through her hands, but the white shine of Sax gave her new life.

She hung on. He hauled her up, scraping past the rough wet walls. He would warm her and find food for her and carry her far away from *los gringos malos* that had hurt *el pobre Panchito.* She felt very glad, till suddenly the red fog clotted above her in the *hoyo,* so thick it dimmed the bright love of Sax.

Los gringos again, coming in their ugly *helicoptero.* Sax had not seen them. He kept hauling and hauling on the rope. She wanted to tell him to drop the rope and run, but she had no strength or breath to call a warning, no way to reach his mind. She kept her grip locked, till he had dragged her out into the redness and the roar of the chopper.

She felt his fear that she was dead, but still she had no breath. The feel of danger came down like red rain upon her. She heard the great bray of the gringo machine, commanding him not to move, and felt the sickness in him when he knew they were going to take her.

The chopper came down to the ground and the yelling gringos ran around them. She couldn't feel their minds, couldn't see inside them, because they had no love that she could touch. They were red clouds of evil, red shadow men. All she could see was what they did.

They struck Sax with a gun when he wouldn't drop her on the ground. She felt the spinning dimness in his head. They put cruel irons on his wrists, and cursed him with ugly gringo words and dragged him into the chopper. It roared into the air, and she lost him in the redness when they carried him away.

They had no irons small enough for her, but they cut pieces of the rope to tie her ankles and her arms. They threw her on the ground and pointed guns at her head and let her gasp for air in the foul hot wind of the machine while they waited for another machine. They wanted to keep her far from Sax.

When the chopper came, they threw her on its rough floor and carried her back across the fence, to a place near the terrible *polvo,* the dust that had killed Vic and the whole city called Enfield. There they took away the dress Panchito had found for her—torn to rags now. They laid her on a hard table in a tiny, white-walled room. They found irons to fit and locked them on her ankles and her wrists to keep her there, lying naked under a hot glare of light.

A dull-red danger-cloud hung in one high corner of the room. It was behind her head, where perhaps they hoped she wouldn't see it. It was thick and cold and evil. When she searched inside the cloud, she found a gun barrel jutting through the wall. Beyond it, she discovered another tiny room, clogged with thicker fog. Two men stood behind the ugly killing machine, watching her through mirrors in the wall.

In spite of all the red-feeling badness, she felt sorry for some of the men around her in the room, because they were afraid. She felt them shiver when they had to touch her, heard the quivering in their voices, felt the chill of fear deep inside their shadow-shapes. Afraid of her, they thought she might bring them the deadly *polvo* to kindle its killing fire again and turn them all to crumbling dust.

She wanted them to know she would never hurt them. All she knew about the dust was the terror she had seen and heard and shared. Killing the dear Vic, the dust had hurt her terribly. She knew no way to start it or stop it. Yet she didn't speak, even now when she could breathe, because she was afraid for them to know she could talk. They would want her to tell them how Vic had made her in the lab and what he wanted her to be.

They would kill her and Sax and *el pobre* Panchito when they had learned what they wanted to know. She kept silent, lying still in the irons, but nothing could keep the red haze of danger out of the room, or shut out the red shadow men. They had rough hands and ugly voices and no faces, and they came to do ugly things.

They weighed her and measured her. They pushed cold instruments into her and stuck cold electrodes to her body. They stabbed her with sharp needles to take her blood. They took pictures with flashing light and stinging rays that burned through her body. They shouted hateful questions at her. Cruelly, they tricked her. There was a woman who came to clean the floor. One night she stopped to whisper: *"Ah, niñita! Una palabra de su amigo, Pancho Torres. Él tiene enfermedad. Quiero saber lo que pasa para usted."*

Panchito ill, begging for news of her.

"El pobre!" She felt the badness in the room, but

Panchito lay somewhere in dreadful pain and the woman was not a gringo. *"Dele todo mi cariño.* Give him my love."

"Sí! Sí! Pronto!"

The woman hurried out, and the red shadow men burst in. Shouting curses in their ugly gringo language and curses in their awkward Spanish, they brought machines to catch her words and tried to make her speak again. One of them slapped her.

"Okay, baby!" He slapped her again. "You habla hey? Habla plenty spic to your sick spic friend? Now you're gonna habla to us. Before I'm through, you'll be begging us to let you habla more."

Trembling, she shrank from his hands.

"If you want me to talk—" She had to search for his gringo words. "Bring my friends to me. *El Señor* Torres and *El Doctor* Belcraft. Let me see them well and free where you can't hurt them. Then *hablémos.* Then we speak."

"Fat chance, baby!" His hands began to hurt. "Your friend *Señor* Torres, he ain't in no shape to go anywhere at all. Except maybe to the morgue, where his dirty carcass ought to be. Your pal Belcraft won't be no better off, not unless you habla mucho." He hurt her more. "Savvy that?"

He kept on hurting her, till another gringo voice called him out of the little room. She was alone for a time, enduring her pain. Then another, smaller shadow man came where he could see her through the door. He stayed back from her because he was afraid.

"You there! Hear this!" He spoke from the doorway, his voice a brittle rasp and his quick gringo words hard for her to understand. "Along with your fellow conspirators, Belcraft and Torres, you are now in the custody of Task Force Watchdog, which is a special agency of the United States of America. Our actions are fully supported by armed forces and the President, and you have no right of appeal. Got that?"

She lay still.

"I am Peter Kalenka, recently commissioned a major in the United States Army, now commanding the special science force investigating the Enfield plague. You are now the focus of our inquiry. We want certain information from you. I expect cooperation. We do not intend to cause you needless suffering, but I want you to understand your own situation.

"Here in our custody, you have no rights. We have obtained a summary opinion from the Supreme Court that you are not a human being. Rather, in the judgment of the court, you are a laboratory specimen to be used as we see fit. I am warning you not to expect aid or legal intervention, from any source whatever.

"Understand?"

The long gringo words seemed cold and cruel as his sharp voice was. They carried nothing she wanted to understand. She withdrew into herself.

"We know you were named Alphamega. We know you are a nonhuman genetic artifact, engineered in the EnGene Labs by Dr. Victor Belcraft. We have abundant reason to believe that his insane experiments resulted in the plague that killed your criminal creators, along with many thousand innocent human beings.

"What we require from you is everything you know about the men and the processes that created you, everything you know about the history and the purposes of the EnGene labs, everything you know about the incidents that resulted in the plague. In particular, we must ask what you are.

"Do you hear that?"

She lay quiet, and his voice rose higher.

"We require your own complete definition of yourself. You will assist our team of experts in a complete scientific analysis of your biological and psychological nature. You will have to answer all our questions about the purposes and the processes of your creation. You will describe your powers of perception and action, which appear to be extraordinary.

"Our study of the catastrophe has a top priority. We require everything you know about the origin and the biological nature of the lethal agency—if the thing is biological. Was it designed for warfare? Was its release a tragic accident? A deliberate act? By whom? This Belcraft? Or who else? With what motivation?"

He stepped farther back.

"Or are you yourself the killer?" She felt his fear surge higher. "Murdering your own creators? Are you in fact at war with mankind? Do you threaten that you will start a new contagion to escape our inquiries?

"Speak to me!"

"Puedo hablar." Her voice came thin and small. *"Pero yo no sé—"* She felt his puzzlement and stopped to grope for the gringo words. "I don't know all you want, but I will tell you what I can. But not till I know my friends are safe. *El Señor* Torres *y el Doctor* Belcraft. They must be free."

"Impossible!" Perhaps he saw her flinch. His tone grew calmer. "I'll be honest, because we will require total honesty from you. Regardless of any legal rights they may claim, or any appeals for clemency, Belcraft and Torres can never be liberated. That's because of what they may know. Understand?"

"No entiendo."

"You had better understand. Our mission is to see that the Enfield disaster doesn't happen again. Its origin and nature are still unknown. We expect information from you. We also require Belcraft and Torres to reveal whatever facts they may have learned from you. We can never tolerate the risk that their liberation might lead to some recurrence of the plague. However—"

His red shadow came a little closer.

"Whatever you may be, we are not inhuman." He tried to soften his voice. "We can make concessions. You will want food and water and rest. So will your friends. Torres will continue to need medical attention —his condition is reported critical, from an infection in his shattered knee. If you will help us, honestly and fully, we'll do all we can for them and for you.

"Fair enough?"

"Not fair—" The whisper took all her nerve. "Not fair!"

"If you won't talk—" His voice came low and slow. I'm sorry for you. Sorry for them. You must cooperate."

"*Nunca!* Never! Not till they are free!"

"Means exist." He drew back to look at the shadow men waiting behind him. "Means to make you tell us all you know. Ugly means! I don't like them or those who use them, but we are driven by imperative necessity. You will talk. When you are ready, just call for me. Ask for Peter. Dr. Peter Kalenka. Don't forget."

Then he was gone.

"Okay, baby!" The shadow man who had hurt her was back in the room, a huge red cloud-man with those terrible hands and a face she couldn't bear to see. "You and I, baby—we've got a game to play." His thick gringo laugh rolled like dull thunder in the red-blazing cloud. "When you want to admit I've won the game, you can yell for Dr. Peter. That is, if you're still able to yell for anybody."

When she couldn't bear what he had begun to do, she left herself and reached away for Sax. She found him in a room with no windows, and iron bars to make the door. Two guards with guns stood outside the door. Breathing very slowly, *el pobre* Sax lay flat on a narrow bed with irons on his wrists to hold him there. Reaching, she couldn't touch his mind. A tight bandage was wrapped around his head, and all she could feel was his pain.

She left him and reached out again. She found Panchito in another strange bed-machine. He wore no irons, but two shadow men with long guns watched from the end of the room. His hurt leg was wrapped in white and lifted high. Bottles and plastic bags hung above him. Tubes ran down to needles in his arms, and a nurse stood watching green symbols winking on strange instruments above his head.

He lay breathing hard through tubes that ran into his nose. She felt the dead ache in his leg. Reaching deeper, she touched his sleeping mind. He was dreaming. Dreaming of her. He didn't know about the *hoyo* or Sax or the shadow men. He thought she had been hiding in the thickets near his home. In the dream his wounded leg had healed. When the pain still came, he thought *un avispo* had stung it.

He thought she was hiding in the brush, with the gringos hunting her. He found her and carried her in his arms to an *avión.* The gringos came yelling to hurt them, but the strange flying machine lifted them safely away and far across vaster lands than she had ever imagined, over wide green fields and places of dry brown flatness and long dry brown mountain ridges, to the dear little town that once had been Panchito's home.

The gringos were left far behind, and his fat little mother came running out of the little mud house to meet him, still patting out a tortilla between her quick brown hands. Estrella and Roberto ran after her, fat little José toddling behind, all of them wide-eyed and screaming with joy. He held her in arms and told them she had come to be their new sister, *nuestra hermanita* Meg, and then they were all happy together.

New pain broke Panchito's dream, and she found two doctors in white jackets in the room. No red badness wrapped them because they had come to help, not to harm. Yet one was doing things that hurt Panchito's wounded leg. She tried to feel the meaning of his hard gringo words.

"—desperate to save him." He spoke to the younger doctor. "Afraid they started too late. Shattered patella. Staph infection in the lesion, neglected far too long. Now we've got a bad reaction to one of the antibiotics, running into anaphylactic shock. Prognosis not good."

She tried to reach Panchito again, but all she found was the dead ache in his hurt leg. When she went back to her own poor body, lying where she had left it, the cruel shadow man had gone away. Her hurt body needed her, and she stayed, trying to heal the terrible harm his bad hands had done.

A long time later, the Dr. Kalenka came back to feel her body and study it with his cold bright instruments. A nurse took blood. A young man came pushing a machine on wheels. It had wires ending in cold, sticky patches that he fastened to her body and her arms and her ankles. They all stood frowning at dim-winking dials.

"That animal Harris!" Love shone out of the angry nurse. "He left her a mess!"

"I thought she was dead." Kalenka bent to feel her wrist. "Any human would be. Even she's close to it, with that EKG. But now the vital signs are coming back in a way I never expected."

The nurse asked a question.

"I'll keep him out for now."

"Just for now?"

Love had flickered in him, but now the redness washed it out. "An ugly business, but necessary. If she lives, we'll have to let him back." He moved toward the door and turned to speak again. "Watch her. No drugs. No IV. Nothing. We don't know what might help or what might finish killing her. Just chart everything."

When her body had healed enough to let her leave it again, she reached for Sax. He lay the way he had been, the thick bandage on his head and the irons on his wrists and a needle in his arm. His breath was raspy and slow, and all she could feel was dull throb of hurt.

Reaching for Panchito, she felt nothing at all. He lay very still. His breathing had ceased. A nurse stood staring at the green-glowing dials. Their winking had stopped. A man in white was bending to open one of his eyes and shine a light into it. He turned to snap at the nurse.

"Get Kalenka! I've got to tell him his prisoner is dead."

29

"Billion Dollar Beauty!"

Scorpio had come to the EnGene labs as Herman Doerr, a rootless Vietnam veteran, fond of weapons and outdoor life. Employed as a guard, he moved into a rundown farmhouse just outside the city limits, far from any neighbors. Developing contacts, he became a frequent host for the weekend beer and poker parties of the plant security force.

His target was Arny Carboni, chief of the computer staff and likely to have good access to research secrets. Arny proved difficult. He didn't play poker. He didn't drink beer. He displayed interest in little besides his computers. When Scorpio got to him, it was through another guard, whom he knew as Sam Holliday.

Holliday was a mild-mannered young man with pale blue eyes and straw-colored hair. Playing amateurish poker, always astonished at his own bad luck, he commonly lost enough to keep himself welcome at the parties. Better with computers than he was with cards, he shared hacker lore with Carboni and struck up an apparent friendship.

Cultivating him, Scorpio began offering bits of advice on poker play. Holliday seemed grateful. He admitted his lack of skill. Trying to improve his game, he was writing a computer program to play draw poker. He asked for rules of strategy he could build into the game.

Scorpio gave him hints, tutored him through practice sessions at the computer, lent him money when he lost at the weekend games. When he held several hundred dollars of Holliday's IOUs, he told his cover story that he was actually a private investigator employed by Global Pharmaceuticals to obtain whatever trade secrets he could. He offered to pay for any clues Holliday could pick up from Carboni.

Angry at first, Holliday soon agreed to go along. He got to Carboni, who began selling teasing bits of information, always wanting higher prices. With funds enough from Ostrov, Scorpio kept on paying. Carboni copied Belcraft's lab notes, fed him fragments enough to let him know they were priceless—and finally made his own impossible demand.

Freedom for his father, the dissident Alyoshka. Impossible. Alyoshka had vanished from the media. Carboni feared that he was dead. Scorpio promised to have him released alive from wherever he was under treatment or detention, but promises weren't enough. Carboni held out for a meeting with him, arriving with his wife and daughter in some safe haven.

Playing the tradecraft game, Scorpio probed for weak points and offered larger and larger bribes. More and more suspicious, Carboni refused to settle for anything except his living father. Scorpio searched his house, bugged it, set traps for possible confederates. All failed. Under pressure from Ostrov and the Center, he grew desperate.

One of his bugs had been planted in Carboni's phone, set to ring his own phone when Carboni lifted the receiver. Late on the last night of Enfield, it jarred him out of sleep.

"Holliday? Arny speaking." Carboni was breathing fast, his high voice squeaky with tension. "Hate to wake you, but I think EnGene's about to pop."

Holliday's voice tried to ask some questions, but Carboni rushed on, not listening.

"Likely some genetic hell let loose. How or why, I don't know. Got just enough to frighten me. A damned odd phone call from Belcraft to his brother and another to his girl that scared the panties off her. Could be a false alarm, but I'm afraid to stay in town. You know I never learned to drive. Can you pick me up? The sooner the safer!"

Holliday promised to pick him up.

"Don't talk," he added. "Not to anybody! If nothing actually happens, you can imagine the trouble for us."

Scorpio got to Carboni's ahead of Holliday. The door stood open. He burst in without knocking, to demand the photocopies of the research files. Carboni was white-faced and shaking, but he sneered defiantly, pointing to ashes smoking on the fireplace hearth.

"Okay! All yours! Take 'em home to Moscow!" Clumsily, he was trying to pull a toylike nickel-plated pistol. "Now I know what it was you were bribing me to steal. Genetic poison! Maybe loose already! Whatever happens, I'm through playing games with the KGB—"

Scorpio threw his knife. The little pistol spun into the ashes. Carboni sobbed and fell. Scorpio finished him off and inspected the ashes. Nothing readable was left. Searching the house, he failed again to find anything Ostrov and the Center would care about. Always methodical, he took time to wash the knife and his hands and erase his fingerprints. Two blocks down the street, he met Holliday's old brown Chevy, racing up through the dark too late to do anything for Arny Carboni.

Driving toward the highway, he stopped to bang on the door of Frankie Bard's shabby duplex. Bard was a security sergeant he had come to know at the weekend beer parties. A thick-set man with pale, watery eyes and deep acne scars, he nursed a chronic bitterness because life had seldom given him what he felt it owed him. Their acquaintance had ripened after Scorpio caught him cheating at poker.

Silent then, Scorpio approached him discreetly the next day, offering to work with him instead of exposing him. His first furious denials wilted into mumbling confession. Thereafter, Scorpio taught him skills he hadn't known, some of them legal, and lent him money when he bungled and lost. Now, holding his IOUs for several hundred dollars, Scorpio saw a chance to collect.

A long time waking, Bard came nearly naked to the door, squinting groggily.

"Huh? What the hell?"

"Real hell!" Scorpio dropped his voice. "Loose in Enfield. Drag some clothes on. Anything except your uniform. Fast! We're getting out of town."

Bard blinked and gulped and had to piss, but obediently he pulled odd garments on and stumbled out to the red pickup. A few miles out of town, he pointed at the red-winking neon of the Enbard Mo el.

"My mom's place. Reckon we could stop—"

He braked the car, but suddenly Frankie was shaking his head.

"Let her sleep. Nothing we could tell her. Anyhow, nothing from the lab can get this far."

He drove on for half the morning, however, before they got breakfast at a truck stop out of Little Rock and rented a motel room on Bard's credit card. Bard went back to bed. He watched the TV. Noon was gone before he roused Bard to hear the first confused reports of the Enfield panic.

They stayed two days there, living on Cokes and beer and hamburgers to go, glued to the news. Bard was philosophic about the danger to his mother.

"Don't matter much, not to me. All she ever talks about is how sick she is and how she prays for people to repent their sins. Tell the truth, I'm fed up with all her nutty notions. She's past her time. Just as well if she's gone."

When the White House announced that any possible danger out of Enfield had been safely contained, Scorpio left for Chicago.

"But I'm coming back to Enfield. Or close as I dare. In spite of whatever hit the city—maybe because of it —I get the smell of money waiting there."

"Money?" Bard was groggier than ever, from too much beer and too much sitting. "Money for who?"

"For us. Big money, if we're smart enough to pick it up."

"If EnGene's gone, I don't see how—"

"Nothing it's safe to say much about," Scorpio warned him. "But I was on the trail of something rich the labs were cooking up. Remember Dr. Belcraft? The little guy with glasses that had Lab C?"

"Sure do. Used to work all night." Bard scowled. "Caught me asleep in the guardroom once and threatened to report me."

"Probably dead now, along with most of the rest. But there'll be businessmen and governments keen to pay for whatever they were making."

"You mean—" Bard shivered, abruptly sobered. "Whatever touched off that plague?"

"Whatever." Scorpio shrugged. "Worth a lot of millions to whoever uncovers it. I've got better clues than anybody, but I can't risk my neck around Enfield. For reasons I won't go into. Which is why I need you in the game. If you want to earn yourself more millions than you can count."

Bard gulped and said he did.

"Then get back there. Get inside this quarantine line any way you can—you can say you're looking for your mother. Look for another inside job. This task force will want recruits. They'll want to talk to you when you tell 'em you were an EnGene guard.

"One thing." He caught Bard's arm. "Whatever you have to say, never tell 'em I'm alive. Let 'em think Herman Doerr died in Enfield. I'll get messages to you in care of your mother or her motel, but under another name. It will be—it will be Dave Dodd. Write that down."

Bard wrote it down. Scorpio gave him funds for bus

fare toward Enfield. That night, a hundred miles from Little Rock, he took the license plates off the red pickup, set fire to it and pushed it off a bluff, buried the plates in the ditch a mile away, and tramped on toward Chicago.

Ostrov met him there. In a back booth at Kelly's Tavern, they waited most of the night for Carboni to appear with the Belcraft file. Bright-eyed at first with hope, she stirred him to wish the crisis had given him an hour free to do what he wanted with her, and he hated her again for her insolent aloofness. To amuse himself, he spent the time teasing her with possible reasons for Carboni's delay, none of them the real one.

When she decided to give up the wait, he hit her for another twenty thousand of old Roman's money. She gave him ten. A neat brown-paper package of twenties and fifties that he promised to use for another try for the Belcraft files. Leaving her there, looking worry-worn and too old for her years, her fine shoulders drooping forlornly, he couldn't help grinning.

After a couple of nights with more willing women, though none so tantalizing, he went on to Fort Madison to look for Belcraft's brother and the letter he should have received. The best record left of what had hit Enfield, perhaps the only record.

The brother was a doctor, now out of town. No word since he drove toward Enfield on disaster day. Tearful about him, his office nurse prayed he was still alive. Scorpio waited for him most of a week, playing the role of an unemployed hypochondriac in search of a medical miracle. He haunted the hospital, talking to doctors and nurses and the brother's former patients, picking up what he could. One night he got into the brother's office and found the letter on a desk.

The computer printouts Carboni brought out of the lab had always been too technical to tell him anything. Not quite so baffling, the letter did give him two clear facts. First, the doctor-brother had known nothing about what was going on at EnGene. Second, Belcraft had created a strange new being he called Alphamega. If that still survived, it could be the key to a future far richer than his difficult past.

He got into the brother's house and set a trap for him there, just in case he did get back to look for the letter. Leaving Fort Madison, he called the EnBard Motel from a pay phone in Hannibal. A male voice answered. The motel was closed, commandeered by Task Force Watchdog. If he wanted to get in touch with anybody inside the perimeter, he could call the post message center.

He called the message center. Two nights later, registered as Dave Dodd at a motel in East St. Louis, he got a call from Frankie Bard. Frankie's mother was okay, gone to live with his aunt in Colorado. He had found work, but he could get the weekend off for fun and games if Dave wanted to meet him at Ozark Falls.

At Ozark Falls, they rented a boat and rowed out across the lake. A quarter-mile from shore, with no sign of trouble, he started asking for news. Frankie had got on as a civilian night watchman at the old Enfield municipal airport, which was inside the perimeter and now reserved for military traffic.

"They gave me a hell of a time!" He had brought a six-pack, and he stopped to open a beer. "Grilled me like a spitted chicken when they heard I'd been at EnGene. Wanted all I knew about the lab and the research staff and the other guards. Especially, they were curious about you."

His bulgy eyes blinked accusingly.

"Your poker parties. Wanted to know who was invited and what we talked about and what you'd ever said about anybody else and where you'd been before you came to Enfield and what any of us knew about Arny Carboni."

Frankie stopped to squint.

"Are you some kind of spy?"

"They may think I am." Scorpio grinned, reaching

for a beer to click against Frankie's bottle. "What they think won't buy us any women. I work for money. Came back to EnGene because I'd got the odor of it. It's got to be still there. Waiting for us to dig it up. You'll have to do most of the digging."

Glancing at the shore, he dropped his voice.

"What have you picked up about the plague research?"

"Nothing—which is all I want to know." Frankie shrank away from him. "They've strung barbed wire along the edge of the dust, with signs to warn people out. Don't ask me to risk my ass in there."

"I won't do that," Scorpio assured him. "Not yet, anyhow. What we want is this little animal Belcraft made in his lab. If it's still alive—"

"I think it is!" Frankie brightened. "The chopper crew was talking about a funny critter they caught. Must be something pretty odd. Supposed to have crawled out of the ashes of the EnGene lab. A big hunt for it, ever since the task force got here. It had gotten outside the perimeter fence. Trying to hide, it fell into an old well.

"Funny thing, how they found it. Belcraft had a brother. A doctor somewhere. A lab technician I met at the new canteen told me about him. The brother somehow knew where the critter was. Came here to haul it out of the well. Chopper crew caught 'em both—"

"Our game!" Scorpio grinned. "The animal? What's it like?"

"I haven't seen it." Frankie looked uneasy. "Can't say I'm keen to. The lab man says it looks like a little girl, maybe two years old, starved half to death. Big-headed and skinny. They're got it chained to a table in a guarded room, with alarms all around and guns trained on it."

"Our baby!" He beamed with elation. "No wonder they don't want it to get away again, because it looks to be the only relic left of EnGene. The only key to what they were doing—maybe making genetic bombs."

"Bombs?" Frankie was alarmed. "They ain't my dish."

"Or mine. But don't sweat that. They'll be taking the beast apart to find out what makes it tick. But listen to this! I've got contacts panting to pay big money to get their own chance at her. Just leave the bidding to me. Old Clegg might top 'em all. No matter to us."

Scorpio lifted his bottle.

"Here's to her, Frankie! There's an old song about a million dollar baby. Once we get our hands on her, she's our own billion dollar beauty!"

30

"Whose World?"

Belcraft dreamed again of Alphamega.

"*Véngale,* Sax!" Her little hand was tugging desperately at his. "*Véngale al pobre* Panchito. *Muerto! Muerto!*" She was calling him to come with her somewhere, because poor Panchito was dead.

He tried to tell her in the dream that the dead were dead forever, but she pulled him with her into a hospital room where the wall monitors no longer flashed with signs of life and a nurse was pulling up the sheet to cover a starkly rigid face.

"Help him, Sax! *Por favor!* He must live!"

He knew there was no help, but she drew him closer to the bedside.

"*Dígame,* Sax! Tell me what to do!"

There was nothing at all to do.

"*Hágale que viva!* Make him alive!"

She pulled him closer. Suddenly he and she were one. Reaching inside the unmoving thorax, they found the stopped heart. Their dream-hand squeezed. Responding, the heart quivered and contracted. They squeezed again and yet again, until the quivering muscle resumed a strong and steady beat.

Panchito lived again!

Sharing her joy, he turned with her to the elevated evil-odored leg. The knee was shattered, severely infected, swollen and draining, possibly gangrenous. Feeling together, they reached beneath the stiffened bandages to palpate the hard-swollen skin, reached deeper to explore the torn ligaments, the lacerated menisci, the shattered patella.

The bullet had been removed, but all its harm remained. She needed him to help her know how the knee should have been. Together, they sensed the badness that had spread from the wound to kill the good flesh. Together, they taught the hurt cells how to live again.

"*Gracias,* Sax!" They were suddenly back in the room where she had found him. "You were wonderful! *Qué marveloso!*" She caught his hand to kiss it. "Panchito *será* okay!"

Time had passed before he woke, lying on a hospital bed like Panchito's in the dream. A tight bandage wrapped his head, but the long pain was gone. He felt remarkably well. Suddenly restless, he wanted to get out of the bed for a cold shower and ham and eggs and then a brisk walk out in the sunshine.

He tried to sit up. Hard steel clicked. His left wrist was handcuffed to the rail of the bed. He heard motion behind him and knew a guard stood there.

He lay back, remembering the desperate drive from Fort Madison, the panicky search the perimeter fence, the cold wet stiffness of Meg's tiny body when he pulled her from the well, his icy certainty that she was dead. But now—

Meg was alive!

Not only that. In the dream—and he knew the dream was real—she had somehow revived the man she called Panchito, who had been clinically dead.

Trembling with awe at what he knew she must have done, he knew her healing power had touched him too. He recalled the flapping chopper landing, the crewmen tramping around him, and then the long dim time that had left no memory except the dazing throb of pain in his head.

That blanket of blackness had been lifted.

" 'Morning, if that's what it is." He turned his head to find a man at the door, a sunburned kid in an Army uniform too big for him, standing with his sunburned hand on a leaning rifle. National Guard, by the look of him. "What's this place?"

"Post hospital, sir. Used to be the infirmary, here at what used to be Enfield College. Three miles out of what used to be the town. Feeling better, sir?"

"A lot better. Can I use the bathroom?"

"Not without permission, sir. Have to call the doctor."

"Do it, please! And then I'd like some breakfast."

A nurse came in to take his temperature and pulse and blood pressure, frowning in silent surprise at what she found. A second guard unlocked the handcuffs and followed him into the adjoining bath. Instead of breakfast, an orderly came to wheel him away for a head X ray.

Waiting while they processed the film, he heard excited voices. One was Dr. Kalenka's. The technician came back for a second shot, then three more at different angles. When he asked what they were finding, the technician gave him a look that seemed uneasy and told him to wait again. Back in the room, still with no breakfast, he sat by the bed till the National Guardsman snapped to attention and Kalenka came in, now in a major's uniform.

"Belcraft?" His puzzled tone made the name a question. "What has happened to you?"

"I'm wondering what your X rays show." When Kalenka merely frowned, he added, "I must have been hit on the head."

"Somewhat too hard." Kalenka squinted at the chart and took his pulse. "Or so we thought. All the evidence of a serious concussion. Large clots forming. Dangerous pressure on the brain. Last night we were considering surgery. Your recovery is—well, unbelievable. Remarkably rapid and complete." He leaned to peer into Belcraft's face. "Can you explain it?"

"I can't. But I do feel good again—if I can get something to eat."

"Later." Kalenka nodded at the nurse behind him. "First, I've got a few questions."

"Okay." He felt too fit to let anything trouble him. "I've got a question of my own. Do you—or did you have a patient here who revived from apparent death? Named maybe Panchito?"

"Torres?" Kalenka gaped and stared. "What do you know about Pancho Torres?"

"Nothing," he said. "Except what I dreamed."

"The man—the man was dead." A slow half-whisper. "Of anaphylactic shock following an adverse reaction to antibiotics given for a neglected infection. No heart action for a good many minutes. He did revive—I don't know why."

He paused for another searching frown.

"Like you, he woke up this morning begging for breakfast. The infection is apparently under control. I have just seen a new X ray of Torres's knee. The major fragments of the shattered patella are somehow back in place and beginning to knit."

Shaking his head, he stopped to peer into Belcraft's face.

"You say you dreamed about that?"

"About Alphamega. The little creature I found crawling out of the ashes of EnGene after the disaster. Do you know . . ." Tension shook his voice. "Is she here?"

"She is." Kalenka nodded slowly, staring at him. "A prisoner, captured when you were. You claim she was with you in this remarkable dream?"

"We were together. . . ."

Recollection washed over him. He sat silent, living the dream again, lost again in that instant devotion that had come with his first glimpse of Alphamega, trembling again with awe at her unknown gifts.

"Together?" Kalenka's voice was sharper. "How could that be? When we have her shackled, lying in a guarding cell?"

"In the dream she wasn't shackled." He wanted to smile at Kalenka's baffled dismay. "She took me to Torres, if that's his name. Acting together—almost as if we were two hemispheres of the same compound mind—we examined the injuries. If she actually needed my skills, I don't know why. She touched injured organs as if she knew how to heal them. A knowledge she seemed to get from me." His breath caught. "How is she?"

"Still . . ." Dazedly, Kalenka shook his head. "Still a prisoner. Still a riddle to us. Now in apparent need of medical care we don't know how to give." He squinted into Belcraft's face as if to find his answers there. "She is, of course, under interrogation. More intense as she recovers from her hardships. She is clearly intelligent, though reluctant to speak and then only in the broken Spanish she must have learned from Torres. However—"

His lean face turned bleak.

"She won't tell us anything. Her unfortunate attitude has placed her life in danger. Yesterday she was badly injured by an interrogator who seems to have displayed more sadism than common sense. I thought she was dead—though we know too little about her vital processes to be certain of anything about her. This morning, like Torres and yourself, she seems to have begun a remarkable recovery. Still, however, she refuses to talk. All of which brings us to one more question."

His probing eyes narrowed.

"About her contacts with you."

"She amazes me." Belcraft shrugged. "I don't understand anything she does."

"There are things we've got to understand." Kalenka bent closer, with an air of dogged patience. "We let you return to Fort Madison. You were hospitalized there for minor injuries suffered in a gas explosion not yet well explained, though it happened around the time the creature is thought to have fallen into that well."

"She saved—saved my life." Belcraft hesitated. "It's nothing you'll want to believe, but if you want what happened, here it is. She had been searching for me—searching, however she does it, from down in the bottom of that well, because she needed my help. She saw the explosion about to happen. Speaking in what seemed like a dream—it's nothing I can explain—she warned me to get out of the house."

"Nothing I want to believe." Kalenka turned sardonic. "Military intelligence reports from Fort Madison that you had abandoned your medical practice and fallen heavily into debt—"

"No choice of my own!"

"Your insurers are charging—"

"Perhaps." He shrugged. "Perhaps I am suspected of arson. But I'm alive. So is Meg—unless you kill her here. Which is all that really matters to me now."

"Belcraft, I don't know what to make of you." Kalenka's frown bit deeper, his stare still accusing. "No matter how you try to rationalize whatever you're involved in, you've got a lot to answer for." He gestured with his finger as if pointing at items on a list. "You were a patient in the Fort Madison hospital. You conferred with your attorney, who admits that he had informed you of pending legal charges. You walked out at night, with no permission from anybody. He let you have his car—he says unwillingly. You drove back here. You walked directly to that well and pulled the creature out. How did you find her?"

"Another dream—if that's the word for however she reaches me. Of course I wonder. I never took much stock in parapsychology, but this has to be some sort of mental contact. It seems to happen only during sleep or half-sleep. Could be the waking mind creates some kind of barrier. Not that I can explain Alphamega or anything about her."

"I don't know—" Kalenka sat down slowly on the

bed, looking suddenly very tired. "I don't know what to think."

"About Meg?" Belcraft caught at a hint of troubled sympathy in him. "Are you—are you going to kill her?"

Kalenka sat silent for a moment as if he hadn't heard. "She's—well, a very difficult problem." He shook his head, speaking half to himself. "Too many riddles with no apparent answers." His baffled eyes returned to Belcraft. "You realize that we've got to learn all we can about what she is and how she's linked to the disaster. She came out of the same lab where it began. If En-Gene was working toward some biological weapon, we need all we can learn about it. For the sake of national defense. In any case, she offers fascinating scientific puzzles. But in the end—"

He paused, with a darker frown at Belcraft.

"In the end, she will have to be destroyed."

"No!" He tried to smooth his voice and frame some reasonable appeal. "She hasn't hurt anybody. I don't think it's in her to hurt anybody. Think—think what she is!"

"I'm afraid of what she is."

"But she isn't—isn't anything to fear. I admit she does sometimes frighten me, but that's only because I don't understand all her gifts. My brother created her. He used to talk about what he hoped to do with genetic engineering. Our own natural creation, he used to say, came about through a random, hit-or-miss evolutionary process that took billions of years. Now, he thought, we should be able to engineer evolution to create some better sort of being than we are.

"That's what he hoped to do. His great dream was to create a new sort of life without the defects and limits we owe to all the accidents of our animal origins. Something closer to gods than to men, he used to say, as we have always imagined gods. To my mind, that's what Alphamega was meant to be. But she's still a child. Maybe less than he hoped to make her, because his work was interrupted. Yet I'm coming to see her as the first try toward a new and better species. The Eve, perhaps, of a totally new order of being. A child goddess!"

"Perhaps she is." Kalenka nodded gloomily. "That's why I'm afraid."

"Of a single harmless child?"

"Because of what she might become." Though the room was cool, he found a handkerchief and mopped his haggard face. "Belcraft, it does trouble me. However she came to be, she's certainly something wonderful. But I'm afraid to let her stay alive."

Staggered by Kalenka's deliberate finality, he groped to recover himself. "Have you—have you talked to other scientists?"

"Of course!" Kalenka seemed oddly angry. "We've debated her. Ever since you found her. Among ourselves in the research staff. With a few outsiders we've had to trust. There is sentiment in her favor, and tremendous scientific curiosity. But nothing else touches the one big issue: Whose world do we want it to be?"

"Whose world?"

"I told you I'm a Jew." Silent for a moment, Kalenka looked almost apologetic. "I've seen genocide. I abhor it. But let's assume she's all you think she is—the first pioneer of a better race than we are, engineered to replace us on earth. Are you ready to say humanity has failed? Ready to let her children crowd us off the planet, the way our own forebears must have pushed a hundred or a thousand older species off?"

"A crazy notion! One baby girl? Do you think Vic engineered her to exterminate mankind? You didn't know my brother. . . ."

"Nor do I know what he did." Wearily, Kalenka sagged where he sat on the edge of the bed. "But I can't forget what happened to Enfield. I'm afraid your brother blinded himself to all that was coming out of his lab. We simply can't afford to take the chance that this little monster could be deadlier than the dust—harmless as she may look to you."

"You're wrong!" Belcraft whispered. "Terribly wrong!"

"Another thing," Kalenka added, frowning unhappily. "General Clegg is following everything we do—he has called me twice already today. He seems more frightened than I am by what he believes about the creature. To him, her abilities are gifts of Satan. He keeps quoting a passage out of the Bible. *Thou shalt not suffer a witch to live.*

"He sees her a literal witch, sent from hell to lure the world toward destruction by science turned Satanic. He's convinced she brought the disaster. Only a warning, he says, of the terrors she has come to spread. He's demanding her destruction—soon!

"Officers on his staff and people in his Cato Club are holding out for time to complete our study of her. Some of them are keen to get a biological weapon. More are hoping we can learn how to defend ourselves against biology gone wrong. But the fact is that we have very little time."

"I . . . I see."

"Something else I must add." Kalenka hesitated, looking uncomfortable. "I don't like to threaten you. I can't honestly promise that either you or Torres will ever be liberated. You both appear to know too much. But I want you to keep in mind that we can make things easier for both of you if you and she cooperate."

Belcraft found no words to say.

"I'm sorry." Kalenka's features tightened as if with genuine regret. "But that's that way it is. You won't be released again."

31

Keri Grant

Anya came back to Kennedy on a Concorde, wearing a curly red wig and more exotic makeup. In her new identity, she was returning to America after five years in Europe. Her passport had been expertly forged to support a cover story based on information Tim Clegg had gathered from the Watchdog files.

She and her twin sister had grown up on an Indiana farm, encouraged by their mother to hope for great careers in art or letters. Liberated by money from an uncle more generous than their hard-headed farmer-father, they both left the farm on the day they turned twenty-one.

Jeri entered a New York art school. Keri, with more wanderlust than any settled aim, had gone on to Paris, looking for the fabulous world of carefree bohemians their romance-minded mother had always dreamed about.

She found the old Left Bank long since faded into mythic history, along with Hemingway and Steinbeck and Gertrude Stein. Even when her own talent proved to be another mirage, she had kept on chasing romantic illusions through an Amsterdam commune and love affairs with a penniless Italian who claimed to be a count and an American drifter who said his father owned a Las Vegas casino and finally a Frenchman who promised to make her a movie star.

Now, in the aftermath of the Enfield tragedy, she had resolved to put those silly dreams behind her. The legacy nearly gone, she would soon need an honest job. First, however, she had come home to learn what had happened to her sister and her parents. In Piedmond, the nearest airport town still alive, she checked into the quaint old Norman Towers, whose red-brick battlements had been laid up the year the railroad came.

Tim Clegg, so their story went, had met her while he was stationed in Europe. She called the number he had given her for Captain Sam Holliday. Two hours later, he came up to her room and stopped a moment in the doorway to study her.

"Different." He nodded, with a smile of frank approval. "You look the part."

"I am—was—an actress." She closed the door and turned to take his hand. "I'm coming to like Keri, but also to feel she's a very risky role to play."

"So far, so good." He scanned her again, the smile still lingering. "The survivors have been interrogated pretty thoroughly about EnGene and everyone connected with the research staff. Jeri Grant and her parents are dead; I'm certain of that.

"Jeri had some hint of trouble coming. An Indiana neighbor says she made a phone call that frightened her folks into driving down here. They must have gotten here just in time to die. Our background for you came from what we learned in Indiana. No survivors in the Enfield area are likely to know that Jeri had no twin. If American intelligence had penetrated your cover, I'd have been informed."

"I hope you're right."

"A lot will depend on you."

Feeling a little easier, she found herself responding to his smile. The room was warm, and they sat beneath a lazy antique ceiling fan. Honeysuckle scented the air from a spray in an imitation Chinese vase on the antique mantel. She had found a kind of comfort in the Norman Towers, because it belonged so much to the past, because it seemed so secure from the faraway Center. She had begun to like Tim Clegg, but his next words disturbed her.

"I must tell you, however, that things have changed."

"How?" His open face seemed to show both admiration and concern. She wanted to trust him. In fact she had to trust him now. Yet she could never quite forget that he belonged to the *Glavni Vrag.* "We've come too far to start changing plans." She frowned in spite of herself. "I let my superiors believe you're defecting to us. It's a story they're sure to suspect. Double agents are too often double-crossers. If I report some new plan—"

She shivered.

"My own risks are just as great," he assured her soberly. "Even if the general is my father—I know him too well to think he would hesitate to have me shot if it came to that, but nothing has changed our actual goal. That's worth any risk." He was leaning urgently toward her. "We're still fighting to shield civilization from genetic war—or maybe something worse. We can't afford to fail."

"So what's the change?"

"Not our aim. We must kill this synthetic being before Kalenka and his team get the secret of whatever hit Enfield. The difference is that ridding the world of her looks a lot harder now."

The big fan spun slowly overhead, its gears humming a monotonous rhythm. The honeysuckle spray was suddenly too sweet. She wanted to toss it out of the window, but she sat where she was, waiting uneasily.

"Here's the problem." He shifted uncomfortably. "Alphamega was killed here in the lab. Or at least mauled so severely by a sadist on the staff that Kalenka announced her death. He went out of the room to arrange for staff and equipment to study the body and came back to find her reviving."

"A medical mistake?" Anya frowned. "Just a coma?"

"Who knows? She's still a riddle to Kalenka. To everybody. Even her chemistry—something he calls her nucleotides. Totally different, he says, from those in any known form of life. As strange to him, he says, as lasers might be to an ape. He admits that he doesn't understand anything about her. Doesn't know what she can do. Or can't. Which is why she frightens him."

A baffled shrug.

"Her own revival is not half of it. She has friends. Two fellow prisoners. Belcraft's brother, the man who found her in the ashes. And a Mexican alien named Torres, who seems to have looked after her while she was hiding. All three—"

He shook his sandy head.

"There's a link between them Kalenka can't explain. Somehow, they're all able to keep in contact, even when kept physically apart. The creature seems to know all that happens to them. She can touch them—heal them when they're hurt—by some means Kalenka has failed to discover.

"Torres was shot at the time of his capture. The wound was infected, and he had a bad reaction to the antibiotics. Kalenka evidently tried hard enough to save him, electric shocks and drug injections when his heart stopped. But he died, and lay dead too long for recovery without brain damage. So Kalenka says.

"But he did revive, or somehow was revived. The infection is gone, and his knee healed amazingly. Kalenka thinks the creature's uncanny powers are behind the medical miracle of his revival, with maybe a medical assist from Belcraft. Even Belcraft himself has made what Kalenka calls a very puzzling recovery from a fairly serious concussion he suffered when he was captured.

"All of which makes our mission pretty tricky."

He stopped to gaze at her again with an absent-seeming approval.

"We've got to be careful, because we don't know Alphamega. If she does possess some crazy psychic gift, she may sense what we're up to. So far she hasn't used her mental powers, whatever they are, to hurt anybody, but we don't know she won't. Not that we can let that matter." He shrugged. "Whatever she is or can do, this display of unknown powers has raised all the stakes."

"Our lives do matter." She shivered again. "But I get what you mean. If the Center gets a hint of what you're telling me, they could want their own chance to squeeze the secrets out of her."

"Even my father—" Frowning, he seemed to share her dread. "In one way, he's bent as much as we are on killing the creature, because he sees her as an actual agent of an actual Satan. But she also excites his Hitler complex. He wants Kalenka to get the biological bomb, if there is a biological bomb, and whatever else she knows while she's still alive to talk.

"So far she hasn't talked. Our best hope is to learn how to stop her before she does. Belcraft—this Dr. Saxon Belcraft—looks like our only possible point of attack. Jeri was living the past year or so with his brother, the one at EnGene, who have been the actual creator of the being. That ought to give you an opening."

"If he—this doctor-brother—didn't know Jeri too well."

"They never met—I'm almost sure of that. The brothers had been out of touch. The thing is risky. I know that, but it's the best chance we have."

They went downstairs to the nearly vacant and peaceful-seeming dining room for a southern-cooked dinner under languid fans. He drove back to the post. She followed next morning. On the basis of a brief interview and a strong recommendation from him, she was given a job in the secretarial pool at post security. Finding no quarters available inside the perimeter, she bought a used Toyota and rented a garage apartment in Maxon, a tiny farm town a dozen miles away.

The pool had been expanded to cope with a flood of demands from people concerned about relatives or property lost in Enfield. Armed with basic typing and filing skills she had learned for her first approach to Jules Roman, she felt fit enough for the job. Meeting Belcraft was not so easy.

The three prisoners were kept in separate buildings now, heavily guarded. The whole perimeter area was under martial law, with guards and staff under strict orders not to talk. Tim Clegg had scraps of news when he called her to his office, but never anything revealing.

"The creature's still defiant," he told her, "in her own passive way. She's on a hunger strike. She still somehow knows all about how Belcraft and Torres are faring. She keeps refusing to eat until they get better food and freedom in the open air. Kalenka won't give in. In fact, he can't. I was present when he reported the problem to my father. Dad jumped up and banged his desk, threatening to have the two men shot at once as a lesson to the creature.

"A stalemate, with no sign of a break."

"We've got to have a break."

In her other role as a loyal arm of the KGB, she had been filing progress reports through a tiny radio built into a cosmetic container. Computer chips inside it compressed her messages into momentary squeaks too brief to be traced and transmitted them to be picked up and forwarded to Moscow from the embassy in Washington.

"My people are worried." Feeling more and more at ease with him, she let anxiety sharpen her voice. "They demand more progress than I can report. They know just enough to terrify them, and they don't trust anybody. Not me, for sure."

"Who else?"

"Nobody." He sat silent, and she went on. "I'm their

only agent here inside, but I can be replaced. If such military biologicals do exist, my Moscow bosses have ordered me to get them. Or else erase the whole discovery. If they don't get positive news—soon—they'll recall me. Hunt me down if they have to."

He shrugged. "We didn't sign up for anything easy."

She tried to carry on, searching for possible informers. A service club and bar now occupied what had been the student union building of the abandoned college. Spending her evenings there, appearing available and talking to anybody indiscreet or drunk enough to talk, she met a security man who liked gin and Coke a little too well for his own security.

His name was Frankie Bard. An EnGene security staffer before the disaster, he had just come back to work on the post, driving a patrol car and drinking in the club on his nights off. She disliked him. Foul-mouthed and dim-witted, his black-haired belly often bulging from the bottom of his shirt, he always smelled of onions and tried too hard to get his hands on her.

She tolerated him because of his gossip. His pet topic was the captive monster-critter, which held him in a frightened fascination. Sitting with him in the bar, she paid for most of the drinks and listened to his nasal monologues.

"Just nigger luck I happened to be off duty on the night she fired the town, or she'd a burnt me to that queer dust."

Exchanging rumors with his friends in security, with drivers and lab technicians and the mess hall crew, Bard had gathered a store of terrifying tales. The critter shone in the dark. People that touched her came down with chills and fever. Could be the Enfield virus, now incubating in them. Deadlier than anything.

"Me, I wouldn't touch her. Pray to God she don't get loose."

The creature was still chained in her cell in the old infirmary. Bard's friend Mickey Harris had worked her over there. Said he thought he'd done her in, squashed the hellfire out of her like the devil's imp she was. Somehow she'd come alive again. Upset about the injuries, the major had transferred Mickey to mess hall duty. Afraid he'd finish killing her before she confessed what sort of hell she'd brought to kill Enfield.

Her hunger strike was over—Mickey knew the cook who had to fix up the special trays she ordered. The major was scared of her, as much as anybody. Maybe afraid she'd plant the death in him. He'd begun giving her all she wanted to eat and doing favors for her friends, that killer spic and the crazy doctor that found her in the ashes. She'd got the major to order the cuffs off the spic. Even got permission for him to walk outside, exercising the knee Mickey had shot from under him.

To pay for those favors, the critter was talking. Anyhow, learning to talk. English now, instead of her smattering of spic. Learning faster than any human, the lab crew said. Nearly like she read people's minds, though she kept asking a lot of questions. But still too stubborn to say anything about EnGene and the killer dust till Belcraft and the spic were set free.

Which would be never.

"Not a Chinaman's chance." Frankie belched. "The general swears he'll be damned if he ever lets them go, or the critter either." He belched again and lifted a wavering finger for another gin and Coke. "Time's a-comin' when the little monster bitch will have to change her tune. That'll be when they have to let Mickey Harris at her again."

When Anya said she had to leave, Frankie wanted to drive her home. She tried to remind him that he couldn't take his patrol car out of the perimeter. He wanted to borrow her car. Escaping, she went to the "she room," slipped out the back way, and left him to his gin and Coke.

Driving out toward the gate, she saw Mickey Harris walking from the mess hall, late and hastening. She had met him in the bar. He was a dark stocky man with a flat, high-cheeked face and long black hair combed straight back; even at night he wore black-framed mirror sunglasses that glinted in her headlight.

He turned to wave and grin at her. She looked quickly away. She had come to hate him for his persistent stupid passes and all the ways he repelled her. His foul talk and something ugly in his voice when he was drunk and something else she couldn't name. The cold flash of those blank mirror glasses and something in his grin sent a shudder through her now.

Eyes ahead, she drove faster.

Late one night soon after, while she was still awake, trying to compose a radio report good enough to hold the Center off a little longer, her telephone startled her.

"Miss Grant?" A flat, raspy whisper that seemed almost familiar. "Want to stay alive?"

"What—"

"No time for gab. Do what I say, and you won't get hurt. I want a ride. Get down to your car and pick me up at the phone booth outside the Exxon truck stop on the Enfield road. You've got ten minutes."

"Why—"

"Move! Unless you want holes in your hide. Try to stall me, and Belcraft will know you ain't Miss Grant. Nine minutes now. Counting down!"

The phone clicked off.

Nine minutes later, breathless and trembling, she stopped the Toyota at the truck stop. The phone booth was empty, but a dark shadow slid out of the darker shadows behind a parked furniture van. She heard the rear door open.

"Don't look back." The same voiceless rasp. "All you gotta do is run me out to the post. On through the gate and the campus to the old Enfield airport. You know the way."

"I know the way. But—"

"No more gab! Keep your cool and drive me there.

Not too fast. Watch the traffic. No funny business—unless you want a bullet in the brain."

The cold muzzle of a gun jabbed hard into the nape of her neck.

"If things go wrong, you die first."

"Ok—okay!"

The gun was gone. She pulled away, toward the post. Glancing into the rearview mirror when the lights of a speeding car came up behind, she made out a dim form crouched down into the dark.

The corporal at the gate raised his hand to stop her.

"Trouble, Miss Grant?" He leaned to peer into the car. "Can I call somebody?"

"Thanks, Jake." Eyes on her, he wasn't looking into the back. "Nothing wrong. Captain Holliday just called me in to type a late report."

He waved her through. She could breathe again.

She started on through the old campus toward the airport. Two couples were strolling slowly toward the dorms from the canteen bar. Another, in mess-hall fatigues, had stopped in the doorway, swaying in an alcoholic embrace. A block farther on, the late movie was just over. She had to slow for people scattering out of the theater.

The streetlights went out. All the lights everywhere.

Trembling, she braked the car.

"Drive on." The whisper again, close to her ear. "Slow."

For a few seconds, she saw nothing except the startled pedestrians caught in her headlamps. Then she heard emergency generators roaring. Here and there, windows shone again. Something jolted the car. She heard the muffled thump of a far explosion.

"Steady!" The gun jabbed her neck. "On toward the airport."

She obeyed. A siren screeched somewhere in the dark, and she saw red lights flashing closer.

"No help for you." She felt hot breath against her hair. "That's our escort to the terminal. All you do is follow. The freight gate will be open. Drive inside. Down the taxi strip. We're taking the general's jet."

The patrol car lurched around a corner on squealing tires, red lights flashing. She followed it on toward the airport, through an open gate in the new chain link fence, down the taxi strip. Her headlamps picked out the white star that was painted on the side of the jet, and a name, *Spirit of '76.* The door was open, the stair down. She parked beside it.

"Lights out! Gimme your keys."

She snapped off the headlamps and gave him the keys. They jingled somewhere. The patrol car went dark. Two men ran for the jet. The one ahead—Frankie Bard? She thought the other had something in his arms. Her captor darted after them.

Lights came on in the jet. The stair retracted. The door swung shut. Engines whined and roared. Their hot blast washed her. The plane swung, rolled away, thundered down the runway. Still shaking, she sat watching the twin tongues of pale fire climbing into the night.

32

The Color of Hope

For far too long, there had been no hope.

Lying always chained in that red-hazed room, the hateful gringos always watching, she had seen no way to freedom. Though she could touch *los pobres amigos,* her two poor friends, that was only with her mind. The gringos would never let her body go, and they would keep on hurting it until she could never heal it.

Los pobres!

She had reached to help when her friends were hurt, but she couldn't break the irons or open doors or stop the cruel gringo guns waiting to kill them if they ever tried to get away. Reaching their minds, she could feel what they felt, share their fleeting dreams of freedom, try to ease their despair and pain. Yet she had no way to shield them if the gringos wanted to hurt them again.

Nor to help herself. If the cruel gringos let their bullets smash her head and spatter her brain, if they let the laughing man named Mickey come again to squeeze and tear her too much with his savage hands, if they darkened too much of the quick-dancing fire that made her alive, she could never teach the hurt cells how to make her ashes burn again.

Dead forever, she could never again comfort her

friends. She could never hope to find why the dear Vic had lit the life in her, never even know the great mission he had planned and hoped for her to carry out. Only empty darkness would be left for her, and for Sax and Panchito, and for all the others Vic had shaped her to help.

In Panchito's dreams, he was always carrying her home to that small mud house in San Rosario, the small mud town where he had lived when he was young. She was to be *la hermanita chiquita.* Roberto and Estrella, fat little José and *la madre,* the mother herself, they always laughed and cried and touched her with tender hands and took her to be one of them, far and safe from all the ugly gringos.

Poor Panchito! He always woke again, to the blazing lights and the new iron bars and cruel truth that the gringos were going to kill him before they ever let him go.

And Sax—*que lástima*!

Sax was never happy, even in the dreams she reached. Once he was back where he used to live, wandering through the empty house on the river, feeling lonely for Midge. She had been his *mujér,* the dark-eyed woman who named the house Tara Two and went away because he had never let her know how much he loved her.

In another dream, he was running through the woods with Vic, back when they both were very young, the dear Vic no taller then than Panchito's tiny *hermanito* José. The limping dog named Canis had gone ahead of them, chasing a rabbit. They tried to follow the dog, but Vic had been too small to run fast enough. He stumbled because his eyes were bad, and cried because he couldn't keep up.

Sax had run on in the dream and left Vic behind him, lost and bawling in the woods. He woke up very sad, because he had never been nicer to Vic. Now he could never be nicer, because Vic was dead.

More often when she reached for Sax, she caught him

dreaming of her, finding her again in the ashes of the lab when she was still a small pink sausage. He was smiling again at her thirsty eagerness when she sucked up the first beer she ever tasted. He was watching her crawl away from him when she was afraid of the soldiers, sad to see her go. He was afraid for her, searching again, pulling her out of the cruel cold blackness of the *hoyo* where she had fallen when she tried to hide. Always he was wondering.

Wondering why he loved her, not the way he used to love Midge, but yearning to comfort and help her. Wondering what she was and what she might come to be, if *los enemigos* let her live to be anything at all.

Always, at the end of the dream, he woke to the heavy blackness of no hope for her. No hope for himself or anybody.

When she did find hope, it was only a tiny spark of brightness, dim in the red fog always around her, so faint and far that it had no color at all. Probing for it, she had to leave herself and reach out of the red badness around her, out far beyond the cruel-spiked perimeter fence.

Reaching, she found the man who had lit that far spark with his own thoughts of her. He had never seen her. She felt no cloak of warning redness around him. He planned help for her instead of harm, yet in spite of the spark of hope, he troubled her. Sometimes his image came when he thought of her. A heavy dark man with sharp dark eyes. His name had been Ranko Barac, but now he called himself Escórpion. At first she found no love for her or anybody that would let her touch his mind.

Not until once when he slept.

In his dreams, she discovered a long-forgotten love for his grandfather, a lame old man who had been as lean and hard as he was. Awakening that love, she touched his sleeping mind and uncovered old recollections he had put away. Later, when she had learned the way, she could sometimes reach his mind when it shone with that strange hope for her, even when he was awake.

The world where she first touched his memories was strange and hard for her to understand. The grandfather had lived in a high rock house on a high rocky hill in a country of strange pits and caves called the Kras. That was in a far land called Montenegro. Himself a war-scarred fighting man, the grandfather had sent seven hard sons to the endless wars of his war-hardened people. Six of them had died in battle to defend their rock-ribbed nation. That was the way men should die, and they had made the old man fiercely proud.

The other son had shamed him. He was the Scorpion's father, who had become something called a spy. Spies perhaps were sometimes useful. Sometimes they had even given up their lives for a cause or a country, but the old man hated them for the way they killed by stealth and deception, with no fairness toward their foes. It had been a woman spy in something called the partisan wars who betrayed the last of the fighting brothers. When the old man learned the truth, he never let the Scorpion eat or sleep in his house again.

The Scorpion's mother had once been a partisan for a warrior named Tito. Following him, she had sworn her loyalty to a hateful ruler called Stalin. The grandfather blamed her for seducing his son to join her ugly cause. They married in a place called Moscow and took their training there.

While the Scorpion was young, they had lived in places that were names in her mind without pictures, Istanbul and Rome and London and Lima and Havana. Using different names and passports, the Scorpion's father always said he was attached to the Soviet embassy as a journalist for Tass or a staff officer for some ministry.

The Scorpion had learned many languages and the ways of many people, and his spy father trained him to be what he called a good soldier of the party, skilled in the art called tradecraft, adept at killing, expert in all he needed to become a master of spies. But neither his father nor his mother had ever taught him any love. They took no time for love, because love for anything except the cause was poison for a spy.

Perhaps his father died as a spy for Russia, but the young Scorpion was never told about it. That gray winter they had been back in Moscow for something called retraining and reassignment. His father was ordered very suddenly to Santiago, with hardly time to pack. He waited with his mother for their permission to follow, but that never came.

If his mother knew why, she never spoke about it. The year he was twelve, she got a divorce to marry a factory manager who had a dacha and a private limousine because he was making imitation Levi jeans for the black market.

He disliked the factory manager, a loud fat man who hated him. They quarreled. He broke the man's arm with a fighting trick his father had taught him. He tried to make his mother understand, but they sent him away to live with his grandfather in Montenegro.

At first he hated Montenegro. The narrow rock house had no comforts. There was nothing to do in the village. He had to herd the sheep and goats. They lived on goat's milk and black bread and goat's-milk cheese. He had no friends, and even the language was strange. He stole a pistol and hid food and made maps, planning to run away, but then he learned to love his grandfather.

That surprised him, because the old man hated spies. He smoked strong Turkish tobacco and smelled of goats and talked to him as if he were a warm new friend, seeming interested in all he said about the cities where he had lived and the different peoples he had known.

Perhaps there had been too much tobacco, because the old man coughed in the night and sometimes gasped for air. He had to ride the donkey when they went down to the village. Drinking strong slivovitz in the café, he talked with his white-haired cronies about the many wars they had known.

His voice was rich and mellow when he didn't have

to wheeze, and the boy loved listening. He talked of his six warrior sons and how they died, fighting in the wars of Tito and the partisans. He never wanted to speak of the other son, the spy. Hurt at first, the boy came to understand. Holding him in his arms while he tried to breathe, trembling and gasping and turning blue, he shed hot tears when the old man died.

Sixteen by then, he went back to Moscow. He learned then that the factory manager had been caught and shot for gangsterism. His mother, they said, had shot herself. Love had been poison to one more spy.

Men who had known his father saw ability in him. At first he disliked them and their loveless world. He sometimes even felt wistful for the barren hills of the Kras and his grandfather's wheezy voice, but at last he followed the way of his father, training for the KGB. He plied the craft now just as he played chess, with conscious skill and total concentration, but moved neither by devotion to the USSR nor hatred for the *Glavni Vrag.* To a spy, hatred could be as deadly as love.

No loyalties bound him. When he began to learn what Alphamega was, or what others believed her to be, he saw her as the prize in a larger and more rewarding game than he had ever played, one which his own nerve and skill and wits might win. Turning against his old companions in the KGB, he felt no regrets.

In Meg's own mind, the color of hope shone stronger.

33

El Momento

She found it hard to understand the glow of hope that washed the Scorpion at the times when she could touch his mind. The memories she awakened in him were nearly too strange for her to picture. Sometimes she wanted to hate him, because the cruel spy work had almost killed the kindness in him. A man who knew no law and valued no life, scarcely even his own, how could he carry hope for her?

Yet she had to reach for him when she could, because no other ray of hope had come to her through that dead red fog. Shut up in her cell, the gringo guns always on her, she followed the Scorpion when she could, looking for understanding. Most of the time he stayed far from Enfield, afraid he might meet some survivor who would know him from a time when he called himself Herman Doerr, but she was touching his mind when he came to speak to Frankie Bard.

Frankie was a security man from the post. The only love she ever felt in him was for money or food or drink, or for showing women the stud he was, never the warmer love that might have opened his mind, never even a gleam of hope. The Scorpion saw him as a dim-witted glutton, but yet a useful tool.

On two or three evenings a week, Frankie drove off the post to fill himself with Chinese or Mexican food at a smelly place in Maxon called Juan Wong's Taco Chinatown. The Scorpion came to meet him there, wearing a cowboy hat and a black patch over one eye. They parked their cars outside the café or at the all-night market across the highway. The Scorpion never left his car. He let Frankie speak with him, and then he drove away.

Frankie was sometimes a balky tool.

"When's my payoff?" he asked one night. "Suppose the little bitch is worth all the millions you say she is, how do we cash her in?"

"Leave her to me." The Scorpion grinned and slapped his back. "We make one move at a time. When we have her where we want her, I'll open up the bidding—for all the millions we'll ever need, and some safe haven where we can spend them. I know the game. When the good time comes, I'll see you get your cut."

Though she could never see into Frankie's mind, she followed the Scorpion till she found the source of hope.

They planned to take her away from the prison!

Seeing that, with neither one aware of her, she was able to aid their planning. They wanted to take her to some far place where she might be safe from the gringos and from other enemies she saw in the Scorpion's mind. Obeying his instructions, Frankie made copies of files the FBI and the special investigators had gathered on her and Sax and Panchito. She caused the Scorpion to search them again until he found a way to escape by *avión*.

The idea, she let him think, was all his own. The files of the FBI reported that Panchito was a twice-escaped convict, under sentence of death for a murder committed after his first escape. A Mexican alien, he had begun his career flying illicit cargo into Arizona from secret airstrips in Mexico. His birthplace was a faraway town called San Rosario, where perhaps he would have family or friends who might be helpful if the bribes were big enough.

The Scorpion built his plan around Panchito. Sax was not included. Meg ached with dread when she thought of him left alone in the hands of men like Mickey Harris, but the red fog always grew thick and dark around her when she tried to think of ways for the Scorpion to make a place for him in the plan.

Late one night when they were ready, the Scorpion drove his rented car off the highway into a lonely arroyo a few miles outside the perimeter fence and climbed the slope beyond to fasten plastic explosive to three of the tall new poles the gringos had planted to carry the new power line into Enfield.

He telephoned Frankie the next day to say that the weather had turned good for fishing at the lake. Uneasily waiting, Meg tried to reach Sax and Panchito. She found Sax on the bed in his room, snoring fitfully. Gringos in uniform were dripping something into him through a needle taped into his wrist, shouting angry questions at his ear. They got no answers, because they had made him too dead to speak or think or even dream.

Panchito had been luckier. Answering questions in English and questions in Spanish for many days, he had told them and told them and told them all he could remember about San Rosario and coming away from it to *la tierra de dios* to fly *aviones* for the *marijuaneros.* He had told them many times about the sad death of Hector on the prison wall and about the bad luck of the girl who died in Enfield and the bad time in the jail before the frightened deputies who set him free.

Sometimes angry when they pretended not to believe, often half *loco* for need of sleep, always aching toward the end from the cruel hands of Deputy Harris, he had sworn again and again upon the honor of his mother that every word was true when he spoke of *La Maravilla* who had come to him out of the little river and the strange months when they had been *fugitivos* together. Even when *los médicos* came to drip the drops into his body, they had found that he had no more to tell.

Now at last they had left him almost alone. The guards were still with him, but they had taken off the irons to let him exercise his injured leg. The knee in fact had grown strong again since she brought Sax to help her touch it. Now it never gave him pain, but he still groaned and limped to prove the need for exercise.

When the time came, she tried to make him ready.

Just past midnight, the lights went out in her cell. She heard gringo curses and then the heavy thump of the explosions the Scorpion had made. She felt weak and cold when she thought of *el pobre* Sax, and the nearness of danger was a red fog around her when she remembered all the risks to Panchito.

Pero ahora!

Now! This was *el momento*! Trembling, she began to narrow her hands and her feet to slip them free. The irons were still too tight. They bruised and tore her skin, but at last they dropped away. She rolled off the cruel table, ran through the red dark out into the corridor.

Flashlights flickered there. Gringos ran and shouted, and she hid for a moment behind a drinking fountain. She was near the outside door before the emergency lights came on. Guns thundering behind her, she dived outside into the dark. Red lights came flashing at her, wheels screaming on the road. A car stopped ahead of her. A man jumped out.

Panchito!

"Aquí, niñita!"

He had no limp. His arms swept her up. She felt the strong thump of his heart, the way she used to feel it when he carried her in his shirt. The wheels screamed again. Roaring fast through dark streets, they passed another car. It followed. They came through a gate and stopped near a dark *avión.* The Scorpion ran to it, waving with a gun. Panchito carried her up the steps into its strange smells. The man Frankie came after them and then the Scorpion, all shouting loud.

"Okay, *chiquita,*" Panchito whispered. "*Con buena suerte,* you will be okay."

With luck! She hoped for luck.

Panchito put her in a soft leather chair. The man Frankie fastened a hard strap around her and took the next seat. His breath had a stink of onions and beer, and his body had a bad smell of terror.

Panchito sat in front beside the Scorpion. The *avión* roared and moved. Cars came racing after them, red lights blinking, but they kept ahead. Gunfire crackled behind them, but she saw no harm. The *avión* roared louder.

They were in the sky!

A long time in the sky. Beside her, Frankie belched and swallowed a pill and belched again. Twice he yelled at Scorpion that he had to go. He came back to belch and scratch his hairy body. In the seat, he sagged against the straps and jerked himself awake and sagged again. Finally he was snoring.

Panchito drove the *avión.* The Scorpion watched him and watched everything. He saw Frankie sleeping and yelled loud at him. Frankie moved and burped and scowled at her and went to sleep again.

The land beneath was dark, but she could feel the shape of it. She wanted to help Panchito drive the *avión* through the dark. He needed help, because he couldn't feel the world the way she did. He had to look at maps and look at shining dials to know where he was. He was too wide awake to let her show him what she saw, yet she could feel his happiness. At last he had left the gringos and their cruel chair behind.

Touching him, she could see the dark land the way it had been in his dreams. She saw the trees and neat fields that would turn green when there was light to show the green. The land that would be green slid slowly back, slowly changing to a wide bare dryness that would be brown when the sun came back.

Sharp brown mountains grew slowly out of the dark ahead and slid slowly back beneath and sank again into the dark world behind. Searching ahead for some new brightness of hope, she began to feel instead the red badness of danger.

"*No, señor,*" she heard Panchito saying. "*No es posible.*"

The Scorpion's voice was suddenly tight and angry, but Panchito still spoke very softly. Whatever *diós* might will, he was not afraid. She heard him explaining to the Scorpion, pleased to be speaking Spanish again. The Scorpion wanted them to set the *avión* down on the strip at the edge of the hills above San Rosairo where he used to land when he flew for the *marijuaneros.*

"*No es posible,*" Pancho said again. The *gasolina* would not last. Instead, perhaps they should stop at the airport near *la Cuidad de Chihuahua,* where perhaps they might obtain more *gasolina.*

Louder, the Scorpion said no such thing was possible. Warnings must have been sent. The *policia* would be waiting. Probably *soldados.* The stolen *avión* would be seized. They would all be shot for kidnapping the child, if it really was a human child.

Were there no other secret strips they could reach?

"*Verdaderamente,*" Panchito said. Indeed, he had known other strips, but they would have no landing lights and no *gasolina.* The *avión* would drink all the *gasolina* before the sun came, and it landed far too fast for them to live through a crash *en el campo.*

Even saying that, Panchito's voice was very quiet. He still felt happy. *Diós mediante,* they might survive. If they were fated to die in the *avión,* that would be *la voluntad de diós.* The will of God, and better by far than going back to the gringo torture boxes.

The Scorpion shouted bad-sounding words in some language she had never heard. The noise woke Frankie, who blinked and listened and stumbled out of his seat, yelling commands at Panchito. He wanted them to land on some safe airstrip, where there were lights and gasoline. He told the Scorpion they could threaten to burn the airplane, with the little bitch inside it, unless they got fuel.

The Scorpion laughed. Frankie shouted louder. The Scorpion told him to sit down and sleep off his beer. Frankie pulled a pistol out of his belt. A bright-bladed knife flashed out of the Scorpion's hand. Frankie belched and sank slowly back into another seat with his own hot-smelling blood running over his hairy stomach where it bulged out of his shirt.

The Scorpion came back to pull his knife out of Frankie's throat. He wiped it clean on Frankie's shirt and slid it back under his own clothing.

"So what?" He shrugged and grinned at her. "Dumb bastard. We won't need him again."

She hurt inside, feeling Frankie's life pouring out, but she had never found any love that would let her reach him to ease the pain or help his body mend. The dimness of his life flickered into blackness, and his pain was gone.

Panchito drove them on.

"*Quizas,*" she heard him murmur to the Scorpion. "*Si la luz viene—*"

Perhaps, if the daylight came in time, they might come down alive. She wished she could help him feel the shape of the land the way she did, but it was still dark to him. He drove the *avión* on and on, until its roar began to change and break. The Scorpion sat beside Panchito, but he had no skill to drive the *avión.*

The roaring stopped. Panchito spoke to the mother of God. The Scorpion twisted to look back to grin strangely at her. He looked ahead again, and she saw that he was ready to die. All she could hear was the soft rush of air around them. She turned to the dark window, searching for the first pale grayness of day, or perhaps the color of hope. All she found was the redness of danger, suddenly so thick and cold that it was all she saw.

The color of hope was gone.

34

Green Eyes and Pale Hair

He woke with a throbbing head and a patch on his arm where the needle had been. The handcuffs were gone, with Band-Aids to show where they had cut his wrists. The nurse taking his pulse was a neat young woman he hadn't seen before.

"Feeling better, Dr. Belcraft?"

It was a long time since anybody had greeted him so warmly.

"I think so." He frowned at her uncertainly. "Is—has something happened?"

"Something has happened." Carefully calm, she nodded. "The major will be coming in. I'll let him tell you."

She let him use the shower, wash off the stiff and bitter-reeking film of drugs his body had sweated out. She found him a razor and the khakis Miss Hearn had brought him at the Fort Madison hospital, freshly laundered now. Feeling almost human again, he came out of the bathroom to find Kalenka squinting at his charts.

"Well?" Kalenka's piercing stare dimmed his hopes for really good news. "Something to tell me?"

"A new situation." Kalenka nodded. "While you were under sedation, the being you call Alphamega got away."

"She did?" He tried to cover his elation. "Still free?"

"Still missing." Trouble bit deeper into the dark, hard face; Kalenka had seen how he felt. "Though the search will continue."

"When did it happen?"

"Night before last." Kalenka spoke slowly, watching his responses. "Details not yet entirely clear, but we have evidence of an elaborate conspiracy. Some outsider set explosives under the power line. In the dark, the creature somehow slipped out of her restraints and escaped from the lab where she was under study.

"They'd somehow enlisted a man inside. One of our own security people. He released another prisoner, this Mexican convict who had been with Alphamega before her capture. The security man drove them out to the airstrip in his own patrol car. The unidentified outsider caught up with them there—he had kidnapped one of our secretaries and forced her to smuggle him through the gate. The convict is a pilot. They got away in the general's jet."

"I see." Belcraft smiled in spite of himself. "Now what?"

"We still have you." Kalenka's narrowed eyes kept on probing. "Our last link."

"I don't know anything—"

"Maybe you don't." Kalenka shrugged. "Our interrogators say they've milked you for all they can. Not that you can hope for release. But—assuming you'll agree to be reasonable—I can arrange to make things somewhat better for you."

"How much better?"

"Enough to make a difference. An office job that should have a certain interest for you—we might call it occupational therapy. The available creature comforts; a very limited sort of freedom, here under guard and inside the fence . . . if you'll agree to be reasonable."

"Reasonable? What does that mean?"

"Accept the fact that you're better off here than outside." A bleak and fleeting smile. "There's a story in

Fort Madison that you've lost your mind as well as your practice. That you've been unhinged by the effects of a chronic but latent infection with the organism that killed Enfield."

"Huh?" Anger shook him. "Who started that?"

"Who knows?" Innocently, Kalenka blinked. "But your old friends would be terrified to see you coming back. Your practice is dead. Suppliers are seizing equipment you hadn't paid for. Bankruptcy proceedings are in progress. Warrants are out for your arrest on charges of arson and fraud. There's a pending request for your extradition to face them. I've been talking to your attorney, Higgs. He will advise you not to try to get back. Nothing good for you there."

"I see." He caught his breath and peered into Kalenka's wary face. "What is this work?"

"Not too demanding." Kalenka softened his voice, trying to be persuasive. "A job that fits your medical qualifications. Not, however, in the research lab. That's fully staffed, and still discovering nothing. I want you on the crew we've set up to cope with the panic."

"Panic?"

"Call it paranoia." His thin-fleshed features tightened. "A graver danger now, on all the evidence, than the actual organism. People live in terror of getting infected from dust blowing out of the Enfield area or water flowing downstream. They're terrified of what the media are calling 'killer carriers'— people carrying latent infections and not aware of it. Those who think they've been exposed are trying to sue everybody they can. For property damage and mental suffering if they can't think of anything else.

"Your new job, if you take it, will be in public relations. Convincing people that all their fears are groundless. Better take the job."

"Why my job?"

"You're a doctor." Kalenka met his searching stare. "Competent to deal with medical inquiries. If you suspect us of some devious plot, I can't blame you. But you're here to stay. You may as well lend us a hand. Why not?"

"Why not?" He nodded. "Nearly anything would be better than your interrogators."

"Okay, Doctor!" Kalenka tried to seem pleased. "Agreed! So long as you observe the conditions I'll have to impose. You'll be working under Captain Holliday—Sam Holliday, who's in charge of special investigations. He'll assign guards to keep track of you.

"You will wear a badge at all times. You will remain confined to the old campus area. You will obey orders and observe a curfew. You will recognize that the job is actually important, and you will give it the time and attention it deserves. Okay?"

"I don't get the sense of it." He frowned at Kalenka. "All those guards, balanced against whatever work I can do."

"Holliday's problem." Kalenka shrugged. "Or maybe the general's. It's what they want. In any case, we have to keep you well secured."

With no better alternative, he shook Kalenka's vigorous hand. They let him shop in the PX for a few essentials and took him to meet Captain Sam Holliday, a lanky young man with an easy smile and an air of firm authority. Explaining his duties, Holliday let him know that he wasn't going to be quite so free as he had felt.

Guards checked him into his new quarters on the third floor of what had been a residence hall at the college, checked him into the mess hall and out again, into his new office and out again. Walking anywhere he was allowed to walk, he always found a man in uniform not far behind him. Willing enough to answer comments on the weather or the mess hall chow, the guards turned stonily silent when he asked for news of Meg.

His office had been occupied by some vanished professor in the school of business. Dusty maps and graphs and uninviting texts on statistics and economic theory still lined the walls. A computer terminal on the desk loomed forbiddingly at him, but he found at least a dim hint of liberty in the windows, which looked across the old quad, its lawns and shrubs now beginning to sear beneath the late summer drought.

Though the computer baffled him at first, the job itself was nearly too easy. Secretaries brought him stacks of angry or apprenhensive letters. Many were similar, and somebody ahead of him had composed form letters that could be combined to answer most of them with fresh assurances that the Enfield incident had been brought to a safe and final close. When he asked for help with the computer, Keri Grant rapped on his office door.

She was a tall young woman with long pale hair and intense green eyes. Her shape brought muted whistles from the guards, and he thought she could have been an actress. He couldn't help staring, the morning she came in, wondering why Holliday had sent her. He wondered again when the terminal seemed as puzzling to her as it had been to him.

"I took computer science back in Indiana." Her slight accent baffled and enchanted him. "Years ago. The machines are all different now. I think we must experiment."

After his cruel interrogation, the hopeless days and sleepless nights, the threats and blows and electric shocks, the thirst and hunger and hard restraints, Keri Grant seemed unbelievable. Her gleaming platinum hair, the hint of a warm caress in her haunting voice, the scent of her body and his thrill when she touched him, most of all her warm and quick responsiveness—everything about her was totally enchanting.

"Great!" he agreed. "Let's experiment."

Together, they found and read the operator's manual. He learned which keys must be struck to call the form letters out of disk memory, which keys would delete sections that failed to fit the complaint and which would call up paragraphs that did, which keys would return the completed reply to disk memory, tagged with a code symbol that would let the secretarial pool call it out again, verify the name and address, and route it on to the printer.

Now and then he thought of Midge, but the bitterness of her departure was already fading into things 'ong ago. All the events and tensions since that night Vic called from EnGene had driven her image away into an unreal dreamworld, along with the peaceful-seeming past of old Fort Madison and the romantic history of the river and the decayed stateliness of Tara Two.

It was strange to think of his elation on the day just a few months ago when Billy Higgs proposed him for membership in the Fort Madison Rotary Club and he had gone home to Midge with the news of his longed-for appointment to the permanent hospital staff. All that had dimmed into limbo.

Alphamega stayed closer to his mind, a mystery unresolved. Had her unknown rescuers taken her to some safe haven, where she might grow up to find her destiny? Or was she dead in the wreckage of the general's jet on some distant mountain peak? When Keri Grant began to seem a friend, he nerved himself to ask if she could tell him anything.

"Very little—even if the general hadn't told us not to talk." She gave him a companionable grin. "The stolen airplane has not been reported anywhere. They believe it headed south. The pilot had flown drugs from secret airstrips in Mexico. He may have tried to reach one of those strips, but high-altitude photo missions have failed to spot anything that looks like the general's jet anywhere at all. We know he didn't reach any commercial airport. Assuming he landed safe, he may have hidden the plane. He may have flown on to Cuba or Nicaragua—assuming he somehow refueled. He may have crashed."

She stopped to look at him.

"Which leaves you." Her greenish eyes had a quizzical glint. "Their only lead—and I think they're wondering why you were left behind." Her voice grew softer. "The creature means a lot to you?"

"Her name is Meg. And she really does." After too many days of hostile interrogation, he liked talking to Keri Grant. "From that first glimpse, when I found her crawling out of the ashes of the lab, I wanted to love and trust and help her. I don't know why." He added. "Certainly I know nothing about how she escaped."

"I'm sure you don't." She grinned easily again. "Entirely sure!"

She tantalized him. Slow at first to talk about her European years, she began to tell him about colorful characters she had known: hungry artists and kings of industry, hitch-hiking students and penniless exiles and relics of the old nobility.

Drinking in those tales and the way she told them, he began to picture her as a carefree and sometimes daring vagabond in a world of glamorous romance that seemed far indeed from Fort Madison and the schools and lakes and hospitals where most of his life had been spent. She came to seem utterly out of place among the dusty charts and reference books and business texts around them. Wondering again what had brought her here, he had to know her better.

"If you're from Indiana," he asked her, "how come the accent?"

"Five years in Europe." Her quick smile lingered as if she really liked him. "Speaking everything but English. Living on a tiny legacy that's now used up. Learning I hadn't been born an artist or a composer or a novelist. I came back when the lawyers cabled the news that my sister and my parents had been trapped to die here in Enfield."

"My brother died here."

"I know about your brother." Her haunting voice grew warmer. "Jeri knew him—"

"Jeri?" He started. "She was your sister?"

"We were twins." She was sitting beside him at the computer keyboard, and now she reached to lay a sympathetic hand on his. "We seldom wrote, but once she sent a snapshot of Vic. An odd little big-eyed imp in his picture, not at all like you." Her exciting eyes approved him. "They were planning to marry, once his big project was done."

"I never saw her. Only talked to her once—"

Looking into the lively brightness of her oval face, he shook his head and said no more. Her hand on his, her voice in his ears, her fresh scent and her electric nearness transforming everything—he wanted her. Her level eyes met his, the pupils wide and dark, kept looking so steadily and so long that he forgot to breathe. He thought she wanted him.

"A sad thing." Her fleeting half-smile faded, and she took her hand away. "The whole disaster—and they still want us to call it just the Enfield incident!"

Her voice changed.

"I came here asking for information about Jeri and my parents, never imagining what would happen. They arrested me. Detained me. Grilled me for facts I didn't know about Jeri and Vic and genetic engineering. Three horrible days before I convinced them that I'd never been here and never met Vic and never even heard that much about him. And now—"

Her slight shiver was so eloquent of dread that he thought again that she should have been on the stage.

"Now they suspect me again." She let him drop his hand on hers. "You see, I was involved in the escape—"

His breath caught. "Alphamega's?"

"Your pet creature's." The quirk of her lips seemed almost malicious, but she went on to report her own adventure. "The plotters had a man outside—the man who set those charges under the power lines. The night they were ready, he called me out of my apartment in Maxon and made me drive him in through the gate, crouched down in the back of my car.

"My usual bad luck." Her wry expression bewitched him again. "You see, I'd known Frankie Bard, the security man who joined the escape. Kalenka and the general seemed to think somebody must have paid me off. They gave me a bad day under interrogation. I might have been in more trouble, but Captain Holliday stood up for me. He's okay.

"Even now—" A grave little shake of her fine-molded head. "They aren't really satisfied. They wanted me to give up my little apartment and move into the women's dorm here where they could watch me, but Holliday saved me again."

"If you're in trouble . . ." Looking at her, rejoicing in this new sense of trust after his long isolation, he nearly forgot to go on. "I'm in a rather more difficult fix."

"I know." Her warm hand squeezed his. "I've been told to report everything I can learn from you. Anything about contacts you might have with anybody off the base, any evidence that you're really in some sort of touch with your dear Meg."

"Thanks!" he whispered. "Not that I know where she went or anything about her. Nor even expect to. That jet would have been too hot to come down safe in some pasture. If it crashed, she could be dead."

"So she could be." She was nodding slowly as she spoke, green eyes growing remote and cold, as if the notion somehow pleased her. "We may never know."

He drew his hand away, that moment of closeness broken.

35

"The Whore of Babylon"

Next morning Belfast was sitting in his office, staring at another angry letter, this one from a farmer threatening to sue because the claims office had refused to pay him even half the value of his seven prize-winning Holstein dairy cows, dead in the dust of Enfield. Instead of punching up a form-letter reply, he was wondering hopefully if Keri would be coming in. He smiled to greet her, when he heard a rap on the door, and started a little guiltily when he saw Captain Holliday.

"Come along, Doctor. The general wants to see you."

Holliday failed to say why, but the waiting guard escorted him across the quad to the old administration building, almost as if he were under arrest. A black sergeant frisked him for hidden weapons and led him down a corridor walled with glass-cased trophies the college teams had won, at last into a big corner room where Clegg sat at the departed president's glass-topped desk.

In full uniform, medals on his chest and silver star shining, Clegg sat ramrod straight. His rawboned face seemed older, Belcraft thought, bitten deep with new trouble-creases. The guards had left him at the door.

Clegg ignored him for half a minute, then looked up at him and paused as if expecting a salute.

"Good morning," Belcraft said.

"Come in." A commanding hand beckoned him closer, with no invitation to sit. There were, in fact, no chairs in front of the desk. "Major Kalenka informs me that you are now cooperating with us." His voice was loud and flat. "Is that true?"

"I am doing office work."

"I expect something better." Clegg scowled, the dark, deep-sunk eyes narrowed as if to probe for his soul. "Perhaps you know your brother's demon is now at large?"

"Alphamega? Kalenka tells me she has been rescued."

"Rescued?" The cragged head jutted at him. "By whom?"

"I don't know."

"I understand that in the past she has sent you revealing visions?"

"I have dreamed about her, yes."

"Call them dreams!" Abrupt impatience. "Do they come since the rescue?"

He shook his head.

"Why not?"

"I don't know. Unless she is dead?"

"She's alive!" Clegg rapped the words. "I saw her last night. In a vision of my own. The whore of Babylon! I heard the voice of St. John like thunder in the dark sky behind her. He was denouncing her monstrous fornications as he denounced them in his own apocalypse two thousand years ago.

"He warned me that she must die again." The general's somber eyes lifted toward the ceiling, and his voice began to ring. "And yet again, as she has died so many times since he first warned the world against her. She has been burned at the stake. Hanged from the scaffold. Racked and drawn and quartered. Forever in vain."

Listening, Belcraft shifted uncomfortably on his feet, uncertain what to make of such an outburst.

"Her evil is eternal," the solemn tones rolled on. "She has been banished to hell and returned again to every whore-hungry nation, to tempt the innocent and corrupt the righteous and lure every soul she can into Satan's blazing maw. Alive again, reborn through your brother's hell-taught arts, she must die again and yet again, until almighty God decrees her death forever."

Half erect, he leaned across the desk, rawboned hands supporting him.

"Hear them now if you never heard before." His eyes fell to blaze at Belcraft, cold with accusation. "Hear and heed the words of St. John, as they are written in the Scripture and he spoke them to me last night in my vision."

Intoning them, his voice rang with a ritual power.

" 'I saw a woman sit upon a scarlet-colored beast, full of names of blasphemy, having seven heads and ten horns. And the woman was arrayed in purple and scarlet color, and decked with gold and precious stones and pearls, having a golden cup in her hand full of abominations and filthiness of her fornication. And upon her forehead was a name written. MYSTERY, BABYLON THE GREAT, THE MOTHER OF HARLOTS AND ABOMINATIONS OF THE EARTH. And I saw the woman drunken with the blood of the saints and the blood of the martyrs—' "

He broke off the chant, glaring at Belcraft.

"Sir, do you challenge the truth of my vision?"

"Your quotation is probably accurate."

"Dr. Belcraft, you hear this!" High on his forehead, his birthmark burned redly through its makeup. "That witch is sent upon us as a curse from Satan, bearing the sword of Armageddon. God has allowed her fearful weapon to destroy one city, to let us see how it can destroy the world. She has taken now it with her, wherever her demoniac minions have hidden her.

"If we suffer her to live, she will wield that sword again, smiting every nation. Therefore she and all her monstrous iniquities must be banished again from the planet. Look now into the depths of your quivering soul. Don't you see that her reign of sin must be cut short?"

"No—no sir." He had to catch his breath. "If I could see Alphamega as anything supernatural, it would be as an angel of mercy, sent to bring us life and hope and peace—"

"Infidel!" Clegg's hoarse boom cut him off. "Hear the judgment of the Lord, in the words of Saint John: 'The ten horns which thou sawest upon the beast, these shall hate the whore, and shall make her desolate and naked, and shall eat her flesh, and burn her with fire.' "

He scowled across the desk.

"Sir, if you remain too stubborn to perceive the truth, let me explicate. Those ten horns are the company of the holy, that blessed group which I am chosen to command. I implore you to grasp the need of our God-appointed mission, which is to recover that mighty sword for the defense of our own sacred destiny, and to kill the witch before she can deliver it to the hosts of evil that teem all across our idolatrous planet. Understand?"

"No, sir." Belcraft straightened. "That's nothing I can understand."

Clegg came to his feet, the handprint flaming brighter.

"Then, sir, let me try to make it clear." Fury trembled in his voice, and he paused as if to smooth it. "With the same hell-given craft that enabled her escape, that whore of Satan has evaded the CIA and the KGB and the police of all our international friends.

"Others are after her, as desperate as we are. The hellhounds of the KGB have been hunting her with all their own Satanic zeal, hoping to seize her weapon for the evil schemers in the Kremlin, but we know that they also have failed.

"Sir, the simple fact is this: To save the world for God, we must find her before they do. Since other means have failed, we must turn to you. Your own past visions have told you where she had hidden herself. When you dream again—"

"I see." Wryly, Belcraft smiled. "Now I understand."

"If you really do, I commend you." An icy smile. "God will bless you for it. When any vision reveals her present hiding place, you will inform us at once. If you do that, we can cut her abominations short, with that holy sword restored to our own righteous hands. If you fail, all mankind may die before the ultimate wrath of God. Understanding God's commandment and your own sacred duty, you may go."

"Thank you," Belcraft told him. "I'm ready to go."

Glowering like a storm cloud, Clegg waved him toward the door.

In bed that night, Belcraft wondered uneasily if another dream would come. The world's future might be simpler, he thought, if Alphamega lay dead somewhere in the wreckage of the general's jet, all her secrets lost. Awake next morning, he felt a gray depression because there had been no dream.

Keri lifted his spirits when she brought in a new set of form letters she and Holliday had devised to answer a fresh flood of apprehensive letters inspired by rumors that governments all over the world were covering up fresh outbreaks of the Enfield plague.

Her sardonic antipathy for Meg still hurt, but he tried to understand. She had never known Meg. All her family dead in Enfield, wiped out by the same biological mischance, she had no reason to think well of Vic or his work. Her smile for him was still alluring, and she cheerfully agreed when he asked her to join him after work for a drink.

The guards let him take her to the new officer's club, just opened in what had been the faculty lounge. She said she drank no alcohol, but Perrier seemed to give her gaiety enough. Enchanted again with her flattering attention, her shining eyes and her shining hair, her shape and her scent and her voice and the hinted mysteries of her past, he almost forgot his own Scotch and water.

Laughing when he asked about her European years, she recalled a time when she'd thought her talents were for the stage. Hitchhiking across half a dozen countries to catch the Bolshoi Ballet on tour, she had run out of money in Rome and nearly been jailed for begging help from American tourists waiting in line for their mail at American Express. Trying out in London, she had finally been offered Laura's role in a revival of *The Glass Menagerie,* only to have the director turn her down. He said her accent wasn't sufficiently American.

"Me! Imagine! Off an Indiana farm!" She giggled. "Not sufficiently American!"

Guards always near, they walked to the mess hall for dinner together. Listening to another story, this time about the Italian banker who hired her to write his life history and wanted to keep her as his mistress when she wouldn't swallow his tall tales about how he'd bluffed out the Mafia to rake in his millions, he hardly touched his dried beef on toast.

Afterward they strolled around the quad and sat on a bench in front of his residence hall. Listening again, or answering her eager-seeming questions about his boyhood with Vic, he sat longing to be somewhere else with her, and no guards watching. In the darkening dusk, the guard stepped nearer.

"Nearly ten, sir."

"My curfew." He kissed her, and her response intoxicated him. "I have to go inside."

"Shall I come with you?"

He blinked and got his breath. "Would you?"

She kissed him again and called the guard aside. What she said he didn't hear, but the grinning guard waved them toward the door. With him in the narrow room, she stripped and posed for him silently, smiling with candid pride in a form still firmly perfect, delighted with his breathtaken adoration. Half undressed, he had stopped to admire her. Laughing at him, she came to help him out of his shirt and shorts.

They showered together, soaping each other, and he carried her dripping back to the bed, her pink nipples hardening against him. For one painful moment, her casual expertise reminded him that affairs with other men must have filled her European years. In another moment, as her magical hands guided his first deep thrust into the warm wonder of her, that melancholy pang was gone. Lost in the taste and scent and feel of her, even in the exotic accent of her breathless whispers, he forgot almost everything.

When the air conditioning stopped at midnight, shut down while the damaged power lines were under repair, he found a fan in the closet and set it to blow on their naked bodies. Laughing once at his unceasing eagerness, she murmured that he must have been missing Midge.

"I loved her," he muttered. "I really did. But she was never—"

Reaching again for Keri, he said no more of Midge. Once when she breathed a half-malicious query about what other women he had loved, he thought of Meg, wondering how she would feel about Keri if she really were alive to reach him again. He thought she wouldn't care.

He woke at dawn on the narrow dormitory bed, Keri close beside him, breathing gently, splendid even in her sleep, the fan still washing their bodies with humid summer air.

"Meg—"

The whispered name died in his throat. Alphamega had come back in his dream, in Keri's captivating shape.

36

La Madre de Oro

The big gringo with Pancho Torres in the cockpit had been a frightened *loco,* never willing to let him land anywhere for *gasolina.* Not even when he begged for *La Maravilla*'s blessed life. Starving the engines, he kept the *avión* in the air until the first daylight let him find the flatness of a wide *laguna* he remembered from his old days with the *marijuaneros.*

It was dry in this dry season, but not flat enough.

The hot *avión* came down too fast, breaking into many pieces, and now he knew he was dying. His broken chest made him want to moan with every breath, but he found no strength even for moaning. Both his legs were numb and dead, the way the one had been when the gringo at Enfield shot his knee. Flies buzzed around his blood when the sun came up, and they crawled in his eyes. Death would be a kindness.

Yet he tried to stay alive because of *La Maravilla.* He couldn't move to find her, couldn't even call her name. Listening, he heard *cuervos* cawing—waiting maybe for the death they would find in the wreckage—but no sound from her. Perhaps *los santos* had intervened to shelter her. If they had not, he thought she must be dead.

La santíssima! Perhaps already returned to heaven, where her soul belonged. Praying for her happiness among the saints, he listened to the crows. The flies crawled and stung. His chest grew worse with every breath, but for her sake he kept on breathing. The sun rose higher, blazing into his face until all he saw was purple light. He was glad when the aching deadness began to spread from his dying legs, because he had no strength to help her and sleep would wash away *el dolor.*

"Panchito!"

La niñita's blessed voice!

"El pobrecito Panchito!"

She was floating in the air above him, a white-shining light with a shape he had never seen. Perhaps an angel's shape. Her high child-voice was tenderly kind. She had felt his pain and come to ease it.

Her bright-shining wings brushed his face with a coolness that soothed the burning of the sun. Shining fingers of her light reached deep into him, feeling what was torn and was broken. Troubled by what she found, she spoke to *El Doctor* Sax.

He was still far away, where they had had to leave him, lying nearly dead on a bed in the gringo prison. A gringo *medico* was dripping a poison of the brain into his blood, while angry gringos in the uniforms of soldiers shouted demands for all he knew about about *la bruja.* The witch. That was their name for *la niñita.*

The gringos got no answers, because they had poured too much of their poison into his brain. The *médico* was begging them to stop, because he said Belcraft was dying, though not yet entirely dead. *La Maravilla* found life left in his mind, and slowed his dying, and brought him with her back to the *avíon,* where it lay broken in the dry *laguna.*

Working together, they swept away the pain. Belcraft guided her fingers of light, reaching deep to teach the pieces of broken bones how to creep back into place and knit together again. He helped her cause the dying cells to remember the life they had almost lost. Together, they made him live again.

"El pobre querido!"

She felt sad again for the Sax, because when they were done, she had to leave him once more in the far gringo prison. She had reached, however, to help his hurt body heal, and the *médico* was soon amazed at the way his life signs had returned. It hurt her to see the soldiers still demanding what he knew about how *la bruja* got away.

When Pancho Torres woke, *el dolor* was really gone. He could breathe with no pain. Working with whatever she had called from Belcraft's faraway mind, *La Maravilla* had healed him. The dried blood was hard on his face, but the flies were gone, and the blindness of the sun. His head could move. He found his voice and called *la niñita's* name.

Los cuervos squawked and flapped, but he heard no sound from her.

The day was ending, the air no longer so hot. The crows still cawed somewhere near. When he turned his head, he found one of them standing on the bloated belly of the gringo called Frankie, tearing at the face where the eyes had been. One of Frankie's hands seemed to be reaching for the pistol he had tried to fire at the Scorpion while they were still in the sky, but the purpling fingers no longer moved. Frankie was entirely dead.

The sun went down. The crows squawked and flapped away. He called again for *La Maravilla* to speak to him. If she could speak. All he heard was the crows. A sad thing, he thought, if she had given *toda la vida* to restore him, saving no life for herself. At last he slept again, a healing sleep without pain or dreams or any wonders.

The engine sound of *un carro* woke him. Hunger had come upon him in the night, and a great thirst. He thought kind people must have come at last, with water and help for *la niñita.* A jagged fragment of the broken *avión* lay across his legs, but he rolled his head to look.

A pickup truck came jolting across the rough *laguna* floor. It stopped. A man got out. A lean, quick man in greasy jeans, wearing a ragged straw *sombrero.* He raised a grimy hand to shade his eyes from the low sun and stood a long time squinting into the wreckage.

Torres tried to call out when he saw the man turning back to the pickup. In a moment he was breathing *gracias a diós* that his croaking call had not been heard, because the man had come back with a rifle. Crouching a little, he peered uneasily around him again and stopped to aim the gun at Frankie's head.

Frankie's face was hard to look at where the crows had torn it, but the man fired two careful shots into it before he came on to roll the body over and rip a thick billfold out of the hip pocket. Squinting into that, he looked up and crouched back from something else.

He had seen *la niñita.* Pancho moved his head enough to find her. She lay very still on the hard-baked clay beside a broken seat from the broken *avión.* Her long hair was spread on the ground, golden where the sun struck it. Her body was thin and small, nearly bare, the same golden color as her hair. Her face was down. She was not moving.

Qué lástima! He thought she must be dead.

The man was not so sure. He aimed the rifle.

Pancho Torres moved. His legs came free of the broken metal on them. One finger reached Frankie's pistol to drag it toward him through the dust. Lifting it took all his strength, but he was able to swing it toward the man aiming at *la niñita.*

"Panchito, *no!*" He heard her small child-voice, screaming faintly in his head. *"Por favor, no matanza!"*

Sick and shaking, he pulled the trigger. The pistol kicked itself out of his hand and spun away across the dust. The man's head came apart, as ugly as Frankie's. The body crumpled down beside *la niñita.*

He thought he heard her voice again, scolding him for killing, yet he couldn't be sorry. Sweating and trembling, he had to lie flat again until he felt strong enough to stand. He limped to *la niñita* and dropped on his knees to touch her, wondering if she could really be alive.

Her body felt cold, but it had not stiffened. He saw no blood, felt no broken bones, but she had been hurt inside. There was no movement of breath, but he found a pulse in her tiny wrist, very weak and very slow. Perhaps, if he could get her to a *médico,* she might yet live.

Pero no!

He must hide her. The gringos would be hunting then, alerting *la policía,* publishing pictures, offering rewards. Any *médico* would have to inform *los autoridades.* They would soon know that he was a convict who had waited to die for one killing in *el Norte,* and who had left two more dead men here in the wreckage.

He must keep her safe, keep her sheltered, hope she could heal herself as she had healed him. Perhaps there could be aid from the big gringo called *El Escórpion.* Or had he died? Pancho walked around the wreckage, searching, and found footprints in the dust. Tracks of *El Escórpion,* limping and stumbling, wandering away.

Had he gone for help? Perhaps. Perhaps not. Perhaps he was dazed, lost in the desert, perhaps already dead. In no case was he a friend worth trusting. No aid would come from anywhere. If one man had found the wreck, another surely would, but none would be a friend. Honest finders, quick to call *la policía,* would be no better than *El Escórpion.*

Desperate as he had been for any chance at freedom, he had never understood the man, who seemed strange and deadly as his name. In the messages Frankie brought, he had promised far too much. He was going to guide them to friends of his own beyond the reach of the gringo law, perhaps *bandidos* he knew, or to Columbian dealers in *narcóticos.* That had never been clear.

Asking Frankie why *El Escórpion* wanted to rescue

them, he had never liked the answers. They wanted to save *la niñita* from the torture, so Frankie said, because she was a holy being sent by the mother of God to open the way to paradise. Meeting *El Escórpion* only when they were in the air, he had found it hard to see him as a lover of the saints.

Searching for any way to safety, he picked up Frankie's billfold, where the dead man had dropped it. American dollars made a thick sheaf in it. Twenties, fifties, hundreds; he didn't wait to count them. In the dirty jeans, he found a switch-blade knife and a big wad of crumpled pesos. Nothing with any name; he wondered if the dead man had been another convict in flight.

The fenders on the old pickup were broken and much paint was gone, but the tires looked strong. There was oil and *gasolina.* A big plastic bottle in the cab was full of good water. He gulped at it till he felt sick again, and went back to *La niñita.*

"Adónde?"

Where could they hide? San Rosario? In his dreams of escape, back at the prison, he had always taken her there, but those were only dreams. *En verdad,* his mother and father were dead, his brothers and sisters scattered. *El tio Eduardo* would report him to *la policia* for any reward or for no reward at all.

La Madre de Oro?

The Mother of Gold? The great mine men said the old *conquistadores* had found and lost again in *las sierras altas.* So *los viejos* said. His brother Hector had learned about it from a rich gringo who hired him to fly for a search expedition. Following the map far up toward the high peaks, they had found the timbered tunnel dug long ago, but no gold at all.

They had flown above it when Hector was teaching him to be a pilot for *los marijuaneros.* Hector pointed out the twisting mountain road the gringo had repaired, and the little wooden *bohio* he had built outside the black tunnel mouth.

Perhaps the tunnel could hide them until *La Maravilla* healed herself. If they could reach it. But it was far away, among mountains too sharp and dry and bare for farms or even goats. The road might be hard to find, and it might be too bad for the old pickup. Yet it seemed *la mejor esperanza.*

Their best hope. The mine was well known to yield no gold, except perhaps to those who sold maps and went to guide those foolish gringos. It would be a place where few people came.

He carried *la niñita* to the pickup. A tiny burden to him since her holy power had restored him, she hung limp and cold in his arms. Too large for her thin little body, her head sagged back against his heart, her long golden hair streaming loose and bright as the halo of a saint.

The pickup cab had a space behind the seat, where he found a roll of odorous blankets on a clutter of worn tools, cans of oil, and a box of ammunition for the rifle. He laid her there, covered with a tattered blanket, where she would not be easy to see.

He drove away at once, picking a way out of the dry *laguna* and on through hummocks of brush and cactus and yucca toward a highway he remembered. Noon had passed before they reached it, and hunger had become a giddy weakness in him. A few kilometers down the pavement, he pulled off again to rummage under the blankets where *la niñita* lay so very still.

He found a slab of hard dry cheese and a little stack of stale tortillas wrapped in an old newspaper whose torn headlines spoke of ENFIELD, LA CIUDAD DEL TERROR. The water in the plastic bottle had grown hot, but he drank and drove on again, gnawing moldy cheese wrapped in a dry tortilla.

Farther down the lonely pavement, he slowed when he saw the skeleton of a car that lay upside down in the ditch, stripped of wheels and glass and engine. It still had license plates. Nobody else in sight, he stopped to change them for the battered plates on the pickup.

When he had to stop for *gasolina,* he paid with the dead man's pesos. To keep *la niñita* from being seen, he got out of the cab and spoke of seeking work he never found in the city of Chihuahua.

He drove till his eyes began to blur, and stopped at last to sleep in the cab until daylight. When they came to another *pueblito,* he stopped again to spend more of the dead man's pesos for bags of rice and dry beans and other things they might need at the mine.

He had been working a smelter in Chihuahua, he told one of the clerks. He was buying these items for the family he had left on his little farm down in *la tierra caliente.* He bought tools and cans for spare *gasolina.* Filling the cans at a Pemex station, he said they were for his water pump, down on the *ejido.*

They were four days on the way to the mine. One whole day was lost when he searched for the beginning of the road. Floods must have come since the gringo repaired it to go there for gold, because new arroyos were slashed deep across it. He had to move rocks and dig the tops from high clay banks to help the old pickup climb them.

Sometimes *la niñita* drank a little water when he held the bottle to her lax lips, but she ate no food. Her eyes were never open. That feeble pulse still beat when he felt her limp wrist, so slow he always thought the next beat would never come again, but he found no other sign of life.

When at last they came jolting to the door of the mine, the gringo *bohio* outside it had burned, but the tunnel was still open. He cleared the rubble from a place on the floor down inside its cool dimness and cut juniper branches to make a bed for *la niñita.* He spread blankets on it and laid her there, wondering sadly if she would ever wake at all.

A pile of timbers inside the tunnel had not been burned. He parked the pickup against a cliff, leaned timbers over it, and spread juniper branches to hide it from searchers in the air. Aching with fatigue when that was done, he stood a long time looking back down the ridges and canyons they had followed.

The rocky slopes rolled and folded down forever, toward the flat brown desert they had crossed. A far thundercloud towered toward a flattened anvil, draping thin blue curtains of rain that dried up before they reached the barren ground. Here and there, he could trace the dim brown line of the road. Scanning it uneasily, he saw no dust, no hint of any follower.

Yet dark forebodings haunted him. He had done the best he knew for *la niñita,* but it was not enough. She was not healing. Even with all her holy gifts, she could not live forever. He longed for help, but there was none. He wished for *El Doctor* Belcraft, the *médico* whose spirit she had called to help her heal him, but they had left him in the prison.

She had begged *El Escórpion* to bring him, so Frankie had said, speaking in whatever manner she had been able to speak from her torture cell. But *El Escórpion* refused, always saying the escape was already risky enough. There would be no help from Belcraft now—not unless *la niñita* could call him again, however she called from far away.

Walking back into the tunnel, he found that she had moved. Her wasting body had stretched and stiffened. Her eyes were wide open, dark and blindly staring. Her bloodless lips yawned wide, her pale face frozen into a grimace of agony and terror.

"Ay, chiquita!" He tried to rub the stiffness from her icy hands. "What have you seen?"

She stayed cold and hard as a wooden doll.

"No hay peligro!" He kissed her frozen face and tried to comfort her. "There's no danger. I'm here to care for you. *Estamos* okay."

But she was not at all okay. He felt no pulse when he tried her wrist and her throat, heard no beat when he listened for her heart. He thought she must be dead.

He stayed with her all that night, holding her bone-hard body in his arms, singing her the lullabies his mother had crooned to him so long ago in San Rosario, trying to work warmth and life back into her sticklike limbs.

Slowly she relaxed. A faint pulse returned. He laid her down at last and slept beside her on the fragrant juniper. The tunnel grew cold at night. He had spread all the blankets over her, and he woke shivering in a narrow ray of sunlight that struck far down the tunnel.

She had turned golden in it, her silk-fine hair still a shining halo. Her staring eyes had closed. That fixed grimace of dread and pain was gone. Her golden lips moved a little as he watched, parting into a happy-seeming smile.

She was alive, dreaming.

37

Hunter Harris

Mickey's mother had been pure Tarascan Indian, a moody beauty from central Mexico. Though his father used to call her a "black spic slut," his skin was darker than hers. He married her out of a Nuevo Laredo brothel. Sometimes, in spite of himself, Mickey found her living in his memory.

He recalled a time when she'd been happy. Glad to escape the pimps and the madams and men more brutal than Blackie, she had loved their home in the Laredo trailer park, loved the strong perfumes and gaudy jewelry she found in dime stores, loved listening to the wailing Mexican records she used to play on the scratchy phonograph. At first she must have loved her big gringo husband.

Mickey never forgot the ripe scent of her, the yielding feel of her breasts and the salt taste of her skin and the sweetness of her milk. That last ugly night was branded on his brain, the night when she stabbed his father with his own bowie knife and escaped across the line. He had been going on four years old.

Blackie Harris was an alcoholic border lawman, once a Texas ranger. He was drunk and threatening to carve his name into Carmelita's yellow belly when she got the knife and cut him with it. The long blade had gone into the gut, and he nearly died of peritonitis. Never entirely well again, he cherished his hatreds and taught them to his son.

The rest of his life he lived along the line, a cop or a town marshall or a sheriff's deputy when he was sober and fit enough to be employed at anything. Drunk, he sometimes searched the slums and dives for Carmelita, threatening to slice the stinkin' liver out of her stinkin' carcass if he ever found her. He never did. Hating her, hating every Mexican, he still spent his weekends in Mexican bars and brothels when he could find the money.

Growing up in those border towns, Mickey went with him into those same bars and brothels and shared the same passions. He had loved his mother once, and cried when his father beat her, but what festered through his boyhood was the way she had abandoned them both, hurting him more than his father. Searching for her as his father did, he found her again in the smell and taste and feel of the Mexican whores, and he avenged himself when he could.

The revenge went best after he became another lawman, first in the border patrol and then whenever he could find the right sort of job after the patrol discharged him. With experience enough, he began calling himself a special investigator, undertaking private undercover missions across the line.

Those missions were seldom legal but often successful. He had grown up at ease in Spanish and Tex-Mex and Spanglish. He was dark enough to pass himself as a native Mexican, and deadly enough with weapons. When Mexican officials were slow to act on gringo requests or sometimes suspected of corruption, he went across the line to recover stolen property and even to kidnap absconders who were hiding or defying extradition, sometimes even to kill them. Men came to call him Hunter Harris.

Though he earned good fees, his real rewards came

from another sort of hunt. The habit of that had begun when he was still with the border patrol, picking up *mojados.* "Wetbacks." The first had been a girl, perhaps twelve years old, who had become separated from her family when they ran away from the river in the dark. With her long black hair and her thin red dress and her strong perfume, she recalled his mother.

She sobbed with gratitude when he offered to carry her back to her friends in Piedras Negras instead of throwing her in the *calabozo.* He took her back across the river hidden in the trunk of his car and drove on to a lonely place he had found. Her taste and her smell and her feel were like his mother's. Even her screams recalled his mother's screams, when his father was teaching her how to love him. He used his own bowie knife, and buried what was left when he was done.

That was the sort of hunt he loved. While it lasted, the job on the border patrol brought him all the game he dared to catch. The hunting was harder for a time after his discharge, until he found that new career as undercover investigator. Often across the border, with contacts enough in the underworld, he was able to stalk his Mexican meat again.

Those good times lasted until a young girl he had snatched off a school playground turned out to have been the wrong man's daughter. Rounded up, some of his underworld associates confessed what they knew or suspected about him. Better evidence lacking, he was robbed and beaten up and warned to stay out of Mexico.

That was when he came to Enfield.

His summons to see General Clegg came as a painful jolt. He asked the sergeant what was up. Claiming not to know, the sergeant marched him into the general's office, almost as if he had been under arrest, and left him sweating in front of the wide glass desk.

Leafing through a thick manila folder, the general didn't look up. The big nose and jutting jaw and heavy thick black brows reminded Mickey of his father. Standing there, wondering what the general wanted, he felt sick at his stomach, the way he had always felt when his father was going to whip him. Behind him, he heard the sergeant walk out of the room and shut the door. He had to stand rigid to stop his trembling knees.

"So you are Hunter Harris?"

The question startled him. He wanted to sit but he found no chair. The general's eyes were on him, hard and cold as his father's, peering from deep caves beneath the jutting brows. He gulped and got his breath.

"I guess so, sir."

"We needn't guess." The general pushed the folder aside and paused to stare accusingly, the way Blackie used to stop and stare and make him wonder what the punishment would be. "I have a new report from the FBI. They inform me that you got the name from your expeditions into Mexico, hunting fugitives."

"Yes, sir." Nervous, he spoke too fast. "You see, sir, the Mex cops are all out for what they call *la mordita.* The bite. A lot of crooks were paying them off, hiding out in Mexico. My business was bringing them back to American justice."

Not impressed, the general laid a rawboned hand on the folder.

"The report also says you gave up that career after you were suspected of sex crimes—"

"Sir—" His voice was a squeak, and he had to try again. "Sir, please! I was up against desperate enemies. Crooked cops and rotten judges were taking bribes to shelter criminals. Trying to get rid of me, they invented crazy accusations, with no evidence whatever. No charges were ever pressed, but I finally had too much—"

"Calm yourself, Harris." The general waved that big-boned hand. "We're not here to drag skeletons out of your closet. Not yet, anyhow. Our only concern is to establish your special fitness for a very important assignment."

"Yes, sir?"

"Your record seems to fit the mission we have in mind." The general nodded, narrowed eyes still hard. "I believe you know the creature—the demon thing—that survived in the ruins of Enfield?"

"I do." Recollection brought a small thrill of pleasure. "I interrogated her."

"Nearly killed her, I believe."

"I didn't mean to, sir." He talked fast again, the way he used to talk to Blackie, trying to delay the bullwhip. "She ain't human, sir. Her body's all different. It was hard to tell what she could take—"

"Never mind the alibis." The general waved them away. "I'm sorry now that Kalenka had you stopped. At the time, we were still hoping to make the little demon confess her crimes. We were hoping for information about the weapon that devastated Enfield. We got nothing useful. Now she has escaped.

"And you—"

The general paused again to make him wait.

"Your new duty is to finish what you started."

"Sir?" He shook his head. "Do you mean—"

"Kill her!" An odd red mark has begun to show through the gray makeup on the general's forehead. "Kill her! Any way you can. The job may be difficult. As you say, she isn't human. A she-demon, full of hell-given craft. That's why I'm sending you. Your background suggests abilities that should match hers."

"I—I see." He shifted uneasily, still wishing for a chair. "Do you know where she is?"

"They stole my personal airplane." A bitter rasp edged the general's voice. "The wreckage has been located where it crashed in Mexico. They found two bodies in it. Bard, our own security man who sold us out, and a dead Mexican, evidently murdered when he came upon them. The survivors apparently left the scene in the Mexican's vehicle."

"That killer spic?"

"Torres? We believe he's still with her." The general

nodded. "Along with this other conspirator, not yet identified. The man who blew up the power line and kidnapped the Grant girl to get through the gate."

"The spic—" Mickey caught his breath, feeling better. "The spic would likely run her back to his drug-dealing pals. Maybe hiding out in some marijuana patch."

"Could be." The general grunted. "The Mexican authorities have been cooperative, rounding up a lot of known drug dealers. So far, that demon-bitch has been too clever for them, too smart for the CIA and military intelligence. That's why we're sending you—"

"Sir, them damn' gizzard-lips—" Alarmed, Mickey scowled and licked his own thick lips. "They hate me. Lied about me and drove me off the border, just because I used to hunt their outlaw friends. They'd kill me—"

Impatiently, the general waved to stop him.

"You will be in western Mexico, where I don't think your past adventures were ever well known. We will give you a new identity if you think you need it, with documents and funds." A smile like Blackie's, when he was summing up sins to justify the bullwhip. "If you get the job done."

"Trust me, sir!" He had always promised to do better. "If you've located them."

"Not yet. Tracing them was difficult. Impossible, in fact, until the demon-bitch gave herself away. She's somehow able to contact Belcraft through sendings we don't understand. You know Belcraft? Our prisoner here, the brother of the man—that apprentice of Satan who called her out of hell. We have an agent who has become intimate with him."

"The tall blonde?" Harris licked his lips again. "Keri Grant? We had orders to let 'em screw."

"My orders." He didn't much like the general's grin. "They screwed, as you put it. She's got him conned. Now she reports that he's had another sending."

"You know where they are?"

"Somewhere in the mountains of western Mexico, hiding in a cave."

"Somewhere?"

"Up to now, that's all we know. The she-demon was hurt in the crash. Lying in that cave, in what Belcraft calls a coma. Conscious, but paralyzed and unable to speak—the devil knows how she sends the visions."

"If she can do that—" Harris shivered. "What else—"

"We don't know her powers." The general's face set harder. "That's why she has to be killed—before she grows to be something worse. You were able to injure her here. If she can be hurt, she can be killed."

"If—if I can find her."

"We have a plan." The general's voice boomed louder again. "The bitch wants Belcraft with her. Grant says she loves him—if you can imagine a demon in love. Since the vision, he's desperate to reach her. We're planning to facilitate his escape. He seems to expect more sending, visions guiding him to wherever she is. Grant will go with him and keep us informed."

"Can't she—"

"You're the killer." A brittle rap. "Grant says she isn't. Her assignment is simply to stay with him and guide you to the monster.

"Yours is to kill her, any way you can."

"Ok—okay!" The word tried to stick in his throat.

"Get it done!" The voice of Blackie Harris. "We're arranging support, and your nation will be grateful. Private sources have put up a reward for you. Five million tax-free dollars, waiting in secret bank accounts, when we know you've got it done."

"Thank you. Thank you, sir!" Thinking about five million dollars, he forgot Blackie Harris. "I'll get it done."

38

Little Sister

She had left her body because it hurt too much. The thread that tied her to it frayed thin with pain, and she drifted now in a dark and dreadful emptiness. Panchito was somewhere far away, doing what he could to tend her broken body and sad because he knew no more to do.

While he slept on the bed of good-smelling tree limbs, she had touched his mind long enough to dip into a dream. It had been a happy dream of San Rosario, in which she came back with him to his happy *familia* in the small mud town, which was still the way it had been that happy time so long ago when he was only a *niñito.* The dream had vanished when he woke, and her link to him was broken.

She had touched Sax once, soon after the *avión* fell. Lying broken with Panchito among the broken parts, she needed Sax. Reaching back through the dark, she found him in the far *cárcel,* sleeping from poisons of the mind the gringos were pouring into his blood.

His mind was still alive, and she brought him for a little while to the place of the accident. He was able to teach her what she must do help Panchito heal himself, but Sax had no knowledge to aid her own body's healing. Only the dear Vic, who shaped it, had ever known its nature and its ways of working, and Vic was dead. She knew no skills to tend herself.

Since Sax awoke, that last link snapped, she had been lost in the dark. In spite of Panchito's anxious care, the thread to her own poor body was worn too thin to last. When it was gone, there would be only the empty dark, with nothing anywhere she could ever reach or see.

A cold and heavy sadness wrapped her.

Longing for Vic or Panchito or Sax, she thought she was more alone than they could ever be. They had all been born from fathers and mothers. Vic and Sax had grown up together, sometimes fighting but always loving each other. Vic had loved his Jeri, who smiled when he came home and called the lab when he was late.

In the prison, she had found Sax dreaming of his Midge, who once had been his beloved *esposa.* Even poor Panchito, growing up long ago in that dark little adobe *casita,* had loved and been loved by *la madre* and *el padre* and *sus hermanitos.*

She yearned for kinship. It was a joy she could never know, because no other being would ever be like her. She had no father, no mother, no brothers or sisters or kindred. No mate for her had ever existed. Alone forever, she could have no children to love her or be loved.

Lost in that dark nothingness, she clung to recollections of love. The dear Vic, loving her at first because he loved his grand dream of what he wanted her to be and then because he felt her love, Vic had been her father and her mother. Though the dear Sax and the poor Panchito had been strangers at first, who might have hated her for being strange, she had found the spark in them that she could kindle into devotion.

But she was not human. She had never been meant to be. Panchito and Sax had been troubled and sometimes frightened by her strangeness. Now even they were gone. Dying alone, never doing or even knowing the great work Vic had planned her for, she was useless, her life-spark wasted.

"Little—little sister?" She caught the voice calling from somewhere in the blackness. It was far away and very slow, because it had to wait while it searched for words in her. "Where—where are you, little sister?"

Trembling, she fled from it, away into the dark.

"Little sister?" The voice was far behind and very faint. "We feel you somewhere, little sister. We may seem strange to you, but you must not be afraid. We search for you with love."

She wanted to answer, because the voice seemed so tender, yet she had no strength to speak, no way even to know or say where she was. Listening, she waited to hear it again.

"Little sister? Answer—answer if you can!"

She tried to speak, but no voice came.

"Where are you, little sister?"

"Here—" She was gaining strength from its glow of love. "Here I am."

"Wait for us!"

She waited, and a shining thing came out of the darkness. It had no shape she had known, though the wings of it made her think of the *mariposa* she had chased one morning when it fluttered across the garden where Panchito had kept her hidden from the gringos. It had no color she had seen, but it was brighter than *el arco iris* he had once pointed out, that great bridge of light bent across the blue rain-curtain beneath a thundering cloud.

"Who—" The strangeness and the beauty of it shook her voice. "What are you?"

"You have no words for what we are."

"Are you *de fuego?*" She tried not to be afraid. "I see you shining like *el fuego en la noche.* Like fire in the night."

"If you see us as fire, we are fire." It seemed happy with the word. "You may call us the people of fire."

"I am Meg," she said. "Alphamega. *El querido* Vic gave me that name. Do you have a name?"

"None that you have learned to say. You may call us—" She felt it touch her mind. "Call us Elder Brother."

"Hóla!" She wanted to smile. "Hello, Elder Brother."

"Hello, dear Meg." It brushed her with its wings, and she felt a glow of love. "We have come to find you because we felt your troubles. We welcome you to live with us, if you can live without your body and leave it where it is."

"No! No! Nunca!" Her voice came like a whisper. "I must not leave it to die alone. Without it, I can never finish the work Vic created me to do. I must not die!"

"Never fear us, little sister. We will never harm or hinder you."

"Can you—can you help me?"

"We wish we could." She heard sadness in the voice. "But your world is unknown to us. We cannot reach it, even to help you save your body. You must learn to live without it. Why should your old world matter to you now?"

"Because of what the great Vic planned me for." Her voice seemed to flicker in the dark like a candle in the wind. "He told me he had shaped me to help that poor world because he loved it. Men around him were making bad mistakes. He tried to warn them, but their blunders destroyed his dream. He died in the lab before he ever told me what I am to do. Now nobody knows.

"A menos que—" Looking again at the being of fire, she felt the warmth of goodness. "Unless you know how to teach me."

The dancing colors dimmed.

"We have no way to see your world." The voice seemed saddened. "Though we had felt the glow of your mind, we could not feel or reach you while you were in your body. We cannot tell you what your task is, but we can give you new strength and understanding if you will come with us."

"Can I ever return to wake my body and learn the work Vic meant me for?"

"Perhaps," Elder Brother said. "If you grow strong enough. If your body lives. If you can find the way."

"Take me. Show me your land."

"We have no land."

"Cómo?" The rainbow wings were reaching to touch her, but she shrank away, afraid of their strangeness. "How can that be?"

"We know of land," he told her. "Many of us were born on worlds not too different from your own. We are those who learned to leave them."

"I—" She trembled. "I have never learned."

"Let us teach you. Let us lead you."

His fire-wings wrapped her, warm with love, and their power moved her fast and far. When they slowed again, great new stars were blazing in the darkness, more glorious than *las estrellas* that Panchito used to show her over the garden at night. One seemed nearer than the rest. They swam toward it. She saw that it was not a star, but a spinning pool of fire.

The wonder of it dazzled her. It was brighter than the sun and flat like a plate. Close to the center, it whirled very fast. Farther out, more slowly. The colors of it were very strange, like none she had known, and more splendid than the rainbow.

She felt afraid again.

"We are safe, little sister. Nothing here can harm you."

"It seems very terrible." She trembled again, and the bright wings wrapped her. "I thought it was a star. Panchito says the stars are terrible fires, like great *bombas* far in the sky."

"Once it was a star." His voice felt warm and calm. "A very great star, greater than your sun. When most of its burning stuff was gone, the star exploded. The shell was blown away. The core fell in upon itself, making something so heavy that it cannot, be seen, because its rays cannot escape. The fire you see comes from broken atoms falling into that dark heart. Perhaps it is a terrible thing, but it also feeds our lives."

They came nearer. The disk of fire spread very large and very bright, even more terrible now since she knew that it could eat a star. She began to find new points of light flying like moths all around it.

"Our city," the bright being said. "Your own city now, if you wish to stay."

The city had no land beneath it, no houses like those she had known. She saw flying bubbles of something like glass, shimmering with colors she had never seen. She saw other shining shapes she had no names for. Some were joined together; others floated all alone.

"The children of fire." He moved a blazing wing to point them out. "Your own people now, if you will stay."

She found the children of fire. They made small swarms like *las abejas,* the bees that had come buzzing one day to a tree near the garden. They moved faster than bees on their own shining wings, which had more splendor than the *mariposa*'s wings. Some looked like Elder Brother. Others were different. All of them changed as they flew. Some came from far away, diving toward the fire as if they had grown hungry for it.

One danced out to meet them. It seemed larger than the rest, the light of it brighter. Its wings opened wide to greet her.

"The Father-Mother," Elder Brother told her. "Coming out to welcome you."

"Bienvenida, hijita!"

Father-Mother's voice was like the songs of *las pajaritas* that used to sing in the trees beyond the garden. She felt glad to hear the soft Spanish words, which it must have found in her own mind.

"I am Meg." She let the strange-blazing wings fold around her, and she rested in the power of their love. "I like you. But how can I be your daughter? *El querido* Vic made me in the EnGene lab. There is no other being like me. There will never be."

"Dear little Meg, you do not understand." Father-Mother spoke with no sound at all, yet with a voice that seemed deep and warm and rich with love. "We are all of us your kindred, closer to you than your Vic or any being on the world where your injured body is, because you are what we are.

"We no longer require feeble body-shells like the one in which your own maker formed you. We live and feel and move in the dark radiance that flows from our dark star. We felt you growing toward our way of being, as most of us have grown. That is why we brought you here."

Feeling too happy to speak, she let the blazing wings caress her.

"Peace, little one. You have come home."

"No—no puedo—" Her heart was torn. "It hurts to say it, but I cannot stay. *Gracias a todos,* but I must go back to my own home to do what I was made to do. If you can help me learn . . ."

Her voice wavered and stopped, because the world of Vic and Sax and Panchito seemed so far away, lost behind her somewhere in the dreadful dark, so far she was afraid she could never even find it.

"If we can," Father-Mother said. "We will teach you anything we can. But your planet is so far that even the glow of your own new life was hard for us to feel."

"—stay." She felt Elder Brother's gentle voice. "You must stay, because your body is hurt too badly to serve your mind again. Here, we can feed your new life until it grows stronger. Without us, Little Sister, you can't survive alone."

"We love you." Father-Mother's radiant wings embraced her again. "We are your people now."

"Not yet." It was hard to pull herself away. "Because my own world needs me. Its sad people are still my own. *El querido* Vic used to talk about its troubles. He created me to heal them, though he died before he ever told me how. I must go back to do what I can, even if I die."

"We want you with us." Their wings grew dim. Darkened, she thought with sorrow for her. "You must stay till you are stronger."

"I must go," she told them. "While my body lives."

Yet she felt too weak to leave. She stayed to let them guide her into their city, which was a great ring of strange-colored wonder, spinning very slowly outside the terrible whirlpool of fire that had swallowed a star. Some of its fire-winged people came out of their bright homes to wrap her in their loving rainbow wings, and she longed to remain here in the shelter of their love.

"We come from far-scattered worlds," Elder Brother told her. "Worlds of land, some like your far planet. Worlds of water, with no land at all. Worlds of gas, whose people have to float or soar forever. We are those who outgrew those planets when our minds learned to tap greater energies.

"You can do that, Little Sister, here in the dark light of our black star. The change to the new way of life may be hard for you, as it was for most of us. When your mother world is all you know and all you love, leaving it is never easy, but—believe us, Little Sister! We can make you happy here.

"You may find us strange at first, but our star is the world you were born for. We have great wealth to offer you, all the wealth we brought when we left our first homes behind. We can teach you their old sciences and their ancient arts. We can help you know and feel the hopes and joys and fears of many different peoples, of empires rising and races dying. We can help you share the history and the drama of many thousand worlds scattered all across the great galaxy, many of them older than your own. Perhaps, Little Sister—"

The bright voice changed.

"Soon, perhaps, the problems of you own little planet will no longer seem—"

"Perdóname!" She had felt a fog of sudden danger growing thick and cold around her far body. "I can wait no longer. You have been *muy amable.* I wish I could

stay here in your world with no land. But I feel great new danger to my own far body. I must go while I can."

"Not yet, *hijita*!" Father-Mother begged her. "Not till you are stronger."

"If I don't go while my body lives, I can never find the way."

"Wait!" Elder Brother seemed distressed. "Please, Little Sister! Wait till you are stronger, and we can guide you."

"I have a guide," she said. "In the new danger-light I feel where my body is."

"If you go, we may never find you—"

"No le hace." She pulled free of his clinging wings. "No matter. I must find my work and do it."

She flew away alone.

"Come back!" His calling voice grew faint behind her. "Come back, Little Sister! Come back if you can!"

The shining splendors of their city faded behind her, and then the dreadful beauty of that great wheel of light around the dark and dreadful pit that swallowed stars. Far from the power of its dark light, she felt her strength and courage draining away.

Again she was all alone.

She had let them take her too far. The thread she must follow was drawn too thin. The danger-cloud she had felt around her body was only a faint red fleck in the world of nothing else at all, but perhaps, *con buena suerte*—

Perhaps, with luck enough, it could guide her home.

39

"Somewhere, Dying . . ."

The airport lights were still out, but Anya heard more sirens coming. The car keys lost in the dark, all she could do was wait—and wonder. Besides Sam Holliday, who else could have known she wasn't Keri Grant? Who had been clever enough, bold enough, to steal the general's jet? Who else had got aboard it?

Patrol cars came roaring and skidding around her.

"Hey? Who the hell are you?"

Post security men were dragging her out of the car. Baffled and furious, they wanted to know who she was and who she had seen and what had brought her back from Maxon after midnight. Alphamega was missing! Clegg had exploded when he heard about it, more perturbed by the escape than by the theft of his jet. Her part in the break had to be explained. Still shaking, still bewildered, she whispered what she could about her whispering abductor, but nobody believed what she said.

Not till Holliday arrived. Grim-faced and edgy, he took her to his office to question her himself. Still she had no answers that pleased him or anybody. Something about the queer, breathless rasp of her captor had been half familiar, but she had seen the man only as a shadow in the dark and she found no name.

"I've no idea who it was," she told him. "The guy knew a lot about me, but he spoke in a queer hoarse whisper and never let me see his face." She shivered. "He really meant to kill me if I didn't go along."

Holliday seemed more sympathetic than anybody else, but the sun had risen before he let her go home. Her head throbbed. Groggy from fatigue and stress, she was still too jittery for sleep. Two aspirins didn't help. She was stirring instant coffee into a cup when her phone rang.

"Grant?" The twangy Yankee drawl of her new Kremlin contact, sharp with impatience. "Where've you been?"

"A problem at the post." That was all she wanted to say.

"Whatever happened, I want a full report." His voice turned imperative. "I'll pick you up for lunch."

"Okay."

She had to agree, though she disliked everything about him. A short, bouncy little man, he wore a neat black goatee and bore a ripe aroma of chronic flatulence never entirely disguised by the Burleigh burning in his underslung briar. Mysterious about his actual name, he signed himself and his books "T. Bradleigh Barlow." A writer of what he called exposés, he had a contract with a small New York publisher for *The En-Gene Mystery: Omen of Doom.*

With no quarters available at the post and General Clegg hostile toward his reputation for lurid sensation, he had set up his word processor in a little house in Maxon, just across the alley from Anya's own garage apartment. They parked their cars on the same vacant lot. Playing a role of casual friendship, he took her out for occasional meals at Juan Wong's Taco Chinatown or sometimes to the Norman Towers in Piedmont.

On those drives, he had received her reports and

delivered new instructions from the Center. She disliked being alone with him in the car. Trying to play the same sort of romantic rogue he had tried to write about in novels nobody would publish, he pushed himself upon her until she looked him in the eye and told him she would kill him if he touched her again. Afterward he appeared to enjoy the harsh messages he brought her from Moscow.

At noon today, she let him pick her up. Juan Wong's place was only half a dozen blocks down the highway. He parked there and turned, scowling through his heavy-rimmed glasses, to talk in the car. Somehow, he had already learned as much as she knew about the escape. Trying to blame her for anything he could, he still appeared pleased with the trouble he foresaw for her.

"So you've fumbled again." Nodding, he paused to relight the briar. "I'm afraid we'll have to find a more competent agent to complete the mission."

"Not yet," she told him. "I'm still the agent in place."

"A double agent." Puffing, he squinted critically through the smoke. "Sometimes we must use them, but we never trust them far. In this situation—" He paused to puff again. "You say you were kidnapped and forced to drive that guy to the plane. Which looks pretty odd. How do I know—how does the Center know you're playing straight?"

"You're a courier." She sniffed at his odor. "Nothing more. You have no authority over me."

"I forward reports." He smirked. "My own as well as yours. I tell you now that I can't continue to express any confidence whatever in you or your mission."

"Reporting on me is not your business."

"It will be." He blew smoke in her face. "When the Center begins to see through your ploys. Look at this Holliday. You claim you trust him because he's Clegg's son. On the face of it, a pretty ridiculous reason. The Center has never really understood why he should defect to you."

Though he had the air conditioner on, she rolled down a window.

"He didn't." Her voice was carefully even. "What we have is a very limited alliance. Clegg was fighting for control of a biological weapon. Holliday and I agreed that the world will be a better place with no science of the sort that killed Enfield. The secret of what happened seems to exist only in that synthetic monster. We agreed that she ought to be destroyed.

"That's the situation as I explained it to the Center. I believe the matter was debated in high circles. Perhaps even in the Politburo. Certain persons were reluctant to abandon our own battle for the weapon. They were told, however, that we had very little chance to beat the *Glavni Vrag.* Better erase the secret than let them get it. The final consensus was to support my present mission. To eliminate that genetic creation."

"With what results?" Rasping the accusation, he stopped to turn the air conditioner higher. "You have let some unknown group kidnap the creature and disappear with her. God knows who they are or where they took her!"

"God?" She grinned at him. "Or Lenin?"

"Comrade, your own predicament is too grave to joke about." He stabbed the pipestem at her. "You have wasted our resources and our time, achieving less than nothing. Unless I can report something more positive within a very few days, the Center is prepared to send a separate force to kidnap Belcraft for our own interrogation."

"Here in America?" She let her eyebrows rise. "That wouldn't be easy."

"Neither was Stalingrad." He might have been quoting the lurid spy novels he couldn't sell. "Mother Russia is desperate. Comrade, have you let yourself forget the unsolved mystery of what killed Enfield? A holocaust that could spread to all the world. You are rolling dice for the life of all mankind."

Forcing a smile for another driver parking beside

them, he was moving to get out of the car. With no appetite, she made him drive her back to the apartment.

"Play your own game," she told him. "I'll play mine."

Watching him drive away, she shrugged and let her thoughts drift back to Saxon Belcraft. Perhaps the world's future would in fact depend on her own loaded dice. Perhaps it wouldn't. She had trained herself not to fret too much over uncertainties she couldn't control. Whatever the case, she enjoyed her game with Belcraft.

As a sex-armed missile of the KGB, she had been targeted on various men, none so exciting. Old Jules Roman had been the only one she liked or respected. She enjoyed his devotion and the luxury he lavished on her, but he had been decades past his prime before she captured him. His occasional attempts at sex had been humiliating failures. She had always pitied him, and his final disposition in Moscow seemed almost an act of mercy.

Belcraft was a far more tempting target, young and vigorous enough, entirely likeable. His naiveté sometimes amused her. All he knew was medicine and the rural Ohio in which he had grown up, a world so different from her own that she found it hard to imagine, but so near the rural Indiana she claimed for her birthplace that she always felt afraid to talk about Keri Grant's fictitious childhood.

He intrigued her with the mystery of his contacts with Alphamega. What sort of thing was the creature? How had she come to rule him so totally? How had she made herself matter more to him than his medical practice and even his life?

Belcraft himself was another puzzle. She had lived in a world of cynics, and she had been moved to surprise and sometimes to pity by his fascinated belief in her tales of Keri's vagabond years in Europe. Spinning them, watching his innocent envy of the imaginary worlds she was describing, she found herself afraid she might come to like him too much. Sex with him was the best she had known, even on that hot night when the air conditioning died.

"You know, Anya, I'm falling in love." He told her that next morning, coming naked out of the shower and erect again with the recollection. He looked at her oddly, shaking his head. "I just woke from a funny dream. I thought you'd turned into Alphamega."

Sitting up in bed, she uncovered her breasts to divert him from her own trembling tension.

"Have you been bewitched?" She tried to seem merely malicious. "Even after last night, you'd really like to exchange us?"

"She haunts me." He sat down beside her, soberly staring at nothing. "At that first glimpse, crawling out of the ruins, still only a little pink worm, she took hold of me. I don't know how she did it. Or what she is. Or what Vic designed her to be. I'll probably never know. I do know there will never be anybody like her."

"Does the dream—" Trying not to seem too eager, she stopped to smile at his jutting penis. "Does it mean she's still alive?"

"Just a dream." He shrugged and drew her toward him to kiss her nipples. "No message. With no trace reported, I suppose she's probably dead."

She saw his penis wilting.

The following night was equally hot, but the air conditioner kept on purring and she found his pent-up vigor undiminished. Talking with a boyish sort of candor about whatever crossed his mind, he had begun revealing a wry wit he had always felt to be dangerously unbecoming in a serious young physician, showing a brain so keen that sometimes she trembled with a new terror of detection.

They woke together in the cooler-seeming dawn, and she hoped he would want her again. Instead, he slid out of her arms to sit bolt upright in bed.

"Another dream." She was uncovered, but he

frowned blankly past her. "The sort Clegg calls a sending."

"A vision?" She tried not to seem unduly anxious. "Do you think that's possible?"

"Nothing I can understand." He shrugged uneasily. "I thought she was calling me. She is terribly hurt and in desperate trouble somewhere."

"Somewhere?"

"That's the problem." His frown bit deeper. "I saw her in a sort of cave. There was a rock roof above her, with rough timbers supporting it. Day was just breaking, gray sky outside. She lay on a pile of juniper branches—I could even smell them. That Mexican she calls Panchito was with her, trying to give her water.

"She's paralyzed. Unable to speak or even swallow. What she really needs is help from Vic. She came to me because I'm Vic's brother and a doctor and because in another dream or vision or whatever it was she thought I had helped her diagnose and heal Panchito. He had suffered broken bones and internal injuries in the fall of what she called *el avión—"*

His breath caught.

"That must—that must have been the general's jet! Down somewhere. Panchito hurt and dying, the way she was. With whatever medical knowhow she thinks she got from me, she was somehow able to save him, but she doesn't understand her own body well enough to heal herself. She was hcping I'd learned enough from Vic to help her."

His whole body drooped in dejection.

"Of course Vic hadn't told me anything useful. The dream was over when I had to tell her that. She had no strength to hold me any longer." His staring eyes looked stricken. "Keri, she's somewhere, dying . . ."

"And you don't know where?"

"Mexico." He spoke slowly, frowning in thought. "That's where Torres would want to go, and I did get a clear impression that the crash was there. If it happened after the fuel had run out on their flight from Enfield, we have at least a suggestion of the distance. The cave suggests mountains. An area high and dry enough for juniper."

Silent for a moment, he looked hard at her.

"All pretty vague. Not much to go on, unless I get another message. But Meg needs me. Terribly! I'm afraid I couldn't do anything, but I'd give anything to get there. If I could possibly escape—"

"Maybe—" She shivered inside. "Maybe I could help you."

"If you could—" He sagged again, shaking his head. "But the odds would be too ugly. Keri, I couldn't let you risk it. No reason you should."

"I—" She had to catch her breath. "I love you, Sax. Reason enough."

His searching eyes probed so deep that she shuddered again, afraid he had seen the truth. But then his own breath went out, and he reached to pull her body to him. She felt the thudding of his heart and knew he believed her.

That morning at work she called Sam Holiday to report a bug in the new letter-framer software. That phrase was a code signal. He called her to bring the latest printouts to his office. She shut the door behind her and told him about Belcraft's dream.

"Very little we didn't already know." Resting his feet on the cluttered desktop, he blinked at her doubtfully. "The Mexicans found what was left of the jet after our search planes spotted it. Down on a dry desert lake. Two bodies in the wreckage. We've got our own agents there. They've identified one of the dead as Bard, the missing security man. The other looked Mexican, but it wasn't Torres. Possibly the unidentified man who kidnapped you."

He scratched his sandy head.

"No sign of Torres or the creature except the tracks of a vehicle that drove out of the lake, to a highway that has a lot of travel. So far, they've got no way to trace the vehicle. It could be anywhere in Mexico by now."

"A cave," she said. "In some dry mountain region where juniper grows."

"Which is nearly anywhere in western Mexico."

"Belcraft's hoping for another dream. He says she called because she needs him. He'd do anything to reach her. I told him I'd try to help set up an escape—"

"You did?" He nodded, admiration in his eyes. "You'd go along to kill the creature?"

"Not that." Soberly, she shook her head. "I've done hard things in the line of duty, but I've got limits. I couldn't murder that creature, human or whatever. What I can do—if I do get the breaks—is to guide some professional to finish the job."

"Maybe—" He took his feet off the desk and sat up to face her. "I see a lot of tricky complications, but nothing else has got us anywhere. Could be—" He nodded slowly, tugging at the lobe of his ear. "Could be our best chance, if I can get the general's okay on it."

40

Agent of the KGB

Two days later, Sam Holliday drove Anya to the old college administration building to get the general's approval. A black sergeant escorted them past the glass-cased athletic trophies into the big-windowed office and left them standing in front of the glass-topped desk. Clegg scowled across it.

"Grant?" His accusing boom startled her. "You are the young woman suspected of complicity in the monster's escape?"

"I am Keri Grant—"

"Sir!" Sam Holliday was already protesting. "She has been fully cleared."

"So I'm told." The deep-sunk eyes pierced her again. "I hope this new scheme is not another such plot, invented to aid another escape."

She felt herself flushing.

"Ask Captain Holliday." She let her voice rise. "I'm not here to be accused."

"Sir, please!" Holiday caught her arm as if to shield her. "They will be under surveillance. Own own hit man in constant contact. I trust Miss Grant. She's aware of our duty to extirpate this menace to every nation."

"That is true." She met the general's eyes. "I know

the mission is uncertain. Unlikely to succeed unless Belcraft gets another vision to guide us to that cave. I suppose there will be danger. But if the creature has to be destroyed to prevent another Enfield, or something worse, I'm willing to face the risks."

"Sergeant!" He called at the door. "Bring Corporal Harris in."

"The hit man," Holliday told her. "You'll be in touch by radio."

She decided not to say she knew him. When the black sergeant brought him in, he gave no sign that he knew her. His thick dark hair was bright with oil and combed straight back. The black mirror sunglasses hid his eyes and made his expressionless Indian face an ominous mask. She shrank uneasily from his unreadable stare.

"Mickey Harris, Keri Grant." Clegg called their names in a loud drumbeat voice. "You may not meet again, but I wanted you to see each other. Captain Holliday will brief you on the mission, but I want you to know its importance. For the safety of the world, that synthetic she-demon has to be destroyed. Understand?"

"I do," she said.

"Trust me, sir!" Harris came to military attention. "I'll slaughter the bitch!"

"We'll trust you for that."

"About my payoff—"

"My staff will set up your guarantees." The general turned from Harris to face her. "Anonymous private sources are putting up rewards. Five million each, payable upon due proof of success." He scowled again at Harris. "But if you fail—"

His heavy voice fell.

"Don't fail!"

He beckoned the sergeant to show them out. Later, alone with Holliday, she protested bitterly.

"Why that—that slimy cockroach! That's what the other guards call him. I see why. Those black mirrors! And the knife he wears under his shirt—I know weapons, and I could see the bulge of it. The way he looked at me! Thinking how he'd love to cut my body up. Made my flesh creep!"

"His special hobby." Holliday made a face. "So it seems. Cutting women up. Young women when he can catch them young. Takes his time, like a very sadistic cat. There's something else in this FBI report. Something so gruesome it's hard to believe. New testimony from a Mexican source that he used to suck their blood while they were dying."

"Clegg—" She shivered. "Does Clegg know that?"

"He's seen the reports. Of course the guy was never convicted of anything. Skipped out of Mexico and left the border to get away from the rumors. The FBI has turned up evidence to nail him, so I'm told. That's what got him the assignment. The general wants that creature hunted down and killed. He's convinced that Harris has the special expertise the job calls for."

Silent for a moment, lips drawn tight, Holliday added: "I didn't want to wish him on you. The general's choice."

That night she left her car with the trunk unlocked under Belcraft's third-story window in the residence hall. Their plans were complete. The escape vehicle was to be waiting at a rest stop on the Maxon highway. Harris would be parked where he could watch and follow. Holliday had arranged funds and travel documents.

Too tense to eat, she and Belcraft skipped the mess hall dinner. He drank two beers and she had a Perrier at the club. They danced a few times to the jukebox and went back to his room to wait for a cold front forecast to arrive at ten. It came late. Midnight had passed before the sudden rainstorm struck. The phone range. Belcraft answered.

"The Maxon police," he told her. "Fire at your apartment."

"Our cue," she told him. "Let's go."

The residence hall had been reserved for women

students, the visiting hours evidently too strict to suit them. Belcraft had found a well-worn rope ladder in the closet. Opening the window into a gust of rain, he rolled it out. She ran down the stairs, told the guard huddled in the doorway that her place was on fire, and darted past him into the driving rain.

A lightning flash showed her the ladder swaying in the wind, Belcraft scrambling into the trunk. She slammed the lid on him and drove into the street through drumming hail. The guard at the gate listened with a half-restrained leer to the story that her place was on fire, but he let her go on.

They were out of the storm before she reached a rest stop. The escape car was a small brown Buick, left standing by a picnic table. She parked beside it and let Belcraft out of the trunk. He gave her a delighted kiss, and they scrambled into the Buick. She drove them away, toward Maxon and Mexico.

The rearview mirror showed her the lights of another car, following toward the highway at a cautious distance. Recalling Mickey Harris, his dark, high-cheeked face and those dark mirror-lenses and the ominous bulge of his hidden blade, she couldn't help shivering.

She lost him when she could in the traffic on the interstate. Their reservations had been made in different motels. She didn't see his car again, but now and then she picked out others, driven, she felt sure, by agents of the CIA. Every night she got away from Belcraft long enough to file a new report on the tiny radio hidden in a jar of face cream.

They crossed at Ojinaga and drove south across Chihuahua. The Mexican authorities had been alerted to search for Alphamega. Police roadblocks stopped them several times to ask their business. Belcraft always said he was looking for a cousin who had brought a map and come to find the lost *Dos Cabezas* mine. The officers grinned and warned them to watch for *bandidos* in the hills.

For her, the drive was a bittersweet adventure. Mexico was new to her. She loved its stark majesties of mountain and desert. More than ever, she loved the days and nights with Belcraft. Yet she suffered an always keener dread of the coming moment when he must learn how she had betrayed him.

He was pushing hard. They took turns at the wheel. He hated to stop at all until a time came when he felt uncertain which way to go without another guiding dream. Even when she reminded him that sleep might invite another vision, he said he was too tense to relax. When she kissed him, with her promise to help with that, they stopped at a dingy little inn that called itself La Fonda Eldorado. In the creaky bed, he seemed reluctant at first, but her old skills soon aroused him. His sudden passion lifted her into ecstasy again.

Afterward, lying relaxed beside him, she had to fight an overwhelming wave of regret. Sick with it, she wanted to tell him what she was, to warn him of Harris on their trail, but the time for that was too long gone. Even if he forgave her, even if he forgot his insane obsession with Alphamega, they could never hope to get away together to any sort of happiness.

His dream did come. Before dawn, she woke with the light in her eyes to find him out of the bed, pulling on his clothes.

"Baby, I've got it!" He pulled her against him, and she felt his rapid heart. "She found me! From somewhere very high. As if she were somehow lost from her body and searching for it from far out in space.

"I felt her touch Panchito. Begging him to help her show me the road he'd followed to the mine—it's no cave at all, but another abandoned mine called *La Madre de Oro.* To get there, we drive on south through the next town and turn right up a canyon just beyond a bridge. It's not all that far. And Meg—Meg's still alive!"

"Darling, I'm so glad!"

She managed to whisper the words. Promising to hurry, she carried the jar of face cream into the bathroom to file her radio report while he was loading the car and cleaning the windshield. Day was breaking before they passed the next town. The bridge was where it should have been, but they had to backtrack and search the rock slope beyond a weed-grown ditch before he found the road.

It looked seldom used, though he was cheered to find fresh car tracks in a patch of sand. Floods had slashed it with deep washes, never repaired. In a mudhole at the bottom of a gully, he hit something that burst a tire. He had to unload the trunk to get at the spare.

Before he had finished the change, a black van came up behind, looming suddenly over the gully's edge and plunging down the rocky slope, horn blaring. It jolted past too fast, splashing him with mud. He glimpsed the driver, a heavy man with sleek black hair and mirror-glinting sunglasses, turning his head to grin at Anya. Showering him with gravel, the van roared up the farther slope and vanished over the rim.

Wiping at the mud on his face, he peered at Anya. "Who could that be?"

"Quién sabe? as the Mexicans say." She shrugged. "Who knows?"

He stowed the jack and the damaged tire. Reloading their luggage, he slipped on a muddy rock. Her toilet kit fell and came open. The cream jar struck the rock and shattered. She was scrambling to recover it, but he had found the radio.

"What's this thing?"

She stumbled away from him, trying to say she didn't know.

"I'm afraid I do." His white face quivered. "I think it explains that car that just ran past us and a lot of things I've been too blind to wonder about. I'm afraid it tells me what you are."

"It's hard to say it, Sax." She nodded slowly, hands raised to defend herself. "But I'm an agent of the KGB."

41

Merchant of Terror

Walking stiffly, as if his joints hurt, Clegg moved to lock the office door and swung heavily back to frown at Tim. There were no chairs in front of the desk, and they stood silent for a moment, face to face on the empty floor. Clegg's deep-sunk eyes were darkly rimmed; Tim thought he looked suddenly worn and old.

"Son—" His raspy voice caught. "Son, you have disappointed me."

"Sir, you have sometimes disappointed me."

"If I have—" Clegg's big hands swung forward and dropped again, a gesture of defeat. "I blame myself." His voice had fallen to a ragged whisper. "There are things it kills me to remember. Things I can't explain, because I couldn't help them. I know I've hurt you. Your mother and your sister, even more than you."

Tim saw the shine of tears in his eyes.

"But I did love you—" He drew a raspy breath and tried to raise his voice. "Believe me, Tim! I loved you and I loved them. I've suffered for the times I lost control. For times when I let my own demon seize me." His heavy fists knotted. "I've lived in hell." His hands came open again, to reach out imploringly. "Believe me, son, I always tried to atone."

"You're hard—" Tim had to catch his own breath before he could go on. "Hard to love, though I've tried. That's why I left a good business job to come back here to work for you." He breathed again, and pulled himself straighter. "No matter. That's all past. I see no need to talk about it now. Mother and Ellen are dead. I've grown up. I try to forget."

"I can't forget." Clegg's voice sharpened, bitterly sad. "I can't help what life has made me. I've been proud of you, Tim. I always hoped you'd be a better man than I am. But now—" He sighed, as if very tired. "I called you here for something more than my own confessions. Tell me—" His voice broke again. "Tell me, have I a traitor son?"

"Sir?" Tim stared. "Sir?"

"Or perhaps a stupid dupe?"

"I hope not."

"This Ostrov woman—" Contempt chilled his voice. "A confessed Russian spy. You led me to believe you had turned her. We have evidence now that she turned you."

"*Turned* isn't quite the word." Hands wide, Tim moved closer. "I told you what she is. A Russian agent, but she shares my own concern to see that Enfield doesn't happen again. When I confronted her in Kansas City, we discussed the creature Alphamega. We agreed on a common duty to make certain, as certain as we could, that no nation can ever make military use of the EnGene technology. As we saw the dilemma, Alphamega has to be eliminated. We joined our resources to dispose of her. If that's treason—"

He shrugged.

"Your story." Clegg's voice had hardened. "Far from what the CIA is hearing now. This new evidence makes you pretty clearly a traitor or a fool."

Tim stood waiting, searching his bleak face.

"The CIA—"

Clegg's angular frame had sagged, and he shuffled slowly around the big glass-topped desk to his chair behind it and sat there for half a minute, breathing heavily, before he continued a little more calmly.

"The CIA has caught another spy. A miserable little rat named Barlow. He writes lurid nonsense he calls documentary exposés. He's confessed that he allowed himself to be recruited by the KGB while he was in Russia working on a book. I met him here when he wanted to come on the post to photograph the ruins of Enfield and interview survivors for another trashy exposé. He seems to hate me now for the way I turned him down.

"A pompous little pup, with the gall to threaten me. He has heard about the Cato Club, maybe from his red friends. Enough, he claims, to do yet another exposé. He says he's going to call it *The Catonian Cabal.* All about how I'm scheming to overthrow American democracy and set myself up as a tinhorn dictator. Unless I let him off the hook.

"I told him to go to hell."

"Good enough for him." Tim tried to grin. "But that shouldn't trouble you. The club has a good grip on the media. It has always been able to stifle such critics." He peered again into his father's face. "What has Barlow to do with me?"

"Enough to hurt you." Clegg's voice turned graver. "He knows you're my son. Ruining you, he hopes to damage me. He's claiming now that his actual business here has been to control Ostrov for the KGB. He's giving his own account of Alphamega's getaway."

"Was he involved?"

"He doesn't admit it, but what he knows or guesses is enough to impress the CIA. A whole chain of ugly evidence—or else very damaging coincidence. Investigating Bard, the guard who sold us out, they learned that he used to drive off the post to meet somebody at that Chinese-Mex place in Maxon.

"Barlow says this contact was another Russian agent. A *Marieleño* called the Scorpion because of his skill with a knife. He seems to have been here in Enfield before the disaster, employed with Bard on the EnGene security force and probably reporting to Ostrov. The CIA has identified him as a man who vanished from a cheap hotel in Piedmont on the night of getaway, leaving an old pickup truck and not much else.

"According to Barlow, he masterminded the getaway. He seems to have placed the explosives that blacked out the post on the getaway night. He got Ostrov to smuggle him through the gate. She drove him to my jet. Torres, the Mexican alien, got Alphamega out of her interrogation cell and Bard drove them to join the Scorpion. They all took off together.

"Barlow thinks the KGB was waiting for them somewhere in Mexico, ready to begin their own investigation of Alphamega. He says Ostrov tricked us into releasing Belcraft to let them get him into their own hands for whatever they hope to learn. The whole object of the plot is to kill our chance at the EnGene weapon and give it to the Red Army.

"An ugly scenario."

"Don't believe it," Tim begged him. "It's the same nasty mix of half-truth and clever horror stories Barlow serves up in his books. Anya talked to me about both men, Barlow and the Scorpion. She despised Barlow—"

"He says she's a skillful actress, able to play any role."

"True." Tim nodded. "That's part of what makes her a competent spy. But I've learned to admire her as a fine human being. Loyal enough to Russia, but even more concerned to save mankind from what hit Enfield. I suppose she had to play along with Barlow to keep the KGB off her neck, but she must have let him know she hated him. Perhaps he's trying now to even a score with her.

"She talked to me about the Scorpion. It's true he was her contact at EnGene before the disaster. But he tricked her afterward—conned her out of thousands of dollars she paid him for documents he said he'd stolen from the lab. In fact, he may very well have been the man who forced her to drive him to the jet, but I can't think she was ever part of this fantastic plot."

"Not so fantastic to the CIA." Clegg's grim voice was edged with accusation. "They're convinced that you're part of it, and they've warned me that my own career's in danger." Clegg pointed a wavering finger. "You can't deny that you got Ostrov onto the base and put her next to Belcraft."

"Please, Dad!" Tim gulped to smooth his voice. "That's Barlow's method. Appeal to paranoia. He picks a few facts and invents frightening implications. He's a merchant of terror, selling his books by crying wolf at everything."

"I've tried to argue that." Clegg sighed and shook his head, leaning with both elbows on the desk as if overwhelmed with trouble. "They don't listen. They're debating now whether to arrest you at once or to leave you free long enough to lead them to your accomplices."

"Give me time!" Whispering, Tim frowned into his stark face, searching for reason. He found a firmer tone. "Barlow has them terrified, the way he tries to terrify his readers. Afraid of the Russians and more afraid of that biological killer. But his plot is pure fiction—it has to be! Just look at the facts."

"If I knew the facts—"

"Here they are." Tim bent urgently across the desk. "Anya has gone to Mexico to kill Alphamega. She has Belcraft with her for a guide and Harris for the killing. Aside from Barlow's fairy tale, we have no hint of any Russian agents waiting for military information. I've seen Anya's reports, and she seems pretty certain of success."

"I'm not—"

"Wait! For both our sakes. With Alphamega dead—proven dead—everything will change. Barlow's story will collapse into what it is, another wild lie meant to save his neck. There'll be no actual case against me—or anybody."

Slowly, as if his joints were painful, Clegg came to his feet.

"I hope so." Hoarsely breathing that, he shook his haggard head. "Son, I do hope so."

Blindly wavering, he extended his lean arm across the desk to search for Tim's blindly reaching hand.

42

After the Crash

Ranko Barac was a boy again, back in Montenegro, chasing a crazy black goat that had darted out of the herd. It zigzagged craftily away across the rocky slope. Sometimes it stopped to stare back at him with wild yellow eyes, but it always shook its horns to mock him and scurried off again.

The old grandfather would be furious if it got away. Desperate to catch it, he stumbled on the rocks and fell into a thicket of poison thorns that stung like hornets. He got up with blood on his hands and raced on again. He was gasping for breath. A pain came in his side. He hated the goat and the ugly country and everybody he had known.

This Kras was ugly, treeless country, full of caves and pits and snakes, good for nothing but the crazy goats he had to herd. He hated his father for never coming back from Santiago, and hated his mother for sending him here when he didn't want to come.

He had loved his father once. A lean, proud man with sharp black eyes and a thick black beard and a rich tobacco smell, he used to sing strange Croatian songs when he was drunk and happy and at home, but all that was too long ago. His father was never at home after he was older, always away on affairs for the nation he would never talk about. You couldn't love a father who left you and never came back.

He had loved his mother more. She was a dark, quick little woman, always working or talking or laughing or crying, never still at all. He'd thought she loved him, till after his father never sent for them to come to him in Chile. That was when she got the divorce so she could marry the pig-jowled Georgian whose factory made *defitstny,* illegal jeans for the black market.

He never liked the way the fat-faced Georgian puffed his long black cigars and bragged about his long black Zhiguli and all the easy comforts of living *nalevo.* "On the left." When they quarreled, he called the man Pig Face. The man tried to whip him. He took the whip and broke the Georgian's arm.

That was when he learned about his mother. She took Pig Face to the hospital and came back to scold him and send him here to his grandfather in the ugly Kras. Because she loved Pig Face more than she loved him.

Panting after the black goat, he came to a deep limestone sink. The goat sailed high over it and stopped on the other side to bleat and shake its ugly horns and grin at him with strange yellow eyes. He tried to jump, but the pit was too wide. He fell sprawling into a tangle of brush full of rocks and thorns and dust and spiders.

His breath was gone and his side ached more and the walls were too steep to climb. He couldn't get out. The goat stood on the rim, bleating with a wicked glee. He lay there a long time, afraid of snakes in the rocks, wishing he could kill the goat, hating everybody—

Till he heard his grandfather calling.

The old man stood tall against the sky, throwing rocks at the goat. One hit the goat in the ribs. The bleating stopped. It ran away. His grandfather lowered a rope and called for him to climb it. He knew then that he loved his grandfather, but the calling was very strange.

Instead of the old man's wheezy Serbo-Croatian quaver, what he heard was Alphamega's child-voiced Spanish.

"Aquí! La cuerda!"

He was reaching for it, but that strangeness woke him from the dream. The rope was gone. He remembered the way he had ducked and caught his breath, waiting for the crash. When he could move his head, he found twisted pieces of the jet all around him. He lay on hard ground, and the pain in his side was real. Twisting to look, he found the handle of his own knife. The point had gone through the thin sheath and into his chest.

He lay there a long time, as helpless as he had been in the dream. Hot sun blazed on him. Moving hurt his head and breathing hurt his chest. The pain from his side spread like a poison through all his numb body. His head couldn't turn enough to let him look for Alphamega or the Mexican. When he tried to call, the coughing seemed to drive the knife deeper. All he could hear was the cawing of a crow.

The crow came closer. Afraid of what it would do, he found strength to reach the knife. It came out of his side when he pulled and fell to clatter on loose metal. The crow cawed and flapped farther away.

He had no strength to do anything else. He felt the blood still coming, hot and sticky on his ribs when he breathed, but he had no way to stop it. Flies buzzed around his sticky hand. The sun blazed hotter. When a breath of wind came, it carried bitter dust that made him cough again. When he felt sleep coming back, he wanted it to take him far away. He felt glad when he thought he wouldn't wake.

But then he dreamed again, again of Alphamega.

"Amigo, no! You must not die!"

"I hurt too much," he told her. "I have no strength to live."

"Por favor, you must try," her bright voice begged him. "Because we need you, and because I feel the love

in you. I see you shining with the color of hope. *El Erudito* Sax will help me find where you were hurt, and we can help you heal yourself."

That couldn't be, he tried to say, because Belcraft wasn't here to help her with anything. They had left him a thousand miles and more behind, locked up with Clegg's interrogators in the prison hospital. But he found no strength to speak again.

Yet, somehow, some part of Belcraft did come to help Alphamega, though not in any visible way. When he looked around him for her, all he could find was a bright shadow dancing in the air. It was thinner than mist, but it wrapped him with kindness.

Somehow, it was Alphamega. He felt her reaching into him. Belcraft showed her where to go and what to do. She stopped the pain where the blade had been. She reached deeper, turning deadness into life.

"Adiós!" he thought she whispered. *"Vive!"*

And the brightness was gone.

He woke again, suddenly strong enough to lumber to his feet and shout at the crow perched now on Frankie Bard. The crow cawed at him, defiant as the yellow-eyed goat in that first dream. The body lay sprawled where accident had tossed it, dead as Frankie deserved to be, already swelling and stinking in the heat. He threw a scrap of metal at the crow and stumbled through the scattered fragments of the jet, looking for the others.

Torres lay near Frankie, flies crawling over the black streak of blood that had come from his nose. Part of a broken wing lay on his legs. Fresher blood oozed from a slash across his throat. The caved-in chest was moving, and his breath was a slow rasping snore, but he was going to die.

Beyond him, beside a seat torn out of the airplane, Alphamega lay very flat and very still. Her eyes were closed. Loose in the dust, her fine bright hair made a golden halo. Her body felt cold when he touched it, with no pulse he could feel. There was no blood he could see. He thought she must have died when they hit the ground.

Her bright shadow healing him—that had been only the ending of the dream that began with the yellow-eyed goat. No longer the billion dollar baby, she wasn't worth even a bent kopeck.

Which was one problem solved. The matter of the auction. Even if the secret of whatever killed Enfield had been somehow hidden in her strange mind or her stranger body cells, finding a bidder for her and closing the deal and collecting the loot had always been the sort of risk he never liked to take. Perhaps her death had been good luck for him.

Maybe for the world.

Yet he thought she looked lovely, even lying dead, and he was suddenly aching with an unexpected sorrow. He had to wipe at bitter tears. His first, he thought, since that bad time when he heard his mother say she had decided to send him back to the Kras because of what she called his crazy rage at her precious Alexei Petrovitch.

That dream of Alphamega stuck in his mind even when he tried to shake it off. He was a grown man now, hard-nosed and sane, believing in nothing he couldn't see or touch or spend. Yet he stood for a moment giddy in the blazing desert heat, wondering how he had survived.

Remembering the pain, he pulled up his shirt to look at his side. Stiff blood had dried there. He found a thin dark seam where he thought—or maybe dreamed—that his knife had been driven through the sheath and into him. It looked like only a scratch. There was no new blood.

He picked up the knife and cleaned it on the back of the broken seat. Frankie's police revolver lay close to one strutting hand. He left it there. The contents of the ripped pockets were scattered around the body. Frankie's payoff was in the billfold. He didn't want to touch it, and he wondered why.

Don't need it, he told himself. The Mexican dying and Alphamega dead, he had no further business here. Nothing left he could do for anybody. If the cops picked him up, he wanted no evidence on him. With Clegg no doubt already stirring everybody up with warnings and rewards, the hounds would be baying. He shook his fist at the crow, hating to think of it coming back to Alphamega, grieved that he knew no way to do for her what he dreamed she had done for him.

Or was it really just a dream?

Maybe—

That maybe was madness. He couldn't afford to go crazy. Not here in this desert, thirst already burning in his throat. He would need all his sanity and all his luck just to save himself. He found the briefcase he had brought aboard and stumbled away through clumps of coarse gray brush. When he looked back once, three more crows were wheeling down from the hot copper sky.

All that baking day he blundered on. The briefcase became a dragging burden. Once, light-headed with thirst, he threw it away. A few steps farther, he turned back for it. If he were picked up, it might betray him, yet it was too precious to leave. It contained most of the last batch of American dollars he had got from Anya Ostrov, the travel papers he had prepared, the letter that even yet might be his lifeline.

In the middle of the searing afternoon, he saw the rippling of water ahead. Near at first, its breaking waves cool and blue and tantalizing, it flowed farther and farther away until it lifted and vanished at last in the dance of heat above the hot white blaze of a dry salt lake. Half-blind from the merciless glare of that, reeling and giddy, he came before sunset to a well-worn highway.

Too weak to walk on, he waited on the edge of the narrow pavement, waving wildly at every passing car and truck and bus. One pickup veered at him till he had to jump for the ditch, but nobody stopped. At last, as the brassy sun was setting, he heard the beat of hoofs and the jingle of spurs. A lone vaquero on a spotted pony came loping along beside the road. He staggered across it to meet him.

"Párate, señor!" His shout was a rusty croak. *"En el nombre de dios—"*

The man laughed and spat a brown stream at his feet and spurred the spotted pony. He pulled his knife. The grinning pig was near enough and no longer looking. Weak as he was, he could have thrown it for a kill.

Something stopped him.

Maybe the giddiness. Sliding the blade back under his blood-stiffened shirt, he shook his head. Maybe the thirst. Maybe—

He spat dry foam. His knife had been the sting of the scorpion, and the will to use it had never failed him. Never before. Schooled to kill as his father had been, and his old grandfather, proud of his emotionless efficiency, he had never hesitated. The sneering vaquero had earned no compassion, and that frisky pony could have saved his life. What had hit him?

He didn't understand.

He slept part of the night in a thicket of weeds beside the road. Slamming thunder jolted him out of an ugly dream of the Scorpion. He had been trapped again in the wet stink of that leaky little fishing boat crammed with convicts and lunatics, most of them fouling the hold and the deck with their vomit on the rough crossing from Cuba. Again he had been marking down the most vicious enemies of the people hidden in the mob, prepared to follow them ashore and knock them off with the cool skill of a bowler knocking down tenpins.

Proud of that skill in the dream, he woke sick and trembling, glad to endure the burst of icy rain that drenched him to the skin, happy to escape the dream. For now, since the shining shadow of Alphamega reached inside him, it hurt to think that he had been that quick-stinging killer. He huddled shuddering in the mud, his back against the driving rain, while that memory faded.

Shivering still, but feeling better when it had dimmed, he cupped his hands to catch drops enough to wet his bitter mouth and lay on his face to suck at a muddy trickle off the pavement until the shower ended. Walking on, too cold to sleep again, he found himself whistling the old Montenegrin marching song his grandfather used to sing. No matter. Whatever he had been, he had grown somehow different since Alphamega touched him. Whatever she had done, he didn't need to understand. Whatever came to him now, it couldn't really matter.

Whistling louder, he plodded down the empty pavement.

43

El Cucaracho

Sorry now that he had ever been the Scorpion, he walked on in the dark. Now and then, when a truck came thundering by, he stood close to the road and waved both arms. The truck always roared on, to leave him in a cloud of suffocating dust and diesel-reeking heat.

A pale moon came out. Before dawn, it showed him a car stopped in the ditch, one that must have passed him. All lights were out, all windows closed. Peering inside, he saw movement. He rapped on the glass. A narrow slit opened.

"What do you want?"

English. A woman's voice, quivery with panic. Needless now, because he was Scorpio no longer.

"I've had trouble," he told her. "I need a ride. Anywhere at all."

"You're American?"

"Jim Gibson," he told her. "From Cedar Rapids."

"Cedar Rapids?" That seemed to relieve her. "What happened to you?"

"I'm a rock hound. Yesterday I parked by the road while I climbed down into a promising arroyo. Slipped and hurt myself. When I got out, my pickup was gone.

I've been hiking since. All day and all night. Nobody gives a damn."

"Maybe—maybe my husband can give you a lift."

"I hope so."

The slit opened wider. The inside lights came on and he saw a pale, anxious smile.

"We're Buck and Martha Tanner. From Nashville. On our way to Gordo la Jara—however you say it. Buck's uncle has a condo on the lake there. He's loaning it to us for a month while he's back at his business. I wish to God I'd never heard of it!"

"I know how you feel. Glad to hear an American voice."

"We wanted to fly, but Uncle Dan talked Buck into driving down. Said we we'd love the Mexicans. Hah! Always jabbering nonsense at us and trying to rob us blind!"

"Where is Buck?"

"Uh—" Blinking in the dimness, she decided to answer. "Gone for help. The car banged and stopped yesterday. Buck couldn't start it. He walked off to look for a wrecker. Before sundown. He's never got back."

She was trying to see him.

"I slid off a rock," he told her. "Tore my shirt and skinned my ribs. Nothing to eat since then. I'm dying for water."

"Maybe—" She hesitated. "I'm afraid of Mexicans. Buck understands a little Spanish, but I can't speak a word. If—" She rolled the glass farther down to peer at him again. "You look worn out. If you want to wait in the car, we've got a case of this Mexican Coke."

"Thank you, Mrs. Tanner. Very kind of you."

She unlocked the car and he climbed into the back seat and gulped a can of warm Coke. Listening to her nervous chatter about the daughter married to a Nashville car dealer and the son studying to be surgeon, he felt a strange relief. His luck had turned. He had no need to kill. Strangely relieved, he couldn't understand the feeling.

Perhaps—perhaps he had no need to understand.

The sun rose. Martha Tanner gave him another tepid Coke. Her chatter stopped and he heard her snoring. He took off his shoes and rolled Buck's plaid jacket up to make a pillow. He felt nearly safe, and there was no need to kill. At least not yet.

Buck Tanner woke him, shouting and hammering on the glass. Bright sun blinded him. His legs ached from his cramped position, and hot sweat had drenched him. Martha stirred and groaned and tried to explain why she had let him into the car.

Buck had brought a wrecker from a town twenty miles away. Hostile at first, he warmed a little to Jim Gibson's story of the fall in the gorge and the stolen pickup. He had walked all night and he didn't trust those grinning thieves at the service station and he wished to Christ he had never seen Mexico.

He rode into the *pueblito* with the wrecker driver and ate *huevos rancheros con jamón* with Martha while Buck tried to deal with those black bastards at the *garaje.* Buck came back boiling. The camshaft was broken, and a new one would have to come from Parral. Maybe all the way from Torreón.

Martha asked how long.

"Quién sabe?" Buck mocked a Mexican shrug, scowling at her bitterly. "That's all I can make the motherbeaters say."

Still with enough of Anya's money, he offered two thousand American dollars for the four-year-old Ford. With Clegg no doubt spreading alarms and roadblocks maybe already set up, the *pueblito* might be his safest harbor. So long as he had a reasonable excuse to stay here.

Eagerly, Buck warmed to his offer. With a fifty-dollar *mordita* to hasten the deal, Mexican officialdom provided a bill of sale, duly stamped and legalized, with a warning of import duty if he kept the car in Mexico.

Their free month in the lakeside condo forgotten, the Tanners caught the next bus north. He rented a room in La Posada Gloriosa, using the driver's license and credit cards he had obtained for Jim Gibson before he left Piedmont. Troubled only a little by his own reckless confidence in the happy turn of his luck, he went shopping for clean clothing and shaving gear and a portable radio.

In the *posada* that night, another ugly recollection shocked him out of sleep. He had been back in the helpless jet, falling blind into the desert, all his skills and plans spent for nothing. Bard lay dead in the aisle. In the seat beside him, Torres was whispering crazy pleas to the mother of God. The silent child behind him was still buckled into her seat and suddenly deadly to him now.

Even if they lived through the landing, he would have no way to hide her while he made the trade. Cool enough through those last breathless seconds, he had sketched out a new plan to be the only survivor. He would knife the girl and the Mexican, fire the wreck to confuse investigation, and move to save himself.

A memory too cruel to be reviewed. Sick and sweating, he sat up trembling in the saggy bed until the nightmare had dimmed. After all, he hadn't killed them, even when they lay naked to his knife. Lifeless as her body looked, some part of that strange child had somehow survived and returned to make him new. Now—and he didn't need to wonder about that seeming dream—he was free to forget all he had been.

Strangely relaxed, almost as if she had returned to touch him again, he sank back into more peaceful dreams of his boyhood in the rocky Kras, where his old grandfather loved him, and he had nobody to fear or hate, and even the rocks and the goats seemed kind.

Asking very patiently every day about the camshaft, he lived at the inn and hiked around the town to look for interesting rocks and listened to the radio for news. Every day there was more about the kidnapped American heiress. A pretty little blond three-year-old. There were wealthy relatives, acting through attorneys who refused to reveal any names, eagerly offering millions of American dollars for her rescue or even for word of her.

Newspapers were always late at the *pueblito,* but when they came, there were drawings of the slender child and smudgy pictures of the renegade security officer and the Mexican accomplice, an escaped convict who had been convicted of murder in *el Norte.* A third man was said to have been involved, but his name and description were still unknown.

That news should have cheered him. As Jim Gibson, footloose rock hunter, he felt comfortably safe, maybe too safe. With Alphamega out of the game, he still had the Belcraft letter. It told more about her origin than anybody else had seemed to know. More, certainly, than he could understand. When the right time came, it should be saleable. To Washington. To the Kremlin. To some private speculator. With craft he still recalled, he could turn it into Swiss bank accounts that should last him forever.

Yet he felt puzzled more and more by a formless unease growing in him. Not for himself; he had learned to live with closer danger than he felt around him now. What troubled him was a curious concern for Alphamega, a feeling he had no way to understand. He had left her in the wreckage, looking as if she had died in the crash.

Yet—

With no need to wonder, he couldn't help himself. He was somehow alive when he should have been dead, that knife wound in his side no more than a fading scar. He owed his life to her return—or had the crash killed his sanity?

His parents had scoffed at all religion. Though his dying grandfather had begged for a priest, he had never seen a better reason for belief in the survival of the human soul than the blind animal dread of death. The human soul—

But Alphamega had to be something else than human.

He found himself pondering all the perplexing evidence of that. Frankie Bard had brought him stories too crazy for belief. She had somehow talked to Belcraft across many hundred miles. She had revived and healed the wounded Mexican after his death under severe interrogation. Mickey Harris, drunk one night at the club, had cursed her as a witch too tough for anything to kill.

The laws of her being were all unknown. He found no way to grasp what she was, nor even any sane reason why she should matter to him now. Yet he felt haunted more and more by that unaccountable dread that she faced new danger, too deadly even for her.

Excitement stirred the *pueblito* when a high-flying American spy plane located what was left of the jet and American agents came to guide Mexican officials to the spot. News of that gave him an uneasy night. The camshaft from Torreón had never come. He was still stuck here, next door to the investigation.

The garage owner drove out in search of salvage and came back to tell of two bodies found in the wreckage. One was the missing security officer, the other perhaps the Mexican convict, though its state of decay made identification difficult. Those offered rewards had grown larger and still larger; many American millions for recovery of the missing heiress; many hundred thousand for the arrest of that mysterious third passenger, or even for proof of his identity.

He wanted to catch a bus or vanish into *el campo,* but he had let that illogical trust in his luck keep him here too long. The time for flight had gone. He had to play Jim Gibson, keep on joking with the *campesinos* and looking for odd pebbles in the arroyo.

Somehow, though the camshaft was always still to come *mañana,* his luck held. The police and the visiting Americans came to doubt that anybody could have lived through the crash. The missing heiress and her captor must have been dropped off to meet confederates at some secret airstrip before it happened.

Next day a truck rolled through the *pueblo,* carrying twisted fragments of the jet toward Torreón. The heiress vanished from the news, replaced by reports and denials that a sudden outbreak of the Enfield organism in South Africa had wiped out the whole population of a black homeland.

Though still he felt curiously secure, that dim concern for the child kept on nagging, until one night he saw her again in another dream. If such visions were no more than dreams. She had been somewhere far away. Trying to return, she was lost in the dark of space, out where she could see the roundness of the planet and the dazzle of the sun on its side.

The thread of her life had drawn too thin to guide her home, and she was seeking help from the man she called Panchito. It was Panchito who had brought her body from the fallen *avión* to the place where she had left it. Searching for him or the path he had followed there, she had come up *El Escorpión* instead.

"No scorpion now."

He saw her happiness to see how completely he had healed, but that faded when she found the color of hope gone from around him. She knew he couldn't guide her home. He shared her sick despair. Not for herself, but for the whole round world beneath her. If she failed to reach her body, to make it live again, to finish her mission for *El Querido* Vic, then his life and hers were wasted.

He felt her joy when she found Panchito's mind and then the path he had taken from the wreck. He followed as she perceived it. The jolting ride across the dry *laguna* to the highway. The long drive south. The turn at the bridge. The climb through the brown foothills toward the saw-toothed summits. The dark tunnel cut into the cliff.

He came with her back to Panchito. They found him sitting on the sharp-smelling green stuff he had cut to make a bed for her, her stiffened body in his arms. After the icy night, it was very cold. He held it hard against his heart, praying for it to live again.

She tried once more to slip inside it, but all the machines of her being had been too badly crushed when the *avión* fell. The sleeping Sax had taught her how to repair the damage to Panchito and to *El Escórpion,* but she knew no skills to remake herself.

Together, they felt Panchito sob and saw the stains of tears across the dark grime on his unshaven face. Sharing her hopelessness and pain, he wept with her for Sax and *El Querido* Vic, and for all the sad world Vic had wanted her to aid.

Perhaps—

He saw new images in her mind, things too strange even for a dream. They sprang from the desperate hope that help might come from the far-off children of fire if she kept on begging the greatness of her need.

Those were images wrapped in strangeness, even to her, shadow-forms shaped more like dancing flame than anything she had known, living in the strange places of their strange city where it turned like a giant wheel of fire around the spinning brightness and the dreadful blackness that had twisted space and swallowed a star.

Those unknowable children of fire had promised life and new learning for her, if she would stay with them. Even wearing no bodies she could see, wrapped in their frightening fire that seemed to cover only beating hearts of fire, they had shone with more than fire, glowing with a love she understood.

They were her own kindred, akin because the dear Vic had made her able to share their strangeness. They were very wise. They would surely know the secret working of her body.

Perhaps, if she went back to beg again—

Red danger flared across the tunnel mouth. Through the fixed and staring eyes of Panchito, she saw a man standing there, his face dark and cruel and grinning.

Bright mirrors hid his eyes, but she knew his cruel hands from the interrogation cell. Stark and black against that red-blazing fog, he raised an ugly gun.

"Misericordia de dios!" Panchito knew him. *"El Cucaracho!"*

The gun jumped, and the dream was broken.

44

"Adiós!"

Belcraft stood blinking at Anya, feeling sick. Clad in shorts and halter against the Mexican heat, she was pink from the sun and streaked with sweaty dust, yet still aglow with a long-limbed perfection that seemed to deny her dazing confession.

"How could you—" He had to get his breath. "Have you told anybody were Meg is?"

"The hit man." Her sun-freckled face grew tighter. "The human rat they call Cockroach. A child killer, who ought to die himself. Clegg picked him for the mission. He's the Indian type with the mirror glasses that just splashed you."

"If he harms Meg—" He stared into her green-eyed defiance. "I've got to stop him."

"No chance." Watching him warily, poised and cool, she shook her head. "A professional killer, armed to the teeth. Ahead of us now, on four good tires."

"I—I—" He caught his breath, staring down at the toy-sized radio in his hand. "And you—" He waved it at her, helpless. "You've been calling that killer every day. Guiding him to Meg. That's why you made love to me. I—I ought to kill you."

"You could try." She shrugged, though he heard a tremor in her voice. "Others have failed."

"Of course I can't." He sagged into bafflement. "I didn't even bring a gun—" He bit his lip. "I suppose that's the reason you warned me that smuggling weapons could land us in a Mexican jail?"

"It really could."

He stood silent, blinking at the grease-smeared device in his grease-smeared hand. A clever invention. He turned it, staring at the removable insert that had held the actual face cream, the nest of wires and batteries and computer chips it had hidden, the tiny mike, the thin antenna that could be unreeled to transmit the message. The broken jar slid out of his fingers and shattered again on the rocks.

"Killing—" He choked on the word. "Killing isn't my business. But if Meg is killed—" He shuddered to a wave of nausea. "I hope you know what you've done."

"Sax, I don't know." Her voice had fallen soberly. "Nobody does. That has been everybody's problem since the whole thing began. Alphamega came out of the same lab that killed Enfield. But why it happened or what she is or how she came to be—"

Her sun-colored shoulders tossed.

"Meg can't be blamed!"

"Who can? We're blind. Nobody knows what new city or what whole nation is to go next. Anybody able to command such disasters can kill the world or rule it. With EnGene gone, that queer child was the only key to what happened. Clegg was trying to wring it out of her. The KGB sent me to get it for the Soviet."

"She couldn't—she couldn't kill anybody!"

"A good many thousand died in Enfield. Clegg believes she has you bewitched."

"Clegg's insane!"

"Perhaps he is." She nodded, and he couldn't help a fleeting pleasure in the sheen of her bright hair where the sun struck it. "But Sax, look at yourself. Captivated by a little pink worm, from your very first glimpse.

Throwing away your whole medical career, for no sane reason. Claiming to be guided in your strange behavior by visions that come to you alone. Any court would commit you."

"Do you think I'm crazy?"

"I don't—don't understand what she has done to you." She frowned uncertainly, her fine eyes graver. "But I haven't been enchanted. She frightens me. When I tried to weigh your hopes for her against the risk of catastrophe, I decided she should die."

"You're terribly wrong."

"Who knows?" Unhappily, she shrugged again. "It wasn't just my own decision. The KGB has allowed me to work with Clegg—with your own government—to put Harris on her trail. Not that I like it." Her face hardened. "A degenerate animal! I can guess how you feel about me, but I was taking orders. I—"

She gulped, and her voice sank lower.

"Believe me, Sax! I've dreaded this. The moment when I'd have to hurt you with the truth."

"Let's get on." He swung abruptly back to the luggage he had been loading. "Meg has this Torres with her. Armed, I hope. Maybe—"

Her eyes had widened. "You're taking me?"

"I can't abandon you here on the desert. Get in the car."

He climbed in beside her and drove on.

Out of the arroyo, he found the black van again. Already kilometers ahead, it was zigzagging up a far-off hill at a rate the little Buick couldn't match. A powerful machine, probably with a four-wheel drive. Both vehicles must have been selected, the bitter thought struck him, to handicap him for just this contingency.

Yet he pushed on as fast as he dared. The twists and rocks and ruts and washes of the neglected road took most of his attention. Keri—or whatever her real name was—sat silent beside him, looking so miserable it was hard not to pity her.

"We've talked about Vic." He spoke at last, almost in

spite of himself. "He used to talk to me. I know what he hoped to create with genetic engineering. It was no sort of weapon, but something good—something that could transform the world toward perfection. His notions were often too dazzling for me. He used to talk about creating a benign virus, engineered to invade and remake our bodies."

"Whatever he wanted, it all went wrong." Her voice seemed small and bleak. "Enfield died."

"I remember Vic's last phone call." Watching the road, he didn't look at her. "A call I still don't understand. Very brief and cryptic. Somehow upbeat, yet I got a sense of desperation."

"He mentioned a letter?"

Surprised, he looked hard at her.

"Written and mailed just before he called. Which makes me wonder now if he foresaw the disaster. Though, if he did—" He paused to steer around a mudhole. "Why didn't he get out? Or at least warn your sister Jeri—" His voice caught. "I guess she wasn't your sister?"

"Call me Anya." She nodded. "Keri was a role I played."

"Played well," he muttered. "You took me in." Pain drew his face. "I thought I was in love with you."

"Love?" Her whisper seemed sardonic. "Love?"

They were jolting and pitching through a muddy wash. Beyond it, he pushed faster, watching the black van crawl up a distant hill. It vanished over the crest. He drove a long time in bitter silence.

"Sax!" she burst out suddenly. "I can't stand it—the way you look. I know you won't believe me, but I never wanted to hurt you. Not this way."

Bent over the wheel, he tried not to hear.

"Listen, Sax." Her voice rose unevenly. "I've done things you'd hate me for, but I'm not wicked. Not the way Harris is. I'm no killer. I told Clegg I couldn't kill Alphamega. That's why he sent Harris—"

"What's the difference if she's dead?"

Anya had no answer. He drove on, up another rocky slope and on across a barren mesa. The black van was out of sight. When he glanced again at her, she was sitting bolt upright, hands folded on her knees, staring straight ahead. Her forlorn expression wrenched him.

"Tell me." He had to speak. "How'd you get into the KGB?"

"To escape something worse." She looked at him searchingly. "If you care," she went on at last, "I'll tell you how it happened."

He had to say, "I'd like to know."

"I'd grown up happy. I was an only child, badly pampered. My grandfather was an engineer who made a fortune under the czars. Come the Reds, he was smart enough to compromise. Built factories and managed foreign trades for them.

"My father managed to inherit his status and some of his contacts. One friend on the Central Committee. When I was a child we had a summer dacha at Nikolina Gora, out in the forest west of Moscow. A Volga with MOC license plates, which meant you were somebody. My father was never a party member, but he stood high enough to let us shop at the party stores. Gourmet foods. Imported shoes and clothing. Fine liquors.

"Mother and I were allowed to go with him on missions abroad. When I decided to be an actress, he got permission for me to study in Paris and London, then pulled political strings to make breaks for me back at home. Of course I knew that most other people were not so well off, but *nichevo*—"

He glanced to see her sad little shrug.

"I never had to care. Not till a silent upset in the Kremlin tossed my father's friend out of favor. Nothing very drastic happened to him. Party members take care of each other. But the people around him—we took the heat. My father died in prison. We lost our apartment and the dacha and the car. My mother killed herself. And I—"

Dismally, she shook her head.

"I don't suppose you can imagine what all that did to me. My stage debut was just about to happen. I'd made exciting friends. Important men were courting me. The whole world looked wonderful, a dream come true."

She paused again, staring away into the dance of heat on the far brown horizon, and he almost pitied her.

"Overnight it all winked out, like Cinderella's coach in your fairy story. No money. No job. No way to live. Nowhere even to sleep. My friends—I'd thought they were friends—were afraid to speak to me. All except two or three *seksoty.* Secret agents of the KGB, assigned to check the reliability of people who might go abroad.

"One of them took me in. A loud, pushy little guy, who scribbled unproduced plays and catty criticism to cover what he was. I'd never really liked him, not till then. But he was better than any alternative. Not bad in bed."

Glancing back at her, he caught the odd little quirk of her lips.

"He kept me as his mistress till his wife found out. By then I knew what he was. He introduced me to the trade and gave me my first assignments."

She stopped to look at him, her green eyes piercing.

"You think I'm wicked. Maybe I am. But I'm a survivor. Glad I didn't follow my mother into the Moskva." The recollection shadowed her face. "It was spring. The ice just breaking. The river still caked with it. A cold way to die."

Her sunburnt shoulders straightened.

"I guess you won't forgive what I am, but I'm not sorry. I've stayed alive. I've learned. I'm good at what I do, and I enjoy success. There have been good times. The best with old Jules Roman—at least till I met you—"

Her mouth quirked again.

"You've probably heard of Roman. An American industrialist who spent most of his life working for peaceful trade with Russia. Going senile when we met, yet still admirable for what he had been. Devoted to me. I got fond of him.

"His murder hurt—"

She must have seen him start.

"He was killed in Moscow." Her voice had turned husky. "By his own doctor, on secret orders from the KGB. I'd set up the Russian trip to let me deliver an early report from our agents at EnGene. Something in it alarmed the Kremlin. I was ordered to rush back and get more of the story. Jules was too sick to travel. The Center arranged for me to bring his ashes."

He turned from the wheel to stare. "You killed your lover?"

"Nichevo." Her shoulders lifted. "He was dying, anyhow—and never much of a lover. I used to pity him when he wanted to try. But please don't think I liked the way he was killed. I couldn't have stopped it."

Silent while they rocked across another new gulley, she met his eyes when he glanced at her again.

"You're appalled at what I have to do. As I used to be. But I'm a Russian. I love my country. If you know our history, it has always been full of cruelty and death. That's still true. We have nearly always been at war. We are now, with your USA. In the KGB, I'm a soldier in that war. When orders are given, we don't ask if they are ethical. We obey."

He heard her draw a long, uneven breath.

"You may hate me, Sax. I've done hard things, but most of them were things that had to be done. I felt sorry for my father, but I'm afraid he asked for what he got. I've had bad times, but they have made me stronger than I ever hoped to be.

"There's very little I regret. Not even the death of your dear Alphamega—assuming Mickey Harris is able to kill her. Perhaps she's as harmless as you think. Perhaps she isn't. Nobody knows the nature or the limits of her powers. She may carry whatever hit Enfield. She may not. The risk is simply too frightening to tolerate."

With that she fell silent. They were climbing a difficult slope that took all his skill. She was staring straight ahead when he could look at her again, fine hands folded on her sun-colored thighs, looking too young and too lovely for what she had said.

"You're hard to hate," he muttered. "But killing Meg is something I can't forgive."

"Nichevo." Her shrug explained the word. "I had to tell you who I am."

From the crest of the hill, he saw a plume of flame-yellow dust climbing from the flat gray mesa they had left far below.

"Somebody behind us. I wonder who?"

"The field support people, I'd imagine. Men from your military intelligence, here with permission from the Mexicans. They'd been picking up my signals and getting orders to Harris."

Noon came. She found the water jug and gave him a newspaper-wrapped taco they had brought from the motel. Accepting it from her as if they had still been good companions, he felt a wry amazement at himself.

The road narrowed, bulldozed out of hazardous slopes. Anya pointed, and he found a white fan of shattered rock poured down the mountainside ahead, the tunnel-mouth a dark dot above it. They crept around a jutting point and he heard Anya catch her breath.

"Mickey! Already back!"

The black van lurched into view, recklessly skidding down the road from toward the tunnel.

"Which means—" He stared accusingly at Anya. "You've murdered Meg!"

If she answered, he didn't hear. For Meg was dead. Dead, dead, dead. He swayed giddily, the word drumming in his mind. He tried to stop that hard word, pounding like his heart, but he couldn't shut it out.

"I couldn't help hoping," he whispered. "Hoping—"

The whisper died. He saw no hope.

Meg had seemed eternal. She had survived shocks that surely would have killed any merely human being. The burning of the lab. The Enfield plague. The fall into the well. Torture in the interrogation cell. Yet a merciless certainty seized and dazed him now, a cold conviction that she was gone forever.

He had loved her more than Midge, more than Anya, more than anything. Never knowing why, he had hardly even wondered. Meg had mattered more than anything. He had done his best to help her.

He had failed. The sun was suddenly too cruel, the air too hot to breathe. The waves of heat all around the brown horizon came rolling closer, dissolving everything into a strangely blazing blackness. He felt the car jolting off the road, but he didn't care.

Meg was dead.

"Adiós, Señor Sax!" Her voice came out of that pounding blackness, but still he knew that she was dead. *"Soy triste—Soy triste—"*

Her voice was thin and small, as if from somewhere far off in the blinding dark. She felt sad to see him so unhappy. His own life had lost its meaning now that she was dead.

"Animate!" Bravely, she tried to cheer him up. "I must go away forever, because my body is hurt too much to let it live again. We must say good-bye forever, because I'll be too far to reach you. But you must cheer yourself. *Animate, querido* Sax! You have been my dearest friends, you and Panchito. I love you both, and I beg you to be glad for me."

He tried to whisper, "If you are dead—"

"No, Sax! *Es de nada!"* Her far-off voice seemed quick and bright. "I can't come back to my poor body, because its little life has ended. But I have received a better kind of life from my new friends. They are the people of fire, who live in a world without land, near a strange black star that swallows suns. I am very sad to leave you, but they are my own people now. I must go where they take me.

"Be happy for me, Sax! I have left the broken body that tore me with pain. My new people love me, and they will let me share the life that comes to them forever in the black light of their black star. They will teach me what I am, and help me become whatever I'm to be, and make me happier than I have ever been. *Por favor,* promise to forget your sadness, so that I need not grieve for you."

He tried to promise, but his throat hurt and he had no voice for her to hear.

"*Adiós, querido* Sax!" Her small voice was fading. "*Adiós—*"

45

"Cold as Stone!"

"Wake up!"

Anya's hands were on the wheel. The car had veered off the road toward the brink of a deep arroyo. He braked it to a pitching stop. The black van was still a quarter-mile ahead, coming fast to meet them.

"Sax?" She caught her breath, staring at him. "Are you trying to kill us?"

"Something hit me—" He felt giddy. "I don't know what. A dream—a vision of Meg. She somehow spoke to me. The first time ever when I hadn't been asleep. She's dead—her body is. But she—her spirit, her soul, whatever she is—came to say good-bye."

He saw the look in her eyes.

"Call me crazy if you want, but I know we'll find her dead. Murdered by your gunman!"

If she replied, he didn't hear. Still sunk deep in the sadness she had brought, he sat blankly staring at the killer's van. His brain felt dazed. Meg's parting words seemed stranger than any dream, because they reflected nothing he'd ever known. People of fire, living in a world without land around a black star that swallowed suns . . .

He shook his head, blinking at the skidding van.

"This heat?" Anya looked hard at him. "Too much for you?"

"I—I'll be all right. "But Meg—"

The van was lurching to a stop just ahead. Mickey Harris got out and stalked on toward them. A dark stocky man with grease-slick hair.

"Careful, Sax!" Anya dropped her voice. "He's deadly."

He sat staring. The flat Indian face and the black mirror sunglasses brought back a sudden drug-dimmed memory of the interrogation cell back at Enfield and Harris mauling him until Kalenka interfered.

"We're okay, babe!" Grinning at Anya, Harris raised two fingers in the victory sign. "Clegg's millions, safe in the bank! I pumped the little bitch full of lead. Her pet spic too. We got it made."

The mirrors flashed at Belcraft. The grin fading, the thick voice faltered into silence.

"Well done!" Anya returned the victory sign. "I'll inform the general. Where are you headed now?"

"I—I dunno." Harris hesitated, shivering. "Something—back there in the dark. I dunno—" He glanced uneasily behind him. "I was taking her head. A trophy for the general. But I got the shakes. Dropped my knife and ran. I dunno why—"

He stumbled to the car and gripped the rim of the window as if for support.

"Mickey?" Anya slid out of the car and came around to him. "Mickey, are you sick?"

"Dunno— Dunno—" He stood there a moment, unsteady fingers combing at the slick black hair. "I've had my share of fresh young meat, and nothin' never bothered me. Even had my hands on the little bitch back at Enfield, and nothin' hit me then. I dunno—"

"If she's really dead—"

"Cold as stone!" He shuddered again, blinking woodenly at Anya. "Funny thing. Chilled me just to touch her. I had a grip on that yellow hair and her head half off—and not a drop of blood. There shoulda been blood." He licked his lips. "I always gotta kick outa the blood."

"Better get along," she told him. "Let the support people know where you'll be, so the general can set up your payoff. We'll drive on up and take photos for verification—"

He stood silent for a time, thick lips working, black mirrors staring.

"Watch out, babe—" His voice had slowed to a rusty creak. "Go in there and you'll be sorry." He swung to shake his head at the far tunnel-mouth. Better stay away. Something I can't shake off." He came back toward Anya, heavy hands trembling. "I need a shot. You got a bottle?"

"No." She shrank away. "We don't have a bottle."

"Something better!" His flat nostrils flared, his broad face twitching into a sudden, ugly grin. "Dunno how she hit me, but you'll do, babe!" The black mirrors clung, and his voice sank to a breathless rasp. "You got the juicy meat I really need to warm that chill."

"Why, Mickey!" Her cool voice reproved him. "You wouldn't hurt *me.* You couldn't. You haven't even got a knife. Not if you left it—"

"Silly bitch! I'll take care of the knife."

"Mickey, are you crazy?"

"Dunno—" Again he peered back toward the tunnel. "But I gotta forget. That's when I always wanted fresh red meat. When things got to eating on—"

Belcraft tumbled out of the car, gripping a tire iron.

"Drop that, bud." Harris backed away, a big revolver drawn. "I'll drill you here and now."

"Better drop it, Sax." Anya's steady voice seemed far away. "You wouldn't have a chance."

The muzzle of the gun looked large and black and very steady. He let the tire iron fall.

"Good girl, babe!" The mirrors flashed at her. "You're the cure for what I've got. And your heroic pal ain't gonna stop me." The idiot grin spread wider. "One thing he can do, if I save him for later. I'll fix the bodies to look like it was him sliced the meat—"

"Wait a minute, Mickey!" She stepped quickly toward him, empty hands spread as if to plead. "Before you get rash, better look behind you!"

"Now, now, babe! I ain't that dumb."

"Listen, Mickey!"

"Hah! You can't fool—"

He heard the whine of gears and backed away to glance toward the sound.

"Hey, you bitch—"

Bare hands reaching, Anya darted at him. He swung the gun to meet her. She dived under its crash, and Belcraft heard it clatter on the rocks near his feet. Lunging to meet her, Harris went over her bent shoulder and came down hard. The mirrors clinked and shattered. Back on her feet in an instant, she recovered the gun and fired two expert shots into his head.

Ears ringing, Belcraft peered at her groggily. He felt humiliated, but also vastly relieved.

"So what, Sax?" Almost smiling, she blew smoke from the muzzle of the gun. "You're a physician. I've trained for the other side of the coin." With a grimace of disgust, she stepped away from the man on the gravel. "If killing had ever been a pleasure, this might be the moment."

The gears whined louder. A car was coming into view above the rise behind.

"Huh?" Anya scowled at it. "I was expecting the support group."

The car was a blue travel-battered Ford. It stopped close behind them. A heavy man in khakis got out. Walking toward them, he stopped to peer at the body on the ground and came on toward Anya.

"Scorpio!" Belcraft saw her hand tighten on the gun. "You're close enough."

"Miss Ostrov!" He seemed more amused than alarmed at her hostility. "Let's forget the Scorpion.

Right now, here in Mexico, I'm Jim Gibson, American." He bent to frown again at the red wreck of Harris's head. "My old friend Mickey?" He shrugged. *"Nichevo,* as you used to say. High time he got dealt out."

"What are you up to now?"

"Nothing for you or the KGB."

"Then, why—" The weapon followed him. "What do you want?"

"Things have happened to me." He waved as if to push the gun aside. "I know you used to hate me, but I'm not what I used to be. You won't have to shoot."

"You robbed me."

"So?" A cheerful shrug. "I never liked taking orders from a woman. Never felt you were paying what my skills were worth. When too many agents from too many places started closing in, I decided to play a lone hand. Followed you back to Enfield and set up the escape with Alphamega—"

"You?" She kept the gun steady. "The man I drove to the general's jet? I did wonder—"

"A trick that worked." He spoke in the flat half whisper she recalled. "One I picked up years ago." He made a face at the gun. "Really, Anya, you won't need that. Not since whatever happened back there on the desert. You can blame me that the jet went down. Torres wanted to land on some lighted field, but I was still hoping to auction Alphamega off for my own retirement fund.

"The crash left me dying—"

Her eyebrows rose. "You look alive to me."

"I'm okay now. Better in fact than I ever was." Suddenly grave, he glanced up the road, the way the black van had come. "But I think we all died. Even Alphamega. There was no sign of life when I looked at her body. Yet somehow—"

He stopped to blink absently at her and Belcraft and the body on the gravel, seeming to search for words.

"Here we come to matters I can't claim to understand. Nothing I say is likely to persuade you, but in spite of all that, Alphamega was—still is alive. Somehow, some part of her. Don't ask me how. With help from Belcraft's doctor-brother—and somehow without her own body moving, because the wreck hadn't left it fit to move—she revived Torres and me."

"Help from me?" Belcraft started. "I never knew—"

"If you're Dr. Saxon Belcraft." Gibson nodded, dark eyes probing. "I knew your brother, back when I was an EnGene guard. Alphamega wanted to bring you when we made the breakout. Not a chance, with you lying drugged in Kalenka's interrogation room."

"If you say she was dead, and you were dying—" Anya squinted at him, shading her eyes against the sun. "How do you explain—"

"I don't." A slow, solemn headshake. "I can't pretend to understand. While I lay there dead, she came to me. Don't ask me how. Or how she and Belcraft put me back together."

His empty hands spread wide.

"I woke up dazed. Only half remembering her visit, I thought it must have been just a crazy dream. I looked at her and Torres. No question she was dead. Torres close to it. I wandered off and found a road. I had no notion what had happened till days later, when she appeared to me again.

"She'd been somewhere off the earth. She was just coming back to look for her body. Searching, she reached me. I followed her back to where Torres had taken her. A queer experience! It ended with her shock of terror. I caught her awareness of sudden danger closing in—she has senses I can't even try to explain. I was hoping to get there in time to help her."

Scowling at the body, he dropped his empty hands.

"I guess I'm too late."

"Too late." Belcraft nodded unhappily. "Harris said he'd pumped them both full of lead."

"Which might not kill her any deader than the crash left her." Gibson squinted again toward the far black fleck of the tunnel-mouth. "We'll have to take a look."

With a scowl at the flies already crawling over the body, he turned back to Anya. "What's with that?"

"Dump it in the van," she told him. "Let the support crew explain it to the Mexicans."

Belcraft helped him heave the body into the back of the van. Back at the blue Ford, they washed their hands with warm water out of a plastic bottle.

"Thanks, doc. Now—" Gibson paused to study Belcraft. "Before we go, I've got a letter for you."

Opening the trunk of the Ford to find a grime-stained briefcase, he dug out a thick brown envelope.

"Sorry, Doctor." He seemed apologetic. "It's to you, from your brother at EnGene. I took it in a midnight raid on your Fort Madison office. After I'd read it, I rigged the booby trap that took out your house." A wry grimace. "That was back when I was still the Scorpion."

He gave Anya a quizzical nod.

"I had a hunch by then that the letter might be worth more than she was willing to pay. The whole situation was getting too sticky for comfort. I decided to hold out for a safer occasion and a higher bid. I'm glad now to get it back to you.

"If you'll forgive me—"

With an odd little bow, he offered the envelope.

"Better read it before we look in the tunnel." Awe in his eyes, he peered again at that far mountain. "I'm half afraid of what we'll find when we get there. Being a doctor, you ought to understand what your brother wrote better than I do. Maybe he's warning us what to expect."

46

EnGene

Gibson went back to his mud-splashed Ford to check the engine and pump air into a leaky tire. Nodding for Anya to follow, Belcraft climbed into the Buick. Both doors open against the heat, he looked again at the letter. It trembled in his sweaty fingers.

Avid to read it, he already dreaded what it might say. The thick brown envelope was wrinkled and coffee-stained, one end slit. Though the postmark was worn dim, he made out "Enfield." With no sender indicated, the letter was addressed to his Fort Madison office in Vic's hand. The neat black-ink script brought him an image of the pesky kid brother he recalled, brighter than everybody and cocky about it, eager to tackle anything or anybody, myopic eyes peering through thick-lensed glasses to pick up facts most people missed.

"Here it is." Sadly, bitterly, he grinned at Anya. "The letter you were trying to buy for the KGB. It really is from Vic. Written from the EnGene lab the night before the city died. I guess you've paid enough to see it."

"Thanks, Sax." An ironic murmur. "You're far too kind."

Reading the closely written pages, he passed them silently to her.

"Dear Sax," Vic had begun, "I should warn you that even receiving this may place you in danger. For your own safety, you should read it in private and consider the possible consequences before you let anyone at all know anything about it. I'd understand if you decide to destroy it and try to forget you ever saw it.

"With only a few hours alone in the lab tonight, I'll have to be brief, but I want to make things clear. This will sum up the story of the EnGene Laboratories, so far as I know the story. The final chapter remains to be written. I can't predict its outcome, but your own survival to read this farewell implies something happier than I feel sure of.

"My involvement with EnGene began the year I finished my doctorate. I'd read a summary report on my own graduate research at the regional AAAS meeting in Chicago. Bernard Lorain came up to me afterward. He's half-forgotten now because they have kept such a security lid on us, but you probably heard of his early work. He'd begun with Jim Watson at Harvard and gone on to Johns Hopkins and later to Stanford. He was a leader of those bright Young Turks who had just begun turning genetic science upside down.

"EnGene was just being planned. I was in hog heaven when he offered to take me aboard. We'd find kindred souls at work there, with nearly unlimited funding and total freedom to dig into the deepest secrets of life. Not to worry, he assured me, about any demands for profit-making or military applications.

"Of course I asked questions. Who was funding EnGene? Why? He didn't know. The best he could offer was a guess, based he said on inadvertent hints from lawyers and accountants. The endowment came, he suspected, from some big industrialist who had come to deplore the way he and his kind had misused technology—stripping the planet bare, wasting resources to build frivolous gadgets and unthinkable weapons.

"This anonymous benefactor was betting some of his millions on serendipity. That, at least, was Lorain's hope. We'd be free to study the ultimate nature of life. With no pressures to sell anything or kill anybody, we had a chance to stumble onto something that could turn civilization toward some saner future.

"That's what Lorain believed. I never got a name for that benevolent idealist, or even found anybody who claimed to know a name. Maybe he did exist, long enough at least to launch EnGene. Maybe he didn't. As things worked out, I was never sure.

"I wanted to know why there had to be such tight security. Lorain's reply seemed reasonable. We would be free to discover whatever we could. The secrets of the unlocked gene might be as explosive as those of the atom. As a hedge against disaster, all our work must be evaluated in advance of publication.

"Who would be doing that evaluation? Our whole scientific staff; that's what Lorain understood. The final disposition of our discoveries—to be locked away in some military safe or published for the world's benefit —that was to be settled by a full staff discussion and a democratic vote. On that basis, I signed up for my first year.

"The look of the place was a painful disappointment. The first of many to come. We're in an old brick building where a TV maker failed. We do have a top-of-the-line Cray computer and adequate equipment—compared to nucleonics, you can do genetics for peanuts. Salaries are low; we could earn twice as much anywhere else. We weren't allowed to patent anything.

"Yet I stayed. Partly because of Lorain. Mostly because we were left free, at least at first, to follow our findings wherever they took us. After the shock of this shabby old firetrap, those early months were great. Lorain was a charismatic leader. He'd recruited a fine team of his fellow Young Turks. The brightest minds in genetics. We got on well together. I began to feel that we shared the same grand dream:

"Directed evolution!

"Natural evolution seems to have been creation by

blind accident, working through endless waste and needless death. A multibillion-year affair of random trial and error. Countless trillions of fatal blunders had to be killed off to get one chance advance good enough to survive.

"We did better, because we had an intelligent aim and we knew the rules. Instead of running haphazard experiments that might take a million or a hundred million years to work or nearly always fail, we could plan what we wanted to do and run it through the computers in fifteen minutes.

"We were creators!

"A great feeling, Sax. We commanded new technologies powerful enough to remake the human race. We could create a race of demigods, or one of demons. Sometimes the possibilities frightened me, but I never thought of quitting. I wanted to make certain—as certain as I could—that nothing went wrong.

"It hurt us not to publish, but at least we could talk. We did, and we reveled in it. Our whole group as a unit seemed keener than any one of us. We worked long hours and long after hours and talked just as long, at coffee breaks and after work and at weekend get-togethers.

"We developed a fine sense for truth, and a vast respect for the cleverness of natural evolution. The process has been glacial, but the wonders it has done—sometimes I thought we'd never match them. We soon came to realize that natural life is more complex than we had ever imagined, its future potentials more amazing. Yet we always dreamed of going further.

"EnGene was the most fun I ever had—the most exciting game I ever hoped to play—till I began to notice that Lorain was changing. His temper got short. His old sense of humor dried up. His brain seemed keen as ever, but he began avoiding our coffee breaks and parties. Too busy, he said, with paperwork the corporation was demanding.

"I thought at first that the company security system

was simply getting under his skin. He was still doing brilliant work that should have been reported in *Nature* or *Science,* making breakthroughs in theory that gave us new models of the gene and new ways to take it apart and rebuild it. He—the whole group of us—might have been up for Nobels if we'd been allowed to publish.

"That security pinch hurt him, and all of us. Other restrictions soon got worse. EnGene executives began turning up to inspect the facility and dig a little too sharply into what we were doing. There were other men, odd characters who introduced themselves as representatives of pharmaceutical firms wanting to know what was delaying the new wonder drugs they said the company had promised them.

"Puzzling people!

"Whatever they were or claimed to be, none of them seemed to know all that much about biology or any other science. They were all in plain clothes, but one day Lorain slipped. Talking about a Mr. Mason, a big-shot coming to look us over, he called him General Ryebold. When the general had finished his inspection and gone, I dug the truth out of Lorain.

"The Pentagon had taken us over."

47

The Pentagon Way

The contact car had arrived. It was a sleek new German minibus, bristling with radio antennas. Besides the driver, it carried a Mexican police official, two technicians, and a Colonel Quayle, the American in command. The air conditioner had died. They were all sweat-grimed and grumbling, the colonel pale and sullen from Mexican dysentery.

He sat in the minibus till Anya went back to meet him.

"Clegg's hit man." She pointed at the red trail across the gravel to the black van. "He told us he'd found Alphamega at her hideout in the old mine ahead of us. Said he killed her. Whatever happened, he came back unhinged. Attacked me. I had to stop him. The remains are your problem now. We're going on up to take photos and verify her death for Clegg."

"We've got our own photographer. We'll follow you."

"Not quite yet," she told him. "Before we go on, we're reading a letter Victor Belcraft wrote to his brother just before the Enfield disaster. He's telling how the whole thing happened."

"I want to see—"

The colonel's face grew paler. He rolled suddenly out

of the bus and ran for the arroyo. Gibson escorted the Mexican cop to look at the body in the van. Anya and Belcraft returned to the letter.

"A hard jolt to me," Vic had written. "Lorain kept me an hour, trying to excuse and defend himself. Claiming patriotism—the obligation to defend his country. Pleading the sheer allure of science. Insisting that we really had no choice except to carry on under Pentagon control.

" 'I do feel trapped,' he told me. 'I guess I fooled myself. In spite of all the evidence, I clung to the notion that we had total freedom to find what we could and control what we found. When you look at how most researchers are tied up with grant restrictions and funding limits and peer reviews and policy objectives and yards of red tape, that seemed to repay what it cost us.

" 'I came here as eager as we all were to engineer a better future for humanity. It's true that lately I've had to mislead the rest of you. But not from choice, Vic. Not from choice!'

"He looked unhappy about it.

" 'I stumbled on the truth just a few months ago, when the Pentagon began calling on the FBI and CIA and military intelligence to beef up security—they were afraid the Ruskies or somebody else would learn what we were up to.' He frowned at me. 'I've been wanting to tell you, Vic, but I was afraid of how you'd take it.'

"Myself, I took it hard. I threatened to quit.

" 'Too late for that.' He looked unhappier. 'I tried, but we're in too deep. All of us, Vic. They act apologetic, but they've made it plain they're ready to kill us if they have to. We're here for the duration—of I don't know what. That's hard to live with, but they're afraid to risk what we might reveal. The best we can do is try to see it all the Pentagon's way.'

"When I said I couldn't, he tried to put a better face on our predicament.

" 'It's an ugly age, Vic. A world with no center. No purpose. No sane direction. Too many selfish forces contending, with ethics and reason commonly forgotten. If a few of us don't stay awake to that, if we don't try to hold one last fort for sanity, the world's done for.'

"He shook his head at me.

" 'Genetic engineering is a race for world dominion. So the Pentagon says. Here at at EnGene, we're still ahead. Just barely. Too many potential enemies too close behind us. People as desperate as we are.' His worn face turned sadder. 'All of us driven by what we don't know about the hell-weapons we think the others are making. All afraid somebody else will beat us to something that will wipe us off the map. Scrambling hard to steal anything they can't invent.

" 'The Pentagon says we're about to lose the race. That could be true.' He scowled and bit his lip. 'If we really do—if we let the Ruskies or some crazy ayatollah or Qadhafi beat us to an unstoppable weapon—that's the end of everything. The worst case would set evolution back to where it started four billion years ago.

" 'That can happen, if EnGene fails.'

"He sat straighter, staring hard at me. He didn't mean EnGene to fail.

" 'Vic,' he tried to challenge me, 'you've got to look at the facts. No matter what we find, genetic science will never be anybody's monopoly. All there is to know about the gene is written in the cells of everything alive. The gene and the atom—the secrets of both have always lain open, waiting for anybody with the wit to read them. Just now, we're ahead—I hope we are. At best, a few years ahead. Maybe only weeks or months.

" 'See that, Vic?'

"I told him I saw more than he did.

" 'You're one of the best.' The old charisma burning again, he was genially urgent. 'Maybe the best brain in the game. We've got to keep you on the team.'

"Yet he didn't seem much surprised when I told him I'd never do weapons research.

" 'That's okay, Vic.' He nodded in a speculative way. 'I respect your attitude. I've talked it over with the general. He has agreed to an alternative, one I think you'll have to accept.'

"He saw my head shaking.

" 'Listen, Vic!' He turned on the charm. 'You're a loyal American. You've got to believe that EnGene exists for the national defense. All we ask for is security from conquest or extinction. Which boils down to the fact that our real goal here is not to make genetic weapons but to discover effective defenses against them.'

"He stopped to look at me.

" 'Can't you turn your talents to that?'

"I had to hesitate, reminding him that defense and offense aren't all that easy to separate. Any defense challenges enemies to break it. Any defensive technology can support aggression. I told him I'd have to think about it.

" 'We'll give you time.' He seemed relieved. 'Think it over, and I know you'll come along. The general has promised funding and full support for any defense-related research project you want to set up. And, Vic, please keep in mind—'

"The charm faded into grimness.

" 'The fact is, you've got no choice.'

"I lay awake all night, looking for any way out. All I could see was prison or worse. Next morning I agreed to go along.

"Mr. Mason was in uniform when I saw him again. Brigadier General Latham Ryebold. A man I had to admire, though I never felt quite at home with him. A plain old soldier, openly contemptuous of West Pointers, and proud of how he'd fought his own way up from the ranks. Not fond of us scientists—I won't quote his phrase for us—but tough as rawhide and totally devoted to his country.

"Cutting his teeth in Korea, he'd scored high in 'Nam and done his bit in Central America. He meant to fight the next war the same way he'd fought the last. To his way of thinking, a genetic weapon would be just another weapon. I don't think he ever asked what a gene is. He'd seen field exercises with phosgene and nerve gas, and all he seemed to care about was efficient delivery systems and reliable data on dispersal and toxicity and possible counteraction.

"To give him credit, he gave me freedom to try any route I wanted toward biological defense. If I undertook the task almost alone, that was my own choice. Most of my colleagues were ready by then to see things the Pentagon's way. One or two of them were so persistent about joining my team that I felt sure they were informants for the general.

"He did give me everything I asked for: lab resources, access to the big computer, routine help at the few jobs I felt willing to share. Most important of all, he had to let me keep up with the work Lorain and the others were doing—after all, I couldn't design defenses against weapons I didn't know about.

"Their research appalled me. Not just me. One day I found Lorain sitting at his desk, face unshaven and eyes fixed on something I couldn't see. He'd been caught by something so horribly compelling in his own imagination that he wasn't aware of me till I caught his arm.

" 'Vic! Glad to see you.' He took off his reading glasses and blinked at me. 'I need to talk, because I've got a problem. We've all got a problem.' He waved me toward a chair. 'We're getting too close to a deployable weapon—one no sane man could want.'

"I sat down to listen.

" 'A bad thing.' He waved the black-rimmed glasses at me, a gesture he must have learned when he was free to lecture. 'Bad! I used to think you were too uneasy about EnGene, but now I get your point. The military gene begins to look worse than the military atom.

" 'A lot worse. In spite of all the peacenik propaganda, the atom never really threatened anything total. Most of the people in the southern hemisphere would survive any probable war. Even if you sterilized the land, life would surely come back from the sea. Nothing atomic could get at all the microbes buried in the deep-sea ooze, and they're complex enough to save a billion years of evolution.'

"He fell silent with that, but his air of brooding apprehension was enough to send a chill down my own spine. He sat there as if he had forgotten me, glasses nervously tapping the desk, sick eyes squinting at nothing. I finally asked if security would let him tell me anything about the weapon.

" 'Sorry, Vic.' He tried to grin. 'There's nothing ready for security wraps. Not yet, thank God. But the lethal agent we're in sight of—it looks like something absolutely ultimate.'

"He forgot me till I prodded him again.

" 'Let's begin with theory, Vic.' He tried hard to pull himself together. 'How did life begin? I think we'd all agree that the first molecular seed was put together out of galactic gas and dust out in space before the stars and planets formed. The original miracle, you used to say, wrought by blind cosmic chance. I know how you've dreamed of working new miracles of your own. Inventing ways to repair nature's blunders.

" 'Here at EnGene, we've revised theory to let us try a different and very dangerous evolutionary track. We're about to start creation all over again, in a way that terrifies me. Vic, we've drawn blueprints for something new in the universe. Not exactly a new sort of life, because it won't be life at all—not in the sense that its basis would be anything much like the double helix that blueprints all of us. We're all of us kin, we microbes and men, sharing a common ancestry.

" 'Here in the weapons lab, we're about to design something utterly alien, yet patterned after our sort of life in ways that make it altogether dreadful. We can design it into cells able to grow and reproduce. We can engineer them to feed on anything organic, make them immune to nearly any harm, equip them to exist anywhere and endure anything.

" 'I'm scared, Vic!'

"He dug into a drawer for a bottle I'd never seen. I waved it away when he offered it to me. He tipped it up, gulped, and shuddered.

" 'Turned loose, it could sterilize the planet forever.' He sat blinking glassily till he remembered me again.

" 'Your cue, Vic.' His haggard eyes seemed to plead. 'They call it Project Lifeguard. I've debated it with the staff and then with Ryebold. They think the lethal effects can be contained and controlled. The general has ordered us to go for it, balls out. I'm afraid they're all still crazy—crazy as I was when I was conned into organizing EnGene.

" 'And you—you're our last chance to stop them.' "

48

Who Killed Enfield?

The crunch of gravel underfoot brought them back from EnGene. Belcraft laid the letter aside to face the fat Mexican cop. Wheezing and sweating in the desert heat, he had come with the gray-faced colonel to question them about the killing. He sneered when Anya told him the dead man had been Hunter Harris, wanted by Mexican law along the Texas border.

"Qué mentirosa! Qué puta infamosa! Qué matadora!"

Too many gringos had been mocking Mexican justice. Mopping his dark face, he paused to give Belcraft a half-apologetic nod, but a man lay dead and no truth could be expected from a gringo killer-whore.

His manner changed when the colonel spoke up to identify her as an American agent. Indeed, stationed once in Tamaulipas, the cop had heard of *el tejano malo,* the bad Texan and his deplorable thirst for the blood of virgins. Suddenly courteous, he congratulated Any on her courageous resistance. With one of the technicians for a driver, he took the body away in the black van.

After another panic flight into the arroyo, the colonel

said he had to see a doctor. He left in the minibus with his driver. The other technician loaded cameras and tripod into Jim Gibson's Ford to ride on to the mine and record whatever they found there.

Belcraft and Anya went back to the letter.

"Pawns of the Pentagon!" Vic had been tired by then, his hurried script no longer so neat. "I can't tell you how I felt, finding out how we'd been expertly conned. *Desperate* is too weak a word. One more night when I couldn't sleep. Jeri was worried sick, but of course I couldn't tell her anything. Except that I was up to my neck in work I couldn't leave.

"Though of course I couldn't warn her, I did urge her to take a week off to visit her folks in Indiana while I caught up. No luck with that—she said they were already on their way to Enfield. Worried about her because she'd told them we were living together.

"It didn't help next morning when I found somebody had gotten into my office. Not the first time. My lab notebook had been moved from where I left it. Copied, I suspected, by the general's agents. He dressed me down when I reported it. He'd warned us our offices weren't secure. Anything secret was to be kept locked in his office safe and signed out when we needed it. A crazy arrangement, considering the hours we worked and the notes we had to keep.

"When he'd finished his scolding, I tried to persuade him to stop research on the Lifeguard device. Absolute insanity, I told him. Some remnant of humanity would surely survive the worst the nukes could do. Certainly some seed of life. But Lifeguard—if it was really going to be as totally lethal as Lorain expected—Lifeguard could erase every natural organism from the planet.

"Forever!

"He listened to me, poker-faced, chewing on that wet stump of a cigar he never lit.

" 'Thanks, Dr. Belcraft.' He nodded, with no expression. "Glad to have a man with your know-how able to confirm the kill-potential estimates we've been getting from Lorain and Kalenka. The weapon looks better than we ever hoped for.'

" 'But, sir—' "

"I groped for a way into his skull. Nobody could hope to hold a monopoly on biological weapons any more than on the nukes. Hostile nations weren't going to sit still. If they couldn't duplicate the weapons in their own labs—which any competent genetic research facility could surely do, given the key fact that they were possible—spies would go all out to steal them. Which itself might lead to the ultimate accident.

" 'What if somebody drops a test tube?'

"He nodded again, seeming bleakly pleased. 'That's the clincher.'

"I don't recall what I said. It couldn't have been anything coherent.

" 'Doctor, you haven't got the whole picture.' He shook what was left of his forefinger at me. He'd lost most of it to a piece of shrapnel in Korea. 'That total kill-potential is the beauty of the weapon, because it means we'll never need to use it.'

"He saw how I felt.

" 'Here's why,' Very soberly, he tried to reassure me. 'When the tests are completed, when we know there's absolutely no chance of any survival, I want the Ruskies to find out we have it—they've got spies enough all around us. Myself, I'd like to let them steal the blueprint. The President and the chiefs of staff will never go that far, but some double agent can make sure they do find out what will happen if anybody breaks that test tube. Knowing, they'll never dare order a launch. Your crew here has given us the absolute deterrent.'

"He waved that cigar to keep me silent.

" 'Listen, Doctor. I know you've never really been with us. Frankly, I've wanted to get rid of you, but they always told me you knew too much not to be watched. I understand you're working on a counterweapon now.'

" 'No weapon, sir.' I tried to let him know how I felt

about it. 'I'd give my life to stop all military research. Lorain has authorized me to work toward some kind of biologic shield. It looks like an impossible assignment; from what he tells me about Lifeguard, I doubt that any shield can be—'

"He didn't let me finish. 'Keep at it! Give it all you've got.'

"With no choice, I kept at it. I called it Project Alphamega. A name chosen to hint at what EnGene was up to. We'd been exploring the processes of creative evolution from beginning to end. Alpha to omega. Maybe writing the end of everything, right here in the lab, unless the project turned out better than I thought it could.

"Worried more than ever about spies, the general shook up security again. He had the CIA recheck us all, made Lorain and Kalenka cut their research group down to those they simply had to trust, and stationed round-the-clock guards to watch his office safe. The Lifeguard team still had orders to keep me briefed. What I learned left me very little hope for Project Alphamega.

"For billions of years, we natural creations have been inventing defenses against one another. Thorns and rinds and evil tastes, nicotine and strychnine and penicillin, teeth and spears and guns. But no such shields had ever been evolved against Lifeguard, because we'd never been exposed to anything even remotely like it. It was engineered to consume us.

"And we'd be naked to it.

"Knowing we couldn't hope to immunize ourselves, I tried what looked like the next best thing. I tried to engineer another new creation, as different from Lifeguard as we were, but immune to it. At best, I was hoping to devise some kind of tool we might hope to use against Lifeguard. At the very least, perhaps I could design something able to survive to give some sort of life a fresh start on the planet.

"Even for that, the outlook was so dim that I went

through days and nights of depression so bleak that I couldn't help alarming Jeri—that's when she called her parents about us. All during that bad time I was only going through the motions, without much sense of creation.

"It's strange to say, but Lifeguard was what turned me around. Lorain's team was inventing ways to design and assemble a wholly new class of self-replicating molecules. Led by the general, they were engineering an eternal destroyer, able to consume everything organic it could reach and wait forever to eat again.

"Their progress horrified me, but it also set fire to my mind. It gave me the notion of my own creation, a design for life instead of death, something as everlasting as the killer molecules they meant to make. I decided to try for something like us in its own new way. A being greater and better than natural evolution might ever give birth to. Something able to grow and learn and change—evolving forever!

"That was my new dream: a way out of racial suicide.

"I had to be careful. I couldn't let it become a rival creation, something as dangerous as Lifeguard, making endless copies of itself to crowd us off the planet. I engineered it to be immortal, endowed with every peaceful power I knew how to design into it. Except the gift of replication. It must exist alone, never breeding another.

"Sax, have you ever wondered what a god must feel?

"A heady thing. I was a god through those months, working twenty hours a day in the shadow of that final holocaust looming over us. The happiest I've ever been. You know I never married. Even back when Jeri was still totally adorable, she was never even half my life. I had to tell her from the first that I'd never have time for all she wanted. The big wedding back at her Indiana birthplace, the big new house she wanted us to build, the kids, the summer travel—the lab had always meant more to me than any of that.

"But Meg—

"That's my pet name for Alphamega, the new creation. Actually sexless, because she wasn't designed to mate, but humanly female to my imagination. Meg became my own dear child. Genes of my own went into her, transmuted toward my ideal dream of what she should be. Transformed genes from Jeri—I'm sometimes surprised that she still tolerates me; genes I needed even from people on the Lifeguard team; reconstructed fragments of genes from a paramecium and a nematode and a dragonfly and a condor and Jeri's pet Persian.

"Not that Meg will ever resemble any of them in any visible way. What she can evolve to be—if she lives to escape all the enemies she's going to find around her—the final form of Alphamega is more awesome than I dare imagine.

"Because she's designed to keep on evolving.

"There's a fanatic named Clegg who has threatened to put us out of business for the way he says we were trying to steal God's sacred power of creation. He preaches against what he calls the blasphemy of evolution. Meg's the ultimate answer to his arrogance. A new creation, designed to be more perfect than we are, programmed to evolve and keep on evolving.

"It kills me that I can't be here to watch her grow.

"There have been months of high elation, mixed sometimes with terror when I thought the Lifeguard device might be completed too soon. The climax was an hour of total joy when I saw Meg—I can't quite say I saw her born, but I did feel all the pride and wonder and fear any father could, on that night in the lab when I watched her squirm over the rim, out of her petri dish.

"I had to hide her and the fact of her creation. I knew from the first that she was never going to be the sort of counterweapon the general wanted. Her unknown potentials would have terrified him and Lorain, and certainly outraged Clegg. She's still terribly vulnerable, and I felt pretty certain they'd order her destruction if they ever learned what she is.

"She—"

A shadow fell over the pages.

"Need a drink?"

Jim Gibson was beside the car, offering Anya a square canvas water bottle chilled by its own evaporation. With a grateful smile, she drank silently and passed it on to him.

"We're still reading." He had seen Gibson's anxious glance at the letter. "My brother's telling us who killed Enfield."

49

Deathguard

"I'd better wind this up," Vic had written.

"Sax, if you're alive to read this, my life has been better spent than our poor father ever expected. I've set down all I dare to about how Meg came to be. This is my farewell to you, and a try at explaining a crime I can't confess to Jeri.

"Home for a few hours with her on that night when the way out struck me, I was feeling far too desperate to make any sort of love. Lying there, with Jeri sobbing in her sleep beside me, I saw a way to rebuild Lifeguard, to impose a limit on what Ryebold calls its kill-potential.

"The answer to the weapon, the one I'm about to try, is simply the molecular clock that runs in all our body cells, counting and cutting off their generations. That's one of nature's earliest and most essential biological inventions. It controls growth and limits life. Erasing each aging generation to make room on Earth for the next, it's what makes evolution possible.

"I suppose you know that cells in a tissue culture generally stop dividing after a few dozen generations, because that automatic clock has turned them off. I saw a way to build that same control into the Lifeguard quasi-organism to limit its lethal range.

"I took that suggestion to the team. Lorain wanted none of it—not just yet. Lifeguard itself was coming too near what he called perfection. He refused to sidetrack research into anything that might delay the effort. When I went to the general, he overruled Lorain—at first I didn't see why.

"The general called it Deathguard—a code name meant to disguise it. On his orders, I got more lab space and more help and more briefings from the Lifeguard crew on their plans and hangups. I found myself in a crazy race against them, the stakes too high for sanity. Tonight, as I write, I'm barely ahead.

"Or so I hope.

"Yesterday, reporting to Ryebold before he left to spend the weekend at Camp David and make his own report, I told him I had Deathguard as ready as it could ever safely be, needing only one final untested step to activate it. His poker scowl seemed to set a little harder when he heard about it, as if he had just picked up a royal flush.

" 'Great news for the President!'

"He called the whole team together, to congratulate us and talk about delivery systems. With Lifeguard far too hazardous for any actual use—even he had always admitted that—Deathguard promised to be the ultimate super-weapon.

"A fact I'd never seen, I don't know why. Working to counter Lifeguard, I had caught myself in an ironic trap. Lifeguard was too monstrous ever to be used—unless, ultimately, by some suicidal lunatic. In the general's mind, Deathguard wasn't. I saw no answer to his hard logic.

"A single milligram of the Deathguard culture would be a thousand times enough. It would be absolutely undetectable by X-ray or Geiger or chemical sniffer or anything else. It could be loaded into a bullet-sized missile or hidden anywhere. A secret agent could carry it in a watch or a button or a hollow tooth. You could target it on a factory or a city or a ship or an army camp, without much risk to anything outside the target area.

"Assuming, of course, that it actually worked.

"The general asked me to work up plans for a test. That horrified me. We couldn't be certain of anything about it. A failure, with Lifeguard set free, could wipe our sort of life off the earth. I told him that. Never a change on that hard brown poker face, he said he had faith enough in my science. He'd already made his own cost-benefit analysis. Risky, he admitted, but the risk was one we had to take.

Though Deathguard was still my secret, I'd talked to Lorain and the others on the team about a possible new mutation to limit the spread of the Lifeguard quasi-organism. Given the idea, that safety gene isn't hard to build. They knew enough to let them duplicate all I'd done.

"The general took off for Camp David and left me to face the grimmest decision I can imagine. Myself, I don't much mind dying—Lifeguard itself had resigned me to that. Investing our lives in such weapons, all of us at EnGene had forfeited our own rights to survival. If we have spies on the staff, and I'm pretty sure we do, I can't grieve for them. As for Ryebold himself, and whoever he reports to, I can't help wishing they were here for the finish, but they know too little to matter.

"Killing Lorain and the rest of the staff—that does hurt. They've been my closest friends, even through all our battles over the Pentagon intrusion. I respect their motives. Patriotism; they're convinced that advanced biological weapons are coming, from some worse source if not from EnGene, and they want America to have them first. The sheer joy of discovery. A crazy confidence that we can control anything we create.

"I admire them all. I might have loved Carole Bliss if she hadn't put our research ahead of love.

"What I plan must look like madness: to murder them; to murder a city. An insane dilemma, but one they've forced on me. It's the only way I know to balk their own more unthinkable insanity.

"But Jeri . . .

"I'm afraid to tell her, because she wouldn't understand. She might get hysterical enough to give me away. I can't even risk making up some new scheme to get her out of town, because she's expecting her folks from Indiana. With the stakes what they are, I can't risk any more than I absolutely must.

"I know I've never been quite fair to Jeri, but this—it's too cruel to think about. Too horribly unjust for her and her parents, and for all those thousands of people in the town, innocent of anything, certain to be caught before that molecular clock turns Deathguard off.

"Assuming that it does. I wish—but I've had no sleep the last two nights, sweating over possible alternatives.

"They don't exist.

"Leaving Meg—that hurts more than anything. Like any proud parent, I've been longing to watch her learn and change and grow. It tears me apart to leave her so young and defenseless, lost in what will surely be a deadly wasteland.

"Yet she'll have a chance. She's engineered to survive the Lifeguard pathogen. Which means she'll be immune to Deathguard too. With luck enough, time enough for her own evolution, she should discover gifts that ought to keep her safe forever. Her genes are designed for infinite change, for the potential to grow forever toward the ultimate goal of life. If she does survive—

"I'm terribly afraid. Her vital processes have never been tested. She has already begun to show tantalizing promise, but she needs tender care and understanding love I won't be there to give—care and love she may never find in the aftermath of what I feel forced to do.

"Am I insane?

"The choices I face are harsh enough to break anybody. Groping for anything saner, I always came back to a reality worse than anything I plan. I know that sooner or later, some computer would malfunction, some command would be misunderstood, some test tube would be dropped, some idiot would make the wrong decision. Once spilled by any such inevitable mischance, the Lifeguard virus would spread to blot our kind of life off the planet.

"Tonight—the fact seems too cruel to face, but this will be the final night for all of us here at EnGene and many thousand others. I'm driving out to Maxon to get this letter into the morning mail. That's upwind and nearly twenty miles away, well outside the probable lethal zone.

"I can't stand to see Jeri again. There's nothing I can say or do to help her now. I'll get a snack at the truck stop—can't remember when I last ate—and come on back in time to say good-bye to Meg. A hard thing, because she won't understand. I must try to explain what she is and she was made for, but I know she's still far too young to get it all.

"Tomorrow morning, Lorain will be calling the team together for our daily planning session. We'll all be there, the half dozen of us they've had to trust with Lifeguard know-how. It's my turn to make the coffee. I'll put half a milligram of Deathguard cells into the pot and drink the first cup myself.

"The stuff will probably be tasteless, but that shouldn't matter. My fellow engineers of Armageddon may have time enough to guess what's hit them, but all they can do is to let those synthetic macromolecules replicate themselves until their internal clocks turn them off.

"That's the story, Sax—

"I've taken too long to tell it, but I had a lot to say. You may hate me for laying such a hard burden on you. It's a poor return for all you used to do for me. I always loved you, Sax, most of all for your everlasting tolerance and for everything you taught me. Believe me, I sometimes even thought of saying so. I never did, never could. Because, I guess, I couldn't bring myself to admit how much I needed you.

"Forgive me, Sax!

"I hope you'll be the first know the truth. I'm trusting you to get it out to all the world, in the surest way you can. Be careful! There are people in the Pentagon and out of it who'd do anything to stop you. Plan against them, and do what you can to play things safe.

"This will be the Deathguard test Ryebold wanted me to make. If you're reading this, you'll know my molecular clock was able to turn the virus off. I've said all I dare tell about EnGene. Whatever may have happened here while this confession is in the mail, I hope you can use it to warn the world against the sort of thing we've done.

"God help you get the warning out, and God forgive me!

"So long, Sax."

50

The Shining Virus

A hot gust blew through the open doors of the Buick, sharp with alkali dust and the pungence of creosote brush. The heat had left Belcraft sticky with grime and sweat. Yet, passing Anya the last page of Vic's letter, he shivered. A hard lump ached in his throat. Staring off at the yellow dust-devils dancing across the brown mesa and the far black fleck of the tunnel shimmering in the heat, he found everything blurred with tears.

Anya finished the letter, and he saw her cracked lips quivering.

"I didn't know—" she whispered. "I couldn't know—"

"Nobody—" He gulped at the lump in his throat. "Nobody could."

It took a long time for him to shake off his pain. The letter had left him crushed under the weight of his brother's hard ordeal, left him wounded as Vic had been by the ruthless necessity to sacrifice Jeri, to kill his fellow researchers and condemn the innocent city, to lose everything but Meg. And now—

"If she's dead—"

His aching throat had closed.

"We don't know." Anya tried to cheer him. "Not till we get there."

Moving to break that cruel spell, he started the car. Anya leaned out to wave at Jim Gibson. The blue Ford followed them, lurching and jolting and grinding up the one-time road toward *La Madre de Oro.*

Outside the tunnel, a shelf had been bulldozed and blasted into the mountainside. Pancho's battered pickup truck stood parked there, half camouflaged with juniper branches. Belcraft found a flashlight in the glove compartment of the Buick and led the way inside.

Damp with sweat, he shivered. The tunnel was a dim pit, sloping unevenly down into the mountain as if the miners had been trying to follow a vanishing vein. Parts of it were timbered with rough logs. Decay had broken many of them, letting boulders fall from the roof. Somewhere ahead, he heard the drip and ripple of an underground spring.

Anya kept close to him. Both of them taut with a mix of dread and lingering hope, they spoke seldom and only in whispers. Maybe even more uneasy about what they might find, the photographer had taken a long time to gather up his gear, and Jim Gibson stayed to help him carry it.

The tunnel was dark ahead of them until they came to a pile of fallen rock. The sound of water was louder beyond it, and they came upon a pale glow of light. The floor here had flattened, and the glow led them to a pile of sharp-scented juniper twigs laid to make a bed.

"Nyet!" Anya breathed. "No! No!"

Alphamega and Pancho Torres lay together across the crude bed. The light came from her body, which shone now like the body of that luckless bicyclist Belcraft had seen overtaken by the advancing dust of Enfield. Her fine gold hair was already gone. Her thin little body was naked, the delicate limbs all turned luminous. The fine-boned head was bent grotesquely aside, and his flashlight glinted on the blade of the knife Harris had dropped beside her.

Torres must have been holding her in his arms when the killer surprised them, wrapped perhaps in the worn blanket which lay near her now. He had toppled backward against the boulder pile from another cave-in. A worn 30.30 rifle with a broken and black-taped stock had fallen on the rocks beside him. The flashlight showed half of his gaunt, stubble-bearded face torn away where the bullets had struck.

Silently, they shrank away together. Anya gripped Belcraft's hand, and he felt her shiver. The dank air was suddenly hard to breathe. Falling water clinked and tinkled in the darkness farther on. Behind them, the photographer slipped on a rock and cursed.

"I'm sorry," Anya whispered. "Please, Sax! You've got to believe—"

His throat closed, he could only squeeze her hand.

The others arrived, Gibson lugging a heavy still camera and its tripod. The photographer set them up and took flash shots of the bodies and the knife and a flat-topped boulder where Torres had stacked his meager supplies—a few cans of food, paper sacks of beans and rice and ground corn. He set up a battery lamp and mounted a video camera on the tripod.

Belcraft heard him gasp.

"The damn stiff! Look at the stiffs!"

The flesh had begun to flow away from Meg's slender bones, turned to a luminous fluid that spread slowly to bathe the juniper brush and gather in a moon-glowing pool on the rocky floor.

"It's slower-acting than the Enfield organism," Belcraft told them. "Maybe different enough to save us. I was there to watch the city dying. I saw a boy on a bicycle, trying to outrun the dust. He lost the race. I saw his body dissolve into the same kind of shining stuff—"

"My God! Let's go."

The photographer snatched his still camera and ran,

yelling back for Gibson to bring the video gear. Gibson stayed where he was, frowning at Belcraft.

"Doctor, what do you think?"

"I don't know what to think." Belcraft found Anya's trembling hand in his. "The Enfield organism consumed nearly everything except stone and soil and metal. This isn't attacking the brush or the blanket. Nothing so far except Meg's body. I don't know why. If it's anything infectious to us, we don't know a cure. It's time to run if you want to run, but I'm not sure running would save you."

"So?" Standing fast, Gibson grinned at Anya. *"Nichevo."*

Edging with her toward the tunnel wall, Belcraft heard him start the video camera. They stood transfixed, eyes on what had been Meg. Slowly turning to molten silver, her flesh ran off her bones. Not quite human bones, they were drawn too thin, shaped a little oddly. For a time they remained intact, a delicate fretwork of palely incandescent metal. Then they, too, began crumbling into that slowly spreading liquid pool.

It reached Torres and flowed over the body, spreading like the liquid helium he had once seen climbing out of a beaker in a cyronics laboratory. It covered the tattered clothing, the unshaven face, the gaping mouth and the grinning teeth and the ugly wound the bullets had torn, until the body became a figure of desperate agony, cast in glowing silver.

But it did not dissolve.

"There!" Pointing, Anya clutched his arm. "The fluid—it's evaporating!"

He saw a bright mist rising from the brush where Meg had been, from all the glowing pool. In a moment he caught its odor, a penetrating pungency, a little like ether, really like nothing he had known.

The whir of the camera had stopped.

"Tape's used up." Gibson took it off the tripod. "I'm getting out."

They followed him around the tunnel bend. The

bright sky in view, Belcraft heard Anya breathing hard. He reached to catch her hand.

"Get back!" she gasped. "Stay away! I think—"

She reeled against the tunnel wall. He caught her in his arms and felt her shivering against him as if from a chill. The warmth and the scent of her body brought him a fleeting recollection of their nights together back at Enfield when he hadn't yet known she was an agent of the KGB. And he caught something different, a hint of the ether-sweetness that had risen from Meg's molten flesh.

Ahead of them, Gibson had come upon the fugitive photographer, sprawled on the rocks, snoring and unconscious. He carried the man out into daylight and came back for the camera gear.

The shadow of the mountain had crept across that boulder shelf outside the tunnel. Belcraft laid Anya there on the ground and knelt to examine her. She was unconscious. Her body felt hot, with four or five degrees of fever. The shivering had stopped. Her pulse was slow, but it seemed regular and strong. The pupils were dilated when he opened her eyes, but they contracted normally.

"Alive," he told Gibson. "She's still alive."

"So's he." Gibson nodded at the photographer. "But he's got that funny smell. Like the child's when the flesh was running off her bones."

The body was hot as Anya's, when he examined it. Pulse slow but normal. Pupillary reflex normal.

"What do you think?"

"We'll have to wait."

"Whatever." Gibson shrugged. "You know, Doc, somehow I can't feel much afraid. I was dying, back there when the plane went down. Alphamega brought me back to life—and I've been different since. I don't know what she is or how she does it, but I just can't believe anything from her could really hurt me.

"Though—"

He looked suddenly around him and found a place to

sit on one of the fire-stained foundation rocks. Shivering, he grinned wryly at Belcraft.

"I guess I'll soon be finding out."

The shadow of the mountain seemed suddenly cold. Reeling giddily, Belcraft lay down beside Anya, his arm beneath his head. The weakness, the fever, the infection from Meg—it was hitting him. Yet, like Gibson, he couldn't feel afraid. What he felt, instead, was a trembling awe.

Meg had been a wonder to him since the day he found her in the ashes of EnGene, but a loving wonder. He felt strangely certain that nothing from her would harm him now. He nestled himself into a little hollow in the ground, waiting with a warm expectation for whatever came. When he woke, perhaps he would know—

"Sax?" Anya was kneeling over him. "Are you okay?"

He sat up, feeling oddly as if a long time had passed, perhaps many days. The shadow of the mountain, however, had moved only a little. Gibson lay among the foundation stones where he had been sitting. The snoring photographer hadn't moved.

"All right. In fact, very well." He caught a deep breath, peering uncertainly at Anya. "How are you?"

"Fine." She looked radiant. "Never better. But . . ." Her smile became a puzzled frown. "Different." She peered into the tunnel, shaking her head. "Something has happened to me, Sax. It's . . . it's hard to explain."

"I think . . . perhaps . . . perhaps I understand." His voice had fallen to a whisper. "Meg has touched me before. She always left me feeling lifted, cleansed, happier—in a way I never understood. This time, lying here, I thought I felt her touching me again."

Still on her knees, Anya looked at him searchingly, her face grave with amazement. It must have tanned while she slept. The pink flush of sunburn was somehow gone, and the cracks in her lips had healed. She caught her breath. He waited for her to speak.

"Sax—" Emotion had hushed her voice, and she

paused again. "I tried to tell you what I am. What I was. I knew you hated me, but I couldn't feel ashamed of anything. Not then. I thought I'd had to do whatever I had done. I was proud to think myself a loyal soldier of my country. I even felt I'd been right, using you to lead that killer here.

"But I wouldn't do it now." He saw tears welling out of her greenish eyes. "Not any of it. I do feel ashamed—"

"Don't!" His own eyes filling, he reached to seize her hand. "This—whatever it was—it has left me different. I'm ashamed, myself, of the way I hated you. Enough to kill you, if I'd felt able. Ashamed of the way I remember sometimes treating Vic—as if he had been no more than the spoiled brat I always thought he was.

"If I'd realized what he was going to do, if I'd encouraged him and worked with him, everything might have been different. He might have been alive today. Meg might have lived to become what he wanted her to be. But even as things are—"

Turning to peer into the tunnel, he pulled himself straighter before he came back to her.

"Don't grieve." He grinned at her. "Meg wouldn't want us grieving. You know—" Frowning, he stopped to organize his thoughts. "I woke up with a notion. About what has happened. About what Meg was, or maybe what she is. I think Vic planned her for this."

She waited, green eyes wide and lips a little parted, so lovely since she woke that awe caught his voice.

"Vic used to talk, but I never imagined . . ." He paused to get his breath and put it into words. "That scrawny little kid, full of ideas too big for him. He was going to create a good virus. A notion he kept nursing as he learned more biology. It was to be an artificial microorganism designed to heal. Engineered to infect everybody, repair damaged or defective cells, transform us into something closer to what we should have been. Once he called it a gene for goodness.

"He must have brought the notion with him when he came to EnGene. He had his problems there. I wonder if Meg wasn't engineered to carry on a project the military wouldn't let him complete. He must have designed her—her body—to become a laboratory in which that virus might be perfected."

Anya stared, lips parting wider.

"When we watched Meg's body melting, I think it must have been dissolving into that benign virus. Spreading into the atmosphere as that shining pool evaporated. I think we're infected now, carrying the virus, doing our own bit for Vic."

"If that's true—" He saw Anya shiver. "It's too big for me to believe."

"We have another test in progress." He squinted at Gibson and the photographer. "If they wake up changed—"

The photographer still lay snoring. Gibson had stirred, murmuring something in his sleep, but before they woke, Pancho Torres came stalking out of the tunnel. Almost a scarecrow, drawn gaunt, clad in tattered rags, but grinning with pleasure when he found them. His torn face had grown whole again.

"Tres veces!" He turned to look back into the dark behind him. *"Tres veces!* Three times I have died, and *La Maravilla* has restored me."

He came on to stand over them.

"Amigos míos." As if in solemn reproof, he shook his wild-haired, blood-grimed head. "I see sorrow on your faces. You should be rejoicing. Perhaps you think you saw *La Maravilla* dead. I remain to testify that she lives. As she will live forever. Today we have witnessed a holy miracle. The blessed angels came to reward her loving goodness. They have taken her alive into heaven."

He lifted a bare-boned, red-streaked hand as if to challenge doubt.

"I was never a believer. Not until the holy *Maravilla* lifted me high, to let me see the true glory of heaven. A stranger place, and far more splendid, than the priests have ever proclaimed. Its shape is a great, blazing rainbow around a black and dreadful pit that must be hell itself, because she says it devours stars.

"She took me to meet *los ángeles.* The very angels! Me, Pancho Torres, who had lain in prison, without hope or love, awaiting a death I had truly earned for killing. These were real and living angels, flying on shining wings, living in floating palaces of rainbow fire. I saw that they love her. She loves them. She is happy that her work for her *querido* Vic can now be left for us to finish, and she says we must not weep for her.

"I begged her to take me there with her, but she says we must stay. To complete the holy task Vic made her for—though she never told me what that is."

"I think I know," Belcraft told him. "I think we have already begun it."

51

Omega

Pancho Torres remained behind when they left the mine. *La Madre de Oro* had become a sacred place, a shrine to *La Sagrada Maravilla.* She must be remembered, and he had made a vow to stay here forever, tending the site of her miraculous transformation and relating the wonders of her life to the pilgrims who would come.

Gibson and the photographer had recovered as suddenly as they had been stricken, the photographer apologetic about his needless panic flight and almost abjectly grateful to Gibson for staying to videotape the transformation and rescue his abandoned camera. Gibson shrugged and said it was nothing. Cheerily humming an old Serbo-Croatian dance tune his grandfather used to whistle, he helped stow the cameras in the Ford. The virus had left them both declaring they'd never felt better.

Gibson gave Torres the camping gear and supplies he had bought. The photographer found a jacket he said he didn't need. Belcraft left his spare clothing and his shaving kit. Pancho thanked them in *La Maravilla*'s holy name and stood alone in the dark tunnel-mouth to wave his *adiós.*

Back in the hot car with Anya, Belcraft found his awe-struck elation fading into troubling tension. Herself transformed, she looked lovelier than ever, as innocent as Meg had been, infinitely desirable. He yearned for the love he had lost—but she had never loved him, merely used him to guide Harris here.

He felt her own troubled glances at him, but he kept his eyes on the road.

"Sax . . ." Her slow whisper was nearly too faint for him to hear. "Do you hate me still?"

"No!" The violence of his own tone startled him. "But there are things I can't forget. Things that hurt too much." He looked at her and flinched away. "The virus may have changed me, but there are things it can't erase."

He heard no answer. Tense and trembling at the wheel, he drove on.

Down on the mesa rim, he saw muddy tracks where a vehicle had gone off the road. He stopped the car and climbed out to follow them down into a deep arroyo. The black van lay there upside down, the top caved in. The doors were open, nobody inside. The driver and the Mexican cop had vanished, along with the body of Harris.

When he got back to the car, Anya stood waiting silently. With only an uneasy glance, he beckoned her into the car and drove on again.

"They must have wrecked when the virus put the driver to sleep." He tried not to listen when she spoke. "The colonel must have stopped to do what he could for them."

He dodged a boulder and flinched again when the lurching car tossed her against him. Every word and every chance touch stirred emotions hard to control, even when he told himself that the past had closed behind him. Meg was dead forever, beyond human help. Anya herself had been transformed—

Yet he couldn't help the chill around his heart.

A few miles farther on, they met Colonel Quayle's

minibus. The man at the wheel stopped it on the road and got out to flag them down. Headquarters wanted an update from Anya. He let them both into the vehicle. Anya spent two hours in a tiny phone booth, while the technician sat frowning over his instruments, keeping her in contact.

Waiting, Belcraft thought of the letter, aching again for all Vic had suffered. He lived again through all they had seen in the tunnel, dazed again by the puzzling wonder of Meg's transfiguration into something still beyond understanding. He felt drained and numb. Too much had come too fast, and Anya's role in it still tore him.

Though he didn't want to look, her pale-haired head was visible through a glass window in the little booth, huge headphones over her ears. Hating himself for the ice in his heart, he found no way to warm it. She came out at last, with a wan glance at him and a grateful nod when the technician gave her a cold Carta Blanca.

"I've reported to Clegg." She spoke to the technician more than to him. "I talked to Sam Holliday. Talked to the Pentagon. Talked to the White House. I'm told that the President has been on the hot line to the Kremlin, explaining the little he knows about Alphamega and trying to convince them that she was never a military threat."

She shrugged and sipped the beer.

"Nobody understands what she was, or wants to believe anything I say. The President and the general secretary have agreed to send teams of experts to collect the evidence and question witnesses and look for confirmation they don't expect to find."

"They'll find it." Belcraft found himself speaking to the technician, not to her. "Whenever their experts begin meeting carriers and picking up the virus."

Following the minibus on down the road, they found Colonel Quayle with a little group of men sitting out of the sun under a bluff, gathered around his private ice chest to make a picnic on sandwiches and beer. The colonel looked tanned and fit again. Scanning the others, Belcraft blinked and shook his head.

Mickey Harris!

Quite alive again, though he had lost the mirror sunglasses. His dark face had been half-washed, but mud and clotted blood still caked his hair. The bullet wounds had closed. Waving a bottle of Tecate in a cheerful invitation for them to join the picnic, he stood up and came to Anya's side of the car.

"Hiya, Sister Anya!" He grinned at her genially, not visibly contrite. "They tell me I was dead. I never thought I'd let a woman knock me off. I'm glad to say I forgive you, no matter what you done. Sister, I've seen the light."

He brushed at the flies crawling over his matted hair.

"Believe me, Sister, I know I've got a lot to answer for, because I've let the devil rule me nearly all my wicked life. I hate to think back to all my hellish sins. Ungodliest of all, the ugly way I meant to kill you if you hadn't got me first.

"But I've got great news for you, Sister.

"I've known the glory! I've learned to bow my head in humble prayer. I'm born again, and all my sins have been erased. It's true I've been laughing all my life at the priests and the preachers and what I thought was their crazy blather about salvation. But my soul has been redeemed. The eternal glory of the gracious Lord dawned on me while I lay knocked out or dead—whatever it was—back there in the bottom of that ravine. Christ came to me, and I was reborn into His holy fold.

"Praise God!" He leaned toward her earnestly. "Sister, are you saved?"

Anya flushed and bit her lip, but she answered evenly, "I've seen miracles today, and they have changed me."

She nodded stiffly at Belcraft, and they drove on.

"The virus seems to hit us differently." He heard her thoughtful murmur. "Look at Jim Gibson. An evil animal back when he used to be the Scorpion, deadly as a snake. He seems decent now. He looks and talks and even walks like a different man. But Mickey—"

She made a face.

"Still a slimy bastard! I think I liked him better the way he used to be."

Belcraft tried to keep his eyes on the flood-ruined road. The rocks and ruts and gullies claimed most of his attention, but she was hard to ignore. When those hazards let him, he couldn't help another glance. The virus had left a radiance in her, shining in her beryl-green eyes and her perfect skin. Though the sweetish reek of the virus was gone, he couldn't help catching her own clean human scent, couldn't help a pang of bitter longing whenever the car jolted her against him.

"The virus." When she spoke again, her tone had a tentative warmth. "Though I couldn't convince the White House or the Pentagon, it really has begun to spread. Even to the cop and the colonel, who had never been inside the tunnel. Which means it can change everybody, everywhere. Forever!"

"I hope so," he told her. *But if I'm changed, I'm not changed enough.*

She kept on talking for a time, groping to picture the world as it might become. If enough people were transformed, transformed far enough, wars could be impossible. Pain and sickness could be ended. Everybody could be happy. Could he imagine that?

Silently, Belcraft shook his head. His mood was too bleak.

Of course it would all take time. There might be conflicts and misunderstandings, but perhaps there were ways they could aid the change. If she could get funding and freedom to make the Roman Foundation the agency for international understanding old Jules had planned, perhaps it could do useful scientific studies of the virus and its effects. She wondered if he would want to help.

"Not yet!" His voice came harsher than he expected. "I'm not ready."

"Sax . . ." She drew suddenly farther from him. "I don't understand you!"

Eyes on the hummocks and pits of a mudhole ahead, he found no answer. He felt her searching stare, but she said no more. The slow sun sank. Darkness fell. As silent now as he, she rummaged through their supplies to share a scanty supper of cold tortillas and canned sardines.

He kept on driving, longing to escape her tantalizing nearness, to end the pain. He wished—almost wished—that she had chosen to stay behind with the colonel and his crew. Midnight had come before the nearly empty gas tank and his own fatigue forced him to stop at a dark adobe building behind a Pemex pump. He parked in the muddy court and clambered stiffly out of the car.

"One room?" he asked her. "Or two?"

"Nichevo." She shrugged as if she didn't care, but her voice had a brittle snap. "Whatever you say."

He hammered on the door. When a sleepy woman cracked it open and shone a flashlight into his face, he asked for two rooms. There was only one, for many pesos. When he had counted out pesos enough, she lit a candle to lead them back to a hot little room that reeked of garlic and pot and mescal.

The narrow bed was still warm, as if just vacated. They got into it, naked in the dark. Lying sleepless beside her, listening to her breathing and feeling all her restless movements, he tried again and failed again to swallow that bitter clot of hate.

"Sax!" Her sudden outcry echoed his own pain. "You know I'm changed. I said I'm sorry. What's wrong?"

"Everything!" He tried to soften his voice. "I'm not Mickey. Not born again. I can't forget."

"Oh, Sax—"

That was almost a sob, and she said no more. They lay a long time there in the stale-odored heat. Her rigid limbs were hot when they came against him, and he caught her own sweet scent. Tormented, he tried to shrink away, but he was already on the edge of the lumpy bed. At last her breathing slowed. He felt her body relaxing. He thought she had fallen asleep, until he felt her fingers.

Playfully, teasingly, they brushed his arm, caressed his chest, crept down to his belly and on below. Taut, breathless, he endured it all until she found his strutted penis. Emotion exploded in him then. Suddenly, savagely, he was upon her.

"So, Sax!"

Though he had crushed out half her breath, she was laughing at him. Her strong arms slid around him, pulled him hard against her—and thrust him abruptly away.

"So that's how you hate me?"

Out of control, he grappled her, dragged her to him. Her writhing flesh was hot against him for a moment, her scent intoxicating, but then he felt her arm twist out of his grip. Clutching, he felt it tightening. The edge of her flattened hand struck behind his ear. Paralyzing pain rang through his skull. Aware again, he found himself sprawled and gasping beside her, gone limp, half off the bed.

He heard a muffled sound from her, more sob than laugh.

Then a different voice.

"Sax! *Por favor!*"

Meg! Or was it? Reeling dizzily to his feet, he wasn't sure of anything. She seemed to be somewhere far away, her high child-voice almost too faint for him to hear. Sinking back to the edge of the bed, he thought he saw a rosy glow in the dark above them. Or was it still that dazing blow?

"Please, Sax!" Her voice seemed stronger. "I cannot leave you fighting with *la pobre* Anya. Not because you think she killed me, for I am not dead. *En verdad,* I am more alive than I ever was."

He looked for Anya, to see if she was hearing anything, but she was only a dark huddle under that pink dimness, still softly sobbing.

"Dear Sax!" He thought he heard that tiny voice

again. "My second father! I must go away to my new people, who will love me and make me happy in their far world of fire, but I cannot leave until you love each other."

In the dark above he thought he saw those pale wings spreading wide to reveal a brighter shape, the form of a woman, lean-limbed and lovely, with long yellow hair.

Alphamega, grown into the goddess Vic had dreamed she would be!

In another instant that glimpse had dimmed. Those glowing wings were closing again, but they brushed him as they closed, and suddenly the pain and the hate were gone from his ringing head.

"Dear Sax! Dear Anya!" He thought the shining wings were lifting. "Show me that you love each other."

Tenderly, he reached to touch Anya's trembling arm. The sound of her sobbing had stopped. He heard her laugh again, happily now, the laugh of a delighted child.

"Thank you, Meg!" she whispered. *"Spasebo!"*

At first very gently they came together, needing no words, hardly even hearing that far small voice as it faded into the dark.

"Adios, queridos! My new Father-Mother is calling me home."